My name is Paula, and I hardly ever miss a day of writing; for me, it's a meditation of sorts for me.

I live in Melbourne, Australia. I love to travel and cook when I'm not writing. My dream is to one day have a writing desk with an ocean view. I'm married, with two grown-up children and my fur baby co-writer, Alby. Recently, I added a new member to my writing crew: Spyro, the bearded dragon.

Loving Grace

P.F. SCOTT

It's not about how you fall.
It's about how you get up.

Family Tree

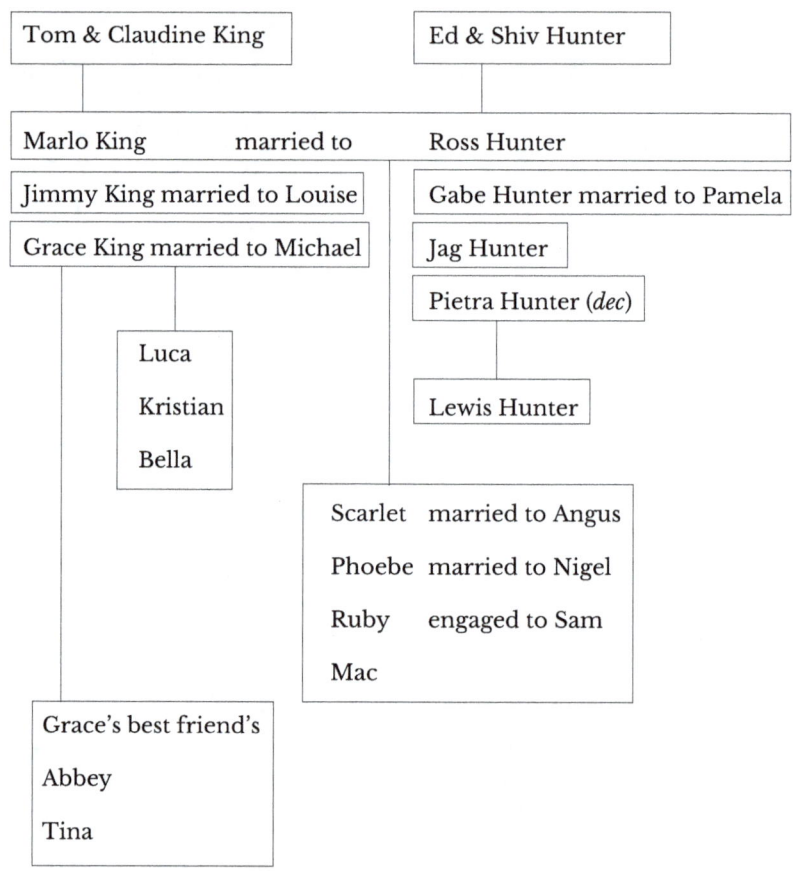

Tom & Claudine King   Ed & Shiv Hunter

Marlo King   married to   Ross Hunter

Jimmy King married to Louise   Gabe Hunter married to Pamela

Grace King married to Michael   Jag Hunter

Pietra Hunter (*dec*)

Luca

Kristian

Bella

Lewis Hunter

Scarlet   married to Angus

Phoebe   married to Nigel

Ruby   engaged to Sam

Mac

Grace's best friend's

Abbey

Tina

Chapter One

Looking out over the mountains in somewhat of a daydream, Grace sat at her work desk enjoying her own company before two of her three children arrived home for dinner. She'd been finalising the wedding collection for her new season release coming up. Grace King the label was at the forefront in luxury fashion jewellery, stocked in boutiques and stores all over the country, and even overseas. Grace had worked hard for years creating her brand, she was the King of Bling! Normally she spent Thursday's working during the day from home, and the night on her own making the most of the tranquil peace and quiet at her sprawling French country style home, at the foot of the blue mountains, just over an hour's drive west of Sydney.

Moving from a small inner-city terrace to five acres and a large six-bedroom house fifteen years ago was one of the biggest changes of her entire life. It was a change Grace never saw coming, it was the surprise of a lifetime, eventually the

Loving Grace

house became a beautiful family home. Her fly by the seat of his pants celebrity chef husband Michael Moore, came home one evening and announced he'd bought a country property; they literally moved a month later. It took some time for Grace to adjust to her knew lifestyle, she'd gone along with the excitement of the move that Michael and the children shared, even though she was secretly devastated. There had been many adjustments and changes in her life, but the move to the country house felt like the biggest, leaving her friends and family in the city, no more quick coffees with the girls or her sister. Michael had enticed her with her own lavish office space in the new country home, he was swept up in how amazing it would be to raise their three children in the fresh country air. The views were to die for, the house a dream, they had a fantastic vegetable garden that made the front cover a magazine. But still, being so far away from the city meant less visitors. Overall, Grace embraced the move and made it her home, she had no regrets.

Michael and Grace had a mutual adoration for one another, they were that couple that people envied, they'd supported one another professionally and personally, in good times and bad times, and they loved each other deeply from the minute they met in Paris twenty-nine years ago. Grace was in Paris studying for a semester, a budding design student discovering the world and herself, Michael had been working in one of Paris's finest restaurants for the past year. The minute he saw the vivacious twenty-one-year-old blonde sitting at the bar sipping her champagne all alone with a smile on her face, he knew he would marry her. And it was love at first sight for Grace too. Michael was charming and handsome. A twenty-four-year-old Aussie chef at the top of his game working in Paris living the dream. From that very first night they never parted for a day, Grace fell pregnant almost immediately... accidentally, they married literally three months later... which was what you did when you were twenty-one, free spirited, a touch rebellious, and in love for the first time in your life. It was a whirlwind romance that never ended.

Tonight, Grace was cooking for her middle and youngest children. Bella was nineteen, living her best life, still living part time at home but spending most nights at her older boyfriend's apartment in the city, and studied business at university.

Middle child syndrome was well and truly alive in Grace's family, as gorgeous and adorable as Kristian was, trouble was his middle name, and all the letters were capitals! Just when Grace and Michael thought their worries were over, along came the next instalment to the saga that was Kristian Moore's life. At twenty-three, he had the world at his feet, his career was on track, he had a girlfriend and plenty of mates, and he was fit and healthy... this was supposed to be his moment to take life by the balls and enjoy. He'd finished a degree in design and technology and was blessed to have a job waiting for him to walk straight into, lucky Kristian had two uncles who founded a multibillion-dollar tech company right here in Sydney. Blessed some might even say.

The kids arrived just after six, they'd have dinner and they'd be staying the night at home with their mother, this was a common occurrence. The problem with living an hour out of town was that the kids left home early when they got sick of catching the train into uni every day, and when they went to uni their social lives took off, which led to them leaving home.

Luca was the eldest at twenty-eight years old, he had been out of home for ten years now, his success was the highlight of his parents' lives. He'd studied law and of course went to work with his billionaire uncles. He was living the high life of a corporate lawyer in the tech scene, traveling the world on private jets brokering deals with his uncles who were not only relatives, but mentors. Last year he bought a lavish apartment in Potts Point overlooking Sydney harbour… Luca was high on life.

Going straight to the cook top, long dark hair falling forward, Bella checked out dinner, she looked like her father with the cheeky smile, she was slender and had Michael's defined facial structure and his height. 'Are these your ravioli?' Bella asked her mother with hesitation, sounding a tad disappointed, she proffered her father's cooking, he was the famous celebrity chef after all. Michael's restaurant was a must for celebrities and foodies when in Sydney. He'd always been career obsessed, from day dot, so Grace was well aware she and the kids came second to the restaurant and his career. In saying that, he never failed to say his family always came first!

Grace ignored her daughter's cooking insult, and yes it was most definitely an insult, Bella was good with those. Instead, Grace went straight to Kristian as he came into the kitchen, her arms out to him for a big warm hug. She knew it wasn't motherly of her, but she favoured Kristian - only because he needed her more than the others. Beneath the buff body and that gorgeous face was a little boy still working out his place in the world.

Bella rolled her eyes as she watched her mother embrace her brother, she'd have to listen to the story all over again, like she'd just done for the past hour in the car all the way here.

'Are you okay?' Grace asked her son, feeling his anxiousness, he felt tense to her touch, and he was huffing and puffing.

Kristian looked down at his doting mother who he adored most in this world. Her fluffy blonde curls in a ponytail, her denim shirt and red sneakers, she was cute, pretty and kind, everything a mum should be, Kristian thought. His mother was his constant, his go-to-person. 'It's not good,' he said, he hated disappointing her.

Grace stepped away from him and raised her brows. *It was never good!*

'He got arrested last night!' Bella blurted out as she shoved a chocolate biscuit in her mouth before Kristian could answer.

This was one of Kristian's best blow ups by far. Jess his girlfriend of a year, who Grace wasn't sure about as it was, had

5

Loving Grace

broken off their relationship last night, she'd claimed she needed to save money to go to New York to study. Fair enough, Grace thought... clearly she didn't love her son. But that was the good part. Kristian hadn't taken the news great; he didn't do rejection well and his temper got the better of him. Whilst he was having one of his famous explosions and throwing all of Jess's belongings over the balcony out onto the street, she called the police. They arrived amidst his tantrum and arrested him. Hauling his arse off to the station and surprise, surprise... Kristian called Uncle Ross to come and rescue him. Again! Grace was surprised she hadn't heard a word from her sister or brother-in-law today. By nature, she was kind and giving, if there was an award for great mothering, Grace would have won it many times over, she was always there to listen, to care, her kids came first above all else, except maybe Michael at times.

She was understanding and calm within seconds of her initial shock, that's why the kids always went to her first with their problems... well the boys anyway... they let her break all their bad news to their father, Michael was known for his long lectures, harsh judgement and punishment. He'd had a hard upbringing and refused to let their kids have it the easy way. When the kids fucked up, he made it harder for them, he never let them off easy.

This indiscretion was bad, but it could have been so much worse, Grace thought as she served dinner. She let Kristian do the talking, tell his side of the story in between Bella's side commentary, then Grace gave him her two cents worth. She understood his frustration but didn't condone his actions, besides he hardly seemed heartbroken although he claimed to be! He'd made a lot of changes to keep Jess happy, and it hadn't been enough, which was disappointing for him. Kristian knew he'd stepped over the line last night with his temper and behaviour, and he was luckier that his billionaire uncle sorted it out, made it go away.

Grace was always very cautious with her words to Kristian; he was a thinker and processed every word she said to him. As a mother she said all the obvious things like, it wasn't acceptable, you did the wrong thing, have you apologised to Jess, did you offer to pay for the things you broke, which he had. The relationship was still over though, which didn't seem to bother anyone really, as strange as that was. The hard part of the conversation was Kristian's violent behaviour; it was a reoccurring issue in his life. From a small boy, Grace knew he was different from his older brother Luca, and it worried her as a mother, especially when it came to women. She didn't know Jess overly well, it didn't matter, her son's behaviour had threatened her so much so, that she called the police, and it wasn't okay with Grace.

The relationship between Michael and Kristian was strained from the minute Kristian took his first breath. Grace went into labour earlier than expected and Michael missed Kristian's birth because he was out on an all-night bender, which back in the day was a common occurrence. Kristian was the only one who harbored negative feelings, not even Grace held

Loving Grace

Michael's early days against him, and if anyone had a right to, it was her. The all-nighters became less and less as the kids got older, he needed to be awake for kids sports games on the weekends, he became a present father, as much as he could, given he was striving for professional success. Eventually, Michael found a balance between family and his career. Nowadays, on Thursday nights he stayed in town at the hotel across the road from his restaurant, it was his one night he was still hands on in the kitchen, and he loved it.

Grace and Bella sat on the long sofa in the living room chatting after Kristian had headed off to bed, they didn't do it often. Grace relishing her time with her daughter, they were mother and daughter, but not quite like the relationship Grace had ever imagined herself having with her only daughter. Bella was a hard nut to crack, she was headstrong and unfiltered, generally Grace was on the receiving end or her daughter's harshness, never her father. A relatively normal nineteen-year-old, she rarely had time for her mother.

'Mum, I'm moving out officially,' Bella broke the news to her mother while her father wasn't home. Because Grace was the soft touch, Michael was the hard arse and Bella knew it, all the kids did. Although she was a daddy's girl, she knew he'd be less than pleased with her announcement. 'It's just getting too hard coming home all the time when I could be living with Dom.' She also knew her father didn't approve of her relationship.

This was the third time Grace had gone through a child telling her they were leaving home permanently. The air left her lungs as she contemplated her reaction. She sighed pleasantly, it was hard not to be emotional, in fact she wasn't able to hold the tears back... mothering was never easy.

'Are you crying! Don't cry, you're being so dramatic.' Bella didn't understand her mother's tears.

Grace took a minute to speak, 'You do what you need to do sweetheart.' Ever the supportive mother with kind and caring words, although she was internally devastated. Many years ago, she had been young, she'd been adventurous and independent too, not necessarily by choice, but circumstances... so who was she to stop her daughter from experiencing life.

'Can you tell dad for me?'

It didn't matter what Grace did for Bella, she would always come second to Michael as far as her daughter affections were concerned, 'So, when are you planning on actually moving out of the house?' she faked a smile.

'I was thinking Monday!'

It was like a thousand daggers to Grace's heart, she wanted to cry, but instead she started talking about how she could help Bella move and offered to help pack her things for her even though she didn't like Dom the boyfriend at all, he was a little older and manipulative from what Grace could tell. She also didn't like the idea that he lived with another older guy who sounded shady as hell. Bella had uni and she was young

9

regardless of how mature she considered herself to be. Her daughter was getting in over her head... so yes, Grace was in an internal spin.

She lay in bed that night, tomorrow was Friday, she turned fifty on Saturday and for weeks she'd been thinking about the enormity of the milestone birthday. Was she everything she'd ever hoped she would become. Did she love the way she wanted to love. Was she the woman she'd always aspired to be. There were a lot of internal questions going on, turning fifty was secretly weighing heavily on her.

Chapter Two

Birthdays were hard for Grace; they always had been. Her father was Tom King, he'd met his best friend Ed Hunter on the ship migrating from England to Australia when he was thirteen years old, the two would be life-long best friends. By chance they lived near each other in inner Sydney, both got jobs doing whatever they paid, rather than going to school, and by the time they were in their early twenties they'd bought their first pub together. Ed Hunter married Shiv, a young second-generation Indian girl who lived at the end of his street, very beautiful and very alone, she'd come to Sydney from northern New South Wales where her family were Cain farmers. One year to the day after Ed and Shiv married, Tom King married Shiv's best friend Claudine, a second generation Australian with a British and French background. The four were inseparable, so it was no surprise that Ed and Shiv's eldest son Ross, married Tom and Claudine's eldest daughter Marlo. It was a mammoth and joyous celebration; only poor beautiful Claudine wasn't there to share in their joy. This coming Saturday would mark fifty years since Grace's mother Claudine had died giving birth to her. Sharing your birthday with the anniversary of your mother's death was indeed a burden, and now the fiftieth anniversary was something that affected Grace in ways she'd never talk about. Her feelings on the matter were so deeply buried she had no idea how to express them. Not that Grace wasn't loved by her family, because she was adored by all. Her father Tom always showed his love until the day he died from a massive heart attack when she was just twenty-one.

When Claudine died, Grace's older siblings were young, Marlo was ten years old and Jimmy seven. They fussed over Grace, she was their baby sister, but funnily enough, the only person who ever spoke openly with Grace about her mother was Shiv, she gave Grace the love and care needed in the absence of her mother as much as she could. It was easy to love little Grace, she was the tiniest little blonde with gorgeous blue eyes and a lovable personality, very much like her mother. The resemblance was uncanny, at times awkward, especially when family friends made comments likening her to her mother. The inner circle of the King and Hunter families never did though... except for Shiv, who loved that Grace reminded her so much of her dear friend. She'd learned most about her mother from Shiv.

After Grace's father passed, she stayed with her older sister Marlo and her husband Ross for a month before going to Paris to study. Her brother-in-law had always been more than a brother-in-law, he was Grace's favourite person, he was tall dark and handsome, her sister fair, blonde and beautiful, they were a great looking couple. Her big brother Jimmy had moved out with Louise two years prior, now his wife, he was always there for Grace too in his own way, his wife Lou was three years older than Grace and was now one of Grace's best friends. She considered her friends to be family. She met Abbey on the first day of high school, she was a bubbly spark, so pretty with long hair and sun kissed skin, smart and full of fun and energy. Then one awful day during science class the principal took Abbey from class, her mother had been hit by a car crossing the road and killed. The two girls became tighter than ever. It was in the following months that Tina came into their world. Some older girls called out, 'look, it's the dead mothers club' to Abbey and Grace in front of the whole lunchroom. Tina saw red, she had a bulldog attitude and more front than Myer. Immediately she jumped to Grace and Abbey's defense scolding the older mean girl, and from that moment on, the girls were like the three musketeers, always together.

When Grace struggled after the birth of Bella, everyone rallied around her. It hadn't been the best of her three natural births, she'd had post-natal depression immediately. Tina moved into their Summer Hill home to help without hesitation, which was greatly needed. Abbey had just had her first baby and was on the phone every single day, Marlo took time out from her own growing family to help her sister too. She now had four daughters of her own. Being that Marlo was ten years older than Grace, she was a nurturing big sister, always there when needed,

Loving Grace

they were close for sisters. Eventually the fog began to clear for Grace, and she became the wonderful mother she is today.

'Fifty, that's a big fucking birthday Grace. Let Michael give you a fancy dinner at the restaurant if that's what he wants to do,' Tina said on the phone from behind her office desk in the city center of Sydney.

'You know I hate my own birthday,' Grace sighed, she'd been internally scrutinising turning fifty for weeks. Sitting at her own desk looking out over her elaborate veggie garden and the magnificent mountain range backdrop.

Michael had been pushing for her to celebrate her birthday in some form, you only turn fifty once he'd told her. 'I'm okay with dinner, but that's all,' Grace told Tina, smiling to herself as she took a gulp of her morning coffee and chatted to her dear friend.

Tina was happy, 'I'm glad you're up for it, we need to celebrate you Grace King.' She was high up in the bank she worked for, had never been married or had children an lived the life of a single woman well. That special one had never come along, despite the efforts of Grace and Abbey trying to find her a man their whole entire lives. Tina proudly remained single and sassy, she wasn't settling for anything but special, she often said. Besides, she was the fun aunty to her friend's children, she had a special bond with all of them, but especially Bella, due to the fact she's spent so much time with her as an infant when she was helping Grace with her hard time. All Tina needed was her friends.

'So can you make it Saturday night for my birthday dinner then?' asked Grace.

'I have a late lunch date, but I'm sure I can make it by mains,' Tina huffed.

'Oh, anyone special?'

A pause, 'They're never special, I don't attract special men, you know that.'

'That's not true,' Grace was sympathetic to Tina's quest of dating, there was always a story that would have Grace and Abbey in fits of laughter, Tina's dating history was legendary.

'Well, then name one special man I've ever dated… that's right, there's never been one,' Tina huffed, 'Sex is all I need,' something she had been saying forever. She, however, did have a mystery man on the side for years now, who provided regular adequate sex apparently and wanted nothing more from her other than that. The girls didn't know his name… they'd never met him. Tina said it would never lead to anything so what was the point introducing him, it was just sex because he was nothing special, and he was committed already, so, the girls took that as him being married… they didn't judge. Their friend had her life sorted; she was confidently independent, she led a full life and loved her career at the bank. Abbey on the other hand was on her second marriage which was different to most other marriages. The first one had lasted thirteen months… no kids… and ended terribly, and all before she'd turned twenty-five. Now she had a daughter Addison who was the same age as Bella, and she was married to Dean, who she seemed happy with despite hardly ever seeing him… but maybe that was why.

Loving Grace

Career was a priority for Abbey, she was finally a partner in the law firm she'd worked in for nearly twenty-five years, Dean, an international art dealer, so, they didn't spend a lot of time together.

'It's a shame Abbey's away for your birthday,' Tina pointed out, Abbey was on a well needed extended holiday in Europe with Addison and Dean.

'She needed this holiday with her family, her New Years resolution was to take more breaks,' Grace laughed, Abbey was a workaholic.

'Poor Addison and Dean are probably doing Europe while she's held up in the hotel on zoom meetings day and night,' Tina was great at sarcasm.

'No, I think she needed this holiday as much as Dean and Addison,' Grace sighed, 'She'll be back soon enough, we can all do dinner?'

'I'm in Perth all next week with a big conference and then I'm in Melbourne I think, I'm not sure yet,' said Tina, she was always on some kind of work conference or trip. 'Anyway, how's Bella?'

'Yeah... umm... she's moving out... I don't really want to talk about it, I'm not ready for her to leave home, but I know she needs to do her thing,' Grace paused with a huge sigh, 'Michael doesn't know yet... he's not going to like it, she's moving in with Dom... the boyfriend Michael doesn't like.'

Tina gasped, 'Oh!'

'Mmm.'

'Michael will never like any of her boyfriends, you know that right. He probably still thinks his baby girl is a virgin too!' Tina scoffed.

'Oh, for sure,' Grace agreed laughing, 'He'd kill me if he knew I let her go on the pill at fifteen, but what choice did I have?' another sigh seeking her friend's approval. She'd caught Bella in bed with one of Kristian's friends, who was a guest at the beach house they were renting for the summer in Palm Beach.

'You did the right thing, it's called being a responsible mum... better to be safe than sorry,' Tina agreed. Grace had never shared the Palm Beach incident with Michael, he'd be mortified.

The friends finished up their call and Grace finished up work for the morning, she had so much to do, and not enough hours in her day. At her own admission, she didn't love housework, she had a cleaner come twice a week, the house was simply too big for her to keep clean on her own, she had a gardener too! Today she picked up the dry cleaning then packing Michael's suitcase for his trip, Grace always packed for her husband when he travelled. Michael always had loads of dry cleaning as he did a lot of guest appearances for charity and corporate events, he lunched a lot, and he demanded his chef whites were always dry cleaned. As she hung up his clothing in the robe, she sorted his cloths for his trip to Singapore next week, he was going to do TV work over there, it was a show he'd worked on for years as a guest chef presenter. He travelled quite a lot; it was all part of being a celebrity chef. Michael had TV clothes as well as his two best suits and two sports jackets, Grace put them all to one end of the hanging space in his robe ready to start packing. Feeling a lump in one of the jackets inner pockets, of course she stuck her hand straight into the inside pocket and retrieved the small red box. She'd accidentally found her birthday present and opened the box without thinking. Gasping at the bling before her, holding her breath... the most fabulous earrings... a drop pearl with a diamond ... WOW! She loved them. Looking at them only for a moment before snapping closed the box. Michael had gone all out, she was overwhelmed.

Carefully putting the small red box back into the jacket pocket and then packing it into his travel garment bag. She didn't want to spoil his surprise.

Grace continued with packing her husband's suitcase, he'd be leaving Monday morning so there was no point in him coming back to the country house Sunday with her, she was driving into the city this afternoon for her birthday weekend, she'd take his suitcase in with her, along with fresh chef whites he'd asked her to drop into the restaurant before she headed off to dinner with her sister Marlo tonight. So, her Friday was turning out to be a very busy one.

Tomorrow Grace was fifty years old, and Michael knew what she loved most of all... fine jewelry. She was a collector, it was her passion, her hobby, and her business. Heading off into Sydney in her car, thinking she'd have to act super surprised when Michael gave her the earrings tomorrow for her birthday, he took great delight in giving gifts.

It got under Michael's skin that Grace never wanted to celebrate her birthdays because of her family and what the day symbolised for them. In his eyes her family were selfish and thoughtless when it came to Grace and the fact it was her birthday too, not just their mothers anniversary. From the moment he met her, he'd made a big deal of her birthdays, they'd celebrated in their own way, he always managed to make her birthdays joyous and inclusive of her friends and even her family. He loved buying her lovely gifts, and the birthday joy went both ways... Michael had gifted himself his dream car for his own fiftieth birthday a few years back, a classic Mercedes that was his absolute pride and joy.

As much as Michael bitched about his in-laws, he loved them all. Marlo was his wife's big sister, she was challenging at times, but fair, he actually really respected Marlo. His friendship with Jimmy, Grace's brother, and Ross, who was married to Marlo, was very social, they were the billionaires. Often they played golf and went to football games and events, Hunter King had corporate boxes everywhere and Ross suffered from tremendous FOMO, so they went to everything and anything. The guy's got on well, often Ross and Jimmy took business associates to Michael's restaurant, they'd gone on more than a few boys trips all together, and they took Michael to Vegas for his fiftieth in the Hunter King private jet... they were billionaires after all!

It gave Grace great joy as she drove the bustling streets of Sydney's CBD in peak hour, particularly on a gridlocked Friday, it took her back years. Back to when she was young and

19

Loving Grace

adventurous and full of life, attending uni in her days and running around Sydney free as a bird partying her arse off most nights of the week with Abbey and Tina. Her mind wandered, she sighed with nostalgic glee as she sat in the beige leather comfort of her luxurious Range Rover on Pitt Street, she had a blissful grin on her face, unlike the other commuters stuck in traffic at the red light. She'd made great time getting into town, and she had every reason to be happy, kicking off her birthday weekend, checking into a lovely city hotel, then taking her sister to drinks and dinner, and then meeting her husband back at the hotel room and maybe having ravishing sex... it had been a while, these days sex didn't always fit into their schedule.

Michael had a permanent booking for suite twenty-nine ten ever Thursday night, and he'd extended it this weekend right through to Monday when he flew out to Singapore. Every now and then Grace joined him at the hotel for a weekend in the city, if they had an event in town or she just needed some hustle and bustle, they stayed at this hotel... in suite twenty-nine ten, always.

Housekeeping had been, the suite was immaculate, Michael's bags were neatly placed in the walk-through robe. Grace stood at the ceiling to floor windows and looked out over Sydney, she really loved this city! As much as her country home was impressive and beautiful in so many ways, she was a city girl at heart. She'd grown up in Darlinghurst, it didn't get more city than that. The Hunter's lived in neighbouring Paddington, Ed Hunter and Tom King owned a string of hotels from

Darlinghurst to Bondi, Ed had sold the last of them off shortly after Tom's sudden death.

After the bags arrived at the suite, she took Michael's chef white's and made her way across Pitt Street to his restaurant. Opening the big oak doors always reminded her of her husband's achievements, Michael had dedicated nearly thirty years to the success of his restaurant, he'd sacrificed so much, so had Grace. In the early days he'd worked hard and played hard, their marriage seemed one sided from the outside, yet it was perfectly balanced to them, and they'd stood the test of time, they'd proven their love could last.

'Grace how wonderful to see you,' said Bree who had worked at the restaurant for almost ten years, she'd worked her way up from waitress to manager, super-efficient and well respected amongst the team. The fact that she was thirty years old and drop dead gorgeous was good for business. Grace had once asked Tina and Abbey if they thought Michael was fucking her... *absolutely not!* Tina had said, like she was insane. Bree was a single mother with five-year-old son, she was doing her best to make life work and she valued her job at the restaurant.

'Hey Bree... I love the red dress,' Grace gushed giving her a kiss on the cheek and a hug. The younger woman would look good in a brown paper bag; she was stunningly from head to toe, Grace agreed, Bree was good for business.

'Thank you, it's an oldie, but a goodie,' she smiled and winked.

'I'm dropping these in for Michael, is he here?' holding up the chef white's, Grace looked around, stylish herself in her soft pink silk pants and blazer, her smooth long blonde waves falling to her elbows.

'He's in the kitchen,' Bree's big smile was pleasant, 'Prepping for tomorrow night, there's a special menu being prepared for a very special birthday gal.'

'Oh, really!' Grace laughed as she headed to the kitchen.

'I believe it's all your favourites,' laughed Bree.

'I hope so!'

Michael was showing a young chef something in the freezer over to the side, Grace got a few waves as she opened the kitchen door, the restaurant was closed before the dinner service began at six.

'Hey you!' Michael looked please to her, going straight to her and giving her a peck on the check and a warm hug.

'I'm on way to pick Marlo up.' She touched his face, her sparkling blue eyes looking up into his. 'Here you go,' she said handing over his chef whites.

'Thank you. I'm meeting Jeff and Frizzy for a drink later tonight, so I'll be a little late getting to the hotel, do you mind?' Michael pushed her hair back out of her face and gave her one of his irresistible grins.

'Not at all,' her smile was cute and easy going.

'You have a good night my beautiful wife,' he kissed her forehead, 'I'll see you when you're fifty,' he had a cheeky tone, 'You'll be my first fifty-year-old,' he joked with a little naughty laugh.

'Well, I certainly hope so.' She kissed his cheek and left.

Pulling up at the front of Marlo and Ross's palatial waterfront home in Point Piper. By any persons account, it was a large architecturally designed luxurious home, sure it had harbour frontage, a million bedrooms and bathrooms, a sculptural swimming pool on the edge of the harbour, manicured gardens, and an underground turntable car park, which was a high-end gallery for their cars. Then there was the rooftop helipad, for emergencies only, Grace had always wondered what kind of emergencies. The street front high black fence was unassuming, which was just how Marlo and Ross liked it. As splendid as the house was, it was foremostly their family home, being billionaires, they needed privacy and most of all safety. Grace text Marlo to let her know she was waiting, it wasn't the kind of neighbourhood you honked your horn in, the entire street would erupt with house and car alarms... if you sat idle too long, you'd have security or the police at your window within minutes. Of course, Ross's super high-tech security system was elaborate, not to mention the actual security guards who worked for them twenty-four seven.

Marlo stepped out from the front pedestrian gate looking a picture as usual. Platinum blonde hair in place, her complexion radiant and taught, not a trace of plastic surgery, although there had been several trips to L.A. for what was termed shopping adventures, but everyone knew that was where her plastic surgeon was based. Marlo Hunter was slender and sleek, she attended the occasional fundraiser, but was invited to them all, she enjoyed the odd luncheon too but focused most of her time and energy on her own self-funded

23

shelter. Marlo Hunter was unique, most people envied her, she was a rare woman who managed to make everything look so easy, she could mix it with high society one day and then peel potatoes and feeding the homeless at her shelter the next. She was generous and kind with not only her money, but her time. Her marriage was strong to this day, although not perfect, she had four gorgeous daughters who she adored. Her mindset was to be present with everything she did, when you spoke to Marlo, you had her full attention.

'I wish my cars had these,' Marlo said swinging up into Grace's Range Rover.

'I'm sure they all do,' Grace watched on as Marlo inspected the hand grip inside the door.

'No, I don't think so,' Marlo looked bewildered, and Grace was bewildered frankly... Marlo and Ross had a collection of cars that put most collectors to shame.

'Maybe you need a Range Rover,' suggested Grace being a smart arse, she often flippantly said things to Marlo purely for the outrageous answer she hoped to receive. Her sister drove Bentley's, Lamborghini's, and Rolls Royce's to the supermarket.

'Well maybe I do... I'm going to be a grandmother soon; I'll need a car like this for a pram and a car seat.' Marlo was serious.

'What about your Bentley, it's an SUV?' Grace humoured her sister.

'I don't want to put the pram in it though!'

That was exactly the kind of thing Grace was expecting, *how fucking outrageous!* she thought as she left the curb. But that was Marlo, she didn't mean harm by it, it was just that her world was so not Grace's world that sometimes it was oddly amusing to her.

'Exactly how long now until you're a grandmother?' Grace asked her sister who's oldest daughter Scarlet was expecting her first baby. All the Hunter girls had dark hair and skin and favoured their fathers Indian heritage; however, they had Marlo's fine features and her goodness.

'Five and a half months. I'm so excited to have a baby in the family, I literally think I've got a disorder. I can't stop thinking about gifts for this baby. I'm obsessed,' Marlo was very matter of fact in an excited way. 'Scar hasn't said anything yet, but I know she's thinking it... Ross says I'm being too much.' Marlo squinted her eyes, 'Am I too much?' she asked her sister, 'You can tell me Grace.' Her little sister was the one person on the earth who could say something terrible to her and get away with it. Grace wasn't a bitch; she was honest and didn't have an issue with the truth when it came to sisters ways. Marlo appreciated it.

'I don't know,' Grace shrugged driving. 'Maybe just don't visit too much when the baby arrives, and don't try and do everything for them, let them be first time parents on their own.' Grace turned left onto New South Head Road.

'Are you saying I'm too much!' Marlo huffed a laugh, knowing she was sometimes very innocently too much in the very best of ways.

'You've been known to be at times... I love your very much, for the record.' It was hard for Grace to keep the smile off her face.

Loving Grace

'Mm-mmm,' Marlo grunted, 'My too much is noted, I won't be an overbearing Granny... FYI, I don't think I want to be called Granny...it sounds too old for me. And I've got to get through another wedding in two months' time before I become a fucking grandmother.' Marlo rarely swore.

Marlo's third daughter was marrying her long-time beau in an elaborate wedding in Italy... *who didn't love an overseas wedding!* Ross and Marlo had bought a luxury estate in Tuscany last year, they'd been in love with Italy forever, so of course they wanted to share it!

'Hey, have you spoken with Bella recently?' Grace changed the subject.

'Sort of. Why?'

'I don't know, there's something going on with her, she's moody, she's moving out, and I've just got a feeling she's not right.'

'Yes, I heard about the moving out thing... I'll speak with her tomorrow night at dinner if I can, and I'll ask Mac if she knows anything.' Mac was Marlo's youngest daughter, McKenzie, she and Bella were best of friends, the cousins were three years apart in age and had a beautifully unique relationship.

'Oh, and I know about Ross bailing Kristian on Wednesday night.' Grace glanced across at her sister. She was still yet to tell Michael about it, she'd do that later.

'I only found out myself today. You know Ross, he's loyal to the point of wrong. And he loves Kristian like a son.' Marlo made excuses.

Again, Grace glanced at her sister, 'How much was bail?'

'Nothing- I don't know... Ross pulled a favour. It's not even on his record.'

Grace wasn't so sure she believed her sister, she really wanted to, but even if bail were posted, Ross would never tell, that was how he rolled, because he was loyal to the point of wrong, he was a man who would do anything for those he loved, and he did love Grace's kids. Ross was the person who everyone went to because his heart was huge, and he never let anyone down, he always listened and gave sound advice and never judged.

'One day that kids going to fuck up and it won't be fixable,' the emotion in Grace's voice was alarming.

'Maybe not, Ross said this really shock Kristian up, I mean it's not every day your girlfriend rats you out to the cops for your drug stash.'

'What!'

'Um.' Instantly Marlo knew Grace had no idea about the drugs. 'So, allegedly,' she began, taking a deep breath as Grace pulled down a side street to pull up. 'When the police came the apartment... well, apparently Jess told the cops to check Kristian's bedside draw for drugs and they did.'

Grace put her hands to her head, 'Oh, my god, and they found something!'

'It was coke from what I know. Nothing to worry about.' Marlo played it down.

'Nothing to worry about!' Grace exhaled, 'He's a kid who can't control his temper at the best of times. He's been arrested and almost jailed twice because he can't control his temper, and you're telling me he's got cocaine in his bedside draw... not to worry!' Grace was nearly hyperventilating.

'It's not as bad as you think, Kristian wasn't charged, Ross made it go away.' Marlo put her hand on Grace's leg.

'Marlo!' Grace raised her voice, 'Drugs! Ross can't keep making things go away.'

'Lewis assured me Kristian only does coke when he goes out, it's not a daily habit, he's not addicted.' Marlo was in damage control, and it wasn't working.

'Lewis!' gasped Grace, 'How the fuck does Lewis know, what is he, a drug dealer!'

'Don't be so ridiculous,' Marlo scoffed, 'Lewis is a mentor and Kristian's boss, they talk about things, he's a cool guy and Kristian relates to him, and he really looks up to Lewis.'

Lewis Hunter was too cool for his own good and a little up himself, as well as Ross's nephew. Michael had never liked him, and Grace wasn't a fan either. His mother was Ross's younger sister. Pietra had been troubled, by fourteen she was using drugs, staying out all night, skipping school. At fifteen she complained one morning to her mother with a stomach-ache, and literally gave birth to a baby boy in her bed twenty minutes later with the assistance of her extremely shocked mother Shiv. Pietra didn't know who the father was. Two years later at just seventeen, she died of a heroin overdose in a city brothel. Pietra was the Hunter family tragedy; they'd never got over her death. It was the loss that changed their lives forever, and her baby, Lewis, was the light to guide them through the awful storm.

Grace huffed and shook her head, it was one thing to perhaps assume that in this day and age, maybe one of your kids might have taken a drug at least once, but to know for sure was unnerving for her. The Kristian saga went from bad to worse, how did she help her son, and why had he not told her himself. What else didn't she know!

'Grace, Kristian's a great young man, Ross said the drugs weren't enough to even warrant an arrest.'

'Oh, really, since when has Ross been in the drug squad?' she snapped at her older sister feeling a bit betrayed.

'He knows about drugs.' Marlo became huffy, and Grace rolled her eyes pulling out of the curb and doing a U turn. 'And Ross loves Kristian, you know that. He's also his boss, and if Ross thought he was heading down the wrong path, he'd pull him up.'

They discussed it until they got to the Watsons Bay hotel where they were having a drink before heading to Doyle's to share a seafood platter. It had been their father's favourite restaurant, so they often went there together. Grace couldn't help but worry about Kristian, she was always worrying about him, but at the same time she needed to let him be a grown arse man on his own terms, well try to be anyway. The next big problem was how to tell Michael, he wouldn't take this lightly. It was going to be awful; she'd have to choose her moment.

'Shiv is excited about your birthday, I've told her it's not a party, just a dinner... so she doesn't go overboard,' Marlo said sipping her champagne.

'Let her go overboard, I like Shiv's overboard, I need some overboard in my life,' Grace sighed.

29

Loving Grace

'I called Michael to let him know they were coming, he was a little cagy with me, you know how he gets around your birthday.'

'No! How does he get?' Grace questioned, her brows raising. The tension between her husband and her family and her birthday wasn't a secret, it was something nobody ever addressed openly.

'I don't know!' Marlo rolling her eyes, wishing she hadn't mentioned it.

Grace gave her sister a long stair as she gulped at her martini, 'I just want a nice evening with the people I love, because it's my birthday.'

Marlo knew better than to bite back, 'Then my darling Grace, that's what you shall have.'

'Do you think our children know how lucky they are to have mothers?' asked Grace with a sigh, her mind wandered from her birthday to her mother.

Smiling Marlo knew exactly where her sister was coming from, 'I hope so.'

'Do you think I would have married Michael if dad had been alive?' Grace was really going into unchartered waters now; her thoughts were getting deep. Something had come over her, she was turning fifty tomorrow and she'd never had this discussion with Marlo, ever. Their father could be very persuasive, he wanted Grace to be with Jag, but Grace had other ideas.

It took a few seconds for Marlo to absorb her sister's words, 'Um, I don't think he'd have liked young Michael, especially because he got you pregnant out of wedlock,' she exhaled with a smile. 'Who knows, maybe you would have married Jag.' Marlo laughed out loud, their father and Shiv really pushed for that union.

Oh, now Jag was a story! Grace had all these little moments in her life that seem to lead her straight to Michael, because they were meant to be. 'Mmm... no.' She pondered her sister's bias opinion as she processed. 'Actually, I would never have married Jag... never... not in a million years. Nobody was telling me who I was marrying.' It crossed her mind briefly that she may be hitting out at her sister, she wasn't sure why, she just wanted to say something to piss her off, she felt like it was because of the Kristian/cocaine thing, it could have been for her attitude towards Michael.

Marlo remained silent, not completely sure where this was coming from, or what the purpose was. Her little sister was not often a bitch. Was it because she was turning fifty? As a family they had these little glitches and twists, the most hurtful ones rarely got spoken about.

'The whole arranged marriage thing worked for you... and well, Jimmy got off easy, because poor Pietra died,' Grace said unable to help her harshness.

'Grace!' Marlo was horrified. *Was her little sister out of her mind!* Their father did heavily encourage the unions between the King's and the Hunter's, and it was when Pietra passed away that it was first suggested that thirteen-year-old Grace and an eighteen-year-old Jag might one day marry, but the suggestion was rejected with tremendous backlash from Grace, she told her dad she'd run away if he ever mentioned it again. The only Hunter child to have an Indian name, Jag... short for Jagdeep. Jag and Grace had never been tight, especially after the incident! A ten-year-old Grace had teased a fifteen-year-old Jag and called him dumb; he'd pulled her hair; she swiftly kicked him in the balls... and then he slapped her face. Any ideas of a future between them had ended right there and then. The two never saw eye to eye from then on, and yet their parents still thought there might have been a chance! Grace would have been more receptive to marrying Gabriele, Ross' twin, had he not been twelve years her senior.

Grace looked at her sister with apologising eyes, 'You were lucky, you would have married Ross anyway, because you've always been in love with each other.'

'Well, one of us had to do what we were told, and you're right, Ross and I would have married,' Marlo said light heartedly, she wasn't forced to marry Ross, it was true love.

'You're such a good girl,' Grace mocked her sister, they were back to normal.

'Yep, I've always been the good one, you and Jimmy on the other hand!'

At least they could see the bright side and got over it fast. Marlo was a wonderful big sister; the two sisters loved each other, despite their words.

'Now let me tell you about Kitty and her latest divorce.' Marlo was ready to change course. They moved on.

Just as dessert came out, Grace got a text from Luca her eldest child, her good child, her easy child. He wanted to talk to his mother as soon as possible, which alarmed Grace as he wasn't that kind of guy, he wasn't an urgent person, he never relied on his parents for anything more than their love and care. Luca needed a face to face at his place, and since she was in the city already, preferably tonight and without his father as he really needed her motherly advice. Grace sighed, he had done this once before, he'd summoned Grace and Michael to his new apartment so they could help him choose new carpets, so tonight, Grace was expecting another decorating emergency. Luca's life was dreamy, he had everything, he lived in a fabulous apartment, he drove a great car, so the little things were sometime huge things in Luca's life.

Deciding to swing past Luca's on her way back to the hotel after dropping Marlo at home, Grace pulled into the curb outside Luca's building around ten thirty. She'd always loved Potts Point, the old buildings, the tree-lined streets, it had a coloured past, what was not to like!

Luca had been in L.A on and off brokering a new deal for Hunter King the past few months and he'd only been back in town for just over a week, he'd come to the house for dinner earlier in the week.

His art deco building was lit up with soft night lights, Grace missed living in the city, she thought how wonderful it must be to be young and living her son's lifestyle, for a moment she felt very old as she waited to be buzzed up.

Loving Grace

When Luca opened the door, arms opened wide for a hug from his mother, she loved his big loving hugs, she loved hugs in general, especially from her sons.

'Mum, I know it's late, I promise this won't take long,' he said appearing anxious. Luca was tall, dark and handsome, his shoulders were broad, he was manly and very good looking. All three of her kids looked so very different to each other. Luca had dark hair, olive skin, dark eyes, and a placid nature, not to mention outrageously intelligent. Whereas Kristian was fair-haired, stocky in build, and not as tall as his older brother and certainly not as calm and easy-going either. Bella was Michael through and through, the eyes, you could tell she was his daughter just by looking at her. She had the same nature too, self-absorbed, and not in a bad way, it was part of their personality.

'It's fine sweetheart, your dads gone for a few drinks with Jeff and Frizzy tonight, I probably won't see him until the morning anyway.' Her smile was warm and kind.

'Mum!' Luca was troubled as he looked down at his mother.

'What is it,' her smile and sparkling eyes loving.

'Please. Sit. Do you want a cup of tea?' he sighed gesturing to the sofa.

'No tea for me.'

Luca sat on a chair facing his mother, 'I've been seeing someone.' Finally, a smile came to his face and Grace breathed a sigh of relief. She wasn't in the mood for anything heavy, although in Luca's world this was huge, he was non-committal when it came to women, he liked to play the field and didn't like to be tied down. So, seeing someone was a big step.

'Oh, that's lovely for you.'

'Mm.' His dark eyes narrowed as he watched his mum, he wanted to squeeze her, his mother was still great looking for a woman turning fifty, she was warm and caring, he adored her. 'I was seeing this particular girl a few months ago and then we caught up last month while I was home for a few weeks again... do you remember?'

'Mm, hm.' She nodded, but didn't really remember.

He never gave details about any of the women he dated, ever, this one must be different, maybe he was ready to settle down, commit to someone other than himself, Grace thought. She didn't necessarily think he needed to settle down, she just thought that at twenty-eight he might consider it in the future at some point.

'You'd like her I think.' His expression didn't change, he still looked anxious.

'I would! Are you brining her to my birthday dinner, is that what this is about?' Grace asked. 'What's her name?' now showing some interest.

'Her name is Jasmine and she's not coming to your birthday dinner Mum.'

'Okay, well maybe you can bring Jasmine to the house for dinner or a Sunday lunch... when you're ready of course. Your dad would love to cook for her.' Grace didn't quite get Luca's anxiousness. 'Is there something else you need to tell me?' her settling smile letting her son know he could trust her, it was a secret weapon she often used on her kids, it had always worked, especially on the boys.

'She's twenty. She's studying teaching,' Luca gushed.

His mother looked at him, her eyes still at him for a moment, 'Twenty!' still Grace didn't understand her son's angst. Yes, twenty was young, but it was probably just a fling. 'Try not to break her twenty-year-old heart,' she added. 'I'm sure you're having fun together.' She could tell Luca was feeling absolutely awkward. 'Does Jasmine think you're too old, do you have a problem with her age?'

'No, I don't have a problem with her age, she's very mature intellectually.'

'Okay!' Grace raised a brown with an easy tone. 'She kind of sounds sweet.'

'Jasmine is pregnant Mum.'

Oh, and there it was. Grace was in shock before she was able to process her sons' words and considering her reaction and her response. There were no words, she didn't have any, nodding so he knew she'd heard him, then waiting for him to say something.

'She's not sure if she's keeping the baby,' he took a moment, 'I've told her I'll be there whatever she decides, but ultimately it's her decision,' he said it like he wanted his mother's approval.

'I see.' Was all Grace could manage.

'What else can I do... I... I don't know what to do Mum.'

Grace knew he wanted her to say something, he wanted her wisdom, 'Luca,' she took a deep and thoughtful breath in, then took a few seconds to center herself. 'You need to do what you think, and feel is right,' a few seconds of pause, 'The one thing you don't want to do is have regret in a situation like this. You never want to wonder, what if I said this, or if only I'd done that.' It was her first instinct to be completely and boldly honest with him. 'Do you at least like this girl?' She was still in shock; it came out harsher than intended.

'Of course, I do!' Luca was offended.

'Are you sure this baby is yours, it's just you've never been committed to a woman, let alone one who's supposedly carrying your unborn child.' It hit Grace second by second.

'Mum!' he seemed surprised and somewhat even more offended, 'I know it's my baby.'

'Well, my love, you've never brought the same woman home twice, I had to ask.'

'I *like* Jasmine a lot,' Luca's voice was heartfelt. 'I just feel so out of control. This is so massive for her; she's really freaking out and I don't know what to do.'

'Yes, you do know what to do,' Grace had that certainty in her tone that her son needed, 'You do what feels right. You're a smart man. Be compassionate to Jasmine and be true to yourself.'

Luca gestured like he got it, like his mother gave him some kind of confused clarity, 'I will... I am.' Running his hand through his hair he sighed.

'I'm here for you, whatever happens. You'll never be alone.'

37

Loving Grace

Grace flopped down on the hotel bed, her head was pounding, her heart was heavy, it had been a big few days of mothering. Her boys were good sons, she adored them both with every ounce of her being, they were each so special to her in their own way, and to see them both unhinged, was painful. Being their mother was Grace's most cherished job. After Kristian's behaviour in the week and now finding out about the drugs... she'd had no idea. *Did that mean she was a bad mother, or just a naive one!* And now Luca. Her chest felt tight. She'd been twenty-one when she fell pregnant in Paris with him, right after her father had died, she'd been reckless in every which way she possibly could in her younger years. It was as though falling pregnant had been a clear sign from above, to stop, take stock of her life and grown the hell up. As young as Grace was, it was exactly what she did. But this wasn't her, it was Luca, and she knew she was powerless.

Sure, she could take Kristian home and try to cleanse his life... at the end of the day, he was a twenty-three-year-old young man living his life in this day and age. And as for Luca, she had not control whatsoever over his unborn child's fate.

'Sorry I'm so late,' Michael said snuggling into her back under the sheets, his touch was cold and yet welcomed.

'Hi,' a smile of relief and comfort filled Grace's heart. Michael soothed the feeling of unrest. He was always the light in her storm. He nudged playfully into her neck, pulling her hair back so he could kiss her, 'You smell amazing.' His hands wandered under and up her singlet, her skin tingling

'I'm glad you're here,' she managed a soft laugh smelling the alcohol on his breath. She couldn't tell Michal about Kristian because he'd been drinking, and Luca had made her swear she wouldn't tell his father. So, Grace laid there letting Michael turn her on... what else could she do! Exhaling as his hand went down her front and into her knickers, his familiar fingers pressing firmly into her wetness knowingly as her back arched to him. This was just what she needed, distracting sex.

Rolling her onto her back with a touch of force, which she loved... Michael was clearly in a dominant mood... it was the alcohol, 'I love fucking my wife,' he said moving over her with that look in his eye that meant she was in for great sex.

'You're about to have your first fifty-year-old... it's officially my birthday,' she grinned.

'Happy birthday sweetheart.' He said pulling her knickers off, he liked the power in bed. Grace let him go, watching him, she liked it when he was in this mood, he set the pace, and that was fine by her, she was more than happy to let him do all the work. As his tongue licked her from anus to clit with a roughness that was almost too much to handle right off the bat, she let out a sigh followed by a groan, it was distracting, she loved it. Hands fingers at her nipples, naughty little tweaks that hurt yet made her cum immediately. After all these years, their sex was still pretty good, a touch complacent, but they still knew exactly what the other needed and wanted. Grace pulled Michael up to her, she needed him to plunge his hard cock inside her pussy, she was buzzing inside now... she really just needed penetration... she needed to be fucked. They had two

Loving Grace

styles of sex patterns, they either made love and it was powerful and emotional, or it was like tonight, careless and a touch desperate... which was Grace's favourite.

Licking and kissing her nipples on the way up, Michael knew he could fuck Grace any which way and she'd always be up for it. His wife was amazing on every level, a pleaser by nature. 'Leg up,' he instructed pressing himself inside her wet pussy. One thrust and he was in. Taking one of her legs and bringing it up to his shoulder, stretching her so he could feel her tight pulsing pussy scissoring his cock, the feeling engulfed him as he pounded into her with the gusto of a young man. As he held firm to her body, Grace clenched to him, she was cumming again and so was he.

Michael wasn't the type of guy who like to fuck for hours, for the first few years, he had been that way inclined, but then as time went on, life got busier, the kids came along, he became an in and out man. Grace didn't mind so long as she got off first, which she did ninety percent of the time, the other ten she usually finished herself off when he jumped up to go to the bathroom. She'd use her fingers or if she thought she'd been ripped off, she wasn't shy getting her vibrator out to let him know he'd left her hanging.

Tonight, hadn't been a great orgasm... fast and furious, she'd offloaded some tension and just the fact that she'd cum, would help her sleep.

Maybe in the morning before they went to breakfast with the kids, she'd tell Michael about Kristian, oh, and there was Bella moving out too. Her head hurt again.

Chapter Three

Grace woke to the biggest display of green and white flowers, a silver tray with a hot pot of tea and the morning paper.

'Thank you,' smiling and sounding croaky first thing in the morning.

Sitting on the edge of the bed, Michael held out a smallish white gift bag, 'For the woman who has everything,' his grin was telling.

Grace didn't think she had everything... but anyway.

'I thought about getting you something random like a ride in a fighter jet or a week at one of those stuck-up health retreats you and your sister love. But I know my wife, so I decided to play it safe.'

Grace took the small white square box from the bag and looked at it... not the box she's been expecting, not the box she'd found in his jacket pocket. Opening the box was the biggest surprise of all. Thick yet feminine golden links encrusted with

41

sparkling diamonds. Grace marveled at the exquisite bracelet; she'd never seen anything so beautiful. Gasping, her eyes flickered, not what she'd expected, but gorgeous and possibly better than the earrings.

'What do you think?' Michael was eager for her answer.

'I-I'm,' she was speechless.

'This is just the beginning; I've got the day planned for you, my love.'

'Michael it's beautiful!' This was extravagant bling!

'There's a few more surprises coming your way,' his smile was cheeky.

'Really, I'm blown away, I don't know what to say,' she was still taken back by the bracelet.

'Honey, you don't have to say anything, just enjoy your birthday,' he nodded hoping his wife would just chill and savour the day he had planned for her.

Breakfast was at the hotel, just the kids and Michael having some family time at a round table. Kristian devouring the full buffet, demolishing a plate of hot food, then pancakes and syrup, followed by fruit and muesli and then topped off with French pastries and two cups of black coffee. He ate like no other Grace had ever seen. Yes, he was an athletic guy, he was well built, she wondered if his appetite was because of drugs, Grace didn't know a lot about drugs.

Bella was staying in the city at Dom's house of course, the boyfriend she had utterly devoted herself to in such a short time. Grace couldn't think about Bella moving out of home permanently today, it would truly ruin her birthday if she did. They'd always had a delicate relationship, she tried to be the best mother she could, but Bella's relationship with Michael seemed to outshine her at every turn. He was Bella's favourite and Grace felt it, still she was completely devastated her baby girl was leaving the nest.

Luca seemed noticeably quiet to his mother this morning, maybe it was just her, because of what he'd shared with her last night, Grace didn't know. It seemed everyone had something going on, yet they all managed to make Grace feel special, they'd given her a designer handbag, one of her many loves in life.

'Well, haven't I been spoilt,' she said lifting her wrist to flash her new bracelet and then hugging her new bag into her front. Michael put his arm around the back of her chair.

'You three are so lucky to have a mum like this one,' he sighed looking at all three of his kids, all of whom he loved and adored beyond words. 'She's dedicated twenty-eight years to you guys, never forget that.' Michael sang his wife's praise.

'We know,' Kristian sounded a tad defensive; he didn't like being called up on what his mother meant to him, especially by his father.

Bella blinked her eyes at her brother Kristian with annoyance, 'Let him talk Kristian, he's saying nice things about mum.' She would always fiercely protect her father.

'This woman would do anything for you three, she lives for you guys.' Michael was proud of his family unit, he had divorced parents and no siblings, he'd never known family until

Loving Grace

he married Grace. 'It's not all about Chanel bags, be nice to her, be nice to each other, that'd make her day too.' Michael loved to preach to his kids, he only wanted them to be good people.

Kristian looked at his mother, he worshiped her, he didn't need to be told his mother was the best.

Bella just wished someone would bring up Kristian's bad behaviour and put him back in his box!

Luca just sat back and observed, he was lost in his own thoughts, Grace could see he wasn't quite right, she gave him a smile across the table of support and love. Today the impact of his position had come to her with full impact. They needed to talk some more; she needed to tell him she was in his corner no matter what.

'Dad, can we go over to the restaurant so I can set the table for tonight?' Bella wanted to put her stamp on tonight's dinner for Grace, and to help her father out, they wanted to make it extra special and a little different. 'See, don't say I don't do anything for you,' Bella looked at Grace for recognition.

'Thank you!' Grace sighed with a super sarcastic smile to her daughter, then looked up at Michael, he understood, only parents could love such a bitch!

'Let's go,' he glared at his daughter shaking his head, she had the power to turn gold into shit in a second with her words. Bella was the twinkle in his eyes though, he cherished her from the second he knew Grace was pregnant. 'I'll be back in time to take you to lunch Grace.' He bent forward and kissed her forehead.

She loved her life; her family were her everything - even if her daughter was an upstart.

'I gotta go mum, Jess is coming over to pick up some stuff I forgot to throw out the window,' he said rolling his eyes, 'Can I bring someone to dinner?'

'Who?'

'A date – not Jess.'

'Kristian!' she scoffed at him, 'No!'

Kristian smiled like he'd been teasing her, 'Got ya!'

Luca was looking on with slight amusement.

'I don't want you bringing a random to my birthday dinner.'

'I'm joking Mum,' he had a mischievous smile, 'But I have met someone pretty awesome. I spent the whole night with her,' he teased some more, he couldn't help himself.

'Great. I'm happy for you. I don't want to meet her tonight though,' Grace had a grin on her face, bringing the conversation to a humorous ending.

Kristian got up in his jovial mood and kissed his mother on the cheek giving her a hug as he so often did, he was the most affectionate of her children, 'I love you mum. See you tonight.'

'I love you too. Be safe.' She looked up at him with love and concern in her eyes, so much worry for a child who she did her best to raise right. Had she, Grace couldn't help but wonder if Kristian was the way he was because of her, or something she'd done. She'd read an article that said a child's foundation for life was set in the first five years of their life.

Luca shook his head as his brother left the restaurant, 'Blatant favouritism,' he teased his mother.

Loving Grace

'Never. Absolutely not!' Grace had a soft spot for Kristian, but she didn't love one child more than the others.

'Mmm, sure.' Luca gave his mum a smile. 'He's single now, he'll have a different girlfriend every day of the week like the old days, you know that right?'

'I hope not.' She didn't find it funny at all, she was too concerned. 'Tell me, do you know anything about your brother taking drugs... cocaine?' Grace knew it was wrong to put Luca on the spot; but her kids were now adults, they could speak freely with her.

'I don't know, not really,' he said uncomfortably... which meant yes, he did know something.

'Sorry, I shouldn't have asked.'

'I'm pretty sure he dabbles sometimes, nothing big.' Guilt got the better of Luca.

'I see,' Grace sighed, 'Thank you.'

'You know about the arrest the other night,' Luca said to his mother.

'I do. I haven't told your dad yet,' her tone was prickly.

'Lewis and I had a chat with him yesterday in the office, he could have gone to jail you know.'

'Why is Lewis so involved with Kristian?' Grace huffed.

'He is Kristian's boss and a good mentor for him,' Luca sighed. 'We're both close with Lewis, he's really cool,' Luca was matter of fact. 'He's a good influence on Kristian.'

'How so?' Grace was skeptical.

'To start with, Lewis is the one who got Kristian in on the new gaming platform design, if this comes off mum, it could be just the beginning for Kristian, they're designing groundbreaking technology.' Luca seemed very proud.

Grace huffed her disapproval but didn't say anything else on the matter, 'You've been quiet this morning, are you okay, any news?' changing her tune and focusing on Luca.

He hadn't moved in his seat for ages, he sat low and somewhat chilled out, 'I'm good. I didn't sleep much. I'm waiting.' Luca was the kind of guy who women gave a second and a third look at, he was hot, olive skin, and dark intriguing eyes. He had this style that was very cool and very suave, Luca was an attractive guy with everything going for him.

'If you're not good, let me know,' Grace said warmly, she could see the angst in her sons' eyes. 'We can talk anytime.'

'I'm just waiting mum,' he sounded drained and a touch sensitive, and with good reason. Grace didn't say anything, she nodded to let Luca know she understood.

Michael and Grace walked arm in arm to the Royal Botanical Gardens, near Victoria Lodge, the view of the harbour was breathtaking from the lawn on the perfect Sydney day. They used to come to the park when the children were small, they'd run around barefoot on the grass until they were worn out.

'Remember how much we loved coming here with the kids,' he said taking Grace's hand and walking her down past Victoria Lodge. Set up for just the two of them was a beautiful picnic on the grass, only a little more elaborate than their old blanket and Tupperware plates. Everything in whites and neutrals, a low table, real plates and cutlery with linen napkins and the most beautiful flower arrangement. Grace gushed at the sight, it was very special, and she was overcome with Michael's effort.

'Take your shoes off, you know how good this grass feels underfoot,' he said taking his shoes off and his jacket, putting his hand out to Grace, 'I don't know, I thought this was a good way for you and me to spend some time alone today.' His smile said it all.

'I love it, this is the best thing you could have done, it's exactly what I needed today.' Looking over the table and the intricate detail someone had gone to, Grace sighed, she smiled as Michael poured a glass of sparkling water for her. The soft cushions relaxing, she wanted to lie down and think of absolutely nothing, enjoy her time with the love of her life before her birthday dinner tonight.

The rays of sun penetrating, Grace was relaxed as Michael opened the picnic basket and unwrapped two amazing meals, placing them on their plates with such perfection, he could serve up baked beans from a can and it would look gourmet. She debated whether to tell him about their sons and their current situations of concern, and of course Bella moving out. The longer she held out, the worse Michael would take it, she knew that, but it still didn't feel right getting into it on her birthday. And as for Luca's predicament, she'd been sworn to secrecy on that one anyway.

'I'll miss you when I'm in Singapore,' Michael said as he finished his lunch.

'I know. Me too.' Grace loved the first few days of Michael being away, then she missed him terribly. Their schedules just never seemed to align. Whenever he had a business trip, she had a deadline or a meeting she couldn't miss, and whenever she was away on business, he couldn't leave town. Once a year they took a month off together, normally September or August to go to Europe and soak up some wine and sun.

'Oh, and I might have to stay an extra few days now, there's a dinner thing that I apparently have to attend,' Michael sounded exhausted, as much as he complained, she knew he secretly loved the dynamics of his career.

'So, you're away for how long?'

'Roughly a week or so... I'm sorry.' He scrunched his face up regretfully to her.

'It's fine,' Grace smiled, she didn't want him feeling guilty for working, God knows she worked long and hard at times when she needed to. 'I've got loads to do anyway.' That wasn't exactly true, her workload was now under control, she planned on helping Bella move out, having some time at home doing absolutely nothing while Michael was away. Marlo had told her about a few new TV series she should definitely be watching, so that was what she planned on doing.

The lunch was everything it was supposed to be, the two sat enjoying the fine weather, Grace laying with her head on Michael's lap, chatting about the past twenty-eight years they had spent together. The talked about the good times, they made plans for their next trip overseas, this time they would venture to Spain and the south of France.

Loving Grace

Kicking the hotel door shut, Michael and Grace striped off their clothes, by the time they got to the bedroom they were naked. Sex for Grace with Michael was more often than not repetitive these days. The last ten years had been a ritual of what worked. There were no complaints though. She didn't need sex every day, she didn't even need it every week.

As Michael held himself over her, his thrusting was firm and intent, he didn't mess around now he was getting older either. More often than not it was a race to the finish, working each other up fast and hardly any foreplay. Getting to the point! Grace thought this was pretty normal for married couples.

As Michael's body stiffened to hers, she pressed herself into him so she could hurry herself along and not miss out on her own birthday orgasm. Sex without an orgasm was a lost opportunity, she hated missing an opportunity. Sometimes she wondered if they needed to spend more time trying when it came to intimacy and sex.

Lucky the bathroom mirror was large in the hotel suite, Grace liked elbow room when she put her makeup on, and Michael splashed a lot when he shaved. They'd come back from their park picnic, had a quicky and taken a nap, now they were getting ready for her birthday dinner. Grace never understood naps, until she got into her late forties, then she appreciated the value of a good half hour nap. Refreshed and ready for her special night, she questioned Michael.

'What kind of cake did you make me?' She knew he'd made her cake yesterday; he always made their family birthday cakes the day prior; he made fantastic birthday cakes.

'If you must know, it's white chocolate mud with strawberry French buttercream.'

Her mouth dropped open; a gasp escaped. She loved cake of any kind, especially Michael's cakes. 'I'm so happy. You know I love French buttercream.' Her eyes watered at the delicious thought.

'I know what you like,' he said feeling the shave on his face.

'And just so you know, I love my bracelet. I really do.' Grace watched his reaction in the mirror as she applied blush with a way oversized makeup brush.

'I'm glad you love it, now let's get that new dress on you, or we're going to be running late... you can see how bad that would look considering we're only across the street and it is my restaurant,' he joked.

Grace walked in holding onto Michael's hand, balancing in her once before worn heels that she bought online, maybe a size too small... but they looked great! She was fashion conscious but not obsessed, her clothing wasn't anything like her sisters designer wardrobe, and she never thought she looked awful, nobody had ever said she looked awful to her face.

'Happy Birthday Grace,' Bree greeted her with a kiss on the cheek and a smile, standing there very efficient and beautiful. 'Your sister is already here.'

Loving Grace

'Thank you, Bree.' Of course, Marlo was there, she was ten minutes early to everything.

'Michael, can we have a quick chat in the kitchen before you sit down,' Bree said like there was an issue she needed him to sort out.

'Give me five,' he kept walking toward the private room the dinner was in, 'Just let me get in the door and seat my wife on her fuckin birthday,' Michael said under his breath so only Grace could hear him.

'She's just doing her job,' Grace nudged him. The two large sliding timber doors were half open as they got there, 'Can't you be late once!' Grace smiled as she went straight to her sister for a birthday hug.

'Happy Birthday Darling,' Marlo was emotionally cheery. 'I love your hair curly.' She fluffed out Grace's long blonde hair, then stood back.

'Happy Birthday Gracie, you still look twenty-one to me gorgeous girl,' Ross gave her a bear hug of a cuddle as he always did. He was a tall man, not as slim as he used to be, unruly now salt and pepper waves, and a cheeky smile, and for a guy in his early sixties he was still handsome. He looked every bit a billionaire, distinguished and intelligent, his half Indian blood line was ever prevalent. Money hadn't changed him much; he was still the same old Ross that Grace had known her whole life underneath his fancy clothes and billions of dollars.

'Here you go, it's from Ross and I, the girls have bought their own gifts for you.' Marlo handed Grace an envelope. No fancy bows or wrapping, just a big heart drawn on it.

Opening the envelope, she lifted out the card which had an itinerary inside, 'This is right before the wedding,' Grace looked at Marlo stunned.

'Yes, I know, we'll get there just in time for all the fun.' Marlo said with a smile. 'You. Me, Mac, and Bella in the Mediterranean for a week... Michael can fly over with the boys and Ross. I'm taking you to Italy and Malta for a girls trip you will never forget; I'm going to spoil you... And don't say you can't come because I know you can, I secretly checked your schedule.' Marlo was buzzing with excitement. 'Oh, and there's this too, Ross wanted you to have something today on your actual birthday, he picked it out for you,' she said getting a gift box from her Birkin. 'You've got guest arriving, put it in your bag, open it when you're back at the hotel tonight,' she said tapping her sisters hand to hurry her up.

Marlo's holiday itinerary was outrageous and jammed packed... a private jet to Rome, then to Malta, a super yacht to Sicily and Sardinia, then finishing back in Malta before flying to Florence then driving to Marlo and Ross's estate in Tuscany for their daughter's wedding. Grace's mind boggled. Marlo didn't give normal gifts, she was extravagant, and Ross encouraged her extravagance because he could.

'Umm,' Grace was baffled, she could hardly believe it looking at her sister. 'Did you say Bella's coming too?' The opulence of this gift was overwhelming.

'Of course, and Mac, oh and Louise too if she can.' Marlo was making it a family affair. 'I thought it would be kind of nice the week before the wedding for us all to bond... oh, and Abbey and Tina are invited too.'

'What about Scarlet, Phoebe and Ruby?' asked Grace, they were Marlo's older daughters.

'They'll be busy with the wedding and being pregnant, this is just for us.' Marlo had it all sorted, she'd enjoy planning trips away more than anyone Grance knew, she had it perfectly planned out.

Grace, who was still in shock, she'd received extravagant gifts from her sister and Ross before, but never like this, 'Marlo. Ross. Thank you, I don't know what to say. Thank you both so much.' A happy face suddenly appeared, this was great, she'd been expecting to head over to Italy a day or two prior to her nieces wedding, but this was awesome.

One by one, the dinner guests arrived whilst Michael visited the kitchen to make sure all was as planned. Bella had arranged the table and added a few touches of her own, flowers, elaborate glasses and plates with personalised napkins embroidered with Grace's initials, and name tags so everyone knew their place at the table of seventeen. She'd done such a great job that when she'd arrived, Grace hugged her and told her how wonderful everything looked. As she hugged her daughter, she remembered she was planning to move out on Monday, her chest hurt at the thought... and then she remembered she still hadn't told Michael. That would have to be amongst the conversations for tomorrow.

Just about everyone was there, her family, her kids, Bella's boyfriend Dom who'd slipped in late, Ross and Marlo, their girls all except for Phoebe who lived in London. Her brother Jimmy and her sister-in-law Louise, and of course Ed, and Shiv. When they arrived, Shiv hugged Grace for a long time. They both missed Claudine presence tremendously today, and being in each other's arms, they felt spiritually connected to her in some strange way.

'The happiest of birthdays to you my sweet girl, my gosh you're just gorgeous,' Shiv squeezed Grace in tight. She'd been at the hospital the day she was born, waiting outside the delivery room door, listening intently as her best friend gave birth and then left the world. Shiv's love for Grace was as strong as the love she felt for her own children, she'd treasured her from the second she took her first breath.

'Thank you Shiv... I love you.' Grace felt the warmth that only Shiv gave her, her eyes filled with emotion, she couldn't stop the tears escaping.

Shiv wasn't overly tall, she was Indian and very beautiful, she dressed impeccably with great style. She was born in Grafton and didn't have an accent; her family was amongst the first Indians to migrate to Australia back in the late 1800's. Nevertheless, she still faced modern day racism.

Smiling at her best friend's baby girl, who was now a mature and wonderful woman, Shiv touched Grace's face, 'Oh, my goodness I love looking at you. You look so much like her.' Now they both had tears as everyone around them tried not to notice their touching moment.

Loving Grace

Ed Hunter was in his eighties and still as fit and strong as an ox, 'Gracie my girl, you don't look a day over twenty-one.' All the Hunter men called her Gracie, they were all charmers.

She laughed, Ross had just told her the same thing, 'Well, I'm starting to believe I could be twenty-one now.' She looked at Ross who was standing next to his father, both smiling at her.

'I hope that husband of yours knows he's a lucky man,' Ed's gruff voice said as he rubbed her arm with a gentleness that reminded her of her own father. They were gentlemen, old school Englishmen. Good men.

'I'd like to think he does by now,' she smiled as Michael overheard and made his way in behind her, wrapping his arm around her waist.

'Ed, I'm the luckiest man alive.' Michael kissed the side of her face.

Most people who knew Grace adored her, she was kind and caring, and funny at the most unexpected moments. So, yes Michael knew he was lucky.

'Okay, stop hogging the birthday girl,' Jimmy came through and scooped his little sister away from her husband and into his embrace. 'Fifty! It just seemed like yesterday you were fifteen and sneaking down to the Cross to misbehave... Happy birthday! You look absolutely amazing Grace.' Jimmy was always one to compliment women, he loved making them feel good about themselves, he cherished his sisters, his wife and his nieces, he was a ladies man, but in the loveliest way.

'Thank you.' She smiled; her heart was completely full of love. All her favourite people were in this room with the absence of a few.

Jimmy slapped Michael on the back, 'Hope you've got a good dinner in store for us mate – I'm starving.' Jimmy was bubbly and happy.

'Oh, happy birthday my beautiful girl,' said Jimmy's wife Louise, she was loud by nature, pushing her way close to Grace and gave her a big kiss and warm hug, all the men taking a step back. 'I love this bracelet,' Lou grabbed Grace's wrist and held it up, pulling a face at Michael, 'Nice one... Very nice!'

He raised his brows, 'She's worth it.' He and Louise got along great, he liked her, she was an in-law too, they understood each other.

'This is something I just know you'll love,' Louise handed over a gift bag, 'This is from me, not your brother!' It was a large gift bag with a box inside it. Grace sat the box on a dining chair and opened the lid. 'I hear you're heading to Europe soon!' She winked at her good friend who was so much more than an in-law. Grace gasped as she took the vibrant print Valentino kaftan from the box and held it up.

'I'm in love!' Grace sighed with pleasure.

'It's a silk and cotton blend, great for those hot evenings on the yacht,' Louise winked, she was very fashion forward, she too like Marlo, had very expensive taste, they could afford extravagant things. Grace on the other hand, like beautiful things, but she could never justify spending four thousand dollars on a kaftan ... and there was a matching headscarf too!

Loving Grace

'Lou, I love it, thank you.' Grace gave her sister-in-law another hug.

'You know that's not from me,' Jimmy interrupted them, 'I'd never give you a kaftan for your fiftieth,' he said giving his sister an A4 envelope. It was gifts galore and having billionaires as family made for great gifts. 'You only turn fifty once, and you are my baby sister.'

Inside the envelope was a print of tropical florals with brightly coloured birds, an oil painting in beautiful pinks and oranges with subtle greens and limes, it was breathtaking. A note paperclipped to it saying, 'Delivery is Monday.'

'I saw it, I thought of you,' Jimmy had a soft smile as he spoke to his siter. 'I hope you have a place for it, but I wanted you to have it.'

Grace took a big breath, she knew this painting was something special, her brother new art, he was a collector, 'Jimmy, it's gorgeous,' her voice soft as she marveled at the beautiful colours. Jimmy and Louise didn't have children, they lived a wonderful life full of travel and riches. They lived high up in their luxurious Sydney CBD penthouse, sometimes she envied their life, they appeared to have it all.

The room was filling fast, Grace made a fuss over her niece and business confidant Scarlet, and her tiny weeny baby bump, being pregnant had been a wonderful time in Grace's life, every time. Her niece was having the first baby in the family since the birth of Bella, so the excitement for everyone was high. Scarlet was married to Angus, and he was everything any parent would want for their daughter, he was practically perfect in almost every way. Marlo loved making a fuss about Angus, which Grace had thought at times was probably embarrassing for poor Angus. The fact that he was normal... he was a builder, not rich, his family were average working-class people from the northern beaches, and he was perfect to Marlo and Ross, he was normal. They treated him like he was one of their own, they tried not to overstep the boundaries with offerings of their good fortune, they really did try to be good in-laws, and Angus appreciated that.

'Hey, you,' Mac was a ray of sunshine, a delight and yet she couldn't see her own beauty. 'How does it feel turning fifty Aunty G, do you feel that old?' Mac was twenty-two years old and had her own issues. She'd had a substance abuse issue for the best part of her teen years, in and out of the best rehab clinics all over the world. Thankfully now she was straight and just a gorgeous girl to be around. Grace loved Marlo's girls, they were special, and they loved their aunt, they looked up to her and respected her like an older sister more than an aunt, because Grace was ten years younger than Marlo.

'You know Mac, until right now, I didn't think fifty was that old.' She smiled.

'Fuck! Okay, so it's not great feeling fifty,' Mac winced as she hugged her aunt. At twenty-two she was intriguingly stunning, tall, large blue eyes, and a mass of thick wavey dark long hair. University wasn't on the cards for Mac, unfortunately she'd spent too much time in rehab rather than studying in high school. Life was different for her now, she didn't have a job as such, her job was to stay clean and well, a homebody these days with hobbies such as painting, drawing, and sewing. It wasn't easy being Marlo and Ross Hunter's daughter all the time, the money meant there was always the threat of kidnapping and extortion, trust issues with friendships and wondering if people just liked you for your money.

Ruby was the last niece in attendance with her fiancé, soon to be husband, Sam Rutherford, a merchant investor and apparently ruthless according to Luca and Ross. Ruby had always been a leader, the outspoken one of the sisters, a go getter and sometimes too bossy, but she couldn't boss Sam around, she'd met her match. Grace liked Sam, although Marlo wasn't sure... not that she'd ever breathed a word to anyone but her sister. Ruby seemed happy and Marlo and Ross were happy for her, it was hard being mega wealthy and trusting your children's choices. Grace was close to all her nieces, and they had good relationships with her children, the cousins were all very tight.

As everyone took their seat, the only empty seat was Tina's, she was renowned for her lateness, or lack of commitment to a social occasion. It was her only flaw as far as Grace was concerned. Tina had gone on a lunch date and God only knows where that had led her. She'd told Grace she'd be late; she'd text to say she be there by the time the mains were served.

'Why can't she just be on time?' Kristian questioned as Tina's empty seat sat between him and Luca. If anyone was calling bullshit out, it was Kristian.

'Someone said she's on a date,' Scarlet raised an eyebrow to her cousin.

Grace chatted with everyone up and down the table, she sat in the middle between Michael and Marlo, with her brother and Louise opposite.

As she sat for a moment quietly observing all the people she loved, she looked at Bella nestled up beside Dom, someone Grace wanted to believe was in love with her daughter but had an inkling he actually wasn't... There was just something about Dom that she couldn't put her finger on. The relationship didn't feel right to Grace, she kept telling herself she was wrong, that she was being persuaded by Michael's negativity and not giving her daughter enough credit. Dom did nothing to endear himself to his girlfriend's parents during dinner, he went outside for cigarettes and only spoke with Luca and Scarlet's husband Angus, his clean-cut black hair was too perfect, he had facial hair that was like a permanent after five shadow, and that annoyed Grace for some reason! She tried so hard not to be that mother, but she just couldn't help it, the thought of her daughter sleeping with Dom, gave Grace an unsettled feeling inside.

The drinks were flowing, and Michael was enjoying himself, he had one eye on the table service at all times. It was hard for him to shut off, he was a control freak at the best of times. 'How's the champagne?' he asked Grace for the second time.

She looked at him with sparkling eyes, 'Great, thank you.' He looked preoccupied. 'You can relax now, everything is perfect.' Giving him a kiss to the cheek. As she looked at everyone, she admired the way that Shiv sat back and watched over her family with so much unconditional love in her eyes, it made Grace mushy and warm. This was her family too. Kristian teased his sister about something, while Marlo chatted with Mac, and Ross and Louise laughed loudly while Michael told a story, Grace loved her family.

Then Tina slid through the door and into the private dining room, Grace giving her a wave, everyone saying their hello's, she'd stopped to view Scarlet's baby bump and was chatting there for a while, Grace sipped on her champagne, letting Michael fill her glass again, then she heard Marlo at her side say something.

'Tina, those earrings are magnificent!'

Before Grace even looked up, she knew her world was about to change. It was the heaviest feeling of dread and devastation all at once... it consumed her immediately.

'Thank you, Marlo. They're new actually!' Tina had a glint of mystery to her tone, there was something about her words that made Grace look up quickly, Tina was standing on the other side of the table making her way along the table, she wanted to see her best friend's expression... the earrings! 'Happy birthday Grace, sorry I'm late, my date was fabulous. I'll tell you all about it!' Tina winked.

Grace managed a smile; she could feel the tension all around her... They were her earrings. She could feel Michael looking at Tina and Tina looking at him. The room felt like it was closing in on her like a vice, her heart was pounding so hard it hurt inside her chest and throat. Her temperature was bubbling over as she hung onto the strained smile at her lips.

Her husband was fucking her best friend!

They were having an affair!

Her mind a mash, unable to think or breathe, so much so, she could barely keep her eyes open.

Michael was Tina's mystery man!

Tina reached Grace and put her arms around her, placing a gift bag on the table, 'Happy birthday!' she said something else, but Grace could only see her lips moving in the faded-out sound of the room. Still, she managed to smile. Tina began chatting with Marlo until she went down the table to her own seat. Grace sat there in a daze, everyone was talking, the sounds were hurting her head as her worst possible nightmare sank in.

Michael had got up and left the table and gone to the kitchen. Grace sat in a stunned coma for what felt like forever.

'Grace!' Marlo said softly at her side, bringing her back into the land of the living.

She looked at her sister and gasped for breath, 'My head hurts, I've got a headache, I need to go!'

'What's wrong, are you all right, you look weird?' Marlo whispered, she immediately knew something was up, her sister was suddenly pasty and looked clammy.

'I need to go!'

'Have a drink of water.' Marlo was concerned, handing her the water glass, keeping things on the down low as to not cause a scene. 'Do you need some air; can I take you to the bathroom?'

'Mmm,' was all Grace could manage.

Marlo sat looking at her, if she didn't know better, her little sister was having a medical episode.

63

Loving Grace

'What's wrong?' Now Louise from acrost the table was in on it, and then Jimmy questioned Marlo as she sat in this strange moment of not knowing what was happening.

'I think I need some air.' Grace breathed, she stood quietly and couldn't see anything, it was all a blur as she made her way out of the room without a fuss. Marlo followed. They went out onto busy Pitt Street. Grace gasped and gulped for air, feeling like maybe she needed to throw up or pass out, she held her head and turned around on the spot.

'What is happening, is it your head? Do you need a doctor?' Marlo asked mid panic.

'I'm going to the hotel; I need to go to bed.' She needed to run as fast as she could away from the restaurant. *How could this be, but then it was like she knew exactly how it could be, and exactly when it began and why. Fuck!* Grace felt sick.

'What's going on?' Now Michael was out on the street with them, which sent Grace into an internal spin.

'She's got this awful headache, she looks terrible.' Marlo scoffed at him.

Unable to look at Michael, Grace took some deep breaths, closed her eyes, and said, 'I'm sorry, I sorry. I need to go to bed, my head is pounding, It's a migraine.' She'd had migraines before, it was believable. They'd come on suddenly in the past, once Michael had even called an ambulance to the house for her, so he believed her.

'Sweetheart, are you sure, I mean everyone's here for you.' He could see she was out of sort's big time; she looked unwell.

'I need to go to the hotel; I need to lay down.' She couldn't bring herself to look at him. 'I'll be fine.'

'I'll take her, you go inside,' Marlo told Michael who couldn't believe this sudden turn for the worst in his wife.

Michael objected, 'I can take her. Do you want me to come with you honey?'

'No, no!' she gasped looking across the road, 'You go back in and make sure everyone enjoys their dinner. Marlo!' Grace said putting her hand out to her sister, managed to dismiss Michael without looking at him again, then she crossed the street, Marlo at her side to assist.

'I think you need a doctor?' Marlo said as they crossed the floor of the hotel lobby together.

Grace suddenly stopped and turned to her sister, 'I'll be fine from here.' She stopped walking. 'Please go back to the restaurant and finish your dinner.' She needed to be on her own, desperately.

'Grace!' Marlo sighed, 'You don't look well. I'm worried.'

'I just need to sleep. I need to go to bed,' she said finding a fake smile to ease her sister. 'Tell everyone I'm fine, I need to sleep this migraine off, and I don't want anyone bothering me, I really need to sleep.'

Marlo took a few seconds, 'Do you think you ate something? Could it be food poising?'

'No. Marlo, please. My heads pounding, I need to go up to bed,' Grace gushed. 'I'll call you tomorrow.' And with that she briskly walked around the corner and straight into an awaiting lift, leaving Marlo standing there. If she'd left it another second, she would have burst into tears and God knows what she would have said to her sister.

The second the suite door closed, Grace began hyperventilating, without even stopping she went straight to the bathroom basin, she could barely hold herself up, her entire body was in shock, in a cold sweat. It was as if she was looking at herself from outside of her own body, her beautiful new dress was strangling her, she unzipped it and let it drop to the floor, then kicked her heels off.

And this was fucking fifty!

Her world had just come crashing down around her in what felt like a split second. Her head actually was pounding. A few sharp breaths in as she stood in her underwear, then a dash into the toilet, holding her long hair back, she threw up until there was nothing left.

How could this be, how could they do this?

Tina's earrings were most definitely the earrings from Michael's jacket, there was no mistaking them... it was all starting to come together but in rapid visions in her head. Holding her hair back from her face, spitting into the toilet bowl, Grace questioned her own sanity.

No, this couldn't be happening. It was crazy. It simply couldn't be true.

Back up at the basin she splashed cold water on her face and rinsed her mouth. The more she tried to settle herself, the more she thought about all the questionable moments in time. Hot burning tears ran down Grace's face. The things they'd both done and said over the years, times when they'd avoided each other, or not! It was all falling into place and Grace couldn't stop it. She let out a scream of frustration as she took her bra off and threw it across the bedroom, she put a t-shirt on and got into the big, oversized bed on the side she always slept in. The drapes had been drawn, the bed was turned down, pulling the covers up over her face she softly whimpered, the pain was excruciating. Taking sharp breaths as the weight of it all fell over her. Slowing her thoughts down to get some perspective was taking all her energy, staying with one thought seemed impossible, it felt like she was literally going crazy.

Her husband was fucking her best friend! Her best friend was fucking her husband! And she was more than sure it had been going on for years! Michael was the married man Tina was sleeping with all along, it had to be him. Why did he stay married to her, why didn't he just leave if he wanted Tina? Was she losing her mind... How could this be. How had she been so blind and so stupid! So many things made sense to Grace. All the business trips and nights spent in town, and the times she'd been unable to contact Michael for one reason or another. At the time, she'd just let it go thinking he was busy with the restaurant, but now she knew. Grace hated those wives who kept tabs on their husbands every move, she'd never wanted to be that wife. Then another thought, had it been Michael and Tina's game plan to make out like they dislike each other... did they purposely give off red herrings? the more Grace thought about it, the more it made perfect sense. Then as if she were a crazy woman, she'd doubt herself in the very same moment. *They wouldn't do it to her... to the kids!* But the facts were all there, so much so, she could almost pinpoint when it all began, it was as clear as day now and she'd let it happen right under her own roof!

Luca's birth was a twenty-four-hour battle, Michael just made it to the hospital for his arrival. Grace had been terrified she was going to die... it was hard not to think that way, her mother had died in childbirth... why couldn't she? Marlo was a pilar of strength, right until Michael turned up smelling of whisky and cigarettes, literally minutes before Luca was born. Things weren't great for some time after that, but Grace did her best to be a new mother and wife. Then when Michael had pulled a no-show for Kristian's birth. Grace forgave him because that's what she did, she was hell bent on being a good wife, and having a family, her children having both parents. There was a lot of outside noise, Marlo, her friends, even Shiv had it in for Michael, but Grace sucked it up and let him off the hook. Things weren't normal for quite some time though. Michael was always at the restaurant, she had two little boys, Luca was at kindergarten, and Kristian was a hard baby for the most part. Out of the blue, and unexpected, Grace fell pregnant with Bella four years later and Michael had his chance to redeem himself with baby number three. To his credit he became super husband and a great father from that moment on, he doted on Grace and miraculously, the marriage was back on track and better than ever.

Nobody expected Grace's third birth to be as difficult as it was. Michael was at Grace's side the entire time. From the moment Bella was born it was evident that Grace wasn't herself, she wasn't right! Unable to even feed her new baby. Marlo and Michael were concerned immediately, one of them was there by her side in hospital at all times, Grace was vague and out of it with no interest in Bella or her own wellbeing. When it was time to go home, it was clear Grace needed help, that's when Tina stepped up. She'd just arrived home from a long trip to Europe and offered to move in and help her best friend out. She slept in the nursery so she could get up to Bella, she'd fed the children, cleaned the house, and looked after Bella while Grace slept most days. Marlo came by every day even though she had her own young family to care for. Abby had just had her first baby and was busy navigating motherhood, but still she managed to talk to Grace on the phone every day. Michael would come home from work, and help out, he and Tina spent a lot of time together, alone, and mostly at night while Grace was drugged out in bed. Then one day out of the blue, Tina told Grace she had to go, she literally left the house that morning. Yes, the girls remained friends, they saw each other regularly, but things felt different for some time for Grace. Tina leaving snaped Grace out of her baby coma as she called it, life went on. Tina never had anything nice to say about Michael from that time on though, in fact she told Grace many times back in those days that she could have done better than Michael, that she deserved better. And as for Michael, he said her friend Tina was hard work! It was as though for a long time the two kept out of each other's way, as if they didn't like each other… or so it seemed.

Bella's first birthday party surprised Grace most of all. Tina was very close to Bella, but she made up a lame excuse not to attend. At the time, it seemed ridiculous, now it all made sense. Tina hadn't wanted to come to Grace and Michael's home, she didn't want to see them together playing happy families... Certainly not if she was fucking Michael behind Grace's back!

It was so awful that Grace couldn't comprehend it. It was inconceivable. The more she allowed herself to think, the worse she felt. Getting up and going to her toiletries bag, she took out the box of sleeping pills. There were three left, so she took them in the hope she'd zonk herself out before Michael came back. Lying in bed, she now actually had a real migraine, she fought the urge to throw up as her chest physically ached. A numbness slowly invaded her body, the thoughts slowed, hot tears still fell from her eyes as she laid motionless until she fell asleep.

Chapter Four

The next morning when Grace woke, the night before was immediately with her. Michael was in bed next to her, his body warmth made her nauseous, she'd never imagined in her wildest dreams she'd ever feel this way in bed with her own husband, who until this day she had worshipped and adored with the fullest heart. It was the most awful feeling, wondering who the man beside you really was.

Grace hadn't had a chance last night to think about what she did next. This morning felt worse than last night, today she was numb from head to foot, her mind was super fragile, she was scared to open her eyes, scared for Michael to know she was awake.

Today he was expecting her to go home so she figured she could get up and do so. She'd play the headache card, and get the hell out of there, she doubted he'd want her hanging around town anyway.

Loving Grace

Did Tina stay with him in this hotel every Thursday night, or did he stay with her. And then it came to her... another slap in the face. *Tina was away on a business trip all next week... and Michael was in Singapore!*

Grace needed to get out of bed and leave, she couldn't stay, she had to go, with the least amount of contact with Michael. Her state of mind wasn't ready to accuse, debate, or fight with her cheating fucking lying husband. A fast swift exit was what she needed. Turning herself over to the edge of the bed, lifting the covers and getting out, her head foggy, she still felt like she needed to throw up. Her stomach was churning, she was flushed and hot, thanks to her being perimenopausal and dosed up on sleeping pills. Emotionally spent, Grace moved quickly to the bathroom, shutting the door behind her and locking it. Peeing, and then going through to the walk-through robe, putting on her bra, undies and then her soft pink pants and top, as she pulled her top on, Michael appeared.

'How are you this morning, better?' he asked standing there naked in front of her, which now felt wrong to Grace.

She didn't look at him, 'No, actually. I'm not great, I've got an appointment today with my doctor, so I'm heading home early.'

'Maybe you should stay here. Don't drive when your unwell, I'll call a doctor to come to the room to see you,' Michael sounded insistent.

'No, no. I'm fine, I'll be fine.' Scurrying, packing her belongings quickly, passing him and going to the bathroom to get her toiletries.

'Are you having breakfast? Have you got time?' he asked her.

Hah! What the fuck do you care! 'No, I need to get to the doctors.'

'Okay!' he sounded dumbfounded. 'Bella took all your presents with her last night; she'll bring them home for you. Everyone enjoyed their dinner, and they were all shocked at your disappearing act.'

He had her attention, 'I didn't disappear, I was really sick.' Glancing at him for the first time, he was still standing there, still naked.

'Well, I guess you're not coming back into town after the doctors.'

'No, I'll say goodbye now.'

'Okay,' he sounded a little wary of how strange his wife was acting. 'Grace, are you sure you're right to drive all the way home? I don't have to go to the footy with Luca and Kristian, we can stay here all day, and you can relax in bed, I'll order food up and we can watch the footy together.'

Was he onto her! The thought entered her head. She doubted it.

Turning and looking at him like he was insane, her bag over her shoulder ready to leave. She wanted to punch him in the ugly fucking face and then grab him by the hair and bash his head into the marble wall, over and over. 'I can drive myself home; you go with the boys,' she said calmly.

'Well, I'll call you later,' he came close to her, 'I guess you'll tell me how you get on at the doctors,' a pause. 'I'm off to

Loving Grace

Singapore early tomorrow,' Michael sounded lost as he leaned in and kissed his wife on the cheek, going to put his arm around her as she backed towards the door.

'Yep, sure, we'll talk later,' she did her best fake smile just to get out the door, she needed to go, now!

Pressing the lift button ten times, like her life depended on it, Grace didn't allow herself to think twice, she had to leave even though it seemed like one whole mistake... Michael would never do this to her, was she delusional! Walking briskly to the valet she then waited. Michael hadn't put up too much of a fight for her to stay. She knew exactly what his game was now, how he operated, how he had fooled her all these years. Her stomach felt like it was turning inside out as she stood waiting. Then her phone rang.

'Are you okay?' Marlo asked with great concern.

'I-I'm on my way home, I'm okay,' Grace stammered.

There was a weird silence for a few seconds, Marlo was confused, 'Should you be driving home after a migraine, can't Michael drive you?'

'My car has just pulled into the valet, I have to go,' Grace's voice was about to faulter, she was about to crack.

'Sure,' Marlo said, 'I'll call you later. Drive safe.'

'Bye.' Grace hung up and got into the familiar comfort of her Range Rover, she took a deep breath, and headed home, no music, no radio, just her and her car.

The hour drive home was spent on the phone to her three children, they each called her to see how she was feeling this morning, they were all worried. Luca sounded as lost as she did.

He said he was going to head home to see her for dinner tonight, straight after the football. Kristian was doing the same once he found out Luca was going home for the night, they'd drive together. Bella was coming home today too; she had packing to do for her move tomorrow.

By the time Grace made it home, she'd missed four calls from her brother, Shiv, her niece Scarlet, *and Tina*. When Grace saw the missed call from Tina, she was angry. Standing in her large perfect French country style kitchen, she pondered calling Tina back and questioning her straight up, but she was smarter than that. Since last night, her mind had gone back and forth... *her husband was having an affair with her best friend... her husband was not having an affair with her best friend.* Even though the earrings were her only proof at this point, Grace felt it in her soul. The affair had been going on for nearly twenty years, she needed to process it, then act on it. As much as she loved her kids, the last thing she wanted to do tonight was having them all at the house. She'd find a way to push through.

Grace showered and went to bed, her bed, it was eleven am. She looked over at Michael's side, it was the weirdest feeling. She suddenly hated him!

How could he cheat on her? He was such a great husband, everyone thought so! Perhaps she wasn't such a great wife? Why hadn't he left her years ago for Tina, and why was he still playing happy husband when she clearly wasn't enough!

Her confusion was next level. Their sex life had faded over the years, she'd been perimenopausal for a while now, her libido had gone and come back a few times. She'd lost her orgasm and found it again, just like Samantha in Sex and the City. There were times Grace didn't feel like sex, but then once she got into it, she was always a happy participant. Michael was a good lover... not her best ever if Grace were completely honest! Oral sex had never been high on her to do list, and she didn't like anal sex unless she was drunk, and it was fair to say she was happy to receive more than give. Overall, she rated their sex as normal. *But was it!* Critiquing her own sexual performance wasn't going to change a single fucking thing at this stage, the horse had bolted... Besides, she knew she wasn't bad in bed, before Michael she'd had a few lovers, experienced lovers at that, and she'd held her own rather well, or so she'd thought.

Did it matter if she was a crap root, anyway... No!

Grace knew she didn't deserve this betrayal; she knew she'd been the best god damn fucking wife she could possibly be in every aspect of her marriage to Michael. He'd played in his restaurant for most of their time together and she'd never not once complained. She'd been the stay home mum, their children were dropped off and picked up from school every single day, they had fresh lunches every day, they had dinner on the table every night, they had a clean warm and loving house to call home, so did Michael. Her business made money, and she financially contributed, good god... she'd floated his fucking restaurant for years should the truth be told! Grace had done everything in her power to be the best wife and mother she could. The only time she'd ever faltered, in what she thought was her obligational duties as a wife and mother, was after she gave birth to Bella, and it seemed that had been her downfall. That was when Tina the rat snuck in!

She'd experienced waves of emotion, sadness, confusion, and anger. Right now, she was angry. Tina was a brazen thief whilst she was suffering postpartum depression... unforgivable and completely inconceivable. Grace went into doubt mode again. *Maybe she was completely wrong, maybe she had her wires crossed and Michael had given Tina the earrings as a gift for some other reason.*

Grace tried to think of every excuse imaginable as to why her best friend was wearing those earrings.

The sting of tears fell down her face as she lay in bed, a new wave of sadness filled her entire body. What was she supposed to do now? She'd never had to deal with such an intense personal issue within her marriage before. She needed to get some kind of clarity so she could process her thoughts. By dinner time she needed to be on her A game, she couldn't show any signs of her own internal dilemma, her kids had enough of their own shit going on.

'Mum, you're snoring!' Bella said as Grace opened her eyes, 'Are you feeling okay, how's the headache, dad's worried about you.'

It was too much for Grace, 'Mmm.' Bella was standing at her bedside waiting for her to answer.

'Okay, well I'm going to start packing,' she looked at her mother thinking how unwell she looked.

'I'll get up in a bit and help if you like.'

Loving Grace

'No, I can do it, you look awful,' Bella stood there. 'It's one bedroom, I've got it,' she said ready for the challenge.

When the bedroom door shut, Grace's face crumbled, and she began to silently sob. The pain in her heart was like a knife digging at her, she now felt worse than she had this morning, it felt like as every hour passed, reality sank in. Two of her most trusted people had betrayed her. Nobody would believe Michael could ever do such a thing, he was loyal, he was a family man who always portrayed himself as the loving husband. A pair of earrings and her word didn't quite seem like enough proof. As for Tina, she'd been nothing but the perfect friend for nearly forty years. That hurt! Then the worst thought in the world came to Grace.

What if Abbey knew all along and never told her! it was more than Grace could handle right now. She debating calling Abbey who she'd spoken to just yesterday for her birthday, she had this overwhelming urge to do so, and yet the longer she kept it to herself, the longer it wasn't actually reality... In her head anyway. The one thing Abbey the lawyer was a firm believer in was facts and evidence. If she were here, she'd say get your facts and find some evidence before you accuse anyone of anything. Grace knew what she had to do but didn't feel any better.

When the boys arrived around seven o'clock, Grace had cooked the pasta sauce and had garlic bread ready to go. At the dinner table she was present, however not following the conversation. As she looked at her beautiful children sitting at their family dining table, it hurt. Michael had cheated on their family, not just her.

'Mum, you don't look well,' Luca said bringing his bowl to the sink for her, 'Maybe you should go to bed. We'll clean up and I'll bring you in a cup of tea.'

'Yeah, we'll clean up. Go to bed mum.' Kristian stood up and started to clear the table while Bella just looked on with a questioning look on her face.

'Great. If anyone needs me, I'll be in my room.' She gave a smile and headed off without question. Closing her bedroom door and looking around the bedroom was nauseating, everywhere she looked in this house was Michael, the kitchen had been full of him too, he was everywhere. When she climbed into bed, she now felt a stranger in a place that had been so sacred, her one place of rest where she'd felt protected and loved.

Had it all been a crock of shit, a fucking lie? she had so many thoughts, comparing herself to Tina, which she knew was bullshit, but it was nearly impossible not to do. Tina had always had a great body, beautiful long dark hair, she always wore clothes that evoked a suggestion. She prided herself on the allure of sexual mystery. Grace couldn't help it; she found herself comparing every component. *Tina might have been sexier, but she was also a two-faced bitch!!* The mere thought angered Grace; it infuriated her to the point of madness. One minute she wanted to call Tina and have it out with her, tell her how despicable she was, the next minute she wanted to sleep for a week. She laid there scrutinising Tina's personality and moral compass for signs of deception. Grace's usual kind and caring soul had now been compromised by a single pair of earrings, and the more she thought about the past nineteen years, the more she was convinced, Tina was fucking her husband!

'Tea and a shortbread,' Luca said as he brought it to her bedside.

'I don't want the shortbread, thank you sweetheart... You eat it,' she tried to smile and sound pleasant, but the fact was Michael had made the god damn shortbreads, and she'd rather starve than have ever eat his food again.

'What did the doctor say today?' asked Luca as he ate the shortbread, sitting on the edge of his mother's bed.

She hesitated, 'Um. There's nothing wrong, I just needs some rest.'

He nodded his head, 'Dad was pretty worried about you today.'

'He said that did he?' Grace's doubtful tone was a bit too quick off the mark. Michael hadn't called, he'd text her instead, and she never replied.

'Yeah, he did,' Luca looked at her.

'Well, there's no need for anyone to worry, I'm fine.' There was a second of silence. 'How are you?' She was a concerned mother; she spoke softly and gently to her son.

'I don't know yet.' He was powerless to his own future.

Grace nodded her head, 'Life is full of surprises Luca.' Her eyes sparkled as she held back tears, her emotions were unpredictable, 'I like to think it never throws anything our way that we can't handle.'

'It feels more like a test of my integrity or something.' His frustration was on the brink of boiling over.

'Why?.'

Luca huffed a laugh, 'Maybe I'm not father material.' He lost his smile.

'And maybe you are!' Grace smiled.

'I'm not a relationship kind of guy mum, you know me!'

'Having a child is more than a relationship. A child is a lifelong commitment.' Grace wondered if she was saying the right thing, she hoped she was.

'I'm not great at either.' Luca was too negative for Grace's mindset.

'You don't know that, and you don't have an option. If you are to be a father, you need to be a good one. It's that simple.' She was sure about that.

'Wow, what if I'm not, you're talking like you'll disown me if I'm a shitty father,' he laughed.

Grace smiled, 'I will. It's not hard to love your child Luca."

He smiled at his mother, 'Not very inspirational Grace King,' Luca laughed, 'Your headache's getting to ya, ha!'

Unsure of what her son wanted from her, 'Just lay with me, breathe in and out. You'll be okay, I can promise you that,' she said softly closing her eyes, she was borderline hyperventilation. Their conversation was intense, her head space wasn't allowing it.

'Thanks for everything mum!' Luca laid beside her.

Loving Grace

If Grace thought she'd wake up Monday morning and feel better, she was mistaken. The two sleeping pills she took before bed meant she missed Luca and Kristian leaving for work at seven thirty am. When she woke at ten thirty with a foggy head again, all she wanted to do was go back to sleep, her chest still felt tight, she woke angry, she wanted to kill Michael and Tina. The mere thought of what they'd done to her, behind her back, behind her families back, their children! Well, it was too much today, so Grace did something she would never normally do, let alone on a Monday morning. Sitting in the peacefulness that was her bedroom patio, she looked out over the rolling hills, misty and chilly, but very tranquil. Wrapped up in her plush velvet nightgown, she sipped on a tea mug full of smooth red wine, she opened the bottle last night whilst she cooked. The fresh air in her face was helping, the gulps of wine were nice too! The warm tears that rolled down her cold cheeks, not so nice. Wiping them away with her palm, she wondered if Michael loved her... Clearly, he wasn't in love with her, but maybe he still loved her in some pathetic way, he'd stuck around for something, was it money! They each had a personal account and then they shared the joint account that they each deposited into monthly to pay for things like the mortgage, holidays, and bills. She rarely checked the account balance; she was just sure it always had money in it. If it wasn't money Michael had wanted from her, then why did he continue to come home to her, and why did he still want to sleep with her. He was having sex with her and with her best friend... Maybe that was his thing... Why did Tina go along with it? Grace's head was again filled with difficult thoughts, they just wouldn't stop.

The mug of wine had numbed things a little, she loved wine. Grace didn't take drugs, never had, however, she was fond of her sleeping pills and red wine, often together. After a shower, she put on a jumper and track pants, sneakers and tied her long hair up on her head in a ball that looked more like a dead cat on her head.

'What can I do to help?' she asked Bella as she stood in the doorway of her bedroom which now looked bare.

Without turning around, her daughter began, 'I need my clothes put in those cases... they're Dom's cases, he let me take them to put my things in. Then my shoes need to be put in that box there, and everything from those draws in that big bag there,' Bella said pointing here and there. 'I can't take everything, not straight away anyway,' Bella said as she piled her pillows up.

'Why is that?'

'Well, just in case,' she paused, 'Who knows, I could be back in a month.'

Grace didn't say a word, at least there was some doubt in Bella's mind. Dom was twenty-six years old, not exactly ancient, but old enough to question what he saw in a young nineteen-year-old. Well, Grace knew what he saw... the same thing older guys used to see in her when she was that age. If she questioned her daughters decision, she'd only push her towards him.

It had been all systems go all afternoon, they'd packed Bella's car to the brim with suitcases and bags and boxes, with a few still left in the room, Bella wouldn't let Grace drop them to Dom's city apartment tomorrow, which was another thing for Grace to stew on... her daughter made sure she kept a decent distance between her boyfriend and her family most of the time.

'I'm not moving overseas mum,' Bella smiled just before she got in the driver's seat, 'I'll be back to see you and dad for dinner all the time, I'll sleep over occasionally too, you'll see, you won't even know I'm gone.'

'Well then why are you going at all?' Grace lost her nerve and burst into tears.

'Mum!' This annoyed Bella, 'It's not about you... Why are you so dramatic?'

'I'm sad that my baby is leaving home, you don't have to be angry at me for missing you already,' she sniffed hard to regain composure.

'And you don't have to make me feel guilty... God!' Bella slumped into her car. 'I love you, even though you've totally ruined my vibe.'

What a little bitch! Grace couldn't even bring herself to stay and wave Bella off as she left the property, her daughter was such an ungrateful shit. It killed Grace who had never had a mother of her own to love and spoil her, her daughter took her for granted and right now she was sick of people abusing her good nature. Storming in the house and slamming the front door closed, she went to the kitchen bench and stared out over the mountains for a while... lost in thought. A sudden urge came over her, she grabbed her house keys and handbag and went to the garage, got in her Range Rover, opened the roller door, and sped out, kicking up the toppings on the drive as she sped off down the tree lined drive.

Chapter Five

It was time to get the evidence and the facts she needed. Coming to a holt outside Marlo house, Grace took a deep breath in, it felt like she'd held her breath the entire drive-in peak hour traffic to her sister's home. It was just past seven and she was still pumped with adrenaline, for the past day she'd been like a zombie, and suddenly it was like she knew what she needed to do. Pressing the buzzer out on the street with an impatient flicker of her finger.

'Grace!' it was Marlo, she was watching through a security camera, they literally had one in every room of the house.

'Let me in,' Grace barked impatiently. The gate began to open. Marching up to the front door on a mission, not at all in the head space to accept any shit from her sister.

The super large front door opened, Grace thought the size of the door was unnecessarily oversized.

Marlo stood there surprised to see her sister, 'What's wrong?' she said moving aside as Grace whisked past her leaving her to follow on through her own home.

'I need to speak with Ross. Is he here?' Marching into the living room she looked around, which was strange.

Marlo squinted, 'Why, what's going on, are you okay?'

Looking her big sister over, amused at how over dressed all in black for a Monday she was, 'Have you been to a funeral?' Grace couldn't help it, she frowned at her sister's fancy black clothing.

'No, I've been to a luncheon.' Marlo knew this mood. Frantic, rude with a calm tone, classic unhinged Grace. Something was wrong.

'Ross is he here?' she repeated, yes, she sounded rude, but it wasn't her intention. 'It's important.'

'Not until you tell me what is wrong with you.' It was a standoff, they often did this when they had a disagreement, it was a tactical move, silence unnerved the other. As close as they were, they did this often. Marlo didn't like being wrong or being told what to do by her sister, and Grace could go the distance, she could string her sister out for days if need be.

'Ross!' Grace yelled out for him, which infuriated Marlo. 'Ross!'

'Oh, my gosh!' Marlo shook her head in a huff, 'He is here, and I'm sure he's heard you by now,' she said like Grace was crazy. 'Is everyone okay?' Marlo hated not knowing what was going on. 'You're acting weird.'

'Fine. Everything's fine.'

Loving Grace

The standoff continued, they stood looking at each other, squinting, pouting lips, huffing, glaring at each other for the minute it took Ross to appear.

'Hey Gracie.' Even Ross was surprised to see her, 'I heard you yelling,' he chuckled giving her a kiss on the cheek. He was a big man, he was large, tall, and solid.

'I need to speak with you,' Grace felt an instant wave of relief at the sight of him. 'In private.'

'Sure,' he said gesturing to the hall towards his office, glancing at his wife.

When Marlo began to follow them, Ross stopped still in his tracks, 'Marlo!'

Grace never said a word, Marlo huffed with annoyance as they walked off into Ross's office with him closed the door.

Standing looking up at her brother-in-law, for a split moment Grace wondered if he'd believe her, if he'd think she was utterly nuts, if he'd tell her she was crazy... She felt crazy.

He sat on the edge of his desk, 'Sit down.' He offered; Grace shook her head. 'Is this about Kristian, Gracie, because I-'

Grace cut him off, 'I need a private investigator, I know you have one.'

He looked at her for a moment, 'Okay!' he was evaluating the situation, he was a smart man and had known Grace her entire life, 'Business or pleasure?'

'Neither!' her tone was flat; she didn't give anything away.

'I might need a little more information Gracie if I'm going to help you.' Whatever it was, he knew it was serious, rarely had he seen his sister-in law like this. She was a sweetheart to the core, he loved her like a little sister, he'd do anything for her. He'd fight, steel, and even kill for her if need be.

'Umm,' she breathed deep in her pause. It pained her to actually have to say it aloud. 'I need some information on someone and it's highly confidential.'

'So, is it personal?' She was making him work for it.

'Very personal. It's Michael,' Grace said.

'What's happened?' he came back immediately.

'I think he's cheating on me,' she held her nerve.

Ross rolled his head to one side, and then narrowed his eyes at her, 'Who do you think he's cheating on you with?' he was cool and calm, which made Grace think that Ross wouldn't put it past Michael. Ha!

'Tina.'

'Oh!' he sighed, not what he was expecting.

There was a huge silence as she gathered her composure, 'I need to know if she was on the flight to Singapore with him today, and I'd like someone to dig into his flight history and hers, like years back.' Grace felt like she'd lifted a very small weight off her shoulders by sharing her angst with someone.

'You think it's been going on for a while,' Ross asked, curious mostly.

'You don't think I'm crazy then?'

He moved uncomfortably, Ross didn't want to hurt her, 'I try not to let anyone, or anything surprise me… Gracie I don't know what to say,' he wasn't happy, 'I will help you.'

Just then Marlo slowly opened the door, 'Can I come in?'

Loving Grace

'You're in aren't you?' Ross huffed; he was stressed. What he'd just heard bothered him a lot. Grace looked at Marlo, then to Ross, he didn't want to upset either woman.

'I need to know that you're all right!' Marlo said to Grace as she closed the office door behind her.

'Marlo!' Ross began, 'Can we just have a few more minutes alone?'

'Ross!' Marlo was devastated. 'No!'

Grace looked at him, she didn't expect him to keep secrets from her sister and when she turned and saw Marlo's face, literally borderline tears, she cracked, 'You can stay, it's okay,' Grace said and then continued to tell her sister what was going on with her.

Marlo seemed to take the news as bad as they expected her to, 'That fucking arsehole!' she was instantly enraged. 'And her!' she spat the words with fury. 'That bitch! I can see her doing this to you... she's not like Abbey. Tina's got that thing about her, you know... Like she'd sleep with your husband! Oh, that bitch!' This was a lot of swearing for Marlo. Ross looked at her with bewilderment, waiting for her to finish, but she was far from finished. 'How could they do this? I could kill them. Can I kill them?' she looked at Ross like it might actually be a possibility for her.

'Marlo!' he frowned like it was ridiculous. 'You can't kill people.'

'How can they do this to my sister?' Marlo shouted at him like he was to blame, 'She's had his babies, she's done everything for him, so he could have the family he never had, and this is what he does to her,' she was so worked up, 'And her... I'm going to kill her, that fucking bitch!' And with that, Marlo began to cry, she was beyond upset. Grace didn't say a word, she let her sister go, this was what she needed to hear, someone who wanted to kill them as much as she did, it made her feel a little less crazy, it was almost comforting.

'I think you need to calm down Mars,' Ross let her go as long as he could. She went to Grace and hugged her head to her shoulder, as uncomfortable as it was for Grace, she let her big sister do it.

For the next hour, the three of them talked it out rationally, Ross got all the information he needed for the P.I. He'd get onto it tonight, if there was dirt on Michael, Ross knew exactly how to get it.

After lengthy discussions in the privacy of the office, the girls went out to the living room, Marlo's housekeeper Fiorella made tea for them, while Ross stayed in his office. Marlo and Grace had a heart-to-heart sister talk as they looked out over the sparkling Sydney harbour lights, it was one of Grace's favourite views, she loved her sister's home. It took on so many forms, it was this sophisticated and stylish harborside mansion that actually had been in a magazine, then it was a cozy family home when everyone was here, it was the ultimate party house when needed, and it was also a comfortable sanctuary at times like this.

'Please stay the night, I don't want you driving home at this time of night on your own,' Marlo insisted, she had loads of spare bedrooms.

Loving Grace

'Thank you, but I'm heading home, I feel like the drive,' Grace told her sister.

'I'm not taking no for an answer.' Marlo said.

'I'm not staying!' Grace smiled, knowing how much she was annoying Marlo, 'I've got things to do first thing in the morning.' And she did, she had so many things to do, where to begin was the problem.

'I'll let you go, only if you call me when you get home, so I know you're safe.' Marlo hugged Grace in, she was devastated and beyond angry still, she had calmed down quite a bit since her rare outburst in the office. Ross told them the P.I work was vitally important, he made them both promise to keep their lips sealed and to remain calm at all times, no crazy phone calls or outbursts.

The next morning, which was Tuesday, Grace woke up feeling less than great, she'd kind of expected it after she had three glasses of red and two sleeping pills before she went to bed last night, but it seemed to be the best way to put herself out of her misery and get to sleep.

For years Grace had left the banking and bills up to Michael, she just made sure her hefty deposit went into their joint account every month from her business account for their living expenses and savings. She had an auto payment set up, she never missed a month, and she just expected Michael to do the same. She'd had no reason to check the account, she'd always trusted her husband of twenty-nine years to pay the bills. Until now.

Sitting at her desk figuring out passwords was frustrating; she had a notepad in her safe with all the usernames and passwords she and Michael had ever set up. She was keen to see the balance of their joint bank account, and more so their credit card statements attached to the account, to see what Michael spent their money on.

By mid-afternoon, she was into their joint account and the balance was frightful. She began a Grace style audit, seeing only her own substantial monthly deposits going into the account... Michael hadn't made any deposit for over five years! The outgoings were interesting, their mortgage payments for the country house were minimal because it was nearly paid off, and for some reason there seemed to be another mortgage payment, but they didn't own two properties. Grace figured if she just called the bank, they could tell her what the second payment was for. There had to be an explanation. The not so funny thing about calling the bank was, Grace wasn't listed as one of the account holders anymore, so the bank wouldn't tell her zip. She only had online access to the account because she had the username and password, but that was as far as she was getting. Her blood was boiling, pulling off her jumper and T shirt, in the midst of her hot flush crossed with a panic attack, Grace looked at the withdrawals made from the account and saw a whole bunch of things that horrified her. Besides large cash withdrawals from Michael, she couldn't see the credit card being paid off monthly, just some random payments every few months, so the credit card account balance was astronomical. Then getting her diary out she flicked through the pages, she always wrote down when and where Michael took business trips to. The dates and the places he'd been to weren't always matching up with where he'd spent money. Large cash withdrawals in Queensland when he was supposedly in Melbourne, from Brisbane when he was apparently in Perth, Singapore when he was in Dubai. Random hefty payments into the restaurant account, not so alarming.

Grace's heart was pounding in her chest, she racked her brain trying to remember when Tina had taken business trips, which was all the time, she was forever interstate – apparently! Her heart sank, then the buzz of her mobile phone interrupted her thoughts. It was Marlo.

'Ross has asked if you can come for dinner tonight, he's already got something for you,' Marlo said as if it was important, 'You can stay the night, Maria's cooking a roast, your favourite! And she's promising to make us a French breakfast on the terrace in the morning.'

'I'll be there at seven,' she said giving herself some time.

'Six, six thirty would be better for us,' Marlo added.

'I'll see you at seven.'

On her way into town, Grace called Bella, she missed her terribly already, and when it went to voice mail, she started to cry, not leaving a message, instead just hanging up. Her daughter didn't need her anymore, nobody did. The idea of getting older and having the kids leave the nest was supposedly to explore the world and grow old with Michael. *What happens now?*

Panting in and out as she drove, crying loud and openly in the privacy of her car, Grace had never felt so disconnected from her life. Fuck!

As she stopped at a red light she could see a glimpse of the harbour out to her left, she immediately stopped crying. On occasion over her twenty-nine years of marriage Grace had wondered what life would be like if Michael ever died, God help her! How would she cope with three kids, what she'd do on her own, would she be able to go on.

Sniffling to clear her nose, dabbing her red eyes with a tissue, and giving her hair a brush before getting out of her car at the front of Marlo's, prolonging the inevitable by sitting in the car as long as she possibly could, until her clock struck seven. Once Grace knew things about Michael, she could never unknow them, and she was most certain she could never forgive. Her own loyalty would make that impossible, for how could she forgive Michael and Tina for a sin she herself would never ever commit. How could she ever erase the fact that her husband had an affair with her best friend.

The gate automatically opened, they were expecting her, Marlo was waiting at the door for her, 'Let me take your bag, I'll get Fiorella to put you in the bird room,' Marlo said taking Grace's underwhelming overnight bag from her.

'Can I please have the butterfly room?' asked Grace.

'Butterflies it is!' Marlo had a strange smile on her face, a cross between sympathy and frustration as she led the way to the living room and kitchen.

'What is he doing here?' Grace raised her voice rudely.

95

Loving Grace

'Lewis handles our P.I, he's the connection between us and them,' Ross explained seeing Grace's instant horror.

'Nice to see you too Gracie.' Lewis Hunter gave her one of his looks, of which she ignored, huffing dramatically to show her dismay. He was the impeccably groomed nephew of Ross, who also knew her sons super well apparently!

Lewis sat on a stool at the bench, his short dark hair was perfect, his eyes had a certain sparkle that Grace again chose to ignore. He was stylish, she'd give him that much. If he didn't think he was so good looking she might think he was, tall and masculine, jet black hair and dark features, darker skin than the rest of the half cast Hunter Indian/Poms... The Hunter men all had the same mix race look going on, olive skin, dark hair and eyes, they were great looking men. Lewis had a little of something else happening too though, nobody knew what, because nobody knew who his father was. The fact that he'd been on Australia's most eligible bachelors list twice didn't impress Grace one bit.

'Does he know my personal situation?' she snaped, glaring at her brother-in-law, 'I told you in confidence because I trusted you Ross. Not so you could go off and turn it into a Hunter collaboration. Jesus. Fuck Ross!' Her angst was evident.

'Gracie!' Ross began in his firm yet calming tone, 'I can assure you Lewis will be discreet.'

She huffed and turned to Marlo who stayed silent for the first time ever, then she turned to Lewis and gave him a long distasteful stare - a warning shot. The problem with Lewis Hunter was he was too smart for his own thirty-seven-year-old boots. Michael had never liked him, and it seemed suited that Grace didn't either, not that Lewis had ever done anything to deserve her angst or rudeness, but she thought he was up himself, too good looking for his own good, which annoyed her for some reason. He was spoilt by all the Hunter's, even her sister and Jimmy adored him. Sure, his mother died when he was a baby, and his father was a mystery, but Shiv and Ed along with the rest of the family seem to put him on a ridiculously high pedestal like he was so special. That gave her the shits too! What really pissed Grace off, was that Abbey, Tina, and even her sister-in-law Louise all secretly had a thing for him, they were like ridiculous cougar marshmallows in his presence because he was hot, but not Grace.

Lewis Hunter was a little shit!

He was a cool guy, who just happened to be rich thanks to his uncle bringing him onboard in the early days with Hunter King, Lewis, a super smart teenager designed the initial platforms that got Ross and Jimmy off the ground in the first place, he'd help them design a secret online international cyber security network that took them to the next level with governments all over the world, but none of this impressed Grace... Who cared if he was rich, smart, and hot. Big deal!

She looked directly at him, 'So, how do you know this private eye guy anyway?'

He moved on the stool at the kitchen bench, 'I just do.'

She narrowed her eyes looking at Ross and Marlo, then back at Lewis for a long moment, 'I'm hoping you're here because you have information for me, I'm not in the mood to be bullshitted around.' Her tone was still pissed, she could be a bitch in moments like this, her nerves weren't helping either.

Marlo cleared her throat, 'Just so you know, Lewis eats dinner here every Sunday and Tuesday night, sometimes Friday too. He lives a few streets away.' Marlo felt she had justified herself, or somehow make it less like another betrayal to Grace right at that moment.

'Good for him!' Grace huffed like she was in pain. 'Whatever you're about to say, my kids aren't to know, ever, you got it.' She looked around at them all.

Lewis huffed a huge sigh, 'Michael is in Singapore with your friend Tina,' he said partly to get up Grace's nose, and partly to put her out of her obvious misery. Lewis had met Tina numerous times and didn't think all that much of her. 'They flew out together yesterday on the SQ 212, they're staying in a deluxe king suite at The Westin, they've stayed there before together,' pausing to give Grace time to breathe. 'Michael is listed on the property title with Tina of her Glebe townhouse, and they also co-own an apartment in Brisbane.' Again, Lewis looked at Grace giving her a moment to absorb his barrage of information.

It was as though she hadn't taken a breath, just one long excruciating exhale out. Grace was already shell shocked, unable to speak as if a higher power had come over her body and was paralysing her. Marlo and Ross were still processing, they were hearing some of it for the first time too.

Lewis understood the gravity his information was having on everyone, especially on Grace, he'd always like her even though she wasn't particularly nice to him. Revealing that Michael was a sneaky piece of shit wasn't hard for Lewis, he didn't like Michael at all, so the feeling was definitely mutual between the two good looking guys of the family. However, Lewis was fond of Michael's sons, and they of him, which probably only exasperated the disdain between the two men. He cleared his throat, 'Their flight history together goes back years, I can get exact details if you need them, but I can tell it's years and years long,' he blinked to Grace apologetically, he could see her ship sinking slowly. 'Um. You mentioned the regular Thursday night hotel bookings.' Lewis looked at Ross and then Grace. 'The bookings don't exist, there's been three stay this year for Michael at that hotel, and they were all booked by you Grace.' He looked at her as she took it all in.

In a bid not to get emotional or cry, she lowered her eyes to the floor. How much more was there, her head was suddenly pounding, 'Is there anything else?' she huffed at Lewis like it was his fault, still giving him a hard time.

'Yep,' he was short with her, 'The restaurant is in the red and has been for some time.' His eyes went to Grace, 'And the shared joint account is the only money he has... basically you are funding him and his secret life.'

She immediately winced at him; she'd found that out for herself today but didn't like that Lewis knew her finances. 'You looked into my finances!'

'My connection is thorough. If there's anything off limits, then you have to tell me now,' Lewis was matter of fact, there

99

was an urgency to his words. 'I don't want to tell you things you don't want or need to know about your dickhead husband.'

'Seriously!' Grace questioned him, he *was such a little shit*.

Ross intervened, 'Well, I think what Lewis is trying to say, Gracie, is that if you have a limit to the information you want, you better say so now.' It was uncomfortable for everyone; they were all shocked and a bit dazed and confused.

'There's more,' Lewis warned them looking at them all.

'Of course, there is. Go for it. I need to know everything,' Grace scoffed.

'Are you aware Michael has a four hundred and fifty K gambling debt?'

'No.' Grace sighed, she was stunned, 'Now if that's everything I'm going... sorry Marlo, I need to go home, I'm not staying for dinner. Bye Ross. Send me the bill Lewis.' She literally turned around and walked to the hallway. 'Fiorella, can you get my bag from the butterfly room please,' she said loudly, not knowing where Fiorella was. She couldn't stand still; her skin was crawling, and a vomiting feeling was swirling in her gut. 'Fiorella!' Grace shouted, desperate to leave before she lost her shit.

'Grace!' Marlo came rushing into the hallway.

'I need to go,' she tried to hold it together as she looked up the stairs as Fiorella came rushing down.

Marlo reached out and held her sisters shoulders, 'I don't think you should leave; I don't want you driving like this.'

Breaking free, Grace gasped for air, her lungs about to collapse, 'I have to go, I need to be alone. Please don't stop me.'

She was frantic as Fiorella handed over her bag. 'Thank you. I'll text you when I get home.' Then she left. Hyperventilating, unsure if she was going to vomit or melt fist, she was in a wet hot sweat from head to foot, sitting in her car with her eyes closed, trying to think of a worse day in her life. The day her dad died was the clear worst day, this followed closely. Waiting a few minutes until her vision cleared, and she felt focused enough to drive, Grace drove home listening to Fleetwood Mac, crying. Driving was taking all her energy, and she needed to concentrate on the dark roads, if she thought too hard, her head hurt. Her mind was a complete mash. As she drove into her property and got closer to the house, she slowed down and took in her beautiful home. It had been their dream home, nestled into the bottom of the drive, the emotions consumed her, this had been the happiest home for the past fifteen years, it had been their pride and joy and now Grace wasn't quite sure how she felt about it. Pulling up in the garage, then going inside the house, she stood looking around the large living room that lead into the most spectacular kitchen. Michael had falling in love with the house at first sight because of the kitchen, he'd sold Grace with the office space and the views. They'd absolutely loved this house together; it had been their home. But did Michael ever really love it, did he ever really love her? Grace didn't know.

It was time for a plan. One thing she was very certain of, her kids weren't to know... not now, not yet. Grace would tell them when she thought the time was right. They each had their own problems right now; they didn't need to be worried about their parents' marriage. The next thing she was certain about was that her marriage was absolutely over. Full stop. She'd never be with Michael again in her entire life, she was done, as hard it was to consume.

Wandering into her bedroom, she couldn't bear it, walking into the bathroom going to the basin and studying herself in the mirror was awful, she looked dreadful. Her blue eyes brighter than ever from crying, her nose red, her skin blotched with emotion and her hair looked drab. Staring at herself, an urge came over her, opening one of the vanity drawers and taking out the scissors, holding a clump of hair out to the side of her head, she chomped into the thickness at her shoulders. Then repeated cutting over and over until her hair was in a very uneven bob. Michael loved her long hair, that's what he always said, and he'd always demanded her hair be long even though she wanted it shorter.

Who the hell did he think he was! When she thought about it, this was very controlling behaviour. Her hair was gone, and it didn't make her feel any better, but it did make her feel empowered in the strangest of ways. For many reasons Grace was insecure of her looks, even thought she was a woman who knew who she was to a point, she had been wrapped up in this cocoon Michael had made for her, a house where she felt safe apparently, when all along it was a house to keep her under control... Contained! He liked her hair long; he insisted on the local gym membership and the exercise equipment that she never used.

Grace went to her office, she logged into her laptop and took every last cent out of the joint account, as dismal as it was, and she stopped all future deposits. She changed the password on her business account. Next, she took her large work bag and began to fill it with important documents like her password notepad, her crucial workbooks, she packed up her laptop and began to pack all her design pads and of course, her passport, which was everything she needed.

At midnight she was in the robe packing her clothing into two large suitcases. Her shoes and bags into another along with any other belonging she couldn't live without, she'd even packed her bathroom belongings. Grace made harsh decisions there and then. In the hours she spent scurrying around the house packing her life up, she never shed a tear, she was on a mission. This was her doing what she had to do. She needed to go, leave the home she now felt had been her cage. Michael had moved her out to the country to keep her away from the city, from Tina, from his secret life!

Chapter Six

The next morning, Grace packed her Range Rover with two large suitcases, two boxes of belongings and two bags from her office, and of course her knew painting from Jimmy that had arrived on Monday. Besides her children, her life was now packed up inside her car, and in her head she was leaving the country house for the last time.

When she drove out, she never looked back, it wasn't until she got onto the road that she realised she didn't know where she was going. Heading into the city seemed like the natural direction, but not to Marlo, not to her children, and not to her brother. If Abbey had been home, maybe she'd go there, but she wasn't home and besides, she didn't know how to tell Abbey, because what if she already knew! The thought made her feel ill.

It was like subconsciously Grace knew she needed a few days on her own, she needed to plan her next moves, to come to term with her reality... the demise of her marriage. It felt like it wasn't just the end of her marriage though, it felt like Michael had made a mockery of all that they were, their children and everything she thought they stood for as a family. She needed to figure out how to move forward whilst respecting her children. Even though they were adults, Grace was very aware of how this would turn their lives upside down too, she was also conscious of how much Bella and Luca idolised their father, and of the possibility that they may not hold this against their father. She'd have to deal with that, it would kill her, but she'd understand. Kristian, on the other hand, would turn on Michael, she was certain of it.

Her finances were weighing heavily on her mind, money wasn't an issue at this point, her personal account was healthy. Of course, they'd have to sell the country house and pay off the credit card. Michael's dept was his problem now. Grace knew she could live independently on her own money, she wasn't rolling in it, but she did okay for herself.

Not wanting to be too far from things, and definitely not wanting to be in the heart of the city, Grace found herself at the Watsons Bay Hotel, a place she knew well, a place she could stay and feel safe as she took time for herself.

From her room she could see across the harbour to Marlo at Point Piper, she felt connected and not too far away or alone. She could ponder her life whilst wandering down to Camp Cove beach and sitting in the sand with a coffee figuring it all out. Grace needed serenity; she needed a familiar space. She needed to let her brain rest.

Loving Grace

Sleeping most of the day, it felt like it was the first time in days that Grace had actually been able to relax. Sitting in bed looking out the window to what she thought was the most beautiful harbour in the world, was peaceful, yet she still felt angst in her veins now she was awake, choosing to ignore the three calls from Marlo and two from Jimmy that she'd missed... And one from Michael.

As absurd as it sounded, she missed Tina. In times like this, Tina and Abbey would be her first point of call, they often did emergency dinners when there was a crisis or sometimes a three-way phone call if it were super urgent. Tina was always there when Grace needed her and now she was not. The grief was beyond anything she'd expected, if the world could swallow her up, she'd be happy to go.

The thought of food made Grace want to throw up, so she slid back under the covers and lay there in a dozy coma until she fell back to sleep. Emotionally it was all too much. Normally Grace would be consumed with her children's problems right now, but as important as they were, she didn't have the headspace. Luca was a grown man, and he was in a holding pattern with some young girl who had the power to decide his future. Kristian was floundering and erratic, but he was also his own worst enemy. And Bella, well her daughter wasn't really happy with something in her life. Grace's head went into a clouded spin just thinking about her kids. She'd left Michael, her life was in disarray, and she didn't know what to do, all she knew was that she had to leave. She'd left her wedding band and engagement ring at home on her bedside table.

Wednesday morning Grace put out spot fires as she sat in her lovely cozy room overlooking the harbour from the Watsons Bay hotel. She ordered breakfast and picked around it as she pretended to be at home to Marlo on the phone, then she did the same to Jimmy, then to Luca and Bella. It wasn't uncommon for her children to call her several times a day, Luca was considerate, and he was calling to see how she was feeling. Bella needed money to buy a new dress, she'd taken a job at a bar in Darlinghurst. Grace's first initial reaction was horror, and then she went into worried mother mode. 'Darling, you've never had a job before, what's bought this on?'

'Can't you just be happy that you won't need to pay me an allowance anymore!' Bella was annoyed that her mother didn't seem to have much faith in her ability to be grown up.

'I'm glad you're taking on responsibility, but a bar!' it sounded worse than it was meant to.

'I'm going mum, you've really ruined my day.'

This didn't faze Grace, she was so used to her daughter being dramatic, and disrespectful. Bella was tough, she'd make it through life because she was driven, and she was sassy, underneath the bitch exterior was a smart and caring young woman. Bella had wanted a job when she turned sixteen and Michael had knocked it on the head, saying she needed to concentrate on her studies, not work. He'd even controlled his daughter; he was an oppressor as far as Grace was now concerned.

Loving Grace

Walking down to Camp Cove beach, a place she used to come to with Marlo and Ross when she was a kid, they'd swim all day and be home just in time for dinner. She had great memories here, that was why it bought her so much comfort to be here, just sitting with her coffee from the kiosk at noon on a Wednesday, just her and some young mothers with their babies in prams having a catch up, and an old man with a tiny little old dog. Grace got tears in her eyes as she watched the old man with his little, tiny dog at the water's edge, it seemed like they did this every day, one day they would not. She felt the warm tears streaming down her cheeks. Then she looked to the young woman and their babies, it looked like a mother's group of sorts, something Grace never did herself, she wasn't great at making friends, she had two of the best, a sister, and a sister-in-law who she confided in, she didn't need more friends. These young women on the beach looked like super models, with expensive prams, high end active wear and caps to protect their perfect complexions from the sun. Grace hadn't been one of those mothers over there on the sand, and yet she still felt like she had lived her best life as a young mother, married to the man of her dreams, three healthy young children, their family was her world. *Had it all been a fucking façade!*

Back in her hotel room, she sat looking out over the harbour from a comfy armchair by the window, the serenity was exactly what she needed, her plan was to hide out there until Friday when she was supposed to go to Marlo's for the weekend as it was Ross and his twin brothers Gabe sixty second birthday, the Hunter's liked to celebrate birthdays, every birthday was an event.

Thursday Grace woke up in a panic. *How could it be that her husband, the love of her life, and her best friend had betrayed her!* She leaped out of bed and went to the bathroom, throwing up like she'd eaten something rotten. Gasping to catch her breath she flushed the toilet and sat on the floor wiping her mouth and watering eyes with toilet paper. Not the ideal morning! Choosing between going back to bed or showering seemed like a do or die decision. Making the decision to get into the shower, pushing through her tears and grinding her teeth, swallowing the hurt and heartache she felt, and taking the day on... for her own sanity. Today would be spent lazing in her hotel room trying to read a book or watch a movie, or she could go back to Camp Cove beach and do some meditation in the sand, take in the fresh air on the not so warm day, and ground herself. Maybe the old man and little dog would be there again!

Trying her best to relax, washing her short new hair, blow drying it and watching it bounce up into a wavy mass of blondeness, of which she quite liked. The new hair cut she'd given herself felt like she'd partly disassociated herself from being Grace the wife of Michael Moore. She was now just Grace King. Surprisingly, she actually had no regrets about her new look.

Venturing out for a walk around lunch time and ending up having a seafood lunch for one at Doyle's which was kind of nice, but she was a little unnerved when she saw a friend of

Loving Grace

Ross's come in with a group of men. She did her best to face the other way and go undetected, sipping her two glasses of red, enjoying her own company. Her mind seemed to always revert to her doing something wrong to deserve her husband turning to her best friend for sex, she was trying to justify their shitty behaviour with her own faults. It was ridiculous, what could she have done so wrong to warranted a grand affair such as this, and anyway, why didnt Michael leave her years ago if Tina was who he wanted to be with, and why did her so-called best friend tolerate his polyamory!

Until now Grace had tried not to think about Tina's comments about the mysterious man she'd had on the go for years! For just sex... apparently! When all along it was Michael, no wonder she'd never met him or known his name, it was sickening. The thought triggered her to a point of emotion she couldn't control, and she found herself leaving Doyle's to rush back to the safety and refuge of her hotel room for the rest of the afternoon and night.

Paying for a late checkout, Grace didn't want to turn up to Marlo's too early, Friday night was normally a social night at the Hunter's, the girls would be there, sometimes Grace's kids would swing by, and dinner was always a fanfare, they either ordered in big from some fancy restaurant or Fiorella and Maria cooked up a storm, people dropped in and out, drinks started early. Marlo made a big deal of her Friday night open house gatherings. *Oh, to be a billionaire!*

Grace wasn't sure she was up to it though, pretending everything was all A okay! She'd agreed to stay the weekend at her sisters' request, Marlo rarely took no for an answer and Grace knew if she didn't go this time and stay, Marlo would send a search party out for her. The street was full of cars, making Grace anxious from the start, she saw Bella's car and got a sudden chill, for she had this massive emotional lifechanging secret, and her kids didn't know yet. Mustering up all her happiness and good mood vibes, Grace buzzed the street buzzer, ready to pretend all was well.

'Coming Grace,' said Fiorella as she stood on the footpath holding her overnight bag. The gate opened for her, and she made her way to the front door where Fiorella the most well-paid housekeeper in Sydney awaited her arrival.

Walking into the heavily occupied living room was like she'd appeared from outer space. Her welcoming committee went quiet. Her daughter, sister, nieces, Ross, his brother Gabe, and sister-in-law Pamela, even Lewis, all stared at her like she was from Mars.

'Gracie!' Ross was first with a gasp of shock. She stood with her lips pouted to one side, daring them all with her eyes... they all seemed horrified.

'Mum, your hair!' Bella looked like she was going to burst into tears.

Her niece Scarlet stepped forward completely shocked to say the least, 'Aunty G... you cut your hair!'

Loving Grace

Then Marlo went to Grace to welcome her, 'I love it, it's very cute.' Putting an arm around her baby sister and waving for Fiorella to take her overnight bag.

'Mum,' Bella cried out. 'Did you cut it yourself?'

'Yes, yes I did.' She tried to ignore that her daughter was beyond shocked.

'Why?' Scarlet smiled as she asked as politely as she could.

'Because I felt like it,' Grace said matter of fact.

'I like it,' Lewis smiled like it was entertaining. Grace ignoring him.

'Well, its suites you darling. Doesn't it?' Marlo said looking at everyone for backup.

'Grace, you look ten years younger, you look amazing!' sister-in-law Pamela said, a compliment from her was rare, which made Grace wonder who'd said what about her, why was everyone being nice?

Grace smiled at Marlo, 'Well then, maybe I should have cut my hair off twenty years ago!'

Marlo read Grace's mood immediately, she could sense the fragility, 'Let me get you settled into the butterfly room,' she said putting an arm around Grace and following Fiorella out to the stairs.

'Who told Pamela?' Grace whispered as they walked into the butterfly room. If it were anyone, it would be her sister, she loved to talk.

Marlo let Fiorella leave and then shut the bedroom door, 'Nobody told Pamela, why did you cut your own hair off?' Marlo looked concerned. 'I like it, but...'

'Because!' Grace cut her sister off. Marlo was still in shock; she hadn't seen her little sister with hair that short since she was a little girl.

Then the door burst open, 'Mum, why did you do this to yourself?' Bella was obviously disturbed by her mother's home haircutting skills.

'You know Bella,' Grace sighed with great exaggeration. 'It's my hair, and I can cut it if I want to. I'm a grown woman.'

'I know you are.' Bella sensed her mother's offish vibe; she backed off for a minute.

In came Scarlet, 'Aunty Grace,' she was the eldest of her nieces at thirty-six, the closest to Grace, and she knew something was going on, she knew her aunt wouldn't normally cut her own hair. 'I think you look beautiful with shorter hair; I do actually really like it, it's just a little lop sided, nothing I can't fix in the bathroom in five seconds.' Scarlet was a sweetheart, Grace adored her nieces way, she was smart, sincere, and kind.

'Or you could do what normal people do and go to the hairdresser.' Bella still seemed disturbed. 'Dad will freak out; does he know about this?'

'Bella!' Marlo interjected before Grace lost her crap. 'Sometimes people...'

Grace cut her sister off again, 'I don't particularly care what your father thinks of my hair.' She couldn't control herself.

'He'll hate it.' Bella was rattled, taking revenge with her words. Things hadn't been going too well for her of late, she'd quit her new job already.

Loving Grace

'Good for him!' Grace huffed, almost sounding relieved, she smiled at her daughter who promptly turned and left the bedroom.

Marlo gave Scarlet a look like she needed to leave too, so she did as Grace stood there holding her head, 'Darling your hair looks fantastic,' Marlo smiled lovingly as she spoke. 'Even if it is crooked.' Her smile turned into a little laugh. 'I love it though, really I do.' It was hard to keep her emotions in check, she knew exactly why her sister had cut her off. 'I'm glad you're here.' She hugged Grace, 'You can fake another headache if you don't want to come downstairs, I'll cover for you,' Marlo touched her hair sensing a mega meltdown on the cards.

'Hmm, scared everyone will know how crazy I really am, aren't you?' Grace had to smile; she was over crying for now; she was exhausted to be frank, all she needed right now was her loving sister to sweep her up and have her back, which she did.

'I'm just a little concerned Grace. If you don't want Bella and the boys to know about Michael yet, you need to try a bit harder to be normal, or they'll start to ask questions,' Marlo said softly, pushing Grace's new hairdo out of her face, she really did think it looked great, and Pamela had been right, the way her blonde waves bounced around her face really did make her look younger and more current. 'Are you thirsty darling? I've got some Jam Jar Gin direct from London downstairs, just waiting for us to drink it all.' Marlo had failed to mention the Jam Jar Gin was Morus LXIV, and it was a seven-thousand-dollar bottle, she'd had a box flown in this morning, it was her knew favourite drink. Marlo was human just like her sister, but her world was so different on many levels.

The gin was going down well, it was smooth and refreshing as Grace stood beside the kitchen bench wishing she were invisible. Trying to pretend the sympathy glances from Ross weren't happening from across the room, but they were. Only Marlo, Ross and Lewis knew what she was dealing with, and it felt weird, like an outer body experience. Watching Lewis in his fitted white shirt and tailored black jeans chatting with the girls was interesting, he was putting on the charm as she watched him look at Bella... *Was he making fuck me eyes at her daughter. Oh, so help her god if he was!* She rolled her gin lips squinting her eyes, huffing to herself.

'Hey Gracie, long time no see.' Gabe was right there giving her a wink. The Hunter man she should have married, the Hunter man she would have married had he not been twelve years older and already taken, that was. She'd secretly admired him her whole life, he was the Hunter everyone knew, Gabe was the rock star with all the famous friends, literally! The front man for one of Australia's best-known bands ever. He was Gabe Hunter, what was not to like. He played most instruments which led to him joining a band in high school, then he joined a real band, and by the time he was twenty-two they were touring the world. Of course, it helped that he was sexy and full charisma.

Gabriele Hunter was the sexy hot twin with the talent as Grace saw it, Ross was the smart one with the brains. The two brothers were as thick as thieves given their differences. Both had a natural sophistication and presence just like their father.

115

Loving Grace

Ross was borderline old school gentleman, again like his father, were as Gabe was a naughty boy, his fame and lifestyle made him edgier than his billionaire twin. These days Gabe toured with his band only a few months of the year, they still had it! He was an icon of Australian music and lived a good life up in Palm Beach where he lived comfortably with Pamela, his long-time suffering wife who adored him. They'd been together since high school, on and off to be fair until the last twenty odd years.

'Gabe. Hi. I don't think I've seen you and Pamela since Christmas!' Grace smiled wondering if she looked like she'd just left her cheating husband... *Could anyone see that she was having an internal breakdown?*

'I've been hiding away in Europe.' All the Hunter men had this inner charm, half from their Indian mother and half from their father who was a strong character.

'How lovely,' she smiled as Pamela came into the conversation.

'Grace, I'm serious, the hair is fabulous,' Pamela said on her third wine, 'You look chic.'

Now that was stretching it Grace thought, she wasn't chic, maybe a little hip, but definitely not sheik with her apparent crocked haircut, 'Thanks Pamela.'

They were all staying at Marlo and Ross's for the weekend, it was like a luxury hotel. Tomorrow night was the big sixty second birthday gathering at the house, not that Grace felt much like being around people let alone a party, although now enjoying her second gin, she was feeling less anxious. Spending the best part of the night at the long kitchen bench on a stool trying not to engage with others were possible. But as hard as she tried to be inconspicuous, everyone was in a chatty mood. All except for Bella who ignored her mother like she had tattooed an obscenity on her forehead. Grace knew cutting her hair would be a bigger deal to everyone else, than she, her long locks were her trademark in a way, and not one she'd wanted for the last fifteen years. So, if her hair offended her daughter, she didn't give a single shit. In fact, she was happy she'd cut it off.

After a mound of fresh seafood and multiple salads had been cleared from the bench where everyone ate buffet style, Lewis made his way eventually to Grace. He knew she didn't rate him highly, so he kept his distance, especially given her circumstances, he knew her inner private turmoil and that must have been killing her from the inside out, given how she didn't like him an all.

Grace liked to deny Lewis of the Hunter traits, but she had to admit he was just like them in every single way, good looking, better looking – not that she'd ever tell anyone that. He was fit and manly like his uncles and grandfather, clearly he kept in better shape given he was almost three decades younger. Lewis had this air to him, like he knew he was visually superior, which aggravated Grace immensely to the point of rudeness.

'I like the new hair!' he said sitting at a stool next to her.

Huffing, she looked at him, 'I wish everyone would stop talking to me about my hair,' she winced at him like he'd absolutely pissed her off.

117

Loving Grace

He smiled anyway, sarcastically, 'Maybe people have got nothing else to talk about with you, have you considered that?'

Her mouth dropped open. *The gall of this little shit!* 'Then, I'd prefer they just keep the fuck away from me.' Grace didn't care that she sounded obnoxious.

The smile faded from his face just slightly, 'Are you always like this?'

'Obviously,' she took a big gulp of her gin and glared at him, 'That might be why nobody has anything to talk to me about other than my hair,' she sighed, 'And maybe it's why my husband's been fucking my best friend for the last twenty years.' She surprised herself with her openness, nobody could hear them except for maybe Fiorella who was clearing food away from the bench.

'Or maybe, your husbands just a fucken dickhead.' It gave him great pleasure to say that again.

'Hmm!' she sighed thinking how much Michael hated Lewis, she could see why too, he was a smart arse. But then the feeling was mutual no doubt. His comment was blunt Grace thought, she didn't know exactly how to take him. *Ballsy and harsh!*

'For the record, I've always thought Michael was a dickhead, and that you could have done so much better than settle for a dickhead like him,' Lewis antagonised her a little.

'Great!' Grace wasn't giving him much.

'Hey Aunty Grace,' Scarlet came in next to her aunt and put her arm around her. 'I love your new look,' she said with her sweet soft sympathetic voice, she was so much like her mother.

'Thank you sweetheart,' Grace said glaring again at Lewis like everything was his fault. She kissed her glowing niece on the cheek as she got up and then went up to bed, leaving poor Scarlet standing there wondering what was going on with her aunt.

Watching the sunrise over the harbour was therapeutic, if Grace lived in this house, she'd do it every single morning. It felt like she was watching the world wake up, she was on Marlo's terrace drinking hot lemon water and pondering the thought of what this fresh morning was bringing her for the day. She'd literally gone to her bedroom and fallen straight to sleep last night, Marlo had let her go, she appeased Bella when she thought it was rude of her mother to do so without so much as a good night.

'I love this time of the morning,' Marlo said breaking Grace's silence, resting her hand on her sister's shoulder. 'You okay?'

Grace smiled, 'Yep, fine, good now that I've seen the sunrise.' Looking at her sister she realised she looked extra casual. 'What are up to?' asking because it wasn't often you saw Marlo Hunter in jeans, a hoodie, and sneakers.

'I help serve breakfast on a Saturday at the shelter,' Marlo sighed, she took her shelter very seriously, it was her good deed to her town, and it was the most rewarding task she'd ever done besides raise her girls. 'Want to come with me?'

'Sure,' Grace was up for it.

Loving Grace

As they got into Grace's Range Rover out on the street, Marlo turned and looked around at the car, 'What's all this?' she saw the suitcases and the boxes, she was dumbfounded.

'I've left home. I've left Michael.' She was hoping to keep it to herself.

'Grace!' shocked to her core, she'd expected the marriage was over, but her sister had a home, she had a house that had been her pride and joy, it was the family home. 'What are you doing?'

'I've left. I don't want to be there. I can't be there. It's not my home anymore.' She was flustered and finding it hard to explain herself.

Marlo gave it a moment, 'Okay. I understand.' And she did. 'You can move into the butterfly room. It's all yours. We'd love to have you.' This was a big move for her little sister. 'I won't take no for an answer.'

'Thank you,' Grace sat in the car, letting it idle as they had their discussion. 'Marlo?' she asked, 'Can we keep it between us a bit longer. I really don't want the kids to know what's going on.'

'Of course, you have my word.' Marlo promised resting her hand on her sister's. They had a deal. Grace had no other place to go besides her sister's house. Her situation was delicate and so very private, and the only people she knew she could truly trust were Marlo and Ross.

Grace was on juice duty, she made teas and coffees and chatted were needed. She was a natural, and Marlo felt her sister was benefiting as much as the clients. The non-for-profit shelter was her baby, she and Ross funded it one hundred percent. The facility had thirty beds, four full-time staff and ten part-time, with various volunteers. They also had two nearby homes that helped woman with children in crisis. The shelter ran programs to rehabilitate and educate, as well as giving safe shelter and food for inner city refuge. Grace was beyond proud of her big sister. She'd bought an old apartment building and converted it with such love and care, Marlo was hands on with every detail, working closely with her PA Paulette who at the time was a young woman living it rough in the Cross. Her capability and skill set was evident to Marlo, and so she took Paulette under her wing and changed her life. Today Paulette was one of Marlo's most trusted and valuable employees.

Helping at the shelter gave Grace a few hours of not thinking about herself. Marlo's work had always intrigued her in the most positive of ways, their father had been a very compassionate man, and he'd taught them to be gracious and kind. At the end of the morning, Grace had some perspective on life. There'd been a few women at breakfast who were around Grace's age, who looked like the needed a good old fashion hug and a chat. It was hard not to wonder how they ended up at the shelter. Whatever her own problems were, they felt somehow insignificant to what these women may be dealing with. Every one of them had a story.

When they arrived back at the house just before lunch, Fiorella and her two I.C Judy, had everything covered, giving Marlo the run down as she came in. Going from one extreme to the other from the shelter to her sister's lavish home was strange for

Loving Grace

Grace. Sometimes comprehending her sister's lifestyle and wealth was difficult. After this morning, she completely understood her sister's devotion to the shelter, she was a good person.

'Okay, that sound great,' Marlo was a good boss too, one not to be messed with all the same, she ran a tight ship when it came to her life and her home, she had housekeepers, chefs, drivers, gardeners, and a personal assistant Paulette. Paul her sometimes driver/security and Paulette kept Marlo's life in order. 'Grace's car is in the driveway, she's going to be staying in the butterfly room for a little while, please have her suitcases and belongings taken upstairs, and can you kindly bring in the valuable painting currently on her back seat, maybe put it in my office for now... Oh, and we're keeping this between us ladies. Not a word.' Marlo made herself clear; she knew her trusted housekeepers were on the job. The two ladies immediately went out to Grace's car and brought in the suitcases, taking them up to the butterfly room themselves and setting up the room for a long-term stay. The house was large and high tech, the ladies had a system in keeping it in order and running, there was a daily schedule.

Grace spent the day on her laptop in her room changing her address on anything of importance, getting distracted by the harbour view. She was separating herself from the country house, if she didn't have to ever go there again, great! On her to do list was a credit card of her own, she applied for that in less than five minutes, the way things happened these days were astounding. To think she'd actually have the physical card delivered to Marlo's in two business days was amazing.

Soon enough though, her kids would know something was up, they'd wonder why she wasn't at home, then Michael would come home from Singapore and things would really get hairy. Grace had to remind herself to breathe. In and out, she told herself. Keeping it at a one day at a time basis was the only way she could function right now. It was simply all too much.

Fiorella, Judy, and Maria were like angels all day. Marlo got them up to speed in private, they knew their job was to look after Grace, her stay was indefinite, and she was fragile and needed some love and care. Those were Marlo's instructions. So, as they prepared for the evening party with a team of event specialists, they checked in on their special house guest throughout the day.

Grace didn't have to leave the peace of the butterfly room the entire afternoon. Maria brought up lunch fit for a queen. Judy hung up her clothing in the ridiculously large closet and arranged her bathroom for a long-term stay. Fiorella gave her all the access codes to the doors and gates and set up her touch pad with the internal door security system... Every door in the house had a small shiny black wall pad, if it was closed the only way to open it was by placing your hand on the pad, the doors only opened for the hands in the system. Judy gave her the house schedule which Grace had never seen before, then in the late afternoon, she popped back in to see if Grace needed any washing or ironing for the evening. Maria asked if she wanted to eat prior to the party or if she was happy to wait to eat with the guests. It was all lovely and much appreciated, the service was superior. Five stars.

By six o'clock Grace was feeling the pressure of attending the party and pretending her life was peachy... especially with her kids. Marlo came in to make sure Grace was ready, guests would start arriving in fifteen minutes. When she saw Grace sitting on her bed with her bathrobe on and her hair wrapped up in a towel, she freaked out, 'Grace! what are you doing, it's showtime,' Marlo said clapping he hands in a beige Dolce & Gabbana ruched midi dress, looking slender and tall, her blonde hair slicked back, her makeup on point.

'I'm not feeling it.'

'No!' Marlo sighed, 'Get up, get dressed and come downstairs, you'll be fine when you see everyone. And it's Ross's birthday, he's looking forward to celebrating with you,' a smile came to her lips. She could see her sister was struggling. 'Oh, and Kristian is bringing his new girlfriend apparently... maybe!' Marlo shut the door on her way out.

Grace went into the amazing bathroom and locked the door. About an hour ago she'd let a call from Michael go to voice mail. When she'd listened to it, he gave her this story of how busy he was, how he missed her, and he told her that he loved her. Straight after the call, she'd showered and looked at herself in the mirror naked when she got out. Grace didn't hate what she saw, her body had been good to her over the past fifty years, carrying her around this life, giving birth three times. It had been loyal to her all these years. Comparing herself to other people had never been her go, but how could she not now.

Had Michael been more attracted to Tina's physical appearance?
Emotions and hormones were flushing her face, she was mid
hot flush as she took the hair wrap off her head, her new short
blonde locks were uneven and springing up into curls, so you
couldn't tell it was so crooked. Grace could see no way out of
this heavy mood that had set in. Tears stung her skin as they fell
down her face, she brushed her hair and then fluffed it out with
the hairdryer, not even using a brush. Redness had overtaken
her normally fair complexion as she sank down to the
bathroom floor and sat there wondering if she could get away
with just staying in here all night, would anyone even notice!
Her head was in a fog, like she'd taken a pill or two, everything
seemed too hard to think about. She wanted to call Abbey and
hear her voice, but she was in no state to be doing that. Abbey
was switched on, she'd notice Grace's vibe immediately, and
then she'd call Tina and get her to check in on her. It'd be a
disaster!

Nothing felt right anymore. As she sat on the Italian marble
floor in her sister's exuberant and luxurious home, Grace had
never felt so alone. Her walls had been torn down; her life was
unstable. Her husband had dishonored their marriage in the
worst of ways, it was shameful. It was Grace's shame though, like
she perhaps hadn't been enough for Michael. It was as though
she'd let the kids down, like she'd ruined their happy family.
She knew it was ridiculous, but she couldn't help the thoughts,
she couldn't block them out. And Tina obviously didn't think

Loving Grace

enough of her as a friend. Grace thought she'd always been such a good friend to both Tina and Abbey.

Chapter Seven

Marlo Hunter was the ultimate host; she made entertaining in her harborside home look like it was something she did every day of the week. Of course, she had many helpers, she like to oversee everything from the caterers to the glasses her expensive French champagne was drunk from. Marlo was known for entertaining her guests, she liked music, and tonight she'd gone for a four-piece sophisticated jazz funk band. Mid party she often turn things up with a surprise, she'd been known to have fire performers, belly dancers, street performers, fireworks from a barge on the harbour, but tonight she'd decided on sexy roaming magicians that looked like they may actually take you around the corner for a lap dance.

All the guests had arrived, the food was coming around and the drinks were flowing, the band was playing, and the weather was mild, everything was perfect besides the fact that Grace hadn't made an appearance, and it was almost eight o'clock. Both Bella and Luca had asked where their mother was, Marlo played it down by saying she was getting ready, she'd been busy all day and was running late, but now it was getting ridiculous, so she decided the only thing to do was send someone up to her room to coax her down.

The knock on the door alarmed Grace, she'd fallen asleep on the bed in her bathrobe. Getting up in a hurry, it was dark outside, so it was late, she had no idea of the time.

As she swung the door open, 'Your sister's freaking out downstairs,' Lewis said standing there looking very comfortable with himself in another fitted white shirt that showed off his physique, a black blazer, and black pants and super shiny shoes. 'She sent me up to get you, I'm not to go back down unless you're with me,' he ran his eyes over Grace in her bathrobe, her hair all curled out. 'So, I suggest you get dressed,' he said entering her bedroom uninvited, shutting the door behind him. 'Oh, and your kids are asking after you too, so hurry it up.'

'Excuse me!' Grace didn't like him just walking into her bedroom, and she didn't like his tone.

'Gracie, I know you hate me, and I couldn't give a fucking shit,' he sighed like she was being a complete baby. 'But I was the only person Marlo could send up here because I'm the only one beside Ross who knows what your deal is right now, so don't make it hard for me,' he took a breath and sighed. 'Put that pretty green dress on and let's go.' Lewis pointed at the dress she had hanging up and did a snap thing with his fingers.

'I'm feeling less than great right now. I don't feel like partying,' she stood her ground.

Lewis turned to her and looked her in the eyes, 'I know, it's crap. I've been in love and lost it too,' he took a softer approach. 'You don't have to party, hang out in the shadows, go to bed early if you want. But at least just make an appearance,' he huffed and smiled.

'What if I really don't want to go down there,' Grace blinked as she spoke, she felt like crap, she didn't see how she'd feel any better dressed in her lovely new olive-green dress with a splash of makeup.

'Well, if you don't go down, I'll have to stay up here with you.'

'I'll put some makeup on and get dressed, you can go now, I'll be down soon.'

'I'm not leaving this room without you, Marlo's orders.'

Grace took her dress and went into the bathroom closing the door behind her. She put it on and couldn't do the zipper up... 'Lewis! Would you?' she opened the door and asked him to assist.

'You know your hair really does look good like that,' he said casually sliding the zipper up her back, she was soft and womanly, and a touch sexy... the way her back came in at the waist.

She turned and gave him a frown, 'No more hair talk.'

'I think it's the curl, have you always had curly hair or is it just that it's cut shorter, it's kind of bouncy and fluffy.' Lewis watched her through the open door of the bathroom, she ignored his comments and put her makeup on whilst he stood in the doorway. 'You know, Bella is a great kid.'

Grace stopped doing her makeup and looked at him via the mirror, 'I know, she's my daughter.'

Loving Grace

'I know the boys so well, but I've never spent a lot of time with her, we were just chatting downstairs, she's growing up fast.'

'She's only nineteen.' Grace turned and looked at Lewis.

'You should be proud, she's a nice girl.'

Ignoring his comments seemed the best tactic, he was trying to push her buttons by using her daughter. *He was such a shit!* This was why she didn't like him, he always managed to get under her skin. 'What do you know about Kristian taking drugs, should I be worried?' Grace put her lipstick on, she was ready to go.

'It's recreational as far as I know,' Lewis sighed, he didn't want to talk out of turn, he had Kristian's trust, and he didn't want to break it.

'That's bad though right?' She slid into her nude heels.

'Um,' he huffed like he didn't really want to get into it, 'I don't know, he's probably the kind of kid who shouldn't take drugs to often.'

'So, I should be worried?' They were talking like friends would, without the tone and sarcasm.

'Gracie, I don't know. I mean, a lot of people do drugs now, half those stuck-up dickheads downstairs are high tonight,' he paused, 'I think Kristian's okay, I'll keep an eye out for him.'

'You don't give him drugs do you?'

'WHAT!' he scoffed and exaggerated laugh, 'Are you kidding me!'

'You're a rich guy with lots of connections.'

'I don't get Kristian drugs. I don't touch drugs myself,' he was offended.

'I didn't mean that to sound accusing,' Grace felt she needed to apologise, for a moment she'd forgotten that Lewis's mother Pietra had died from a drug overdose. Grace was regretful that she'd been so careless with her words.

'If I thought your son had a drug problem, I'd be the first to help him. You know I'm close to him right, I-I would never give him drugs.'

'Lewis, I'm really sorry. I didn't mean to...' Her apology was genuine.

'I know. You knew my mum; you know the story.' His guard was coming down.

'I loved your mum,' she said looking straight into his eyes, she'd offended him terribly. They'd never had a serious conversation like this before. 'And I too know what it's like not to have your mum around. Everyone around you tries to fill the void, but it's not the same.' Their eyes locked, they had something in common that had never been apparent to either of them until now.

Lewis took a moment as he held her eyes, 'I like the dress by the way, it looks good with your new hair,' cracking a smile as he held the door open for her.

'How much does your wife love you!' Grace said to Ross, her eyes glazed over the almost naked and very sexy female magician performing to his right.

'What can I say.' Ross smiled at his sister-in-law, pleased to see she'd joined the party. 'You okay?'

'Yep, never better,' she said with humorous sarcasm.

Loving Grace

'It's a shame Michael's not her tonight,' Gabe, Ross's twin brother said, it was his party too, everyone liked Michael, he'd normally be the life of the party if he was there. Michael got along well with Gabe.

'Mmm,' Grace managed. 'Happy birthday Gabe,' she said leaning up and giving him a peck on the cheek.

'Can you believe I'm sixty fucking two,' he gushed.

'No!' she smiled. It was a feat; indeed, he'd partied harder than anyone she knew. He was a rock star and as she looked around at the party, she saw a bunch of their old school friends and some famous faces.

'I heard you turned fifty, make the most of it, you'll be sixty in a blink kiddo,' Gabe bumped her.

'Great, something to look forward to!' They often had light-hearted digs at each other.

'Gabriele, are you giving Grace mistruths about aging? Shiv overheard their conversation and joined them.

'Sorry for the language ma, didn't know you were listening,' he pulled her into his side and kissed the side of her head.

'I'm always listening,' Shiv smiled, she was the matriarch of the family and the one who nobody wanted to disappoint.

Grace saw her kids with a group of their cousins, she put on her best fake smile and motherly mood and went over to say hello. She knew how lucky they were to have such a big loving close family, it was something she never took for granted, living out in the country had taught her to value the time she spent with her sister and the Hunter's, even though she saw them often, she still appreciated them immensely. Marlo whisked past and gave her a kiss on the cheek, a support kiss of sorts. They didn't need words, they had this sister thing going on, and it was unconditional, they could feel the others energy. Kristian introduced Grace to his female friend, the girl seemed nice enough, Grace doubted she'd ever see her again. She drank another red wine and then another, observing as the cousins all entertained one another with tales and stories of a trip to Hawaii as kids, it was lovely, Grace didn't have cousins, she'd just had the Hunter's. Her father always said the Hunters were their family.

'Aunty Grace!' Scarlet was at her side looking as feminine as one did when pregnant, she and Grace were extra close.

'Oh, Scarlet,' Grace winced, 'I'm sorry for how I just up and left you last night. It wasn't you, it's me,' she said apologetic. 'The whole hair thing got to me; I was oversensitive.'

'It's okay,' Scarlet was serene, a tender person. 'My offer still stands to even it up though,' she laughed, 'Or we can see my hairdresser to sort you out. It's up to you.'

'Would you just do it for me, I don't want to see a hairdresser right at the moment,' Grace said not giving anything away, and accepting her niece's kindness.

'If you're up to it, I'll do it tomorrow night at dinner... will you still be here or are you going back home?'

'Umm... I'll be here. I'm here in town for a few nights.' Grace explained. Sunday night dinner was the Hunter's dinner night, everyone had to be there unless they were out of town, no excuses. Sometimes Grace and Michael would make it in if they could be bothered driving all the way in and then home again. Shiv normally cooked all day at her home and bought over whatever her specialty was for that evening meal, and Marlo cooked up a storm too. It was their thing.

'Aunty Grace,' Scarlet said softly looking at her, 'Is everything okay, you don't quite seem yourself?'

'I'm fine sweetheart. Everything's good, thank you for asking.' Grace was putting on her best performance, she felt like shit, a little drunk, not comfortable around all these people... She'd rather be naked in Antarctica right now. 'What about you Scar, how are you feeling?' smiling like she wasn't completely absorbed in her own misery. In actual fact, she adored her niece.

Scarlet just looked at her aunt, 'I'm good,' she paused, 'I'm scared to be honest,' she huffed nervously with an odd look on her face.

'What are you scared of?' The moment had become lighter even though Scarlet's fears were real, and Grace was now concerned about someone other than herself.

'This baby has to come out, and well, I'm scared.' Her eyes were glassy.

Grace could hear the fear in her niece's voice, 'I know, I get it. Believe me I get it.'

'I thought you might,' Scarlet's smile had sympathy. Graces' mother, her own Grandmother died giving birth, it was a family fear shared by all when it came to childbirth. 'I just can't talk to mum about it, she doesn't like to talk about it.' The moment got heavier. 'I know you might not want to talk about it

either, but I need someone to tell me it's going to be okay.'
Scarlet looked terrified.

Alarmed and a little drunk but honored her niece would
speak to her about such things. The fear was real. 'Sweetheart,'
Grace was prepared to be the beacon in the dark for her
beautiful niece. 'I think being scared is normal for most women,'
she paused and put her hands on her nieces arms. 'But you
need to always remember that women give birth thousands of
times a day. Our bodies are made to do so, and of course, there's
modern medicine now.' It felt like the right thing to say, it was
true. Things had come a long way in the past fifty years since
Grace's mother had passed. Grace was the last person to give
birth in the Hunter King family when she had Bella, now Scarlet
was going to bring the next bundle of joy into the world and the
anticipation was bubbling.

'Thank you, I knew you'd understand,' Scarlet smiled
kissing her aunt and leaving to find her husband.

Grace's thoughts went to Luca for a moment, not that his
situation was one of a happy couple together bringing a baby
into the world, but even if he were going to be a single dad,
there would be excitement and joy in the family. At this point
Grace downed another glass of wine. By the time the speeches
were underway, Grace was drunk, all night she'd felt alone, it
was odd being without Michael at such an event. After the
speeches, the music started up and the dancefloor filled up, all
the cousins were dancing together, everyone was enjoying
another extravagantly successful party hosted by the amazing
Marlo... Grace was now standing in a group with her sister in-

Loving Grace

law Louise, her brother Jimmy, Gabe, and his wife Pamela and a few of Gabe's music friends, she wasn't in on the conversation, but watching Shiv and Marlo dance with the kids to a song that was actually making Grace feel queasy... *Was it the music or the wine!* Walking inside from the party she took a bottle of red from the makeshift bar by the kitchen and then went upstairs to the upper terrace where the bedrooms were. Sitting herself on the extra comfortable sunbed, looking out over the harbour and all its glory, still with a half a glass of wine in her hand and the full bottle at her side, Grace sat back, now she was really alone, her face crumbled, and she began to cry. The bizarre thing was that Michael had no idea she was onto him; Tina was oblivious too. Right about now she needed Abbey, which upset her even more. Abbey had tried to contact her today, and she'd had to ignore it, because she truly felt if she spoke with Abbey, she'd have to confide in her and then she'd react one of two ways. Abbey either wouldn't be surprised which would gut Grace beyond belief, or she'd react badly with terrible anger and call Tina immediately and blow it all out of the water. Grace pulled her dress up to her thighs and kicked her shoes off, she was settling in for her own pity party up on the terrace. Michael would be back in a few days and as each day ended she felt it looming closer. He'd arrive home to no wife, her stuff gone, his reaction bothered Grace, would he even give a shit, would he be like, who cares, good riddance, or would he try to find her and pretend she was delusional and swear black and blue nothing was going on. *Would she want to believe him, or would she want to stub him in the eye?* All these thoughts spun around in her alcohol affected brain as she poured another wine from the full bottle, letting out a sob as she used her strength to screw the bottle top off. *Fuck Michael, and fuck Tina. They could both rot in hell!*

'Here you are!' it was Lewis coming out of her bedroom sliding door, startling her in his white shirt that was unbuttoned too far, jacket off, he looked relaxed.

'Get out of my butterfly room,' she slurred giving him a frown.

'Are you drunk?' Lewis stood there looking at her with the bottle in one hand and her glass in the other.

'Oh, my god. Don't act like you care Lewis, please!' Grace mumbled with sarcasm raging in her tone.

'I don't care,' he scoffed, 'But Marlo sent me to look for you again. I don't love being her little go-fetch Grace boy all night you know!' he threw his hand through the top of his short dark hair; he'd had a couple of drinks too.

'Well, go then,' Grace gasped, 'I don't need fetching, I'm not a stray cat.'

He came closer and saw she'd been crying, 'Give me the bottle, and then I'll go.'

'You better just go,' Grace said sitting up and putting her feet to the ground. 'I'm fucking fifty, I can do what I want now.' Managing to stand up, she stumbled a little.

'Give me the bottle Gracie, I think you're about done.'

She moved closer to him, 'You look here Lewis,' swinging the bottle in her hand and pointing it at him. 'You think you're sooo fucking great; you always have, and frankly you're giving me a pain in my arse. So go!'

Loving Grace

He stood there with a stunned smirk on his face, 'I think you're giving yourself a pain the arse,' he laughed.

'Yeah!' she scoffed, 'All the while my husband is probably giving Tina a pain her arse with his cock... And she's probably fucking enjoying it,' she scrunched up her face at the thought, now clearly very drunk. 'I mean...' she shook her head. 'I'm here and Michael my husband is in Singapore fucking my friend Tina... Maybe up the arse, how should I know.' She was serious but comically drunk, she gave it a beat. 'While I'm pretending everything is okay here,' Grace cried a sniff, 'But everything is not okay. I'm not okay Lewis,' she sobbed a big breath.

He was quiet, just listening, he didn't know what to say, Grace was mid meltdown.

'I think I'm going to be sick.' She took a breath in and held it, she'd drunk a lot, and somehow she was still holding her glass and the bottle.

Coming in Lewis took both the glass and the bottle out of her hands, he put his free arm around Grace and under her arm, 'Okay Gracie, let's get you into your bathroom.' He held the wine bottle and her glass in the other hand and tapped her door open with his palm that was around her body. He was one of the special ones with a palm code in the system.

Lifting Grace into the bathroom adjoining her bedroom, he'd had a little experience with drunk women.

'Don't look! Turn away!' she managed to cough before falling to her knees in front of the toilet bowl. Normally she wasn't a chucky person, last weekend it had been from sheer shock, this weekend it was self-inflicted. As she purged at least eight glasses of wine and only two appetizers, Lewis leant in and held her blonde curls back. 'Please don't look!' Grace spat; she could barely hold onto the bowl.

'I'm not looking,' Lewis said looking in the other direction.

Grace let it all out, sobs between her hurls of agony and pain, she was letting out her sadness and of all people, Lewis Hunter was witnessing it.

'I'm okay, I'm okay,' she managed as she sat back with tears and snot. Lewis grabbing toilet paper for her to clean up with. 'I'm so sorry you have to see this.' A moment of calm came to her. This was a down and out moment, but Lewis was at her side, now bending down with a hand at her back with a glass of water for her. Marlo had water glasses and bottled water in her bathroom, just like a fancy hotel, which came in handy for moments like these.

'Can I help you get up?' he asked with kindness.

She nodded, if she could get off the floor that would help, her head had stopped spinning although she was still sobbing softly, makeup like a panda and hair all over the place, her blonde curls bushed out like a madwoman. At this stage her looks didn't matter.

'How about some air?' Lewis said offering to take her back out onto the terrace mainly because he didn't want her throwing up again in the bedroom. Grace was happy to go back out to the terrace. Lewis sat opposite her as she sipped on water and got her wits about her, wiping her face with tissues.

Loving Grace

'I just can't believe Michael has done this,' she paused with tears still streaming from her face, 'To our beautiful family, our kids... I thought I was a good wife,' she sobbed.

'I think you were a good wife, from the outside anyway,' Lewis said.

'I mean, I know Tina is way hotter than me to look at, but I truly think I'm a better person.' It was the eight glasses of truth serum she'd drank.

'He's a dickhead, I've already told you how I feel about him.'

'I don't know what I did wrong,' she was trying to stop crying. Here she was with Lewis, pouring her heart out for lack of a better listener.

'You don't always have to do something wrong for someone to shit in your face Gracie. My two big break-ups were because one of us cheated, nobody did anything wrong to deserve it. The first time I admit it was me, but the second time, which broke my heart, I loved her too much I think,' he sounded sincere, and Grace could hear it.

'I'm sorry she cheated on you!'

'It's okay.'

'What about Immy, poor sweet Immy, why did you cheat on her?' Immy was the first long term girlfriend who'd been his high school sweetheart and then girlfriend for years.

'I don't know, we were more like friends. We were always out with our friends partying, I didn't feel like I was it for her, so I think that made me pull away, not that I'm blaming her... I'm not.'

His depth and truth surprised Grace, 'You could have left before you cheated. How'd you get caught?' This pepped her up a little, she smiled.

'She walked in on me and the housekeeper in bed. Not my finest moment,' he admitted. Not something he was proud of.

'Maybe you're not as great as some women think you are!'

'Who thinks I'm great?' he questioned her with curiosity.

'I don't know. Tina, she thinks you're hot... she thinks everyone is hot.'

'Tina!'

'Yes, you should hit on her, she'd probably do you, she's like that,' a laugh that was covering up her immense pain was more of a huff.

'Nah, she's not my type,' he smiled.

'Well, she's my husband's type,' Grace gave a sad smile, 'So, what's wrong with me?'

'Nothing is wrong with you Gracie, it's all him,' he gave her a smile, and for the first time, Grace thought Lewis was a half decent guy.

'Thank you for your kind words. For everything,' she was till slurring. 'And I'm so sorry you had to see me throw up,' her mood was better. 'Please don't tell anyone that I threw up.'

'It'll be our secret,' his smile assuring her.

Grace still denying the fact that Lewis was utterly sexy and hot, 'It better be,' she warned him.

'I'm surprised Marlo hasn't come searching for you yet,' he said, the scene was much calmer now. Not so heavy.

Loving Grace

'I'll sort her out and make an appearance, then I'm going to bed.'

'Mm, hmm, maybe fix under your eyes before you go down there,' he smiled.

'I don't need you to tell me how bad I look, thank you... Shithead!' Grace huffed.

'No worries, you're welcome. I'll leave you to throw up on your own next time, you can spew in your own hair and possibly choke on it.'

Grace stood up, 'Wow. You're such a lifesaver!' she gasped, 'See, this is why I don't like you. You're a smart-arse Lewis Hunter, and if you breathe a word of my unravelling to anyone, I will hunt you down.' She turned and went into the bathroom.

'I know you will,' he was amused, they were back to normal as he followed her inside.

'You don't have to watch me; I can clean up on my own.'

'I don't have anything else to do.' He wanted to make sure she was okay.

Grace looked at him for a minute, he'd been surprisingly down to earth and low-key tonight, not at all the person she thought he was, 'I'm done. Let's go,' she snaped at him.

Maybe Lewis Hunter was a decent guy.

It was like they'd never left the party; they slid back in without anyone noticing. Grace let Marlo see she was okay, she said good night to her kids and then she went up to bed.

Waking up in a hot sweet, confusion for a few seconds, and then she saw the butterfly pictures on the wall, and it all came to her like it did every morning. Michael and Tina! Then the kids and their issues, last night's party, Lewis and the throwing up. She had a mild headache and needed a wee. As she stepped out of bed and looked at the bathroom, her eyes closed... Grace remembered throwing up. It could have been worse, she told herself, she could have not made it to the bathroom and thrown up on Lewis, or worse... Marlo's floor.

Today was another day closer to Michael returning home and that didn't sit well. Taking a bottle of water out to the terrace she stood at the rail and looked down, there was no trace of the party, it was like Marlo had clicked her fingers and it was all back to normal. Ross stood out by the pool in shorts while her niece Mac lounged on a sunbed reading a book under a super large sun hat. Ross had just swum his morning laps.

'How's this weather?' he waved up to Grace, like he was on top of the world.

'It's special,' she paused, 'Where's Marlo?'

'She'd gone for a walk to see Lewis, something about his new dining table,' Ross shrugged.

Grace didn't know how she felt about that, was Lewis going to dog her out to her sister, or could she trust him?

'Hey Gracie, my mums coming over this afternoon, we're all cooking dinner, you gotta help out,' Ross said chirpy and bright looking up at her as he got his town and headed inside. She wondered if he did drugs!

She really didn't want to help cook dinner; she was over pretending to be normal and okay to everyone. Maybe if she went out for a drive to do some pretend shopping that would

143

get her out of being with everyone. Today she was avoiding humans. She didn't have the energy or mental capacity for too much interaction, in her head, she was laying low until Michael came home, his return was stressing her out. Normally she'd try catching up with Luca, check in on him, making sure he was doing okay, seeing if there was an update on his possible parenthood. Maybe she'd do the same for Kristian, although he was probably still busy with his new friend. And then she had Bella in the back of her mind, she wasn't content or settled, Grace could tell, it was mothers' intuition. She'd come to the party without Dom last night, it didn't seem like a normal relationship.

Marlo's house schedule was good, but also now getting on Grace's nerves after forty-eight hours. Breakfast and lunch was whatever you felt like, it just magically appeared, dinner hadn't been too formal so far. If Fiorella wasn't around, Judy was, and Maria was there most days. Grace didn't get a chance to make her own bed or straighten her room up, somehow, these ladies did it without being seen or heard. Grace wasn't complaining, she just wasn't used to it as she hadn't spent more than a night at her sister's home since she was twenty-one, and there'd been no housekeepers back then.

After lunch, which Grace ate on her own in her bedroom, Shiv and Ed arrived along with Scarlet and her husband Angus, Ruby, and her fiancé Sam. Mac was up and about preparing food with her father when Lewis arrived, and then Bella walked in. Immediately Grace thought her daughter looked offish or maybe even unwell. For a moment it looked like Bella and Lewis had arrived together, this was Grace being a cautious mother, she was watching Lewis Hunter, her Bella was stunning, and he had an eye for younger woman, so she'd heard. Unexpectedly, Bella came to greet her mother with a kiss hello, Grace was instantly emotion. She hugged her daughter in and held back the tears as hard as it was.

'Mum, are you hungover?' Bella pulled away from her.

'Why do you think I was drunk last night?' Grace asked quietly.

'Weren't we all!' Marlo came up and put a hand at Grace's shoulder and moved Bella and Grace to the side of the kitchen, 'You two will be here, this is your spot,' she said placing them at the large kitchen countertop ready to help cook. Marlo prepared the tandoori chicken, Grace, Scarlet, and Bella chopped things for Shiv's dishes, Lewis and Ruby made samosas, and Angus was washing dishes at the sink. Sam and Ed were watching the sailing boats out on the harbour and having an in-depth chat.

'Lew, how come you didn't bring a date last night?' Ruby teased her older cousin. She was just like her mother, only darker. 'I thought you were seeing that wannabe actress girl.' She continued with Lewis.

'No, not seeing the wannabe actress girl,' he said trying not to get into it.

'Why not?' Scarlet asked, delving further.

He put his hands out uncomfortably, he looked casually handsome today, 'Um, because I'm not.' Smiling because his cousins were always into his love life. Scarlet was a year younger than him, she was more like a sister, and Ruby was like a painful little sister ten years his junior.

'You didn't like her, did you?' smiled Mac, she was the inquisitive one who would get to the point. Lewis had grown up with his cousins and he was literally like a big brother to them all, they'd taught him many lessons.

'I'm not telling you!' he joked with Mac who he adored, she was also his goddaughter, so he felt a special connection to her.

'I hope you let her down with kindness.' Now Shiv was on his case.

'I didn't let her down!' he huffed with frustration at the interrogation. 'Can I get a bit of back up here guys?' he said to Ross and Angus who were happily watching on like it was a soap opera. Lewis wasn't one to divulge his personal life, the girls all knew it and they all pushed the boundaries with him all the time.

'No more actress?' Ross questioned, which made all the ladies laugh.

'I never said no more actress,' Lewis laughed at their curiosity.

Grace noticed Bella was so very quiet, she hadn't spoken a word and didn't seem at all interested in the conversation, 'Do you feel all right sweetheart?' she asked her daughter quietly as she stood beside her. 'You don't seem yourself.'

'Mmm Hmm.'

That wasn't really an answer, but Grace knew now was not the time or place, every time she saw Bella she seemed to be a little less herself.

Dinner had been cooked with love and laughs as always, then eaten with joy and happiness, it was over by eight, Grace sat on the long charcoal sofa and listened as Marlo, Shiv, Ed, and Ross discussed the coordination of flying all the guest to the wedding in Italy via private and commercial aircraft. All the kids had gone home, it was just Grace and Lewis sitting on the sofa quietly.

'So, will you be staying here for a while?' Lewis asked her, nobody could hear their conversation in the large living room.

'I think so,' she sounded flat, 'I'm fifty, living with my sister again, I need a place of my own, but I can't rush into anything.' As much as she was grateful, she was drained already with schedules, door codes, and parties at Marlo's.

'What about your house, you're not going back?' he asked with his long legs crossed in faded jeans and his loose t-shirt and slides, very casual by his standards.

Giving him a look like he was a mad man, 'Never!' she said softly.

'Are you ready to live on your own somewhere new?' his eyes narrowed like he was seriously interested.

'I'm a grown woman Lewis.' Grace was baffled at what she interpreted as sexism, or perhaps she wanted to interpret it as that.

'Mmm.' He wasn't about to argue. Grace made it a point to get up in his grill at any given chance, she took nearly everything he said the wrong way, almost like she was looking for an argument.

'Have you ever lived with my sister Lewis?' she almost hissed at him.

'Er, not technically... She loves you more than anything you know.' He watched Grace sip her iced water.

'I'm not one of her daughters. She doesn't need to keep tabs on me.'

'She's worried about you. You're in a life crisis.'

Grace just glared at him, 'Oh, that's very observant of you.'

'I'm going home,' he said getting up and going to his grandparents and kissing them both goodnight without even so much as a goodbye to Grace. She watched on at his display of love to his family, he kissed Marlo and gave Ross a tap on the shoulder, and then he left.

Chapter Eight

Monday had been a week to the day that Michael had left for Singapore, she'd managed to avoid his calls and responded with short text messages to keep him at bay. Come Tuesday she was super anxious, staying in the butterfly room all day drawing new designs for her next collection, in the midst of turmoil, her creative juices were flowing and keeping her mind occupied.
Marlo came to ask if she wanted to have lunch with her and Kitty, one of her society friends, but Grace was desperate to limit her human contact once again.

Avoiding Michael wasn't easy, he'd asked her via text twice today what was going on - was something wrong. He was due home first thing on Wednesday morning, by noon, he'd arrive home, and he'd know she'd left him. Grace couldn't help but wonder, did he still love her at all? Could she ever look at him again without wanting to tear his eyes out? And then sadness took hold, they'd been married to for nearly thirty years.

Loving Grace

Early afternoon she got back in bed, under the quilt where it felt like nobody could get to her, and it was working well until Marlo came in after her lunch date and woke her.

'Grace, are you awake?' Marlo sat on the bed, she couldn't see her sister face underneath the covers, 'I bought you something while I was shopping with Kitty after lunch.'

Grace was now awake. Her sister loved shopping more than anyone she knew.

'I bought you this head scarf, well actually I bought two, one for you and one for me, you can choose which one you like.'

Throwing back the covers, Grace looked at Marlo, 'Is my hair that bad you think I should cover it up with a scarf?' she was horrified.

'I don't think you should cover up your hair,' Marlo's eyes grew big with her words. 'It's a beautiful scarf, I thought you'd like one.' She could tell Grace was in a shitty mood.

'Hermes! Wow. Fancy. I like the pink one,' Grace said, 'Thank you Marlo.' She felt the scarf in her hand, thinking how lovely it was and how thoughtful it was of her sister, her phone buzzed. Lewis.

'I'll leave you to it,' Marlo blew her a kiss and left.

'Yes!' Grace said answering her phone, looking up to the ceiling.

'Can you meet me tonight, I've got something to tell you, and I kind of want to keep it between you and I,' he asked her like it was very important.

'Is it Kristian?' Her heart sank.

'Michael,' he confirmed.

'Oh,' she said relieved, but still getting a sharp pain in her chest, 'What's it about?'

'Gracie, can you meet me, come to my place, we can kill two birds with one stone.'

'I don't want to kill any birds, Lewis. Just tell me now!'

'My place, I'll see you about seven.' He hung up on her.

The thing was, she knew his building but not his exact apartment. She got up out of bed and went into a panic. It was five and she had two hours to dress, do her hair and makeup, eat dinner, and then set off like she was going to perhaps meet a friend for a coffee. Getting out the house was a sinch, Marlo seemed pleased she was going out, doing something productive with herself, she didn't even ask Grace what friend she was catching up with.

When she arrived at Lewis's building, which was right at the end of Marlo's Street, a one-minute drive, she sent a text to let him know she was there.

Grace felt a little mysterious, a tad excited, especially because she was sneaking around with Lewis Hunter... Abbey and Louise would flip their lids, if only they knew. He buzzed her in, she got the lift to level six, there was only one door, and it was open.

'In here!' Grace heard Lewis's yell out, so she entered. Her eyes were taking it all in, this was his home, and she was shocked, not that she knew what she was expecting. It was clean, white, and super modern with hints of natural timber and black iron and it all looking out over the harbour, surprise, surprise. Grace was impressed. And then the biggest surprise of all...

151

Loving Grace

Lewis had an apron on over jeans and a T shirt, slipper like shoes that looked like he really should have been wearing a cigar jacket and smoking a pipe, on a closer look she could see they were Gucci slippers, she wasn't sure what she thought of the slippers. Odd.

'You're cooking!' the surprise in her voice was evident, and the spicy aromas were bliss.

'I have to eat, so I cook.' Everything was said semi-sarcasm between he and Grace, 'Follow me,' he walked, Grace following behind him back out to the lift.

'Where are we going?' She held her bag in close to her body as she got into the lift with him, like she was unsure.

'Fifth floor,' he said, and the lift door opened, they got out and he unlocked the first door and held the door open for Grace. 'Its two bedrooms, I think it's perfect for you, and my tenants have just moved out, I haven't had time to look at the agents' new applicants yet. It's yours if you want it.'

'You own this?' she sounded suspicious.

'I own the building. I bought it from Ross at a good price.'

'Of course. How silly of me.' She wasn't surprised, the Hunter's were a clicky clan. 'I wasn't really thinking of spending this kind of money on rent.' The apartment was fully renovated, modern, and perfect.

'How much were you thinking of spending?' Lewis asked as Grace took a look around.

'Lewis, I can't afford to live here!'

'How do you know... What's your limit?'

'I don't know. Eight hundred.' She plucked a number out.

'Done. It's all yours.'

'You'd take eight hundred a week for this?' She didn't believe him.

Lewis was serious as he stood looking down at her. 'Hey, you said you can't stay with Marlo and Ross forever, this is a good offer, and you'll be right near your family.'

'What makes you think I want to be under you.' She watched him smile. 'In this building I mean.' She tried not to be irritated. His loose neck t-shirt was throwing her; she could see more of his chest than she needed to.

'Gracie, you could do worse than being under me!' he said raising his brow and leaning back on the wall, trying his best to keep it casual and without pressure, he knew Grace was edgy and dubious about his offer.

She narrowed her eyes and huffed disapprovingly, 'I know you could get so much more for this place. I can't take it.'

'I'll let you think about it,' Lewis said opening the door for them to leave, he didn't push the issue with her, instead he took her back up to his penthouse directly above for a chat.

Grace looked around his apartment a little more, a lot of glass and thoughtful design, it was an entire floor of opulence and views. The large kitchen was impressive, and she should know, considering she'd lived with a professional chef for nearly thirty years.

'Can I get you a drink?' Lewis pressed his hands together, which intern flexed his forearms. Grace tried not to notice but she was a sucker for good arms, even if they were Lewis Hunter's.

153

Loving Grace

'No thank you.' She wondered how many women he'd slept with; she could see what attracted woman to him now, he was kind for the most part, and not at all like she'd imagined him to be in private. They'd had a few moments now, were they'd been honest and frank with each other, and he had surprised her with his depth of character. And as much as it pissed her off, she was starting to see why he'd been listed as one of the country's most eligible bachelors. The line around his pouty lips was defined, his smooth skin looked like he had regular facials, and those Hunter eyes looked right through you. Still, he had this sarcasm with her that she didn't know how to take. Did he dislike her as much as she disliked him, it was quite possible.

'Take a seat, you might need it,' Lewis pursed his lips with an awkward look on his face.

Grace was distracted, her phone was buzzing in her bag, over and over, when she saw it was Luca it threw her. *What if it was important*, she was never one to avoid her kids calls, especially when Michael was out of town. 'Do you mind if I take this quickly, it's Luca,' she said looking up at Lewis.

He gestured a wave and went over to the kitchen and tended to his cooking that seemed to be simmering on the cooktop.

'Luca!' Grace walked to the far side of the room and listened to her son tell her how Jasmine his twenty-year-old fling was definitely having his baby, and how she didn't want him to have anything to do with her or the baby, she's taking the whole 'I don't want to burden your life' approach.

'Mum, I don't know what I've done that makes her think she's a burden,' he sounded flustered. 'She said she's leaving the country. She said she's not going to tell me when the baby is born. She's treating me like I've done something terrible to her.'

'Okay, keep your cool with her,' Grace could hear the frustration in Luca's voice. 'Don't give her anything to hold against you or to be frightened of. Luca, you have rights in this situation, but first just give her a little time,' she said looking over at the kitchen, Lewis had his back to her, however he could probably hear her.

'Mum, I have no rights if she vanishes of the face of the earth, that's what she said she'd going to do.' He was distressed. 'I told her a baby is not a burden. It's my baby!'

'Well, is it yours?' Grace had to ask.

'Mum!' he raised his voice.

'Sweetheart, it's a valid question, how do you know for sure?' she whispered going far into the corner so Lewis couldn't hear her.

'I know it's my baby mum.'

'How do you really know?'

'Mum, listen to me. I know it's my baby,' Luca pleaded with her, 'I'm the only guy she's ever been with.'

'WHAT!' Grace said loudly nearly dropping her phone. 'She could just be saying that to you.' She was mortified, it was so shocking she couldn't believe it.

'I can't believe you would say that Mum!' Luca gasped.

Grace put her hand to her head, 'Luca Moore, that's the most irresponsible thing you've ever done in your life.' Grace

155

gasped, 'You should know better at your age than to sleep with a virgin,' she hissed in the softest voice possible, scolding her adult son for his sexual behaviour that she knew was really none of her business, but she couldn't help herself.

'I didn't go out looking for a virgin, I didn't know she even was until it was happening.' He wasn't in a great place, and Grace was making it worse. 'And I really liked her.' His mother could hear the pain in his voice.

'I suggest you get your legal obligations and rights in order before anything else,' her tone was unpleasant.

'I'm coming home for the night, I need to see you,' Luca said.

'No. I'm out,' she said quickly and louder.

'Well, I'll come over tomorrow night.'

'No, I'll be out then too! I'll call you tomorrow night, I'm in town, maybe we can have dinner together,' she said trying to put him at ease.

After a lengthy pause, Luca agreed to tomorrow night as a maybe.

Grace hung up her phone and looked at Lewis, maybe he had heard as now he was looking at her with this strange look on his face, maybe he hadn't. 'Sorry,' she said going back over to the kitchen bench, 'The older the child, the bigger the problems.' Trying to disguise that she was flustered.

'All good?' he asked innocently, Grace knew he'd heard some of it.

She nodded and stood with her hand out on his kitchen countertop, 'Now, sorry, what do you have to tell me, why am I actually here?'

He winced at her, 'Come. Sit down,' he said going over to the large fawn coloured sofa. 'Um, I wanted to tell you this information alone, just in case it's something you didn't want Marlo and Ross knowing, you know it's kind of private.' He was very serious.

'Out with it then,' she was brash with him.

Lewis looked at her as he tried to ignore her rudeness, 'It's about Tina and Michael and their relationship.'

'What, are they secretly married!' she laughed at the awkward moment.

He had to say it right and with sensitivity, 'Ten years ago, Tina underwent several rounds of IVF.'

'Go on,' Grace didn't move a hair.

'Michael was the only sperm doner,' he paused to give her a moment, 'I've got copies of the receipts, and medical records.' He huffed a big sigh. 'Tina became pregnant, but she had a miscarriage at six weeks.'

Grace took a gasp of air, so she didn't drop dead on the spot, 'I know!' she looked at Lewis expressionlessly. 'I mean I remember... I took her to the hospital, and I took care of her all week,' a pause, 'She told me the father was a one-night stand.' Remembering it so clearly. 'Tina was devastated though, so upset, how could I forget.' Looking at Lewis she knew he wasn't surprised.

Loving Grace

For a moment he thought she was taking it all too well, 'Well, Michael was the father.'

'Okay.' She got up. 'I'm going to go.' Grace was rattled, all she could think about was the abortion Tina had when Bella was five, it stuck in Grace's mental calendar because her friend had missed Bella's birthday party because she'd had the abortion the day prior.

Had it been Michael's baby too? Of course it was! Grace knew he would never have let Tina abort his baby; he'd literally told Grace there was no way ever in hell she was not having his baby when she'd become pregnant at twenty-one in Paris. The mere suggestion had horrified him.

'Are you okay Gracie?' Lewis broke her thought.

'Yep, thank you,' she said slowly, 'I've got to go. But thank you for the update. And let me know how much I owe your private eye friend,' she said backing towards the door.

'Are you sure, you don't look okay?' he was concerned.

'Um!' She stood there in a blank haze.

'Do you want to stay and have dinner with me... Have a drink?' it was a duty of care offer.

'No. I'm going to go. But thank you anyway Lewis.' She backed out the door and closed it.

The next morning Grace woke up with a sore chest and puffy eyes, she cried herself to sleep last night in what could only be described as true heartbreak. Mostly she was bewildered as to why Michael had never left her for Tina. If he loved her so much that he wanted to give her a baby... Even though he already had three, then why didn't he just leave their marriage and do so. Partly Grace felt as though now her very own children with Michael were insignificant in their fathers' eyes... Had they not been enough for him. *Who was this man!* How did he manage to live a completely separate life with two women who were so close to each other? It felt like she was mourning Tina, like she'd died. The hurt and heartbreak of the betrayal was beyond her anger right at this moment.

At breakfast down in the kitchen, she sat silently as Marlo and Paulette confirmed details of the weekend trip out to an exclusive island on the Great Barrier Reef. Ross was thinking of buying the island, so he was taking Marlo for a quick weekend away so she could check it out.

'Now, Grace you know you're welcome to come with Ross and I,' Marlo looked up from her laptop that was beside her plate of fruit as Grace shook her head. 'Well then, Mac and Judy will be here this weekend with you. Maria will be taking the weekend off. We'll be gone for two nights, and if you need me for anything, you can call me at any time.' Marlo was worried about leaving Grace, and with Michael coming back into town today, she was hesitant to go away at all.

Spending the morning sitting out in the sun gathering up as much vitamin D as one's eyes could, Grace thought about a random swim in the pool. The water didn't feel warm enough and the sun was delightfully replenishing.

Just as a late lunch had finished at the living room dining table, Fiorella came rushing into Marlo, Grace, and Mac, she seemed flustered and upset. 'Michael is at the gate; he wants to see you Grace!' she said looking between Grace and Marlo.

'What's wrong?' Mac asked curiously, she'd been told her aunt was staying at the house because she had some things to do in the city for a few days, but Mac knew her aunt wasn't herself.

'I'll go,' Marlo said standing up from her seat, her tone authoritarian like... She marching off down the hall towards the front door before Grace could speak. Sitting for a few seconds, heart racing, stomach churning, it was the most awful feeling. Contemplating seeing Michael, her husband who until this past week she'd utterly cherished and been so in love with. *Oh, God she wanted to see him, she wanted everything to be like it used to be!* Then the thought that he'd been sleeping with her best friend and coming home to her bed and then having sex with her, repulsed Grace immediately. This double life he'd selfishly been living had shattered her being, and now he was here.

She stood up and headed off down the hall towards the front door in what felt like a slow-motion walk, brain fog consuming her. Barefoot and casual, Grace could hear Marlo and Michael yelling out the front by the entry gate. Paul, Marlo's driver was standing at the front door watching on. Grace walked past Paul and to the gate, and the minute her wary eyes set upon her husband; she stopped in her tracks just a few feet behind her sister.

Michael stepped forward through the gate, 'Grace, what are you doing? This is ridiculous. Come home,' he said trying to sound like he was confused. He'd returned home late in the morning to find her wardrobe in disarray and mostly empty and then the bathroom had been cleaned out as well as her office, the safe, the bank account, it was soon apparent she'd left him, and of course Marlo's was the first place held look.

'You don't have to do this Grace,' Marlo said, then she looked at Michael with daring eyes, 'Don't you step a foot inside this property... Paul!' Marlo called out with urgency to Paul at the front door who was ex British SAS, he'd squash Michael flat in a second.

'What the fucks going on, and what the fuck did you do to your hair?' Michael stepped towards Grace who'd decided to move in front of her sister. 'Don't listen to her,' Michael pointed to Marlo. 'She's manipulating you like she always does,' he was pretending his dirty little double life didn't exist and that Marlo was the problem, deflecting to Marlo who'd always had it in for him right from the start. 'What has she said to you?' he looked at Grace as if he were devastated, like she'd been brainwashed by her sister, like his heart was broken. 'Your hair... I told you never to cut your hair!' Michael's tone was getting aggressive in a way Grace wasn't accustomed to.

The hair! Grace saw red. 'You did this!' she wanted to vomit. 'I can't believe you would do this to me. To us, to our kids.' Grace said with a distant look in her eyes, her devastation was obvious for all to see.

'What the hell are you talking about Grace, have you've fucking lost your mind!' He wasn't giving up without a decent effort to deny his dirty filthy lies that had clearly been uncovered by his wife somehow. 'Get your things Grace and come home with me. Now!' Realising he was in deeper shit than first expected, he took a step to her and looked down over her intimidatingly.

'You-you were in Singapore with Tina.' Grace had all his mis comings manifested in her brain. 'I know everything Michael,' she said, her voice quivering, yet she was not scared of him. 'I know you don't stay at the hotel on Thursday nights. I know the restaurant is in the red. I know you own property with Tina for gods' sake,' Grace took a breath, 'I know you have huge gambling debts and that you have spent my money on her,' she started to cry at the reality, 'You've been with Tina for years, behind my back. She was my best fucking friend!' Grace began to lose her cool as she raised her voice, she was crying. 'Oh, and I know about the IVF... Were our three amazing children not enough for you?' she hissed through gritted teeth. There was the longest of silences as both Marlo and Michael comprehended her accusation. For Grace, it had been the final knife in her back twisting with humiliation and hurt, their children had been their life, and his actions would hurt their hearts tremendously. 'Why don't you ask Tina about the abortion she had the day before Bella's fifth birthday.' Grace had a sudden glint in her eye. She could see he was totally blindsided by her knowledge. 'I know everything Michael!'

Marlo stood there listening in complete shock as Paul appeared at her side, this was the first time she had heard about IVF.

'You are my wife, now come home, get in the fucking car, NOW GRACE!' Michael pulled at her arm; he was bamboozled and flustered. He'd finally been caught out and yet he was still denying his wrongdoing like some kind of narcissistic pathological liar.

Without a word, Grace pulled away from him, turned around and walking a few steps, but then turned back around, 'Go fuck Tina! I hope you both fucking die!' Then she continued on inside the house.

Marlo's mouth fell open as she stood with Michael at the gate, she was completely gob smacked.

'Yeah!' he yelled out to Grace as she got to the front door, 'Maybe I wouldn't have had to fuck Tina if you had been there for me instead of trying to be the mother you never had,' his words were venomous.

'Don't you dare talk about our mother,' Marlo gasped in horror, 'You need to leave now.' She gave Paul the look to remove Michael. The IVF revelation had floored her, it had hurt Marlo that Michael, a man she trusted her sister life with, had betrayed her. It was the unthinkable. No more nice sister-in-law.

Paul stepped forward and pushed Michael back out onto the nature strip, then shut the gate locking him out. Marlo went into immediate damage control, she found Mac in the kitchen and made her swear on all her sisters lives that she would not breathe a word of this to a sole, a big call Marlo knew, asking her youngest daughter to keep quiet, but Mac seemed to understand the gravity of the situation, she'd heard it all and was in as much shock as anyone. When Marlo found Grace out on the back terrace staring out over the harbour, she was in a silent cry, she put her arm around her sister. Grace was smaller than Marlo, she always had been, from the moment she'd seen her little

163

Loving Grace

sister, Marlo had been her protector above anything else. This had thrown her though, she'd consoled her sister the best she knew how to over the past week, and now this. Grace had been a wonderful wife and mother, she'd been born to raise children, her life was devoted to them and to being the best wife she could, which was pretty damn perfect, and this was the thanks she got! All along her husband had been a two-faced devil. Marlo couldn't begin to imagine her sister's pain, but Grace was strong and resilient, she had to be from birth. Sometimes when Marlo had felt hard done by because she lost her mother when she was ten years old, she thought about how Grace never knew her mother at all. The love Marlo had for her sister was beyond sisterly love, it was in some ways a maternal attachment. When Grace was hurt, Marlo was hurt, she couldn't fathom living without her little sister.

'You will get through this,' Marlo said softly as they both watched a boat go past in the distance. 'We're only given what we can manage in life.'

They stood watching over the harbour for a while, no words, just the comfort of each other. Grace in a complete state of sadness, and Marlo coming to grips with the IVF revelation. She wanted Michael and Tina to pay... Wait until she told Ross! He was at work and then out for dinner, there was no way he'd let Michael get away with this, neither would Jimmy. Never in all the years that she and Ross had had their good fortune had she ever wanted to use their money in a revengeful way, until now.

Later that night as she lay beside her sleeping sister in the peacefulness of the butterfly room, Marlo imagined just how she'd bring Michael and Tina down, it was endless when you had billions of dollars.

Chapter Nine

Every day seemed like Groundhog Day to Grace. Wake up, realise it's not a dream and then get through the day as best as possible. Ross kept giving her sympathy looks down the dining table as they ate breakfast, obviously Marlo had updated him on the IVF saga and Michael's visit yesterday. It all seemed like a mess and Grace wasn't exactly sure what she needed to do next.

'How would you like to come with me to the hairdressers today?' Marlo asked Grace, it was just the three of them at the table.

Grace took a deep breath in, 'I don't think I want to; I think I'll wait for Scarlet to cut it.'

'Scarlet!' Ross was amused, 'Remember what she used to do to all her dolls. I wouldn't let her cut your hair Gracie.' He did his best to brighten the somber mood.

'Well, I trust her,' she was low, her voice didn't have much expression. 'Um, and I have to start looking for a more permanent place to live.'

'Why? You can stay here as long as you need.' Marlo was surprised by this. 'We love having you here, you don't have to leave.'

'Gracie, you can stay as long as you like.' Ross put his spoon down and gave her his attention. 'Please don't feel you need to hurry up and leave, you can move in, the butterfly room is yours,' his voice had a warm and exited tone to it, which made her smile.

They made her feel special, 'Thank you. I'm really grateful, but there will come a time when I need to move on with my life, be a grown up.' She looked at both of them. 'I might just need a little bit of time to settle my head, I've got a permanent headache,' her voice wavering.

'Stay as long as you like,' Marlo said lovingly.

'The butterfly room is all yours,' Ross smiled knowing Grace loved it when he referred to the bedrooms by the names Marlo had given them all. It had been a little joke between them.

'Oh, and we're having dinner at The Boathouse tonight, that'll be nice,' Marlo added as she got up from the table.

Grace didn't know what she wanted to do in five minutes, let alone tonight for dinner. Today she thought she'd go for a drive to see one of her loyal sellers down in Wollongong, she'd been promising for months to visit the store and today just felt like the perfect day to go for a drive on her own. Getting dressed in black pants, beige shirt, and black shoes, putting her uneven hair back in a ponytail and then grabbing her new handbag the kids gave her for her birthday, she was ready for her drive, it would give her time to be away from everyone,

167

time to think and time to breathe, and she'd be working on her business, which was her favourite pastime before her life fell apart. As much as she loved her sister, Grace just needed some time where Marlo wasn't trying to make her better, because she didn't want to be made better, nobody could make her better.

Once she got in the car she wondered if visiting her seller was a good idea, given her vulnerability, maybe the drive was all she needed. Deciding to head to Wollongong all the same because she needed the driving time, just her, her car and music.

One thing that was bothering her was Tina had not called, and by now Michael would have told her that Grace knew everything.

Halfway Grace pulled over to make a call of her own, she simply couldn't wait another minute, 'Abbey it's me!' Grace felt raw and emotional. She'd caught Abbey on the way to the airport to come home.

'Oh, my god I can't wait to see you girls, I've missed you so much,' gushed Abbey.

'I miss you too. I really need to see you Ab's. When will you be home?'

'Twenty-four hours babe,' said Abbey.

'Okay,' Grace gave it a beat, 'Ab's I need to ask you something now if it's okay.'

'I've got ten minutes, go for it,' she said from inside her cab with Dean and Addison, her phone to her ear. Once Grace started, to say Abbey was devastated and shocked was an understatement, and never once did she say to her distraught friend that it was impossible or had to be untrue, that their best friend since high school would never do such a thing! Abbey new Tina as well as Grace, she didn't want to believe this awful accusation, but it did make sense, and yes, the mystery man in Tina's life sure did sound like Michael. Tina was always so vague when it came to this secretive guy she's been sleeping with for years.

Abbey needed to speak with Tina, she needed to hear it with her own ears from the horse's mouth. If it was true, it was not only a deception to Grace, but a deception to the friendship that all three shared. Tina had lied to them both, and the fact that she could do something so awful to Grace was unforgivable.

'Grace sweetie, I'll be home as soon as I can, you hold tight babe, I'll be there soon.' Abbey didn't know what else to say.

Pulling up to Marlo's around three o'clock, Grace saw Luca's car parked across the drive, it was alarming, she immediately panicked and raced inside. Marlo, Mac, and Luca looked at her as she made her breathless entrance as if something were wrong. 'Is everything all right?' she tried to catch her breath. Still silent stares. 'What's wrong?' Panic set in, was it Kristian. Bella. Who was it?

Luca stepped forward, 'I had lunch with Dad today and he's flipping out, saying all sorts of things about you that he probably shouldn't be saying.' Luca looked concerned. 'He said you left him, and that you didn't tell him about Bella in bed with some friend of Kristian's at the beach house years ago,' Luca said with confusion. 'Dad was saying how you'd kept all these secrets from him.'

169

Loving Grace

'What! what did he say exactly?' her face screwed up and then Ross came into the room for a calming support for everyone.

'Um, well he said you had a thing with Avi... You know Avi Roth?' Luca felt like he was suddenly put on the spot, he said the first thing that came to mind after his father had barraged him with accusations about his mother at lunch.

Tina was revenging Grace, because she'd outed her to Michael about the abortion. Grace knew exactly why. Michael was upset Tina had the aborted all those years ago. So now, Tina was telling Grace's secrets. The vault was open. And worse, Michael was telling Luca.

'Grace, you didn't?' Marlo scoffed with horror.

'We weren't cousins Marlo!' Grace snapped as Ross stood there looking at her, he hadn't moved an inch, not even a blink. Mac was wide eyed. Avi Roth had been a good friend of Ross and Gabe's; he was always around back in the day. Avi was known as the it guy, super good looking, a player, a rich kid who broke every rule and law known to humankind until his untimely death ten years ago.

Grace took a breath and held it, blinking her eyes and then pulling a pained face, Michael was still betraying her, and Tina had stabbed her in the back again.

'When?' Marlo gasped. 'How long ago?'

'My Avi... My Avi Roth... You and he had a thing,' Ross was astounded. 'What kind of a thing?'

'Oh, my god!' Grace yelled grabbing her keys and handbag, she needed to get air. 'It was a million years ago, and it happened once!'

'When?' Ross questioned, he was half amused, and half horrified.

'I slept with Avi the night of dad's funeral in your spare bedroom if you must know.' She stated for the record to Marlo and Ross.

Grace left them all standing there with mouths open as she headed to the front door. 'I can't believe Michael is telling my child things like that after what he's done!' She waved her hands with frustration in the air. Luca was a grown man, but he was still her child, and you didn't divulge information like that to your children. She left the front door open as she left.

Starting her car, Grace asked herself who did she despise the most, Michael or Tina? They'd both done this to her on purpose, and fancy telling her son she'd slept with Avi Roth! They'd been calculating and consistent in their betrayal. Frustration overwhelmed Grace as she drove in the traffic, she felt like her sanity was literally teetering on the edge. It was one thing to target her, but to involve Luca was going too far! Tina's apartment was right at the end of a leafy street Grace was speeding down, cars park along the side of the road, she was approaching the T intersection and to her dismay, there was Michael's Mercedes parked straight ahead... It was then that Grace finally snapped. All the betrayal, hurt and frustration had been too much, it was as though a switch had been flicked as she put her foot flat to the floor.

171

Chapter Ten

Grace's confusion was met with unbearable pain. From her arms to her chest and head, even her face hurt, the pain was everywhere.

'Grace, can you hear me, open your eyes.' The voice was not familiar as she struggling to open her eyes amidst all the pain. Her eyelids flickered, as she thought about Bella, if anything happened to her, she'd be leaving Bella to face life without a mother as she did. The boys would be fine, they were surrounded by good men. Grace's whole life was flashing before her.

'My name is Vicky, I'm a paramedic Grace, we're on the way to hospital, you've had a car accident.' The voice was still there, she flickered her eyes trying to open them, trying to give a sign she was fighting. 'Where does it hurt Grace?'

'Hmm,' she sighed unable to speak. Taking small shallow breaths in, the pain in her chest was sharp like a knife, like she was being stabbed in the heart, and then she took another breath in, and the same pain made her wince with agony. In and out she kept telling herself with every breath even though the pain was outrageous, she could hear the voice asking her again, her pain wasn't going anywhere. 'My chest. My head,' Grace managed to say as she felt something brushing against her face, her eyes opening just enough to see bright lights and a person.

'Anywhere else Grace?' asked the voice.

'My face,' she gasped. Every breath hurt, so did every word, she was tired and yet desperately wanted to wake up out of this confusion.

'Okay, I'm just wiping your face so I can see you better,' the voice said.

Grace could feel the cold on her face, her noise hurt, her eyes hurt, and her head had this intense fog and ache that was making her feel sick. All she could think about was Bella, Kristian and Luca, her babies, she loved them so much. Warm tears slipped out of the corners of her eyes and ran down into her hair. Then she fell asleep.

'It's Jimmy. Grace I'm here with you. You gave us a scare.' His loving soft voice was an immediate trigger. She cried before her eyes were even open. 'It's okay, you're okay,' Jimmy told his baby sister, 'I love you. It's okay.' His sister's face was a terrible shock, her nose was swollen, her eyes swollen and black like she'd been in a fight. The airbags had gone off in her face, and saved her life, but it had still damaged her face, it could have been a lot worse.

173

Loving Grace

Grace couldn't speak, her body hurt from head to toe. Her brother's voice was soothing though, Jimmy was the one she knew would never be angry with her, Jimmy was always so beautiful to her, he was her big brother, and she knew his love was unconditional.

Jimmy rubbed her hand, 'Marlo's outside bossing the doctors around, making sure you get everything you need,' his voice had a nice tone to it, he was calm and reassuring. 'Lou and Ross are downstairs with the kids, you're in the ICU kiddo, but our sister's arranging a fancy suite for you when you ready to be moved,' he laughed softly, 'She's being a pain in the arse as you can imagine.'

Grace's eyes flickered open and there he was, her beautiful Jimmy, a gorgeous smile that was comforting and loving even though she was scared to death and still so confused. Taking a painful sob, her chest was sore, her head still ached. It was brain fog of all brain fogs... Grace couldn't think or speak. She was okay though, she was breathing, and she just needed to see her kids, all she wanted was her kids. Fading out and then back to sleep was the easiest thing to do.

Half an hour later she opened her eyes again, something bad had happened, she could feel it. Blinking she saw Marlo at her side, Jimmy behind her, the worry on their faces was frightening. 'Bella!' Grace managed a whisper, 'My boys!'

'Don't talk my darling,' Marlo leaned in. 'The kids are downstairs with Ross and Lou.' Marlo reached out and took Grace's hand in hers, 'What were you thinking Grace!' Tears in her eyes, emotions beyond her control. 'You could have killed yourself.' She truly didn't think that had been her sisters intention. She'd simply been pushed too far. It had all become too much for Grace. 'I can't lose you Grace,' Marlo said letting the tears fall from her eyes. 'I don't know how I'd live without you.' And in a rare display of emotion, Marlo Hunter let herself cry.

Grace was too weak to say anything as her sister rubbed her hand. 'Close your eyes, go back to sleep.'

And that's exactly what Grace did for the next twenty-four hours.

A doctor had explained her injuries, concussion, a swollen nose, bruising to her face, she'd fractured three ribs and sprained both wrists. Grace was lucky.

She knew what she had done. Pressing her foot to the floor and smashing into Michael's precious Mercedes in her Range Rover outside Tina's house. It came to her slowly as she was told about the accident. She'd speed though the T intersection to do so. Endangered innocent people. Grace had asked the doctor if she'd hurt anyone else in the accident, of which to her great relief, she had not.

Marlo came into the room with Abbey at her side, which was a strange feeling. Grace was suffering from a thumping headache. Abbey went straight to her and wrapping her arms around her, sitting on the bed so she could hug her. Grace didn't want to let go of her, through thick and thin they'd always had each other.

175

Loving Grace

'Oh my gosh, I'm so glad you're alright!' Abbey had relied on Grace since they were kids. She'd landed and received a call from Marlo, Grace was in an accident, it had truly shaken Abbey, she'd showered and dressed and rushed to the hospital.

Struggling to speak, Grace was dizzy, she felt lightheaded and most of all, so tired. 'I need to get out of here Ab's. Where are my kids?' she managed with a huff and a puff. The fact she hadn't seen her children was distressing to her.

Marlo looked at her with a smile of apprehension, 'You'll see them soon.'

Grace sighed with regret, 'I need to see them now. I need to go.'

Abbey squeezed her hands, 'You're in a psychiatric ward babe's... You smashed your car into Michael's at high speed. You can't just walk out of here.' She was as gentle as possible with her friend, there was no way her friend was trying to kill herself when she speed towards Michael car.

'What's going on Ab's?' Grace was still confused and upset.

Abbey waited a moment, 'The police are charging you with reckless driving and speeding. You're so lucky you're okay Grace.' She paused. 'The doctors are another story; we have to wait for them to assess you.'

Grace didn't respond or understand any of it, just silence as tears welled in her eyes. Blank eyes looked up at Abbey and Marlo, although she was fully aware of the car crash, she couldn't remember it, only the moments before.

Marlo took a breath in, 'Umm, Abbey and Ross will deal with the charges,' Marlo said looking stressed out, 'The doctors did some test already and they want to assess you as well.' It was awful having this conversation with her sister. 'You hit Michael's car at high speed on purpose Grace… Do you understand?'

Abbey could see Grace's confusion and distress, 'Grace!' she said thinking she'd have to lay it out for her friend straight, 'The doctors are going to do a mental health assessment on you over the next few days, over the weekend. They're not releasing you just yet, and because of the circumstances, there's not much we can do until they do their assessment.' Abbey could see Grace wasn't computing her words. 'The police will be coming in this afternoon to get a statement, and I'll be right here with you, I promise you.' Abbey already knew what she needed Grace to say and do.

Everyone knew Grace smashed into Michael's car deliberately, and that wasn't something a stable person did. The past week had been dramatic and traumatic, but Grace's actions were telling and no matter how much money or power Marlo and Ross Hunter had, they seemed powerless in this situation right at the moment. Marlo had pleaded unsuccessfully with the doctors to let Grace come home into her care, anything to get her sister out of the psych ward.

For Marlo, it was devastating, how did she not see Grace was at this point, she was right under her roof.

The kids came to visit but Grace had been sleeping, they were taking it hard; they now knew everything about their parents, and Tina, and it was a huge shock. Their family had been torn apart. Their mother was in hospital, their father had hurt them all, Tina had betrayed them too, they were all confused and bewildered. All three kids had spent a rather distressing night at their aunt and uncle's home with their cousins all supporting them through this awful time. The shock of Grace's accident compounded with their father's betrayal was nothing short of devastation, even Kristian was too traumatised to lash out and lose his cool. Bella was notably distressed in the arms of cousins Mac and Ruby on the sofa just listening to all the conversations as Marlo and Ross tried to give comfort.

It was like being trapped in a bad dream, a foggy sedated dream. Grace was powerless to her own fate; she could only hope Marlo and Jimmy along with Abbey were doing their best in convincing the hospital that she wasn't crazy... Because at the moment she sure felt crazy, she looked crazy, and she most certainly had acted crazy. She'd snapped after Tina and Michael pushed her too far... Yes, she'd lost her shit, pure and simple, but Grace wasn't crazy, just a little broken. Now, slowly she had to begin to mend for her kids, for herself.

Worried about what her kids were thinking and feeling, Grace questioned Marlo, who answered the only way the beautiful big sister could, assuring her they were okay, and that everyone was doing everything they could to be there for them. For Grace, her concerns were evenly spread as a mother. Luca was the most level-headed and also not without his own private turmoil. Grace stressed to Marlo that she needed to keep an eye on Kristian, he was volatile and unpredictable. Then there was Bella. Grace broke down and started to cry when she said her daughter's name, this would be a lot for Bella to consume, her bond with Michael had always been strong and she didn't know which way Bella would turn now. Grace also didn't underestimate Bella's connection with Tina, they were tight.

'Don't you worry about the kids, we're all over it, I promise,' Marlo said everything Grace needed to hear as Abbey sat at her side rubbing her hand.

Have you talked to her yet?' Grace looked Abbey; they all knew who *'her'* was.

'Briefly, on my way in here.' Abbey's eyes said it all, it hadn't gone well. 'I'm here for you Grace. Just so you know.' It was like it was too painful to say her name. Abbey had been disgusted that Tina had spent almost twenty years screwing Grace's husband, and lying to everyone, it was unforgiveable on so many levels, and she'd told Tina so, along with how she felt betrayed and disappointed. Now, Abbey's first priority was Grace.

Shaking her head, Grace sniffed her tears, 'Ab's, I'm sorry for you, she's your friend, you shouldn't be in the middle of this.'

'Are you kidding me!' Abbey scoffed clearly disturbed. 'I'm not letting her do this to you, this is the most terrible betrayal anyone can ever do to their friend. My god Grace, I will never forgive her.'

Grace had a heavy heart all the same. It had been the three of them forever and now this had torn them all wide apart. Abbey was losing a best friend too. Grace looked at her sister, 'I know the Avi thing disappointed you, but I was a kid.' Grace looked at her best friend, 'That was in the volt!' Marlo didn't know what to say, she didn't know how she felt about the Avi sex thing, it didn't really matter now.

Abbey cleared her throat, 'It was just one night, it was nothing.' Abbey was feeling very protective of Grace, it was after all now just the two of them.

Marlo's eyes grew, 'Thank you Abbey!' she said sincerely with a hint of sarcasm. 'So, let me get it right Grace, you slept with Avi. The day of dads funeral. At my house.' It was judgmental and Marlo knew it, normally this wouldn't bother her so much, but because of the circumstances and the fact it was Avi Roth who was an older man at the time, she felt it was her right to get the full story.

A tired sigh from Grace, 'Yes-yes I did. I was twenty-one and I was grieving. I had sex with Avi. What's the big deal!' Grace was justifying herself; she was not going to accept any shaming from her big sister. 'You know what, my head is fucking aching right now,' Grace was now upset.

'I just want you to be okay, and you're not. I'm not mad at you for sleeping with Avi, he was a very interesting man. God bless his gorgeous soul!'

'Okay, let's see if we can get this assessment done today,' Abbey changed the subject, 'I don't want to have to threaten the hospital with legal action.' She looked at Marlo. 'So, maybe you could go see if they can speed it up or give us an indication of when it might happen,' Abbey's voice of authority was hard to ignore, she was a persistent person when she needed to be, and she wanted Grace out of the psych ward before they found a valid reason to keep her here. She'd seen it happen before, a perfectly sane person who'd had a lapse in judgement, be deemed mentally unstable.

Marlo kissed Grace on the cheek, 'I love you. Everything's going to be fine,' she said leaving to get the assessment underway.

Now it was just Grace and Abbey, they looked at each other knowingly.

'Give it to me straight Ab's, do the doctors really think I'm crazy?' Grace said to Abbey.

'Well, you crashed your three hundred and fifty-thousand-dollar Range Rover into your husband's classic Mercedes,' Abbey smiled bringing humour, 'And that haircut isn't helping your cause babe,' she was lovingly joking, 'And they don't even know that you fucked Avi at your dads wake.'

Grace couldn't help but laugh, 'I'm not crazy,' she had to laugh because it did sound all rather crazy.

'Have you seen your eyes, this one has no white inside, it's all blood. Scary!'

'Don't make fun of me,' Grace looked at her friend. 'I just need to get out of here. What if they decide I'm crazy Ab's... Please don't let them say I'm crazy.' And in a blink, she began to cry again.

'You're not crazy, just a little messed up because your so-called best friend fucked your husband for twenty years behind your back. It's all you got going for you right now,' Abbey chuckled trying to keep it light, 'It doesn't surprise me, remember Jeff Kerr, Tina stole him from me you know! I've never forgotten it.' She'd had a huge crush on Jeff and then Tina went out with him.

Grace realised her predicament, 'I'm scared my kids will blame me and think I'm messed up.' Her emotions were in overload, her voice was wavering and strained. 'And now everyone knows I slept with Avi Roth!' Scrunching her face up to keep her sobs in.

'The best sex you ever had... You've always said that!' Abbey was smiling.

'Don't tell Marlo that, it'll disturb her, she's acting like I fucked my cousin!' Grace sniffed. It was true, Avi had been the been the best sex she'd ever had. Ever. Even if it was just one night. They'd bumped into each other in the upstairs bathroom, Grace was getting ready for bed, she was crying, and everyone was heading off to bed, Avi was staying over in the room across from Grace. She kissed him first and before she knew it, Avi had on against the bathroom door, then they went to the bedroom where she was staying, she snibbed the lock on the door and Avi soothed away her sadness. The bedside lamp was on, she'd never had sex in the light before. He was an experienced older man, and Grace was at his merci. The way his mouth touched her relatively innocent body was mind blowing, sucking her pussy and nipples like a sweet juicy plumb until she couldn't take any longer. Under the sheets he lay over her, spreading her legs wide apart with his manly body, penetrating so deep inside her she cried. It was next level sex. That night Grace became a real woman, she'd orgasmed for real, over and over with no apprehension or inhibitions... Nothing was off limits.

P.F. SCOTT

Chapter Eleven

It was now Monday, and Marlo and Louise brought Grace home to Marlo's house after she was cleared of mental madness. That was the in-joke anyway. The kids had visited over the weekend, that had cheered Grace up. All of them notably upset and not sure what to say or do. Luca being the oldest tried to be strong for them all. Bella was distant, taken aback by her mother's appearance, her face had been a shock, the black eyes and nose, swollen lips, and Grace was very emotional when they'd arrive.

Today was a new day though, and Grace was still weak, but glad to be home and in the comfort of the butterfly room, even if it was Marlo's home.

Fiorella, Judy, and Maria gave Grace special attention. They went the extra mile to welcome her home with the butterfly room fully decked out with a bed tray on wheels for her convenience, a water bottle and a glass, a small posy of flowers on it, a remote for the TV and also an unrecognisable small white disc with two buttons on it. The fresh lavender scented linen was impressive as always, and Shiv had stopped by to drop in a beautiful bunch of flowers for the dresser. The butterfly room was very comforting.

Fiorella picked up the disc and showed Grace, 'Press green, and you'll get me or Judy, we'll be able to hear each other through this device.' Grace nodded, not surprised at all, this was the home of a tech billionaire. 'Press red if it's an emergency, myself, Judy, Marlo, Ross and Maria will all get an alerted that something is wrong.'

'Serious!' Grace was impressed and overwhelmed all at once.

'Mmm, hmm, so don't press red unless it's an absolute emergency. I forgot to mention the police get an alert with the red button.' Fiorella was on top of it all, she ran the house like it was Buckingham Palace. 'Maria will take care of all your meals, and there's been a doctor's visit scheduled for eleven tomorrow morning with your sister's doctor. Doctor Downing.'

'Why?' Grace asked.

'Because your sister requested I make the appointment.' Fiorella knew her boss well, she didn't ever question her.

'Can you cancel that appointment; I don't like Doctor Downing.' She'd had about all she could take for now, Marlo couldn't just make medical appointments on her behalf, that was going too far.

By Tuesday, the shit had well and truly hit the proverbial fan. Michael had summoned his children the night prior to his restaurant in an attempt to win them over with a bullshit

185

explanation, but that's not how it went down for him unfortunately. Bella didn't want to see him, she didn't go. When a reluctant Luca and hot-headed Kristian arrived at the restaurant, Michael didn't have a chance to begin his bullshit stories, because Kristian punched him square in the face. In turn the police were called by a staff member, by the time they arrived, Kristian was long gone. Luca had taken him back to his place, and then there was a knock at the door and the police took Kristian off to the station and Luca called Ross. Michael was a high-profile member of society, a celebrity chef, so the police took the assault seriously.

Tuesday night dinner at Marlo and Ross's was normally the girls and their partners, and Lewis of course. Tonight, Grace was there, and Kristian, who'd been bailed out again by Ross the night before. Bella was coming, and Luca couldn't make it.

Scarlet had come over earlier and finally cut her aunts uneven hair, straight. She'd certainly missed her vocation, just happy that she could be of use in this dreadful situation.

As Grace sat on the long sofa looking at everyone gathering at the kitchen bench going over last night's events and Kristian's run in with the law, she felt like she was a million miles away, on another planet. Sitting alone, she was struggling because she felt Bella was avoiding her, she'd simply kissed Grace hello and disappeared upstairs with Mac.

Lewis saw her staring into the distance looking sorry and sad, and out of sorts, he went to sit with her, getting a close up look at her bruising, 'Well, at least your hair looks better now!' he smirked looking as polished and gorgeous as ever.

Grace looked him over, he made a comment on her hair every time he saw her, because she'd asked him not to... No talk of how her face looked a mess or her loss of sanity, just her hair. And after everything she'd been through, he couldn't help but be a smart arse. At least he was behaving normally.

'I know you've been preoccupied, but have you thought about the apartment in my building,' Lewis said sitting back on the sofa casually.

'I haven't. I probably need to be here right now,' she took a beat, 'But I know I'll need to get away from Marlo soon enough, god bless her, I really do love her.' Grace paused, 'So, if the eight hundred offer still stands, I'll take it. But I don't want to sign a lease, just in case I hate living there.'

Lewis laughed, 'Why would you hate living there?'

'I might hate the view or the location. Or a neighbour.'

'I can assure you you'll love every view and the location. I can't promise anything else,' he had a cheeky grin.

'Mmm,' Grace sighed feeling a little overwhelmed at the decision she'd just made, she sensed a little play from Lewis, a bit of charm.

'Only because everyone is talking about how you slept with Avi Roth at your dads funeral, will I agree to no lease.' Lewis found that story amusing.

She gave him a killer look, 'Stick the apartment up your arse.'

187

Loving Grace

'Oh, come one Gracie, this family needed a good scandal,' he smiled softening her. 'The apartment will be there when you're ready.' Lewis got up off the sofa and walked back to the kitchen as Bella came towards them, Grace watched him walk away, she still wasn't sure how much she liked him, or if she liked his humour, but he was growing on her.

Bella flopping down next to Grace on the sofa, gently so she didn't hurt her mother.

'Hey you.' Grace welcomed the snuggle as Bella unusually showed affection. 'How are you doing?' It was just the two of them in a tender moment. Grace could tell her daughter had been crying, her life had too been turned upside down.

'I'm fine. What about you Mum?' Bella asked softly, 'How are the ribs?'

'I'm fine too.' She smiled as Bella inspected the bruising on her face up close.

'I'm sorry he did this to you Mum,' Bella said at a whisper. 'I will never forgive him, or her.' Bella's face crumbled, burying her head into Grace's shoulder crying, needing her mother's protection and love.

'Ssshhh. My baby, it's okay.' Grace hugged Bella in and rubbing her back, holding her head to her, kissing it. There was nothing she could say to ease her daughter's pain, Michael had hurt them all so terribly. Grace began to cry too, 'You just know, that no matter what happens in your life my beautiful girl, I will always be here for you. You can always count on me; I will never let you down.' It was the first time in many years that she'd had such a moment with her daughter. They hugged and cried for a while, everyone in the distance letting them have their moment, and when Bella had her composure, Grace asked, 'How do like living with Dom?' it was something she hadn't asked her daughter since she'd moved out, and even with everything going on, it was on Grace's mind.

'I don't know Mum,' Bella's soft voice didn't sound positive.

'Really!' Grace was immediately concerned.

'It's fine mum, I'm getting used to it.' She didn't sound convincing, there was something going on, Grace didn't know what, but her daughter hadn't been herself for some time.

Dinner was cozy and nice, given all the people, but they were family. Bella sat close to her mother's side at the table, Kristian on the other side, the kids were like two protective barriers, and it felt nice for Grace to have their support. She'd needed the love from Bella and welcomed it, Kristian was always going to have her back, but Bella may well have gone Michael's way, she'd been a daddy's' girl after all.

There was so much going on, Luca wasn't at dinner and Grace knew it was because he was dealing with becoming a father and the mother not wanting his involvement, which was huge on its own for her son. Grace felt guilty for her children not being happy, suddenly it felt like it was all her doing even though it wasn't. As much as Marlo kept telling her to take time for herself, to not worry about anyone else, Grace really wanted to be there for her kids at this challenging time. Kristian couldn't keep going around being aggressive and thumping his father, even if he did deserve it. Luca's issues were private, and

189

Loving Grace

Bella was hiding something, and it was killing Grace that she didn't have the mental capacity to deal with all of their issues.

After dinner Bella decided to stay the night with Grace, in her room, in her bed. She needed to be near her mother and Grace welcomed it with open arms, they both needed each other more than the other would ever know. As they laid side by side, Grace told Bella she'd left the country house, and she'd found a new place not far from Marlo's, 'It has two bedrooms, so you can have sleepovers whenever you like.' It was hard for her daughter to consume. 'Things are going to be different for a while.'

'Will you be alright living on your own Mum?' Bella sounded worried that her mother would be alone, changes were happening, it was so strange.

'Sweetheart, of course, it's literally just up the road from here... And guess who lives right above me?'

'Who?' Bella looked at Grace.

'Lewis.'

'But you don't like him!' Bella laughed; she found it funny.

'He's not that bad, and he's helping me out,' Grace admitted.

'He owns the building right.'

'I know, he'll be my landlord. He lives in the penthouse above me. His place looks like it should be in a magazine, the views are amazing.' They lived a normal upper middle-class life, and the Hunter's and her brother Jimmy lived like Billionaires.

Bella liked the fact that her mother would be living in town, and so close to her aunt and uncle, she needed all the support she could get right now. Grace was glad to be living closer to her kids, she'd only be a short drive away at any given time, she'd be able to have the kids over for dinners and of course they could just pop in on her without having to driving an hour plus home in the dark. There was an upside in all the gloom.

By the end of the week, Grace was feeling slightly better both physically and mentally. Abbey had popped over every day to see her, Bella had stayed last night at Marlo's again, in her mother's bed... Something was up with her, Grace just knew it. She'd gone back to Dom's today and didn't seem too bothered doing so.

Now that it was Friday night, Marlo and Ross were having drinks with Mac, Kristian, and Lewis out on the terrace. 'The Rolling stones are playing in Auckland on Saturday night... Any takers?' Ross asked as he sat at the table, a questioning look on his face, hoping they'd all say yes. He and Marlo had missed their trip away last weekend because of Grace's accident. Ross needed to be going somewhere, doing something all the time.

Grace was listening in to the conversation from the sofa just inside the living room as they sat with the sun going down on the terrace.

'I'd love to, but...' Grace heard Marlo sigh.

'Grace might like to come. We can fly out in the morning, get there just in time to have an early dinner at that restaurant you love so much Mac. Take in the show. I can book a couple of suites at The Park Hyatt... Anyone?' There was excitement in his voice.

'I'll go, for sure,' Kristian loved all sorts of music, and he enjoyed doing anything with his uncle, Ross had four daughters and had always been exceptionally close to Kristian and Luca. He and Kristian had a bond, perhaps formed because Kristian didn't have such a great one with his own father.

'Well, I'm in, of course,' Mac laughed excitedly, 'Mum, come on, you love Mick Jaggar.'

Still listening, Grace knew Marlo wasn't going because of her, but she didn't want to say it aloud, because she knew she was listening.

'I can't go,' Lewis huffed, 'I've got a lunch date tomorrow. I'm busy.'

'A date with a woman?' Mac asked, 'You're passing up the Rolling Stones for a woman?'

'Yes, strangely enough Mackenzie.' Lewis turned to Marlo. 'You should go, I'll check in on Grace tomorrow afternoon,' he said quietly.

'Come on Mum, come with us,' Mac persuaded her Marlo.

Grace walked out onto the terrace, she'd become a burden because she was mid-breakdown and heartbroken. 'You should go,' she said looking at her sister. 'And I don't need checking in on.' Her eyes fluttered at Lewis briefly.

'I don't want to go,' smiled Marlo.

'Mum, yes you do!' Mackenzie was desperate for her mother to go, she really wanted her there, not that her father and cousin were not fun.

'Please go,' Grace insisted knowing how much her sister loved the Stones and Mick.

Grace was going to be fine on her own, Fiorella was with her, out of sight seemingly, Grace was looking forward to Saturday and Sunday alone, people were starting to piss her off big time, there was always a dinner or drinks, or someone popping in at Marlo and Ross' house.

Michael and Tina's betrayal was now common knowledge, all the Hunter's knew she'd had the accident and made everything worse than it already was. Craving the weekend alone, surely it wasn't that much to ask!

Marlo made a huge deal about leaving early on Saturday morning, she stood in the bedroom doorway of the butterfly room assuring Grace she'd be back tomorrow before the family dinner. A massive sigh of relief flooded Grace when they all eventually left the house to pick up Kristian on their way to the jet, she'd been putting on her bravest face all week, literally an act so nobody thought she was overly insane. The harbour side mansion was in complete silence, she was alone beside Fiorella, who managed to be invisible most of the time. Spending the morning out in the sun on the terrace, Grace could cry to herself and get red eyes without anyone asking if she needed to talk or if she was feeling okay. Early afternoon she had lunch at the table by the pool under the umbrella alone, it was wonderful not having to talk. Fiorella was spoiling her without bothering her, she'd set a place for one, complete with a small vase and a lone yellow rose and the daily papers.

193

Loving Grace

'Grace, while you're here alone carry your disc with you at all times, I'll be in the laundry or one of the bedrooms changing linen and cleaning. I'll be out of sight, but I won't be far away,' Fiorella assured her with a smile like she loved her job. 'Enjoy the sun and relax.' It was as though she knew Grace needed some space, a breather as such.

'Fiorella, I'd like to thank you, I appreciate everything you do for me, I really do,' Grace said, her sisters staff were exceptional.

Watching the boats on the harbour from the lower pool level Grace tried hard to clear her head and let her mind rest, she was a million miles away. Her hands still trembled, she still had black eyes, and she had dropped a dress sized in literally one week.

Michael and Tina had vanished off the face of the earth these past few days, she'd not heard a thing from either of them, not even from the insurance company or the police about her reckless driving charges. If she never had to see or hear from Michael and Tina again in her entire life, she'd be chuffed. In fact, Grace hoped they both would disappear forever, and she didn't feel an ounce of guilt. She was totally unaware that Ross and Jimmy had told them in not so many words to leave town for a while, to leave their Grace alone, to get the fuck out of her life basically.

After barely touching her lunch, Grace curled up on the sofa with a blanket over her head and cried some more. Yes, she was alone, but she was also so very lost and fragile still. Eventually falling asleep, when she was sleeping she didn't have to think about her sadness or anyone else's problems for that matter. As much as she felt like she was on a need-to-know basis with her kids, right now she was finding it hard to process anything.

'I thought I better check in on you!' Lewis said startling her, he was sitting in the armchair opposite Grace as she opened her eyes from a long nap.

How did he manage to get her offside every single time he spoke! Her silence said a thousand words, afraid that if she opened her mouth, only nastiness would come out. Now that she was awake, she looked Lewis over. The navy shirt and jeans looked nice... nice shoes! Grace tried not to see anything good about him, but it was getting harder and harder to push back because he'd been so nice to her.

'Have you been asleep all day?' he had a half grin.

'How was your date?' Grace asked sitting up a little wishing she hadn't woken up; she touched the corner of her eye were the bruising still appeared, it was tender.

'Fine,' he said without expression.

A surprised '*Oh,*' came from Grace. She bet Lewis was fussy, very fussy when it came to women.

He narrowed his eyes to her, 'Fiorella is making us dinner.' As if he lived there, he practically ate every second dinner at his uncle and aunts anyway, even though he was thirty-seven years old and had his own home.

Grace just glared at him, he was sooo irritating, she looked over towards the large dining table at the other end of the living room, near the kitchen, and two places were set. *Unbelievable!*

195

Loving Grace

'I'm hoping this date will be better than my lunch date,' a slight chuckle as he teased Grace, he knew just how to get under her skin and got a weird kind of kick doing so.

'This is not a date,' she grumped.

'When two people eat together, it's a date,' he protested.

'I don't think so,' she wasn't letting it go.

'I do.'

'I don't.' Her head fell to one side, daring him to go her again. Just when she thought maybe he wasn't as bad as she'd always thought, he'd prove her wrong. Lewis Hunter was undeniably sexy, which pissed her off even just admitting it in her own head. Hair dark, deep olive skin, his eyes a lighter shade, he was masculine and had this way about him that literally irritated her to a point of intrigue these past few weeks. She'd never thought of him as attractive. How could one man be so annoying and yet pleasant on the eye. His cheeky nature eating at her bit by bit, inch by inch. Wearing her down with his odd kindness and irresistible charm. Abbey and Louise would kill themselves laughing if they only knew.

They ate dinner in initial silence, Grace sipping a red wine, her first alcohol since the accident, she needed it. Not looking at Lewis was her game, just to see how long she could do it, how much will-power did she have, considering he looked extra enticing tonight.

'I think after dinner, we should go to your new apartment so you can see the view at night,' Lewis spoke first. He thought getting Grace out of the house might be good for her, she looked drawn and pale, hanging around the house twenty-four-seven couldn't be great for her mental health.

'I'm fairly certain it won't look better than this... Why are you so adamant that I take your apartment?' unable to stop herself from asking the question, after all he'd mentioned it every time she seen him, and now she was staring to think maybe it was something to do with Bella. *Did Lewis Hunter have a thing for her daughter!* It wasn't an outrageous thought, but Grace had learned of late to let nothing surprise her.

He huffed, looking at her like she was out of line, 'What have I ever done to you to make you dislike me so much.'

Grace was caught off guard, 'I-I don't dislike you,' she said putting her cutlery down.

'Then just look at the apartment with me. I know you want to.' He continued to stare her out as she gazed back at him with a blank, tired expression.

The next thing she knew, Grace was in the passenger's seat of Lewis's car taking the one-minute drive to his apartment building. He'd insisted, convincing her she needed to get out of the house, and she wasn't in the mood to put up a fight, this was supposed to be a relaxing weekend. Maybe he wasn't as bad as she'd always thought, she'd certainly seen the better side of him these past few weeks. He knew all her personal crap, she just hoped he wasn't pitying her or being nice because she was Marlo's sister, because that would shit her. As far as she was concerned she didn't need anyone's pity, especially not Lewis Hunter's, even if he was growing on her. Slowly.

Loving Grace

They stood in the middle of the living room that would soon be hers. The harbour lights were coming on and the sun had just about set, the view was simply stunning, almost irresistible, Grace liked the apartment a lot. 'I'll need some bank details or an agent to pay the rent to, do you want it weekly, fortnightly or monthly?'

Lewis gave her a curious look, like he wasn't thinking about the rent at all, 'Umm. Whatever you want, I'll message you my details tomorrow.' It didn't seem to fuss him too much at all, he was very casual.

Nodding, she decided to cut him some slack. Lewis had done her a huge favour with the apartment, for some reason.

As they pulled up back outside Marlo and Ross's, she sat in the seat for a moment before they got out, 'Lewis, I'm grateful. Thank you.' There was an understanding between them.

He walked Grace into the house and made sure Fiorella knew she was home, 'You take these,' he handed her two cards that were entry to the apartment and underground garage. 'I'll show you how to set up the security code access when you move in.'

'Thank you, Lewis,' Grace had genuine gratitude in her tone, suddenly struggling to hold back tears. Accepting access to her actual new apartment felt weird. She felt like a foreigner in her own skin.

'Gracie, you are very welcome,' he said with a charming smile, his eyes penetrating right through to her vulnerability. He went to leave, 'I'll see you tomorrow night at dinner.'

Chapter Twelve

Monday morning Marlo and Grace walked to her new apartment that was literally a five-minute walk up the street. The sisters agreed the apartment was perfect, Marlo was onboard, she was excited. Lewis would be right upstairs, so Grace would be safe, and she'd be right down the road.

'This is you all over, I love it!' Marlo gushed as she walked around the apartment checking every little nook and cranny out.

'I know, it feels right,' Grace took a deep breath in, she did feel like she could breathe here. On her own, without her husband. Michael.

Marlo and Grace shopped online all afternoon in Marlo's office. By four pm they'd furnished the entire two-bedroom apartment, and everything was being delivered in two days' time. The new apartment had brightened Grace's spirits somewhat, she was making progress.

Loving Grace

Completely swept up in the big move, Grace had forgotten about the police charges that her brother and Ross had miraculously managed to make disappear. Michael and Tina were consuming less of her thoughts. It hadn't been long, but she felt like she'd come a long way even though she was still in recovery stage from her car accident, and her broken heart. Everyone rallied around her, Marlo, Louise, Abbey, Scarlet, Mac, and Bella all spending the day at her new apartment as all the new furniture arrived. It was like an estrogen overload of home making at its finest. Scarlet was in charge of greeting the deliveries as they arrived, making sure they went to the right rooms, Marlo, Louise, and Abbey along with Grace washed bed linen, unwrapped packages and set up house while Mac and Bella did the heavy lifting as well as coffee and food runs. This was sisterhood in full force, by dinner time the apartment was ready for Vogue to come and do a cover shoot.

'Thank you for thinking of all the extras Marlo,' Grace said to her sister as they stood in the kitchen together filling the fridge with food. Marlo had somehow ordered all the things Grace had not considered, like cutlery, kitchen wear, linen, and groceries. The apartment was literally livable in one single day.

'It's the least I could do,' Marlo never flaunted her money, and she'd insisted she do this for her sister, and you never said no to Marlo Hunter when she was on a goodwill mission.

Abbey and Louise sat on the new grey sofa chatting, Scarlet had gone home to her husband, the younger girls were ordering Chinese takeaway, the vibe was sedate and calm, they were all exhausted after the big day they'd put in.

'I love that you went with blacks and greys Grace, so not you.' Abbey noted as Grace's country house was light and bright with beiges and neutrals.

'Well, the bench tops and the floors kind of set the tone.' Grace rested her hands on the black stone kitchen bench. 'The tapware is all black, and I felt like a change. Marlo showed me some Instagram pages for darker interior design, and we just went from there. It was all Marlo really.'

'Mum, it's amazing,' Bella said looking around at her mother's new apartment, so modern and cool. 'And I love the spare bedroom so much.'

'Good, it's yours whenever you need it,' Grace smiled across the room.

'Can I stay tonight?' Bella's eyes swooned at her mother.

'You can stay any night you like.' For the first time in such a long time, Grace felt good.

As the ladies cleaned up after christening the new dining table, a knock at the door in the background caught Grace's attention amongst the laughter. She opened it knowing who it would be.

'I thought I'd come in and check up on you.' Lewis teased knowing how she hated being checked on.

Had he gone out of his way to look exceptionally attractive this evening! She couldn't help thinking. Grace moved back and let Lewis walk through her front door. 'We're neighbours now, no need to check on me.'

Lewis stopped and looked down at her, 'Oh, all the more reason I'd say.' Winking at her.

Loving Grace

Marlo hugged him hello, kissing both his cheeks and thanking him, 'Hey, I'm so happy your two are neighbours. I'm so relieved you'll be on top of Grace, how awesome is that!'

'Literally on top,' he gave Grace a cheeky grin. 'Hi Lou. Hey Abbey,' he greeted the ladies then gave Mac a wink and a smile to Bella... Grace saw the smile, she was keeping an eye on that situation, her daughter and Lewis.

'Hey Lew,' Louise said pushing her hair back from her face giving him one of her best smiles.

'Hello Lewis, nice to see you,' Abbey said, she'd had two champagnes and had been exited Grace was living under 'hot Lew' that was what Louise and Abbey referred to him as. Hot Lew! It was a secret in joke between the girls, Marlo wasn't privy to this joke, she'd be horrified.

'Lew, do you like what we've done?' Mac put her arms out, proud at how her aunt's apartment had come up. 'The flowers were my idea.' She pointed to the bright pink peony's that looked stunning sitting in the middle of the dark dining table.

Lewis looked around, 'It's amazing, you've all done a great job.' He was impressed that it had only taken a day. All eyes were on him, he stood there, all six foot of him in a white shirt and jeans holding his work capsule bag. Abbey and Louise fixating on him. Lewis Hunter was sexy; they weren't ashamed to admit it. That dark skin and the white shirt with his freshly cut short dark hair, he was a pleasure to their exhausted eyes.

'Let me show you around.' Grace decided she needed to be a little kinder to her new landlord, she waved her arm and lead him into the hall. She loved the apartment. 'The spare bedroom!' Her smile was from ear to ear, Lewis noticed her happiness.

'Maybe Bella will move in with you,' he said as it was just the two of them standing at the end of hall.

Grace narrowed her eyes, 'She lives with her boyfriend,' she paused watching his face, 'You'd be okay though if she did... I mean you are my landlord; I'd have to run it by you of course.'

Lewis laughed, 'Gracie, you can move whoever you want in.'

Moving down the hall she stopped at the end door, 'This is my room.' They stood looking in.

'The palm tree picture... I'm getting a Marlo vibe, am I right?'

'Actually, that was me,' she said walking over and touching the charcoal-coloured canvas with black palm trees. 'The lamp was Marlo.'

He smiled looking at the bronze palm tree lamp, 'Mmm, must be because you're sisters, you like themed bedrooms.' He huffed a laugh at the notion, the room was feminine and stylish.

'Let me show you the laundry.' She changed the subject. 'I had the delivery man hang the dryer, Marlo said it would be fine,' Grace said leading Lewis back through the living room and into a door off the kitchen. 'I hope it's okay.'

'It's your place, do what you need to do.' He was cool as a cucumber about everything.

Abbey and Louise's eyes followed Lewis to the door as he said his goodbyes, he had this presence about him like all the Hunter men, only he was younger and hotter, and he did something to their insides whenever he was around. Grace closed the door behind him and turned around to see Abbey on the sofa give her a sneaky wink, of which she frowned her disapproval to.

'Mmm, very friendly,' Louise said in her soft voice so only Grace could hear.

The ladies left as the night got on, 'Lou and I will be here for drinks and dinner on Friday night about six thirty, feel free to invite your neighbour,' Abbey teased on the sly to Grace on her way out the door.

'Oh, my god! Don't start. Go home.' Grace knew Abbey was going to go on about Lewis, she and Louise couldn't help themselves. Had Tina been here, she would be carrying on too.

Thursday was a weird day, this was Grace's new home, much smaller than her country house and so very different style wise, however, she was in love with being able to see the harbour from her gorgeous living room. The balcony was empty, but then at ten a.m. a delivery arrived for a Mrs. Marlo Hunter. Balcony furniture. How could Grace be upset with her sister; she was generous to a fault, and she meant well... And the furniture was perfect.

Bella had left for university early, Grace had sense things were not going well with Dom. She had tried to open the conversation about her daughters living arrangement when they went to bed last night but Bella was as usual a closed book. If there was a problem she wasn't telling her mother.

By lunchtime Grace already missed Fiorella and Maria, she made her own breakfast and ate a banana out on her balcony for lunch. Her niece Scarlet had been keeping an eye on the business, checking her emails and making any calls that had to be made. Scarlet had worked with Grace for years, she helped set up the current business model and knew the business inside out, so it was in good hands during Grace's absence. She was now in a head space where she could come back in some capacity.

At one o'clock Scarlet and Marlo were at the door, checking up but using the excuse of delivering a freshly baked butter cake from Maria. Grace made coffee and listened to her niece run over some figures and orders.

'So, the new line will be ready for next week's trade fair,' Scarlet informed her aunt.

'The fair!' Grace had forgotten all about the upcoming trade fair, she'd normally go and man her stand with Scarlet and talk with sellers and take orders, but she had completely forgotten about it. 'It slipped my mind.'

'Mac and I will do the fair together, you don't have to even show up if you don't want to,' Scarlet was the eldest of Marlo's daughters and low-key Grace's favourite, she was a pure angel.

'I'd like to go. I should go.' Grace looked at her niece and sister.

'Next week might be too soon,' Marlo interjected with a touch of bossy to her tone as she sat eating butter cake.

'I'm sure I'll be fine if I've got Scarlet and Mac there.' Grace didn't like her sisters doubt, it wasn't that Marlo so much doubted her, it was her being realistic, which right now Grace low key needed, she was taking on too much, too soon.

'I'm just checking in on you,' smiled Lewis as Grace opened her front door. She knew it was him; he was the only person who'd knock at her door, everyone else would buzz from downstairs.

'Still alive!' her smile was big, today had been a good day, she was getting back to some kind of normality. She opened the door and stood looking at him.

'How's the view so far?'

'So far, so good.' She looked him over. Another white shirt with jeans, she'd begun to notice a trend. His hair was getting a little longer on top, still short at the back and sides. As the days went on, Grace was letting her guard down.

'Okay, well you're still alive, that's good. I'll leave you to it.' Lewis stood at the front door, he paused, looking down at her, there was something in his eyes.

'Bye,' Grace said before he could say anything, she couldn't help it, he bought out the bitch in her.

'Have a good night.' He waved without turning around.

'Thanks for checking in on me.' She shut the door.

An hour later her phone rang, and it was Lewis, 'I know you've just moved in and all, but would you have sugar... I'm in the middle of cooking dinner and I'm out of sugar.'

'Sugar! Sure. Marlo had the whole supermarket delivered, I've got a kilo of sugar,' she sighed wondering if he was going to become a pest... Too overly neighbourly. Surely not!

'Could you bring it up to me Gracie, I can't leave my cooktop?'

'Sure.' He was definitely becoming a pest she thought as she hung up on him.

Knocking on his door Grace wondered if he was cooking for a date, he was known for being a ladies' man, Marlo and the girls were always talking about him and the women he dated.

'Come in,' he said quickly opening the door and rushing back into the kitchen, leaving her no choice but to go towards the delicious aroma of his cooking and deliver the sugar.

'What are you cooking?' she placed the sugar on the bench as he stirred his pots now dressed in a black T shirt and tightish track pants, barefoot... It pained her that she kept noticing how good he looked.

'Bolognese, the secret is sugar. Shiv always puts sugar in her sauces.' He called his grandmother Shiv, which was cute.

'It smells good.'

'I told you I was a good cook. You should stay and eat with me, there's plenty here.'

'No. I'm good. Thanks.' She was having a bowl of cornflakes at best.

'Stay!' Lewis turned around with a smile she couldn't refuse.

The little fucker was wearing her down! Grace was in two minds. She liked him, he was surprisingly a nice guy, she liked his humour, he got hers. However, she didn't want to seem too dependent on him or needy... she didn't want to overstep the neighbourly line either. But he had asked her to stay.

Loving Grace

'Okay, sure,' she said wondering what the hell she was doing!

'Take a seat,' he gestured to the kitchen stools at the big bench top, then pushed a glass of red towards her. 'Do you like cooking Gracie?'

'Not really. I mean I'm okay at it, I can cook, I just don't like it so much,' she took a deep breath in, 'It reminds me of Michael.'

'Most people cook, not just him.'

'I know.'

'Shiv taught me to cook, it's a nice feeling when you cook something, and people enjoy it.'

Grace watched him across the bench, she could see he was enjoying himself, a tea towel over his shoulder, his was constantly stirring and adding to his pots, smelling his food, and smiling.

'I had lunch with Luca today at the office, and he told me about, you know,' he spoke hesitantly.

'What?'

'Jasmine and the baby, he told me you know.'

She let out a big sigh, 'Yes, I know. I'm trying to be there for him, but I'm consumed with keeping my head above water at the moment, if I'm being honest,' she paused, 'I don't really know what to do for him, other than listen.'

'That's all he needs, he's a grown man, he'll handle it,' Lewis told her as he set out cutlery on the oversized bench with two water glasses. 'Luca is smart and compassionate... He gets that from you.'

Not knowing how to take his comment she smiled, 'It's certainly not from his father,' she had to laugh.

'You're smart, Luca gets that from you too.' He was now serving up spaghetti and his sauce, it looked amazing.

'It depends on what smarts you're talking about. I'm not too smart when it comes to men. Clearly.'

'So, you married a dickhead, you're not the only one who's ever done that. You've been a good wife and mother to that dickheads kids. You've got your business and your independent... His loss, not yours.'

Wow, Lewis was really polishing her up, was this how he really saw her! Grace was surprised at his glowing review of her. 'Maybe I wasn't the best wife.' She felt her cheeks flush a little. It was the wine, not the great looking man cooking her dinner.

'There's no reason to do what he did to you Gracie. I mean I don't know the intimate details of your marriage; I don't care. You didn't deserve to be fucked over.' Lewis saw the sadness in her eyes as his lingered at hers probably just a little too long. 'Your son is a great guy. He'll work this out because he's been raised right by you.' He smiled as he put the plates on the bench and sat with his wine in hand. 'Enjoy!' he said as he started to eat, Grace observing him a moment.

The dinner conversation went from Luca to her business, and the things Grace had been trying to implement before all her life was derailed. They were having a personal and yet progressive conversation, and it felt great, for the first time in a long time, Grace felt normal. It felt like so much had happened and changed in her life, she wasn't exactly sure how she was coming out the other end of things, it was a day a time situation.

After two hours of fabulous food, wine and great conversation, Lewis stood at his front door as Grace left, he'd learned a lot about her tonight, 'Thanks for having dinner with me.' He smiled looking down at her. She was cute, and much friendlier than he'd expected tonight. Maybe she was coming around.

'Thank you for asking me to stay, I loved the Bolognese, it so much better than cornflakes and milk' she said stopping just outside of his door. 'Good night Lewis.'

'Good night Gracie.'

Louise arrived first for drinks and dinner on Friday night, she'd heard about the Avi Roth sex scandal, that's what the family were calling it, a sex scandal, and Louise had a million questions for Grace.

'It was so long ago; I get my sister is offended because it was our dad's funeral and all but come on... get over it. It was thirty years ago' *She was so over it.*

Louise looked at Grace. This had been the hot topic last night at dinner, she and Jimmy had caught up with Marlo and Ross, who were having a disagreement because Marlo was so bent out of shape over Avi fucking her little sister.

Louise sighed with understanding, 'You know I don't give a shit that it was your dad funeral. I say good for you. I always thought Avi was a sexy man.' Louise was cool, but Grace knew she still loved some good old fashion family drama, and all her scandals of late were keeping the family a buzz with gossip.

Abbey came in the front door and Grace hugged her tight, she was always one hundred percent in her corner, no matter what. There was just this thing between them that never questioned the others integrity because it didn't have to, years of friendship had seen them through some pretty tough stuff. Grace used to think the same about Tina. Never in her wildest dreams did she ever think it would turn out like this. Then Grace started to cry as she hugged Abbey.

'Hey, what's going on?' Abbey asked stepping away.

'I'm okay. I'm just having a moment... Fucking Tina!' She looked at both Abbey and Louise. 'Sometimes I think we had such an amazing friendship, and she's ruined it all. But then I question was it a friendship at all, ever.' She was dumbfounded at the notions; how could Tina do this.

'She was one hell of an actress, that's what I think,' Louise said from the sofa, Tina had been her least favourite of Grace's friends, Tina always made remarks to Louise making her feel like she wasn't worthy of being one of the girls, were as Abbey had always welcomed her.

Abbey stood there looking at Grace, she was teary too, 'I don't know. I'm at a loss.' That was all she could say without crying herself. They'd both lost their best friend, and for good reason, Abbey simply couldn't be Tina's friend for the simple fact she lied and betrayed everyone.

Loving Grace

'On a brighter note,' Louise said changing direction, 'Do you think your landlord might pop by, or has he got a hot date tonight.'

Abbey smiled like an exited teenager with a crush, 'Yeah, did you ask him in for a drink?'

'I did not!' Grace thought they were nuts.

'You know we bought our pj's, we're sleeping over,' Abbey gasped, 'Maybe he'll bring his date home, and we'll hear them having wild sex with her.'

'Oh, my god, could you image,' Louise clapped her hands together, 'Grace, could we hear him, where's his bedroom situated?' They were all looking up at the ceiling in wonder.

'Way over there.' Grace pointed to the wall as her apartment was less than half of Lewis's penthouse. 'And people say I'm the crazy one!' she sighed, 'And listening to him have sex is creepy.'

'What! Don't say you don't find him remotely attractive Grace King!' said Louise walking over to the wall and trying to hear for a noise from above.

Abbey continued looking at the ceiling, 'I don't know Grace, it sounds to me that now that your buddies with Lew you're in his corner a little.' She turned and smiled at Grace.

'His corner!' she questioned with a frown.

'Mmm,' Abbey grinned. 'You're getting very chummy with Hot Lew these days. You've gone from hating him to defending him.' Abbey sensed something, and it was worth a tease. 'Admit that you don't hate him anymore.'

'I never hated him.'

Louise laughed, 'You did too. You used to tell us he was up himself and full of shit and bad manners.'

'And he was. But I think he's changed. Look how nice he's been to me.'

'Yeah,! Abbey couldn't stop smiling, 'Admit you were wrong about Lewis please.'

'I just did. I said he was behaving nicely.' She wasn't about to tell them she'd actually imagined him without his shirt on!

They drank too many champagnes and bypassed ordering dinner, instead eating cheese and crackers with olives, pickles and a packet of cheese Twisties as they sat out on the new balcony furniture so Louise and Abbey could smoke a joint together. It was the laughter Grace needed more than anything. Her two gorgeous friends talking stupidly and keeping her spirits up.

'Would you have a threesome Ab's?' Louise asked just like that as she took a puff of the rather thick joint.

'Of course, I would,' scoffing as if Louise were mad. 'Oh, but wait, not with Dean, it would have to be with two complete randoms. And Dean can watch.'

'Grace?' Louise was getting at something here.

'I don't know, I'm off sex for a while.' She couldn't help wondering why Louise was asking about threesomes, sex was the last thing on Grace's mind, and this had been going on well before the Michael and Tina betrayal... Sure she enjoyed sex once she was doing it, but she was never the instigator, and she didn't even use her vibrator anymore. Her hormones had started to change, and she didn't crave sex the way she used to. 'Sex isn't my thing right now. I don't want it.'

Abbey and Louise looked at her, both frowning at what they were hearing. Then Louise said, 'You're fucking fifty, not eighty. And your too cute and hot not to have sex anymore Grace.'

They could see Grace was dead serious.

'Why are you talking like this and where has my friend gone?' Abbey was freaked out too.

'I don't want it. I don't need it.'

'No, no, no!' Abbey shook her head. 'You've just lost your mojo a minute, that's all.' She was appalled that her friend was basically saying she was giving up on sex. In her day, Grace was a vivacious sexual girl, she'd enjoyed sex.

The laughter stopped and the conversation went to a serious note. 'Do you think maybe you've lost some confidence given what's happened?' Louise asked lovingly.

A slight smile came to Grace's face, she didn't speak, she shrugged as if to say yes. Her life had changed dramatically, Michael cheating on her with Tina had been the biggest kick in the guts she'd ever had. Not only had it been a betrayal, but it was also shameful and embarrassing and something she felt she might not ever get over.

'You're too young to swear off sex,' Abbey stuffed a huge pickle in her mouth. 'And Lou's right, you're gorgeous Grace and funny too, men love you, they always have. I'm taking you out and we're going to find you a sexy stacked random to fuck some sense back into you.'

Louise burst out laughing, it was hard not to, even Grace had a chuckle, Abbey was great at changing the conversation up when need be.

'Thank you for the concern, but I don't want to have sex Ab's. I'm not ready.' Grace took a huge breath in.

'Oh, my gosh. Ever!' Louise whispered. 'I hope you've got an up-to-date vibrator. Tell me you do.'

Abbey shifted on the outdoor sofa to get comfortable, 'Are you scared to fuck someone else?'

'I'm not scared of sex, thank you; I just don't need it in my life right now.'

When it got cold they moved inside, and Abbey and Louise piled into Grace's bed with her, even though there was a spare bedroom with a huge bed. The silliness had stopped, and they talked about the Mediterranean holiday they were all going on. Marlo had extended her offer to Abbey and to Louise, and in a dim light as they wound down they discussed the things they most wanted to do on the holiday together.

As they laid silently about to all fall off to sleep Louise whispered, 'I just heard movement upstairs. Do you think he's alone?'

In the morning Abbey and Louise persuaded Grace to walk around to a popular restaurant for breakfast, set on the edge of the water in a quiet part of the bay, they sat outside in the sun enjoying the morning, overlooking the marina. Grace hadn't left her apartment since moving in. Nobody had forgotten her ordeal, the demise of her marriage and the car accident which

215

led to the psych ward for three days. Getting Grace back to the land of the living was going to be a group effort and they were all working on it.

The girls ate and drank coffee then walked back to Grace's apartment so they could all go and begin their weekends. Louise had an afternoon flight to Silicon Valley in California with Jimmy in the jet for a meeting, then they were going to New York for a day or two of shopping and to catch up with friends for dinner before heading home, because that's what billionaires did! Sometimes Grace forgot everyone around her besides Abbey were mega rich, at the end of the day they were all just people, and they hadn't always been filthy rich.

As the ladies turned into Grace's new street and reached the front of the apartments, along came Lewis almost like it was scripted. He'd been for a morning run, clad in black singlet, tight shorts, and running shoes. All three of them stopped and watched as he took the last few steps to them.

'Morning,' he was out of breath as he slowed down, taking deep breaths in, and smiling at Grace. After some chit chat, Lewis followed the girls inside the building to the lift, 'I'm around all weekend if you need anything,' he said to Grace. 'You know where I am.' He smiled and took the stairs up to his sixth-floor penthouse as the ladies stood waiting for the lift.

Abbey looked at Grace, 'Oh, you're going to need something!' she teased.

Lewis was younger, madly handsome and a charmer by nature and he knew when to turn it onto super charge with a sexy little grin or cheeky muscle flex. Grace had always taken it as him having tickets on himself, and although her opinion of him was changing by the day, she wasn't affected by his presents, the cute smile and those tight shorts holding his phenomenal arse didn't faze her.

Every now and then, reality loomed over Grace like a wet grey blanket. She'd had a terrific night with the girls and breakfast had been nice, they were her inner sanctum for a reason, they knew she'd needed them. The apartment was beautiful with a luxurious flare and so different to her usual style, and the new furniture was a distraction, but at the end of the day she was now on her own, and it was hard to not wonder what she'd done wrong to end up here all alone.

The clouds had most definitely come over the harbour, the safest place for Grace seemed to be snuggled up on her new sofa in her beige lounge pants and a white t-shirt with no undies or bra under her new super fluffy blanket, watching reruns of Sex and the City, her favourite past time. For the most part her mind was a blank, she wasn't thinking about anything but what she was watching, which made a great change. She had better things to do, things like work, preparing for the trade fair, or reading her emails. Scarlet was an angel; she had single handedly kept everything afloat over the past weeks whilst Grace had other more pressing concerns in life. This afternoon she was on the sofa taking a mental health break from life, God knows she needed it.

Just as it was getting dark, there was a knock at the door. There was only one person who ever just knocked at her door.

Loving Grace

'I'm checking in on you. You good?' Lewis asked as she opened the door, standing there with grey track pants and a black t-shirt and a black unzip up hoodie.

'Did my sister put you up to this, has she asked you to annoy me regularly?' Marlo was like a helicopter mother, always having to be in the know.

Lewis stood, his hand resting on the arch of the door just staring down at her, Grace standing firm in her doorway, 'You just had a car accident with a serious concussion, so I feel obligated to check in on you given you are in my building.' He was so very matter of fact.

'Really!' she wasn't buying it.

'Yeah... Do you eat fish?'

'Sometimes.' She loved fish.

'Great because I'm about to get a delivery and I ordered for two, so come on up and join me... Or we can eat here.'

Grace folded her arms at her chest, she just remembered she didn't have a bra on, and she was wearing a white shirt, and he was looking at her with examining eyes which were making her angry. 'I'm not hungry and you can't just come by and ask me to have to dinner with you whenever you feel like it.'

'Why not?' he questioned her.

Oh, for sure he was going to be that neighbour! The pesty one. Who would ever have thought!

'Lewis,' she said standing in the middle of her doorway, 'Shouldn't you be on a date or something. It's Saturday night.'

'I went on a date last night.' His cheeky grin was tempting.

'Great,' she sighed, 'I'm watching something, so maybe another time.'

'I tell you what,' he smiled, 'I'll grab the delivery, and we can eat here, and I'll watch whatever you're watching.'

Grilled fish, salt and pepper calamari, half a dozen prawn cutlets and a hearty Greek salad spread out across Grace's new coffee table as they sat on the sofa, side by side like besties eating fish and watching the untimeliest episode of Sex and the City... The one were Samantha catches Richard Wright screwing around. The strangest thing was that Lewis was riveted to the screen, he hadn't even said a word, he was fixated like he'd never seen it before.

'Need another drink?' Grace asked as she got up to get another bottle of mineral water, the episode had finished.

'Yeah... Who's the dark haired one?'

'Charlotte.' Grace sat back down.

'I like her,' he said.

Grace looking at him, her eyes narrowing, 'Do you!'

'Have you seen Bella much?' he randomly asked.

Grace huffed. Was he keen on her daughter! 'She stayed the first night here with me. She lives with her boyfriend now. She's young, very young, so her life is busy and full.' How much clearer could she make it, her daughter was off limits... *Not for you Lewis Hunter!*

'I don't think Kristian and Luca think much of her boyfriend, what about you?'

Loving Grace

Stopping mid chew, 'How was your date last night?' She wasn't up for discussing Bella with a man old enough to be her father. No way, not happening.

'My date was crap.' He had this curious look on his face. 'What's going on Gracie?'

She huffed, 'What is it with Bella?' Her head went to one side as she narrowed her eyes.

'She's your daughter and I know how much she means to you. I'm just wondering how the two of you are getting on.'

Grace took a second as she tried to read him, 'Did you rent me this apartment in the hope she'd be here more, or perhaps she'd move in with me, and you'd get to see her.'

Now Lewis needed a second, his brows rose, 'I rented you this apartment so I could see *you* more.'

The silence was still, time stopped for the mere moment it took Grace to comprehend his words. They knew what the awkward seconds were all about.

'Thank you!' she nodded choosing to dismiss the intention of his remark, 'And to be honest I'm unbelievably grateful to you.' Grace was internally flustered. 'If I think about everything that's gone on in my life lately, I feel empty and lost.' Tears welled in her eyes. 'Being here in this gorgeous new apartment is a blessing. I might talk like my sister drives me mad, but I couldn't live without her,' she gasped to hold the tears back. 'Being close to her is important right now for me, and you've enabled that. So, thank you.'

Lewis got up and began to clear things off the coffee table, he didn't say anything, like she'd somehow offended him.

'Leave it, I'll do it.' Grace could sense the air between them had changed.

'Well, thank you for eating with me again. It's lonely up there sometimes.' He pointed directly above himself to his apartment.

'Thank you for dinner.' Grace held the stare. Things had shifted between them.

'I'll probably see you tomorrow night at Sunday dinner.' Lewis stared back.

Grace went to the door and opened it for him, 'Sure. And thanks for checking in on me.' Their eyes connected one last time.

'Good night Gracie.'

'Good night Lewis.'

Chapter Thirteen

At midnight Grace was still on the sofa watching TV, there was the wildest storm outside, the windows were rattling, the weather was so ferocious, and the thunder and lightning was making her feel uneasy. It was the fact she was alone, and she couldn't find a single candle in the apartment to prepare for a blackout, Marlo had not thought of candles! The best she could do was a kitchen lighter. As the lightning lit up the room and then the thunder cracked, Grace thought about how complexed life was, humans in general were complex creatures. Everyone had something going on, and if it weren't a Saturday night she'd call Luca to see how he was doing, but she was pretty sure he was with Jasmine trying to work out how to move forward. Grace hadn't even processed becoming a grandmother, it would be another painful gap in her life. Grace wasn't ready to go there.

Suddenly as the storm got louder and then the power went out. She snuggled against some pillows on the sofa and pulled the fluffy blanket up under her chin and watched the storm out over the harbour. Life had changed for Grace, it felt empty and blank, she felt disconnected from everything, not even the upcoming trade fair was sparking her interest. The more she tried not to think about Michael and Tina, the more she did. They had each other and she was alone. How was that fair? *And what was that shit tonight with Lewis, what the hell did he mean by it!* It felt that for some reason she was more distant from her kids than ever, and she knew she was having a sooky emotional night, but fuck! Her life was fucked!

Heavy tears fell down her face as she was powerless to stop her misery. Then there was a knock at the door and lightning filled the room with bright white. It took her a moment to get off the sofa, then she stood looking at the door before she opened it, knowing what may happen if she did open it.

And there he was. They stood looking at one another for what felt like forever. Lewis looked as dispositioned as she felt. In the background the lightning and thunder occupied the sky and without warning or notice, he leaned into her and took her face in his hand, kissing her lips slowly and softly twice.

Wrapping his arm around Grace's back, walking her backwards a step, pushing the door closed with his free hand and moving her all the way over to the sofa whilst he kissed her lips passionately with an eagerness Grace hadn't experienced for decades. Literally.

Loving Grace

No thoughts entered the situation, it was purely actions. They got to the sofa and Lewis sat, taking her down to straddle his lap, his embrace was encapsulating, their lips hadn't parted. All Grace could hear was the breaths of desire, somewhat desperate and wanting, his mouth was dominating hers but not controlling. The feeling in her lower regions starting, something that had been missing for years, excitement!

Their heads went from side to side as they kissed with open mouths, his lips pulling hers in. Her hands brushing up into his short dark hair at the back of his head, his body was hard at her, muscular and somewhat foreign and yet unbelievably fantastic all the same.

Lewis didn't care if it was right or wrong. The thought of Grace had been plaguing him for weeks and now here he was kissing her, feeling her body against his, it was happening. He reached for her T shirt, fully aware she wasn't wearing a bra, he'd noticed at dinner, he'd tried to ignore it, he'd tried not to think about what was under the fabric, but he'd been upstairs in his apartment alone thinking about her for hours.

Off came her T shirt, Lewis threw it to the side and pulled one of her breasts up to his salivating lips, desperately sucking and nibbling at her delectable nipple. Grace losing her breath from the sheer sensation and exhilaration before he meandering his kisses up her chest to her mouth. Their mouths meshing together, kissing with passion Grace hadn't experienced in such a long time, exploratory kissing full of want and desire. She truly hadn't been kissed like this for almost twenty years... As ridiculous as it seemed, it was true.

Lewis reached for her loose pants, his hands sliding inside at her bottom, his warm hands rubbing over her cheeks like he'd been there before, making the throbbing in between Grace's legs so powerful she felt like she was in a dream. Off came the pants. Grace was straddling Lewis Hunter fully naked on her sofa in her apartment, mid storm. His hands exploring her soft body as she pulled and maneuvered his T shirt over his shoulders, then over his head. Only breaking kissing for a second, her hands automatically reached for his pants, tugging at them with a need so intense she was oblivious to all else. Desperate breaths and warm bodies doing what came naturally in the middle of Grace's apartment whilst lightening sporadically lit up the room, his hardness pushing to her moist flesh as she eased down over him, she was a buzz with anticipation. Accepting Lewis inside her as she sank over his manhood like a silk glove. The goodness was beyond comprehension, she'd forgotten to breathe. This kind of exhilarating sensation had been missing from her life, it was like drugs invading her veins... Grace was alive.

Curiosity had been gathering momentum for weeks. Lewis was drawn to Grace, and he could no longer deny his curiosity or urges. He'd had a crush on her when he was fifteen, she'd been twenty-eight and he'd spent the winter living with Marlo and Ross whilst his grandparents went to Europe. Now it was like that fifteen-year-old boy was getting the girl and he, to his own dismay, was full of adrenaline. This was so out of the park for Lewis he was just going with it, the need and want to have Grace was overpowering his logic, almost hypnotic as he kissed the side of her face and sucked at her with nips and sucks, his cock so deep inside her he could feel himself filling her.

Grace was in the moment, nothing else existed in her dismal life as she felt the wetness at her thighs. She'd cum and she would cum again. Not computing the magnitude of what she was participating in, she didn't care, because in this very moment as Lewis held her over his throbbing hard cock, there was nothing she would rather be doing than fucking him. Opening her mouth, her head fell back, she gasped as he held her hips to his, looking at her over him for the first time, completely naked, unbearably soft, her blonde waves unruly, and her eyes closed, a soft moan from her lips as she let herself go to his goodness. Nails digging into his arms, Lewis pulled her face to his and kissed her full pink lips. Her taste was sweet and feminine, she was beyond sexy, like he'd imagined. Lewis wasn't feeling the thirteen-year age gap, not at all. As Grace rolled her hips into his, she did it with a knowingness, with experience. Her lips pulled and sucked at his as if she knew the art of kissing inside and out. Lewis was absorbed with Grace, his hand clenching at her breast, squeezing her nipple between his fingers. She oozed with sensuality as he knew she would. Gasps of want encouraging his now rock-solid cock to delve deeper and deeper into her pussy as her soft rounded boobs and hard nipples rubbed against his chest. Grace wanted him as much as he wanted her, he'd had a hunch, and now he had no doubt.

As she felt herself pulsing around his thick girth, there was nothing she could do to control herself. His sex was invading every part of her, and she was willingly going along for the unspeakable ride. Breathing her way into an intoxicating orgasm that was literally possessing her body, Grace was losing control over and over. Lewis' sexual prowess was so powerful she couldn't keep her cool another second. Groaning and breathing as he laid her on the floor, his was still inside her, never losing contact for a moment.

Lewis was over her, thrusting every inch into her, jolting her with every pump so she moved along the floor. His strength was too much for her delicate body.

Watching her until she watched him back, Lewis was entranced by her ocean blue eyes, the connection was unmistakable.

'Don't stop... not now!' Grace gasped as she felt herself going to that euphoric place of utter numbness that was sex heaven. She was so close, her lips tingling, breaths short and sharp.

Lewis didn't speak, he kept watching her, taking it all in, making sure she got every pleasure she needed. There was no way in hell he was stopping until he'd blown her way, literally! Her face winced, she was holding her breath, he felt her clench to his cock like she was contracting around him, tightening, he could feel her orgasm building inside her.

Grace let a breath out with a big sigh, 'Ahh!' was all she said before going to jelly beneath Lewis, she wanted to cry with relief, with joy.

He'd cum at the exact same time she did, how could he not. Her face had been pure erotic, the mist on their bodies telling of what had just gone down between them. Lewis gently lowered himself over her, not wanting to assume he could lay to her gorgeous womanly body as she caught her breath, and the storm calming to a heavy rain.

Her eyes now studying him. *What did she say to him now!* Was it appropriate to thank him for the fucking fantastic sex, probably not but she so wanted to.

A long minute of silence as they observed each other, Grace lying naked on the floor, Lewis resting beside her. As strange as it was, the weirdest thing was, neither felt uncomfortable. They'd just had mad sex and now it felt good, what was happening between them. Both knew it shouldn't feel as natural and normal as it did. Being naked in the others presence wasn't an issue, and to Grace's surprise she didn't need to grab for her clothing or a blanket to hide her fifty-year-old curves like she often did with Michael because she was ashamed of her own body.

Lewis liked her collected and understated confidence, Grace had an awareness of herself that came with age, and he appreciated it. Once he'd fucked a forty-eight-year-old businesswoman he met in the Cathay lounge, he was thirty, she'd come to his hotel in LA on invite. This was so different to that night! Grace had been an unassuming encounter; he had no idea she was remotely on the same page as him, until tonight. She was hard to read because of all that was going on in her life right now. She was tough, she'd been through a lot and her walls were up, especially with him, he knew she'd never liked him, and he knew it was that dickhead of a jealous husband who'd made her feel that way. Michael's constant need to compare cocks irritated Lewis. Grace was always too good for him.

The buzzer woke Grace up, she had Lewis' arm over her chest, they'd fallen asleep naked under the fluffy blanket on the sofa in the early hours of the morning as the rain sung them to sleep. Rolling sideways off the sofa, she scrambled with one eye open to the door and pressed the speaker button. Panic consumed her... The panic was so much more than just the buzzer and who might be at the door. The thought of last night was this morning overwhelming shock, and that was a massive understatement. Grace had been married for nearly thirty years, and it felt like she had woken up to someone else's life. Suddenly she was fifty, single, nobody needed her for anything, and she'd just had sex with another man for the first time since she was twenty-one years old... he was laying there on her sofa with all his muscles and hotness. And he was Lewis Hunter!

'Yes!' she gasped finally exhaling as she reached the buzzer by the door.

'It's me, I came to see if you survived the storm.' It was Marlo.

'Um... Wait... Hang on,' Grace fumbled as she looked at Lewis who was struggling to get his underwear on. 'Give me a minute, I'm trying to work this stupid buzzer out... I'll buzz you up in a second.'

'I'll take the stairs.' Lewis picked up his things, then leaning in and kissing Grace on the forehead as he rushed out her door.

Loving Grace

Waiting a few seconds before she buzzed Marlo up, she stood at the door wanting to burst into tears. Lewis had kissed her goodbye. Grace rolled her lips at the enormity of what she'd done last night, she had about ten seconds to get her shit together.

'I thought you might feel like a Sunday morning walk.' Marlo looked Grace over as she walked into the living room. 'You look like you just woke up, did the storm keep you awake last night?'

'Yes, it did.' Grace looked around to make sure there were no traces of Lewis or what they'd done together.

'You know a walk would do you good, you need to get out and interact, you can't stay in here on your own all day and night.' Marlo was sympathetic and encouraging, she had a knack with persuasion, and she had absolutely no idea what had gone on last night right there on the floor where she stood.

Dinner was as difficult as Grace had imagined it would be. The entire Hunter clan was there, and it was roast night, Indian style, chicken tandoori with roast potatoes in paprika and spiced vegetables in a rich curry sauce and raite, Shiv had perfected the cross pollination of cultures over the past sixty years, and she and Marlo loved spending the afternoon preparing it. Marlo's huge dining table was full of people and food. Everyone was passing bowls around filling their plates. Lewis conveniently sat directly opposite Grace so she had to look right him, which made her feel more cagy and anxious; it wasn't as if anyone would ever expect they'd had sex last night. Ruby sat on one side of Grace and Bella on the other, there was a lot of wedding talk and then onto the trade fair and Grace's new line coming out. Nobody ever made a big deal about her jewelry, nobody but Scarlet, until today. As much as the attention was nice, Grace felt it was pity attention, which she didn't want.

Then out of the blue, an announcement that threw the table into a spin, 'Pam and I are divorcing,' Gabe informed the table like it was nothing, as he and Pam sat side by side smiling like it was the best news ever. Gabe and Pamela had this long relationship of trials and tribulations for forty odd years that had stood the test of time.

Pamela addressed the table next, 'Don't be sad for us, this has been on the cards forever,' she said looking at Shiv with a knowing smile. 'We're best friends, we shouldn't be married to each other though,' Pamela did her best to explain why it was a good decision they'd made.

'We've stuck it out for a long time, Pam wants to move to Spain and I'm staying in Palm Beach,' Gabe smiled like he was more than content with his future. Normally this would be something they'd talk about as a family at the table for hours, but tonight nobody knew quite what to say, frankly the family was shocked.

As coffee and dessert wound up, Grace was tired, she wanted to go home and Bella had offered to drop her off, Kristian had left early to see yet another new girl. Lewis watched as Grace said her goodbyes and left with Bella, he was going to offer to take her home, but he'd missed that boat, Bella got in first.

Loving Grace

As Grace was leaving Shiv followed her to the front door and requested they meet for lunch tomorrow, she had something she wanted to discuss with Grace in private which sent panic waves through Grace. How on earth could she know so soon about she and Lewis! Of course, Grace catastrophised long after Bella had dropped her off at her apartment. Shiv had been staying in close touch with Grace, making sure she kept an eye on her, but not overstepping her mark, she was very good at keeping things in check and keeping her distance.

The late-night knock at the door wasn't a surprise and gave Grace rather a rush of adrenaline. She'd decided about half an hour ago, that she and Lewis shouldn't have sex again, that last night had been a one-off, and that it was great but not for her. Yes, she'd experienced what Abbey and Louise could only dream about. The sex had been phenomenal!

Grace opened the door and stood aside for him to enter, 'Hi,' she smiled, the look on her face was already regretful. Lewis was a decent man... Oh how her tune had changed! He was everything any woman could want - great looking, confident, generous, interesting and he certainly knew how to please a woman sexually. Grace could go on, but he was in her living room looking out over the harbour lights. As spectacular as he was to look at and as fuckable as he was, they were over before they'd began, she'd seen the light. It could never work.

'I know what you're thinking,' Lewis said turning around to face her.

'You do!'

'Can tonight be any better than last night... Yes, it can!'

Grace's eyes widened, not at all what she'd been thinking, 'How so?'

'Come upstairs with me for the night.'

He was serious and Grace was unexpectedly torn. Last night's sex was like she'd been reborn, an awakening of sorts as to how a man should fuck a woman. It had been apparent to her that she'd settled for mediocre her whole married life. 'Let me grab a few things,' she said with a smile.

Realising, that when it came to Lewis Hunter she couldn't refuse... How could she! His linen was actual linen which normally she didn't like, too scratchy and itchy, but his sheets were invigorating her skin and body as she groaned through her second orgasm, and that was just from him licking her pussy!

Lewis still had his pants on, he was a measured guy who didn't rush things. As she laid sprawled out naked on his bed, her short fingernails pressed into his bare broad shoulders, his darkish skin was smooth, and if she pressed into him harder, she'd most certainly make him bleed. Looking down at his head moving between her legs Grace could feel herself being overcome with everything he was... His tongue was literally brain washing her vagina! Wet down her thighs, Grace panted her breaths, and just as she was about to cum again, Lewis rose up and stood to take his pants off. Rock hard and saluting, it was his turn to receive. Grace moved to the edge of the bed, Lewis

233

not expecting oral sex in return. Sliding down the bed to the floor, to her knees, kissing and sucking at his cock like it was the last cock on earth.

Lewis wasn't one to stand still, he promptly lifted Grace back onto the bed, laying her down, moving over her, so his cock was in her face. His cock was back in her mouth, and Lewis suck at her pussy again! Rolling to their sides, they clung to one another pleasuring with their mouths, Grace's boobs mashing into his lower stomach as he spread her legs wide apart with his arms, his tongue swirled over her folds. When he sucked her clit with conviction, she let him slip down into the top of her throat, no reservations. Then his fingers joined in and plunged inside her pussy as he sucked all her blood to her clit, she was on the edge of gagging, but how could she! His well girthed cock filled her mouth and throat, she sucked at him with the ferocity he sucked at her.

'Grace, you know you've got a great pussy!' Lewis came up for air.

She pulled her head away from him, 'Oh, have I!' She never knew. Nobody had ever told her this before. Her vagina had served her well, given her pleasure at the hand of herself and numerous men, delivered three beautiful healthy babies, and right now so unexpectedly, her pussy was great!

Lewis was surprised at Grace's strong sexuality, not because of her age or her looks, but because she was Grace. For most of his life she'd ignored him, given him nothing, not even so much as a look sideways when other women did. The fact her husband had been having an affair for twenty years, had Lewis wondering. But now he knew for sure Michael Moore was a fucking dickhead because his wife was everything and more when it came to being a real woman in bed. Now Lewis hated Michael even more than he ever had. Grace was gorgeous and always had been, her wavy blonde hair and ocean blue eyes had appealed to him, she was more than just an attractive woman. Lewis' type was young and normally pencil-like and that hadn't worked well for him so far, and now he knew why. He had discovered a real woman, confident within, mature, with a sexy personality and way intriguing. Grace didn't need him, she didn't even like him until this week, they had a chemistry that was different and yet weirdly comforting.

Moving from Lewis, Grace climbed to his lap, the room was warm, their bodies were steamy. Her initial urge had been to sit on his hardness and grind her way to another orgasm. When she looked down at him, she stopped at his face, 'What!'

He just looked up at her, like he was in the deepest of thoughts, 'Nothing,' he said, wondering if Grace was thinking this was just a casual hook up or if she actually liked him, as a person. It had crossed his mind that she was in it for the sex, after all she didn't really like him all that much, even though he'd gone out of his way to be kind to her.

'Are you sure?' she sat on his stomach, her folds wet to him, her body comfortable. 'You look like you've got something on

235

your mind.' And just like that she reached out and touched his cheek as if to soothe whatever was bothering him.

'I was thinking about this,' Lewis said rolling on top of her with care, moving himself into a position so she couldn't escape him, his knees spreading hers as his hard cock submerged inside her, deep and slow he rolled his hips in and out.

Grace was overwhelmed with what his body was doing to hers. The feelings were another situation, suddenly she was looking at Lewis through different eyes, she wanted him regardless of how she'd felt earlier. Now he was this man who she trusted and gave her a certain warmth inside when she saw him, he had been beyond kind and generous when he didn't have to, and now that she did like him, he was unbelievably sexy. 'I'm sorry,' she gushed between breaths.

He didn't stop moving inside her, 'For what?'

'I've been so nasty to you, and you've been so good to me.' She was mid orgasm which made her vulnerable. For Grace, having a large cock inside her was like truth serum. Lewis continued to thrust into her stomach, deeper and deeper. 'I didn't like you, but I do now!' She wanted to feel good, and Lewis made her feel very good.

He couldn't help but laugh, 'Maybe you just like fucking me Grace King!'

'I do,' she moaned like she was in agony. Just when she thought it was too much, he pulled her leg up over his shoulder, then the other, his cock was touching her lungs, it had to be.

Tears of pure elation came to her eyes. This man had literally come to her rescue in the most unassuming way, befriending her in difficult circumstances, although she resisted. Renting her a place to live well under budget, and now making her feel like she was desirable and sexy.

'Are you on the pill?' he asked right before he was about to cum.

'You didn't ask me that last night.'

'I didn't think about it last night,' he grinned with a wince as he held still to her body.

'I'm not on the pill. I'm perimenopausal.'

'You're what!'

'I'm going through the change of life, you know, menopause.' Grace couldn't believe she was having this conversation whilst having sex with a man thirteen years her junior.

He came and it didn't matter whether she was on the pill or not, they finished off their sex romp in the arms of each other on his bed. As they lay enjoying the peace they gave each other at two in the morning.

Grace lay there trying to block all the negative thoughts from her mind. Shiv and her request for lunch. The fact Lewis and she were basically in the same family... Some might say them having sex was almost incestual. Questioning herself and the way she'd fallen into Lewis' bed so easily. She'd just been telling Abbey and Louise she didn't want sex in her life, and here she was fucking Lewis Hunter two nights in a row. But then was it fucking, because it felt like more!

Lunch at Shiv's favourite little French restaurant in Potts Point had been the furthest from the apartment Grace had been. She'd taken an Uber due to the fact she no longer had a car. Not that she wanted to drive, she felt like she perhaps shouldn't drive just yet.

'How do you like living in town again?' Shiv asked as they waited for their drinks to come to the table, she was dressed in all beige with large pearl earrings and a bracelet to match, her dark hair with only a few side greys was pulled back into a neat low ponytail.

'So far so good. I'm still getting used to living alone,' she huffed with anxiety at the end of her sentence.

'This is a new adventure for you my darling. Embrace it, make it exciting.'

'It doesn't feel very exciting.' Grace didn't think anything about her situation was exciting at all. She didn't see it.

'You're a single woman now. You need to watch out for yourself but try new things all the same.' Shiv wasn't one to dilly dally, she was getting to the point and Grace was starting to sweat. If she knew about her and Lewis already, it could only have come from him, and if it had, she was disappointed. He was close to his grandmother, and she was very modern when it came to the ways of the world, however, Shiv wouldn't like anything between her and Lewis. No way.

'I feel like I need a minute to find my feet,' Grace looked with a slight head turn, she was conscious not to reveal anything.

'You're a beautiful woman and men in this town will come for you Grace, all kinds of men.' Shiv was coming in for the kill. Grace knew where this was going. 'Still, you should be guarded, don't let anyone take advantage of you.'

Oh my God! Sighing to release the pressure building up in her chest and throat, Grace was super anxious, 'I'm being guarded.'

'I hope so!' Shive had this weird smile.

'Well, yes I am.' Grace was genuinely scared.

'You know back when you were a girl, I was certain Jagdeep was the one for you, but it wasn't to be. And to be honest I've always wished it had been, you two would have been wonderful together!' Shiv smiled like the thought made her happy, Grace was watching with bated breath. 'But perhaps Jagdeep was the wrong son for you. Perhaps it should have been Gabriel... You know your mother named Gabriele.'

Words escaped Grace. She just sat there. This was left of field. Unexpected. Shocking.

Loving Grace

Shiv continued with her proposal, 'I was thinking now that you are both single, you could go out to dinner. Just the two of you, like a date.'

Grace raised her brows. The second her wine glass hit the table; she took a big gulp.

Still, Shiv wasn't finished, 'I know you're still processing your breakup and the accident, but Gabriele and Pamela have been over forever, Pamela said so herself,' the grin on Shiv's face was alarming. 'They've been putting on a show for their children who are grown up and smarter than they think.' Shiv was being sarcastically honest, she never minced words. 'In time my darling girl, you'll be feeling better, and you'll want someone to share your life with,' she paused, 'I know Gabriele adores you.'

Opening her mouth, nothing came out. Slowly shaking her head Grace smiled awkwardly, it wasn't what she'd expected, and in fact it was almost worse. Shiv was trying to set her up with Gabe the very day after he'd announced his split with his long-time wife... This was horrific. It was terrible for Grace, because no matter what she said to Shiv, she'd be partly lying. 'I'm not ready for dating, and I love Gabe like a brother, so I could never date him,' she said with tearing eyes. The range of emotions were vast, but the biggest one was guild, because she'd spent the most amazing night with Shiv's grandson last night in his bed and if it ever got out, nobody would like or understand it. Grace and Lewis were not the union, Shiv, or anyone had in mind. Everyone would hate Grace.

From lunch Grace went straight to Marlo's to tell her how completely out of her mind her mother-in-law was. Ross was home and he was in on the conversation, 'My mum's old school, I shouldn't have to tell you that Gracie,' he found the whole thing amusing. 'And she loves a good set up.'

Marlo looked at him pulling a face, 'Grace has been through a trauma, and the last thing she need to be lumbered with is Gabe!' Marlo didn't hold back, and she didn't find it as amusing as her husband did. 'My love, no offence to you, but why would Grace want a man twelve years older than her? Not to mention it's not right. They're practically related.'

'Oh, they're not,' Ross wasn't seeing it Marlo's way, 'And the age thing is ridiculous... she liked Avi didn't she,' he teased them both.

'My god!' Grace winced, 'I was a kid, please don't bring that up ever again,' she frowned feeling ill at the thought, if they only knew about Lewis they'd be mortified.

'You forgot about that one, didn't you,' Ross smirked at Marlo.

'Well, the idea of your brother is ridiculous, why on earth would she want him?' Marlo gushed; Ross pulled a face at her, which made Grace laugh.

Loving Grace

'You know what I mean,' Marlo snapped at her light-hearted husband, 'She's trying to find her feet and Gabe and Pam have just split literally this week.'

'They haven't had sex for five years, they split a long time ago, it's just become common knowledge this week, that's all.' Ross wasn't letting up.

'I don't care, I'm telling your mother to leave Grace alone, she doesn't need this kind of crap whilst she's recovering.'

Grace looked at her sister, 'I'm not a victim. Please don't make a thing of it with Shiv,' Grace sighed, 'She means well in her own way.'

'See Marlo. You're overreacting,' Ross chuckled, ending with one last comment to make Grace smile.

Chapter Fourteen

Lewis had convinced Grace to go to dinner with him, he didn't see why they couldn't be seen in public, they were friends and family, not biologically of course, so it wouldn't be unfathomable to see them out to dinner together.

Eating at a table for two with a candle between them seemed like a date, or a romantic dinner. He'd taken her to a quite restaurant in Double Bay that he frequented often. They weren't hiding, they were just laying low.

'Tell me about Shiv and your lunch today.' Lewis knew his grandmother didn't know about them, as much as Grace had been stressing.

'She's trying to set me up with Gabe now we are both single.' She couldn't help but smile.

'What!' he was surprised, but then he shouldn't be, his grandmother loved to set people up, it was in her blood to arrange marriages. Laughing was the only way to react. 'Why wouldn't she want to set us up?' he joked, 'I mean, the age gap isn't really a big deal. Not for me anyway.'

Grace didn't know how she felt about the age difference, she wasn't able to concern herself with too many issues at once yet. The sex was her only focus for now. The age gap would no doubt be just around the corner. 'It seems much more acceptable for a man to be older than a woman don't you think? Tell me, does our age difference bother you?' she asked.

'No, not at all,' he said looking at her, 'You?'

'Um, not right now. I mean how does it feel for you to have sex with a fifty-year-old woman?'

He put it straight back onto her, 'How does it feel to be having sex with a younger guy?'

'I'm fine with it.'

'Yeah, but how does it feel?' He was pressing her, enjoying her discomfort.

'It feels good.' She felt strange answering him. 'I've been sleeping with a man who was having sex with my best friend for the past twenty years... so, fucking you is extremely refreshing.'

Lewis laughed, 'Oh, fucking me!' he teased.

'Yes, fucking you. That's what we're doing.' Grace didn't want to say it was anything more than fucking after just two nights.

'Well then, in that case. I like fucking a fifty-year-old woman very much.' His smile was telling.

'To be clear, I like fucking you too,' she spoke in a soft voice, her eyes sparkling at him.

Graces phone rang in the middle of their meal, it was Bella.

'Mum I need you!' she cried.

'Sweetheart, what's wrong?' Grace's heart sank, she looked at Lewis.

'I need you, can you come pick me up, please mum.' Bella was hysterical.

'Send your location to me, I'm on my way.' Grace stood up from the table in a panic.

Staying on the phone to Bella, they left the restaurant, and Lewis drove Grace to Bella's pin location, which was not too far away. Grace was telling Bella to stay under a streetlight so she could be seen. Bella said she'd had a fight with Dom, and she'd left his city apartment on foot.

When they pulled up and saw Bella standing on the street against a house fence crying, Grace jumped out of the car; her heart was racing as she rushed to her. Wrapping her arms around her daughter who was distressed, holding her tight, for a moment they just stood there, Grace could hear Bella's sobs and knew something bad had happened and it wasn't good. 'What happened, are you alright?'

'I had a fight with Dom,' cried Bella.

245

Loving Grace

'It's okay. I'm here. I've got you now,' said Grace pulling her in tight again. 'What sort of fight?'

'I don't know. A fight,' sobbed Bella as her mother started to walk her over to Lewis's Porsche pulled into the side of the road. Grace put her daughter in the back seat and moved on in next to her.

'I don't have a car, Lewis drove me,' said Grace explaining.

'Hey Bella, what's going on, are you alright?' he looked around from the driver's seat to see them, concern in his voice, he could see she was really upset.

'She's had a fight with Dom,' Grace said giving him a look of uncertainty. At this stage she was unsure of how the fight went down.

'I'll get you ladies home.' He pulled out from the curb not saying anything else, this was a strange situation, very personal.

In the back seat Grace sat right next to Bella and hugged her in, patting her hair and trying to warm her up as she only had on a light top and jeans. Being a mother to a daughter at this age was harder than Marlo ever made it look.

Lewis walked the girls right to Grace's door, he knew he had to leave Grace do her mother thing even though he didn't want to, he wanted to stay and be there for her. 'I'll talk to you tomorrow,' he said as Grace opened the front door and ushered Bella inside.

'I'll call you.' She gave Lewis a look. 'Thank you for tonight.' Her hand pulled the door in, she was grateful. The door closed and he stood for a moment looking at it, questioning the feelings he had for Grace.

Running a bath for Bella and trying to make her feel comfortable and safe, it was now just the two of them and some questions needed to be asked, still Grace knew she had to tread lightly with her daughter. One wrong word and she'd shut down on her. The bathroom was warm, the steam from the water was soothing as the bathtub filled.

'Tell me what happened sweetheart?' It seemed worth a try, her daughter was a closed book, rarely did she let her into her personal life.

'I hate my life Mum!' It was a statement.

'Why, has he done something to you? Move out!' Grace spoke softly as Bella shook her head and scrunched up her face like it was all too much.

'I can't just leave him Mum,' her voice raised. In that moment Grace saw fear in her eyes, she knew not to push the boundaries even though everything in her wanted to. As her mother she wanted to forbid her ever going back to Dom again.

'You get ready for the bath, and I'll go get you a hot drink.' Forever she'd felt like she was walking on eggshells with Bella, only on the odd occasion had they had those heart-to-heart mother-daughter moments and Grace had cherished them because they were rare. She knocked on the bathroom door when she returned with herbal tea in hand, then opened it. Her daughter stood wrapped in a bath towel, she was still crying, which made Grace cry.

Bella slept beside Grace in her bed all night, they didn't discuss details, they didn't need to, Grace figured if her daughter wanted to elaborate she would. For now, her job as Bella's mother was to support, protect, and comfort. That's what mothers did.

Grace was up early, she let Bella sleep while she went out and sat on the sofa thinking about how to go about today. Suddenly her own problems diminished, and she was consumed with Bella and what to do about her daughters' relationship. From day dot Grace's feelings towards Dom had been off, instinctively she didn't like him, and now, she questioned her daughters safety.

Just before noon, Bella came out to the living room, she stood at the window and looked out over the harbour, it was a dismal day and yet the view was spectacular.

Making toast and tea, Grace hummed a song to set the mood, she was going for non-stressful, more relaxing, but Bella didn't speak, eat, or drink the tea. The apartment was warm and cosy with the afternoon sun beaming in the huge wall of windows, Grace sat at the dining table on her laptop, Bella snuggled under the fluffy blanket sleeping, while her phone sat on the coffee table pinging away like crazy. *Was it Dom, and what did he have to say?*

For hours that afternoon Bella slept on the sofa while Grace sat nearby working one the trade fair, it was this Friday coming and she had to make sure all her sample stock was ready, her jewelry had a distinct style which made it recognisable as Grace King, something she was very proud of. She had to order knew cabinets from a supplier because she sure as hell wasn't going to the country house to pick up the ones she had. Online shopping was handy, she bought everything she needed within an hour and was set to go, emailing images and ideas over to Scarlet for her feedback.

Bella slept, whilst her phone sat silently on the coffee table lighting up with messages, Grace got up and went over to look at it. Dom had messaged her many times but she didnt want to be that snoopy mother who invaded her kid's privacy, so she resisted a sneak peek.

Later, mother and daughter sat on the sofa together, no TV, just them and the fluffy blanket huddled up together cuddling, for Grace it was like all her dreams coming true, Bella needing her and her being able to give her comfort, she couldn't help wondering if this would be the case if she was still living at the country house and still with Michael. It seemed to Grace that Michael stood in the way of her and Bella having the relationship Grace had always wanted to have with her daughter.

'Mum!' Bella said as the day turned to night.

Loving Grace

'Mmm,' Grace had been dozing off, she'd not slept much at all last night.

'I need to tell you something.' Her voice was weak and vulnerable.

'You can tell me anything, I'm listening.' Grace patted Bella's hair to her head gently.

The fact that her mother hadn't pressed her for information last night or today about why she fled Dom's apartment last night, hadn't gone unnoticed. She needed to sleep, and she needed to be left alone and that's exactly what her mother had done. 'The reason I left Dom's apartment last night without my purse and my bag was because I'm scared of him Mum,' Bella began to explain that on one occasion Dom had slapped her face and shook her. She told her mother all about how Dom didn't like her going out without him, and how he didn't like her spending time with her own brothers. He said Mac was a bad influence when he didn't even know her, and how he thought her parents were bad examples of relationships! This startled Grace.

Intentionally Grace didn't react to any of the opinions Dom's seemed to have about herself and her family, 'What bothers me the most sweetheart is that he slapped your face and shook you.' Grace didn't give a shit about the other stuff, just that. Bella's big eyes looked at Grace like she knew, 'Slapping is hitting, you know that, right.'

'I know,' her eyes were holding tears back.

Grace wasn't sure she believed her, 'I don't think you should go back to Dom.'

'I know.' She wasn't a stupid girl; she knew this man was not her man.

'You can live here with me, only if you want to.' Grace didn't want to sound too eager.

'Would you mind?'

'Of course not. I would love it. We'll be like roommates.' She winked, unable to hide her joy a second longer, she smiled, her heart was so full. 'When you're ready I can get Aunty Marlo to send Paul to pick up your things from Dom's. Paul lives for this kind of stuff.' Paul was Marlo's driver/security, and he loved serving in a difficult situation. He'd offered to rough up Michael more than once. Bella didn't see why Paul couldn't go over straight away; she was even up for a little roughing up too. 'You're going to be okay here with me, I promise.'

It had been two nights since Grace had seen Lewis, she'd been preoccupied with having Bella move in and she needed to be a mother before anything else. Tonight, Bella went over to Luca's for dinner with Kristian so she could fill them in on her breakup, her older brothers were protective and also on a need-to-know basis with Bella and her love life, they liked to be up on things, and she needed their support right now, the three of them had gone through some changes with their parents breaking up and it had made them tighter than ever.

Loving Grace

Grace took the opportunity to pop up and see Lewis. She told him all about Bella moving in, and how she didn't think it would be a good idea for them to have sex again now that her daughter was so close.

Lewis narrowed his eyes, his smirk was gorgeous, 'Is it just sex between us Gracie?'

'Why, did I do something to make you think it was more?'

He paused, 'It felt like more, that's all.' He wasn't afraid to expose himself.

Her lips pursed as they sat across the kitchen bench from each other, 'I know,' she agreed. And he came to her side of the bench with slow steps, looking down at her on the stool as she looked up into his dreamy dark eyes.

'Gracie, this is more than just sex.' And with that he put a hand at either side of her face and pulled her up to meet his lips, kissing her soft and slowly, but with a forceful passion that was so much more. Their sexual attraction was powerful, it was like fireworks every time they touched one another. Lewis had felt it immediately, there was something between them even before they had sex, a chemistry that felt right, it was easy and soothing.

Lifting Grace off the stool and into his arms, she clung to him as he took her to his bed, laying her down gently. They didn't need to speak; their bodies knew exactly what to do. Fumbling with his jeans Grace unzipped him, then as he sat up he pulled her top off and unclipped her bra watching her as she kicked off her leisure pants and underwear. As he came back down to her body she reached up and peeled his T shirt off and then pulled his warm chest down to hers, their kisses open and slow, savouring, and sensual. She could feel his hardness, his body was exciting and familiar.

Lewis rose over her head, his cock was pressing into her wetness, Grace did something to him that he hadn't felt before. When they were together, there were no years between them, it was like she had this ease about her, and he knew exactly who he was as a man. He couldn't put a finger on it just yet, but it was a connection of sorts, a heated desperation, and when he was inside Grace, nothing else mattered.

His body rubbed against hers as his cock thrusted to her groin. It wasn't just sex, and she knew it, labelling it wasn't something she was prepared to do yet, all she knew was that she couldn't stop. Her body was being awakened; Grace was feeling sexual and alive again. Lewis made her feel younger, she even liked the fact that she felt dirty, gritty, and sexy because he was younger. How could they stop this now, it was just beginning for them. The timing wasn't great, and the family connection was too close for comfort, but they weren't biologically related, and they didn't need anyone's permission. They were two adults.

'I don't want to stop this,' gasped Grace feeling all of him inside her. She had to take charge of the pace, so she rolled out from under him and climbed to his lap, her hot throbbing pussy easing down over him, juices making way as she relished every inch of his cock submerging into her body again.

Loving Grace

Lewis squeezed at her upper thighs, gripping her as she rolled over his cock, he was so deep inside her, it must be hurting her he thought to himself. Her face had ecstasy and pain all over it, her blonde waves were stuck to her sweat, eyes clenched shut as she rode him back and forth, her full boobs arousing him, reaching out he gripped her nipple and gave it a squeeze making her groan. He felt his cock swelling and swelling, her pussy throbbing around him, he was on the edge and so was she. Lewis knew she was cumming, he could feel the warm ooze to him, and he came pulling her hips down hard to his, pulsing his cum inside her with a release of satisfaction.

They lay together peacefully, side by side, both wondering how they were going to navigate this. There were so many obstacles and reasons why it couldn't work.

'I better get downstairs; Bella will be home soon.' It was late.

'Are we going to do this again, is it more than just sex, is it worth it?' Lewis touched her face.

Grace turned her head to him, 'I don't want to *not* do this again,' she said. There was no chance he was getting a commitment of any sort, but she couldn't dismiss how she felt when she was with him.

His eyes looked deep into hers, they had an understanding of sorts, it was more than just sex and it wasn't over.

'Where have you been its late and you didn't take your phone with you?' Bella said sitting on the sofa next to Kristian. They both looked at Grace like she'd missed her curfew, which was certainly how she felt.

'I'm a grown woman... I was up talking to Lewis, letting him know you're moving in, making sure it's okay with him.' She was matter of fact, smoothing her hair down and composing herself so she didn't have *'I've just been fucked extraordinarily well'* written all over her face.

'Were you out with Lewis that night when I called you to come get me?' Bella questioned her, 'And you never liked him... Mum he's being a really good friend to you by the sounds of it. You've judged him unfairly don't you think. I hope you're polite to him.' Bella served it up to her mother.

Grace sighed but before she could say anything Kristian had his say, 'He's done you a huge solid Mum, letting this place to you, he's giving you mates rates you know. You've always been rude to him because dad didn't like him. I hope you've changed your tune.'

Were they kidding! Too surprised to think of an answer. Lewis was giving her a huge solid, and she was very, very grateful... If only they knew.

'And now to more important issues, we're going to be an aunt and uncle. Luca told us!' Bella said smiling like all was forgiven. 'You're going to be a grandmother,' the excitement in her voice was good to see. The three of them talked for an hour about Luca and Jasmine and the baby and how they were going to take it day by day, but whatever happened, Luca would be part of his baby's life, which was a good thing. Grace liked that her kids were spending time together.

The trade fair was a turning point for Grace, she had something special going on, and for the first time in what felt like a long time, she saw the potential for the future. If she did the international trade fairs she could possibly be something huge, it was worth considering. Scarlet, Mac, and Bella had all helped out all weekend and it had been a huge success. For now, she was content running her business from her apartment, working off the dining table and taking in the view.

That Sunday night Grace went to dinner at Marlo's. Scarlet, Mac, and Bella were telling everyone about the weekend with colourful tales, all encouraging. Lewis was giving Grace looks across the table as the girls talked, Grace giving him a smile as the girls had everyone laughing.

'Well, it sounds like our girl's trip will serve as some inspiration for you.' Marlo was pleased Bella had moved in with Grace and that the trade fair had gone well. Her sister needed a break, she needed to focus on something other than her marriage breakup.

Grace went over to get her bag and jacket, she was ready to leave, and Lewis followed her. Nobody could hear them, 'Can I see you later?' he asked.

She looked to see they were clear of anyone, 'I'm not sure I'll get the chance.'

'Then dinner tomorrow night?' He'd missed her all weekend; they hadn't seen each other for over four days.

'I'll let you know in the morning.' She couldn't just commit to him with Bella around, they'd agreed this thing between them was to stay between them. As much as it shouldn't be a secret, it was. Oh, how she'd love Michael to find out she was fucking Lewis Hunter, that would just be the ultimate revenge but given the age difference and the circumstances of the family, it seemed better they didn't broadcast things.

The next night Bella had gone out with Mac for dinner and drinks, which gave Grace the go ahead to go out with Lewis for dinner. As much as their thing was sexual, it was becoming so much more. They enjoyed talking and hanging out, both loved eating and a good glass of wine. When they were together, there was no age gap, they found conversation easy. They sat in an Italian restaurant in Leichardt chatting about life, her kids, and her becoming a grandmother, they talked about Lewis's past relationships and how he didn't feel the need to have kids or be a father. Grace had questioned him, and he'd told her with conviction that he didn't feel the desire to raise kids. She wondered if he said this for her benefit, clearly she wasn't about to have his babies! Had his own life without a father bought these feelings upon him. They talked about him finding his father via DNA testing, it was something he'd thought about but wasn't willing to act on. This was a conversation he'd never had with anyone before.

The lights weren't on in Grace's apartment as they drove in around eight o'clock, they took the lift from the car park up to his penthouse apartment, it was too early for Bella to be home yet anyway, figuring they had at least two hours together. No time was wasted, Lewis took her around the waste and to the sofa kissing her and peeling their clothes off. The want in the early stages of a relationship was always the most heated and exciting as Grace remembered it, it was the time when all you wanted to do was have sex and be with each other. Not that she thought this was a relationship.

The floor became the better option, Lewis kneeled down, Grace sitting over his lap as he sucked at her pink nipples giving her soft bites... sucks that drove her crazy, his hands rubbing over her back and sides feeling her warm soft skin at his palms. Grace's fingers spreading through his dark hair as he held her body to his, resting her elbows on his shoulders. Her body moved to his hard cock as it roused at her moist folds, she wanted him inside her and he was playing a game of keepings off, his lips to her nipple he was fully aware of Grace's need for him as she wriggled in his arms. 'Wait for it. There's no hurry,' he told her as she tried aimlessly to sit over him.

She huffed letting him suck at her again, his hand moving down her back, reaching to her folds underneath so he could give her some relief, she needed it. Grace's sexual tension had become her main tension very much. Sure, she still lived in despair at what Michael and Tina had done daily, her kids still had issues, but Lewis's cock was her release. When he was fucking her she didn't think about anything else but him.

Her nipples swelling at the attention he was giving them, bordering on sore, Grace was enjoying his hand and fingers playing with her pussy, rubbing her in circular motions in a bid to spread her wetness to her anus. She moved back and sat on the floor in front of him, spreading her legs wide open.

Lewis kneeled forward between her legs, looking straight into her eyes and watching her. Grace had no inhibitions with him whatsoever and he found it so fucking sexy, 'I wanna see you cum, let me watch you cum,' Lewis whispered as his fingers touched her pussy.

Grace's deep blue eyes full of seduction and desire for Lewis, she didn't like too much talking whilst they were fucking, it distracted her and made room for other thoughts, so she watched him fingering her on the floor. Her back arching when his thumb rubbed at her throbbing clit, sending her off into a sharp and sudden clenching orgasm. She let herself go, willing her legs to stay open, letting Lewis watch her cum to his fingers. Pearl like liquid seeping from her hole, his fingers spreading it over her glazed pinkness.

Lewis sat up and Grace sat over his big hard cock. Wet, she slid down him with a jolt, his cock was like a drug that she was becoming dependable on. Moving up and down him, Lewis again looked into her eyes like he was searching for something, trying to see her intentions. Pushing him down to lay on the floor Grace put her hands at his stomach and slid around his cock, she liked being on top more than ever. It was her chance to get all her frustrations out in the best way possible, grinding over a younger sexy man, it was her version of therapy!

Holding her hips firmly to his, trying hard to keep his cum at bay. Here he was looking up at Grace King, the girl he'd crushed on as a horny teenage boy... Now she was the woman he was sharing his most private thoughts with and falling for all over again. She had that something that he found irresistibly sexy, something he just had to have. Grace was beautiful, soft and delicate, and yet she could be so feisty and funny. For years he'd watched her from afar, married to that ungrateful dickhead. And now here she was, blushed cheeks and wet pussy, cumming all over his cock!

Grace's lips went numb as her mouth opened, gasping for air. Her folds were burning from sheer utter goodness. Lewis Hunter had given her an orgasm to remember. Cumming inside her with an explosion as she sat on him, her thighs went to jelly, the sweat on her body made her shiver. *How on earth was she ever going to give this up!*

It was nearly eleven when Grace got ready to go downstairs to her apartment. Tonight, things had elevated to another level. They kiss goodbye - not on the forehead - that was so last week. Tonight, the kiss at his door was laced with longing passion, slow open mouth kissing, finishing off with longs gazing eyes.

'Good night Gracie.'

She looked up at him, he was gorgeous, 'Good night Lewis.'

Chapter Fifteen

'How much luggage can I take?' Grace asked Marlo as she sat on the large central ottoman in Marlo's dressing room watching her go through her clothes with great consideration.

'As much as you like,' Marlo replied flippantly. They'd both helped out at the shelter given it was Saturday morning. It was now Saturday afternoon, and Marlo had invited Grace over for lunch, and they'd wound up in the closet with Marlo giving Grace arms full of clothing she no longer wore, one dress still had a price tag on it... Never ever in her life would Grace spend eight thousand dollars on a dress, ever. So, taking Marlo's unwanted clothing made Grace's day. As Marlo searched through a drawer for something, Grace sat twisting the Fendi bracelet at her wrist that her sister and Ross had gifted her for her fiftieth birthday. It had been the gift Ross chose so they had something to give her on the night of her special dinner. Their wealth was ridiculous, absurd to most, yet they were Grace's family, people who she loved, and they loved her unconditionally in return.

'Bella mentioned you've been out three nights this week... Catching up with friends!'

Grace looked up at her sister, this wasn't a casual comment, Marlo was curious, she was always curious.

'I've had a busy week,' she played it down.

They'd been talking about her! Of course they had, she was the family scandal, the crazy one!

A few silent seconds from Marlo, which had Grace on edge, 'Who've you been out with?'

'Abbey!' all she could do was lie. How could she say she'd been with Lewis having the best sex of her life!

'And you're having dinner with Abbey again tonight!' Marlo was also always on the lookout for a trip up. She turned from her drawers and looked at Grace.

Grace tried to be cool, 'Yep. We have dinner all the time.'

'You're so lucky to have such a good friend like Ab's,' Marlo went about her thing, 'I've got to call her soon, I need to put her details on the flight and yacht ledger for the trip.'

Grace made a mental note to call Abbey the second she left Marlo's so she could arrange her alibi. She was going to fill Abbey in on the Lewis situation tonight when they really were doing dinner. But what if Marlo called her before. Grace needed Abbey to cover for her. Now she was in the shit. A panic!

On her walk home, she made the call, telling Abbey she'd explain the reason for her needed urgent alibi at dinner tonight. They'd planned to go to Catalina, just the two of them, Grace needed to tell someone about Lewis, and it could only be Abbey. It also seemed to Grace that Bella was keeping tabs on her and reporting back to Marlo which didn't surprise her.

Marlo was all over everything like a private fucking eye! she'd been worse since the car accident. Grace expected it, she understood it, she loved that Marlo was looking out for her wellbeing, she just didn't love not having her privacy.

'What the fuck did you say?' Abbey asked as they sat at a window table with the lights of Rose Bay glistening in the background. She's stopped mid sip of her champagne.

'I've kind of been having sex with Lewis.' Grace wasn't sure how Abbey would take it.

'Are you fucking kidding me,' Abbey was holding her chest.

'No.'

'And you're just telling me this now because...' Her reaction was clear shock.

'Um. Well.' Grace was hesitant.

Abbey caught her breath, 'Tell me again; did you have sex with Lewis. Lewis Hunter... We are talking about the same Lewis aren't we?' Abbey was still in disbelief as a weird grin came to her face. 'Like fuck sex?'

'Am I really crazy, because Ab's if you think I'm out of my mind, I need you to tell me,' Grace had doubted this thing with Lewis every day since it had started.

'Oh, my god, this is madness!' gushed Abbey, 'How are you having sex with Lewis Hunter?' still stunned, she needed facts, Abbey lived for facts. 'Tell me everything, don't leave a single thrust out!' her words now had excitement.

It took the entire two and half hours at dinner for Grace to tell the story from the start to where they were today, because Abbey kept asking questions and making Grace tell her over and over about how Lewis made her feel and the things he'd said to her so she could come up with a verdict on whether or not her best friend was bat shit crazy, being used by Lewis, or just plain fortunate to be screwing a guy thirteen years younger than she who was fabulously hot. Abbey had known Lewis since he was a baby too, she'd never had the same opinion of him that Grace had, Abbey saw right through Michael's jealousy towards Lewis... He'd probably seen Lewis give Grace the sneaky eye!

'Grace, is this something you're ready for?' Abbey asked as they finished off the second bottle of champagne.

'No,' Grace laughed, answering without a beat, 'But every time I think I'm going to tell him I can't do it, I do it. I've gone

265

from disliking him with a passion to wanting him, and there's no age difference. Ab's I don't even feel like I have to hide my fifty-year-old arse or suck my belly in when I'm naked with him. None of it matters.'

Abbey sat there with huge wide eyes, 'What does he look like naked?'

Grace just nodded her head.

Abbey gasped, 'You are fucking glowing... What's thirteen years between lovers... Zero!' Abbey didn't see the harm, her friend could distinguish someone using her for sex to someone enjoying her company, and if it were just good sex for Lewis, it was exactly what Grace needed. Her friend's heart had been broken; she doubted Lewis Hunter was going to break it any worse than it already was. This was the confidence booster of all confidence boosters in Abbey's opinion.

'You know, right from the get-go, he's been there for me. Getting the lowdown on the cheaters, then renting me the apartment, and let's not forget he looked after me when I fell out my tree at Ross's birthday party,' Grace wanted Abbey to be on board, she needed her approval.

'You go for it. Fuck his brains out. I would... What have you got to lose Grace?'

'Not much,' she shrugged.

'Take it day by day. See where it goes,' was Abbey's take on things. 'And you need to get a little smarter around Bella, she's onto you.'

'No one can know!' Grace sighed.

When Grace got home after her dinner with Abbey, the apartment was empty, Bella had gone out clubbing with Mac and Kristian and some friends, at least she was living life, Bella had good people around her so Grace had no issues with her going out, so long as she wasn't with Dom. Lewis was also out for the night, so she went about her nightly routine getting ready for bed.

Standing getting a glass of water at her kitchen bench looking around the dimly lit apartment out over the harbour lights, Grace had a moment. Her life had changed, her world had changed. Here she was on a Saturday night alone with a champagne buzz, the loneliness was overwhelming, and there was nothing she could do to not wonder what Michael and Tina were doing tonight. She hadn't heard from him, or her, not that she wanted to. A huge part of her life was over. Grace felt empty, the apartment was so quiet, her eyes filled with tears that she wasn't going to let fall down her face. No. Crying was overrated, it had never made her feel better, only worse. A little race of the heart as there was a knock at the door.

'Your home,' Lewis smiled looking into her apartment to see if Bella was home. 'Are you alone?'

Loving Grace

'Bella's out tonight.' She opened the door for him to come in.

'Do you wanna come up to me, just in case she comes home?'

'Sure,' Grace said smiling but without her normal sparkle.

Lewis poured her a glass of wine at his kitchen bench as he told her about his dinner celebrating a long-time friend's birthday at a local pub. He could tell Grace wasn't herself, which alarmed him. Consciously measuring how fast he was falling for her, holding his feelings back because he wasn't confident that she wouldn't pull the pin on them at any given time. He wanted to have faith in her, but she'd been through a lot, and she hadn't recovered yet, he knew that. 'How was your dinner with Abbey?' he asked.

Grace sighed, sipped her red wine, and smiled, God she loved Abbey, the mention of her name gave her a warm feeling, 'I told Ab's about us tonight,' she said as if she'd be in trouble.

Lewis raised an eyebrow, 'How'd that go?' he asked moving to the sofa.

'Umm,' Grace began, sitting herself next to Lewis, 'You know it wouldn't matter what I did, Abbey would be on my side. I could go on a murderous rampage, and she'd find a defense angle for me.' Grace smiled at the thought. Abbey was her ride or die, she always had been. 'She thinks we should take each day as it comes, which is pretty much what we're doing.'

Lewis gave it a minute's thought, 'It's probably all we can do given our situation,' he sighed deeply, 'I mean if by the time Ruby's wedding comes around and we're in Italy and we're still doing our thing, then we can think about what we're going to tell people. Because I'm going to have a hard time keeping my hands off you.' His grin was everything Grace needed.

Narrowing her eyes and studied him, 'I need to ask you something, and it's not something Abbey said, it's something I've been thinking.'

'Ask me anything.'

'I'm not a conquest or some kind of game to you am I? I mean you don't have some stupid bet with your mates about who can sleep with the oldest woman?' She was so serious that the whole mood changed.

'Has Abbey dared you to sleep with me?' he gave her one of his irresistible grins making his point. 'I would never play games with you Gracie. Your age isn't a factor in why or how I feel about you.'

'I'm a big girl, you can be honest with me.'

His eyes held hers, 'My intention was never to fuck you around. I started off wanting to help you, then I don't know, I wanted you more and more, and now I think I'm falling for you,' he paused. 'Do you want me, or are you fucking me around?'

Her eyes glazed with tears suddenly, still guarded, yet somehow able to give something of herself to him, 'I'm not fucking you around. I'm falling for you too.' Lewis leaned over and kissed her lips; she felt something wonderful. Her heart didn't hurt.

For someone who hadn't been that into sex for such a long time, Grace was back to wanting it at any given chance, Lewis did that for her. If she were totally honest, she'd always wondered about him, she'd just never let herself go there. Now she couldn't wait to get him out of his clothes. For all the hangups about her body she harbored with Michael, forever covering her rolls and folds, worrying about her aging skin and the fine lines, being too hard on herself in general. Grace was surprised how liberated a younger man like Lewis made her feel. Not only was he younger, but he was also ridiculously sexy, and so good at sex.

When he got up to get another bottle of wine, she followed him into the kitchen and moved in close behind him at the bench, her hands went around to his front, and she began to rub over his already semi-chub. A surprise to find.

He stood still and let her go a minute, he liked the sensation of her soft chest at his lower back, her hands at his growing cock. Even though there was immense sexual attraction, Lewis knew there was more to their connection.

'Turn around!' she instructed him with a soft voice. He did and she began to unzip his jeans, sliding them gently down his thighs, his underwear too. Grace looked up into his eyes, she focused on them as she took him in her hands and softly began to pull and rub his cock into the front of her body. There was something intense going on between them and she wasn't going to fight it, if he was falling for her, she was falling too. As sure as she was that he'd seen her age spots and lines, she knew he'd seen her vulnerability and genuine heart too. Lewis wasn't a kid, at thirty-seven he knew what he wanted, and he certainly didn't have to settle for just anyone. He made her feel something she'd thought was past her, that perhaps she didn't deserve to feel any longer. As well being a confidant and a friend, he'd woken her desires to be sexual again and as she pressed his hard iron like cock into her stomach, she knew she didn't have to change or pretend, Lewis had seen the worst of her, and now he was going to get the best.

'Hmm,' she breathed him in, with the utmost pleasure. Grace was sucking his cock into an erotic haze. If he lost consciousness it was because she was taking him all the way down into her throat like she had a cock-sucking superpower.

'Gracie. Gracie. Gracie,' Lewis stood there groaning as she gripped him at the base of his cock and massaged him into her mouth.

On her knees, Grace had never enjoyed sucking a man's cock quite like this. She'd consume him if it wouldn't kill him!

'Come up here,' he took her under the arms and made her stand up again. They faced each other, he was in awe of this woman who'd surprised him more than any other woman in his life before.

Loving Grace

'Too much for you?' her eyes sparkled as Lewis leaned into her neck and kissed her slowly.

'Never!' He mumbled taking her and turning her around, so she was against the benchtop. Pressing her with the front of his body into the cold stone, his reached to her front and rubbed his thumbs over her T shirt, to her nipples. His hardness pressing into her back, teasing her with a taste of what was to come. With a caring hand he bent her slightly forward and took her pants down her legs, then her silk knickers very slowly, she stepped out of them and waited. An arm wrapped around her belly as he walked her over to his dining table, kissing her neck all the way then pressing her body chest down over it. With one foot he spread hers apart before leveraging himself to her. Lewis stood behind Grace, his hand reaching down between her legs to find her wet folds, parting them with his fingers then inserting one to stimulate her with long gentles strokes.

Letting her cum, he spread her juices all the way to her arse, circling her anus with his middle finger and delicately pressing inside her, before pressing the other hand down on her back and pushing her to the table. Feeling himself pulsing before he was even inside her, then letting the softness of her folds welcome his cock, sliding up into her silk-like pussy was almost too much for Lewis. Hands at her hips lifting her to meet every thrust, her womanly flesh so soft and morish.

Grace holding the table as she pushed back to meet his groin. Gasping with her mouth open, Lewis deep inside her, his base girth stretching her open so she could feel every inch of his cock now mesmerising her body. She was most positively under his spell. When he gripped her shoulder, she was up for it, ready for more. Fingers digging into her skin as Lewis pulled her back into his thrusts, ramming into her with a force that moved the entire dining table.

Then suddenly he stopped and before cumming, he took Grace by the arms, standing her up, turning her around to him, sitting her on the table, hugging her into his body.

'You okay?' she asked, her cheek at his chest.

'Mmm.'

'You don't sound too sure,' she was panting. Lewis put his hands at her cheeks and kissed her mouth as he maneuvered himself between her legs, Grace reaching up, arms around his neck pulling herself up to him.

'How's this going to work Gracie,' he whispered to her ear as he sunk deep inside her pussy again.

'I don't know,' she said with a soft gasp as he entered her.

Neither of them had to say it, they both felt it. This was more than a casual fling or just sex, way more, and the ever-looming reality of their family and the scandal of their union was hanging over both their heads. It was too soon, there was the age gap, and then they were part of the same family. Even though they had no blood ties, their relationship would not be accepted, not by everybody. In fact, they knew it would be received badly. Forbidden. They'd both had the same thought...

Loving Grace

Were they setting themselves up for disappointment and pain. Could they keep it under wraps from everyone they loved.

Lewis lifted Grace's top off, as she lifted his, they moved to each other lustfully on the edge of the dining table, lips together and wanting, bodies warm and comforting. They had found something within each other so unexpected.

'I can't stop this. I don't want to stop being inside you Gracie,' Lewis mouthed to her swelling lips as he thrust tenderly into her.

'Then don't.' She had no intention at this very moment to stop anything. 'Keep going.' Digging her fingers into his shoulders, cumming as he dug deep inside her and held his body stiff to hers, they'd cum together in a touching climax filled with emotional sex, resulting in the perfect storm.

Grace woke up at five forty in the morning, in Lewis's bed, his warm body beside hers. She looked at him in the dim light of the bedside lamp, she didn't want to leave him, her feelings were real, and this worried Grace.

Was she rebounding at a hundred miles an hour? Her head said yes, her tortured heart said no.

Closing her front door, the kitchen light was on, she didn't leave it on, only the table lamp beside the sofa. Bella must be home. She crept past her door and down the hall only to be alarmed. There were noises coming from Bella's room, she wasn't alone.

Grace froze still in the hall. Her daughter was almost twenty, but if she did say so herself, brazen to bring someone home and into her bed.

The thing was, this was Grace's home, if she wanted to sneak back into her bed from Lewis's at nearly six in the morning, she could, she was a fully grown adult! As she slipped quietly into her bedroom she wondered if it was a double standard, was it okay, or was it not! Bella was a consenting adult and wasn't it better she was home in her own bed with a random, rather than out in some strangers bed.

Before even getting out of bed, Grace called Abbey when she woke up to discuss Bella having a noisy sleep over last night.

'Was it a guy or a girl?'

'Ab's, not now!' Grace was stressing. 'It sounded like a guy, and if she asks me where I was when she got home, I'm saying I fell asleep on your couch.'

'I can't believe your fucking Lewis Hunter.' Abbey was still in shock.

'Should I be letting my daughter have sex in the apartment?' Grace still not comfortable with it.

'I think it's fine, but that's me, I'm different,' Abbey said. She was super relaxed when it came to sex and morals with her Addison and had treated her like an adult all her life.

Loving Grace

When Bella finally got up, Grace looked to see if the visitor was anywhere to be seen, her daughter had a bra and shorty pajamas on, her hair was matted nearly in dreadlocks.

'You were out late last night.' Bella looked at her mother like the roles were reversed.

Grace scoffed, 'And you bought someone home last night.'

'Is that not okay. I thought we were like roommates now!'

She was a smart arse, and Grace should have expected that reaction from her daughter..

It was two weeks until the girl's trip and then the wedding. The relationship between Grace and Lewis was all good planning. Whenever Bella was out, Grace was at his place, occasionally he'd come to hers but mostly when Bella was there or she had visitors over, it seemed very normal for him to be there then, especially if she had family visiting. It had become second nature for them, popping up and down when the coast was clear, having sex at any given chance, sneaking in a dinner at a faraway restaurant and going for walks together locally, pretending it was for leisure and fitness. Things certainly heated up on every front. Grace hadn't had this much sex in her life, and Lewis had never had such an easy-going relationship, besides the fact that it was a secret. Grace didn't expect anything from him, she never assumed his whereabouts and she didn't call him five times a day like most other girlfriends he'd had. They joked that they could literally live like this forever if need be, her in her apartment and him upstairs, they both liked their own space but could see each other whenever they needed. It was the perfect situation on most fronts.

Sometimes Grace felt like an imposter in her own body, the pain of Michael had diminished substantially with Lewis in her life, she kept the bitterness of the betrayal under control – shut off from her everyday thoughts. She'd worked on her urges to kill both Michael and Tina, she was spending time with her kids and focusing on designing yet another jewelry line as the current one went gangbusters in sales. All in all, life was picking up in all aspects.

'Bella's out for the whole night, I think she's met someone,' Grace told Lewis as he kissed her red wine-stained lips. They were cooking dinner in her apartment and spending a quite Saturday night in, he'd had a big week launching a new gaming app that he and Kristian had designed together, it was literally going to be the next big thing. Lewis was close to her kids now more than ever, which was sometimes difficult on a moral level. He hated keeping his feelings for their mother on the down low, but there was no other way, nobody would ever accept their relationship, not yet anyway.

They stood in each other's arms, stirring the pots on the cooktop and drinking wine to soft background music. Tonight was a night they could be like normal people and stay the night together without leaving to sneak back into their respectful beds.

Loving Grace

Grace had changed her bed sheets, the free night was important for her, spending the entire night with Lewis was something she'd been hanging out for. These past few weeks they'd been closer than ever, she'd been feeling great physically and mentally, stronger, and healthier. The strangest part was she'd stop worrying so much about her looks, there'd been no obsessing over her weight, no scrutiny over the lines on her face or inspecting her newly creeping skin in the mirror, her confidence was literally at an all-time high... and why wouldn't it be, she had the affections of a man much younger who was gorgeous and sexy and thought she was all of those things and more too.

The bedroom in the apartment was Grace's favourite room, she loved the walk-in robe and the new furniture, everything was just how she liked it. This bedroom was so different, it was all hers, a lot of things were different now, she slept on the opposite side of the bed to what she had done with Michael, she didn't have to share her walk-in robe. And now she had her very own ensuite, she didn't get bent out of shape about the toilet seat being left up by a man!

They shared a bottle of red and watched a movie and ate some ice cream after dinner. Having the night in bed together it seemed only fitting to start off with sex, they'd showered, and their bodies were warm and relaxed. Tonight, there was no hurry, they could do it all night long if they wanted and then again first thing in the morning and it felt great.

Naked and warm, their bodies meshed to each other face to face, the initial feeling stimulating, they kissed slowly and softly feeling each other as they lay in Grace's cozy bed. His hands gravitated to her boobs, she had good boobs and always had, they were full and high. She sucked at his lower lip and put her leg over his hip, pressing herself against him so he could feel her folds at his skin. Deep slow breaths as the arousal grew between them, slow and well-paced so they enjoyed every second they had alone together.

Grace stopped kissing Lewis; they looked into each other's eyes knowing this was exactly where they wanted to be. Being anywhere else was not an option, someway they'd figure it out.

Grace rolled and Lewis was snug into her back, his hardness pressing into her body as he kissed the back of her neck, trailing down her shoulder and then slowly and softly meandering down her back until his lips reached her hip, then he gently turned her, so she was laying on her back. The same soft kisses went all the way up her stomach and over her boobs to her chest and then her shoulder, he kissed and sucked at the front of her neck, tasting her scent. Grace turned her head and kissed his lips, this time a more erotic kiss to get things moving in a different direction. Moving over her, Lewis knew her body well now, she was soft and feminine in a way that made him want to squeeze her tight, he tucked his arm into her side and kissed his appreciation to her, long slow tender kisses of want. Lifting her leg out to her side this gave him the perfect in, he needed to be inside her. She lifted her body to his and they rolled over once so she was on top.

Staring down into his eyes she still needed to pinch herself every time she was with Lewis Hunter. How had she ever disliked him, it seemed so ridiculous now.

His strong arms pulling her hips to him, her tilting to let him inside her, his tip easing in with an erotic rush of desire that they had become so use to. Grace just knew how to move to his body in a way that got a response immediately. Sex was universal, the fundamentals spoke all languages, the delivery was the only thing that sometimes-needed interpretation. To Grace's surprise Lewis was a generous lover, he liked to please her first, and he knew how to take it far enough without it being intimating for her. Emotionally she wasn't fully recovered, although physically she was, Lewis was an exceptional lover.

With her hands at his chest now, her deep blue eyes looked wondrously into his dark dreamy eyes. Rolling her hips over his, taking him into her stomach and willing herself not to stop even though she thought she might succumb to his heavenly body. Lewis had bought out a side to Grace she had longed for, for so long. She felt vivacious, and youthfully sexual again. Nobody had ever liberated her quite like Lewis. Rolling again, he was on top. Grace let the pillows swallow her up, his arms holding hers to the bed, thrusting in a rhythmic circular motion, stimulating her to the point of no return, she was clenching tight around his cock, she could feel herself contracting to him. Desperate pants were sharp and short, with each motion Lewis had her closer, it was sheer intoxication and emotionally beyond her realm of sexual capability. Grace didn't understand why she was so affected at that moment, but she was. If she backed off now she would never know where he could have taken her, so facing it and taking him on, Grace controlled her breathing and let her orgasm take over. Gaining momentum and spiraling into a numbing orgasm, this was beyond anything she had ever known. Louder, she moaned his name and rolled her head from side to side, trying to save herself from an emotion that was too strong for her. Tears waterfalling from her eyes as her pleasured groans became whimpers.

'Gracie!' Lewis checked in on her, not about to stop as he was there too.

'I never expected this,' she cried as her back arched to his stiffening body. This man was so much more than she'd imagined in all the right ways. She had been judgmental and wrong.

'What did you expect?' he gasped still thrusting away at her.

'Not you, not like this,' she panted. Her emotion had got the better of her, it was a weird sexual emotion that she remembered experiencing only very few times in her life.

Tensing his body as he came, then lowering over Grace and kissing her sweet soft lips, Lewis whispered to her ear, 'Well you're exactly what I expected, and some.'

281

Loving Grace

A smile grew at her lips, a warmth swept over her filling her heart … Lewis Hunter was like a beautiful sunny palm lined beach in her darkest days.

Sundays seemed to come around fast, and tonight's dinner at Marlo and Ross's was special, it was Shiv's birthday and although the family was large, tonight's dinner was going to be bigger and better apparently. Marlo had worked with Maria on the menu all week, she'd invited the entire family and had extra help come in for the night. This was Marlo's thing; she lived for bringing people together. The dining table was decked out with place cards and a full setting of wine glasses and cutlery.

Grace arriving with Lewis was nothing anyone would raise an eyebrow to, they lived in the same building, and they'd become friends in the past month. They weren't the first to arrive, Bella had gone around earlier to catch up with her cousin Mac. Everyone was there except for Kristian, Luca, and Ross, which didn't raise any concerns with anyone, everything went on as normal. Jimmy and Louise were there, which was great, only her brother was in a strange mood, not very chatty and taking Lewis aside as soon as they arrived for a private discussion. Because there was a massive amount of cross-family/work going on they all tried to keep work aside, but sometimes things needed to be discussed, exceptions were always made.

Louise chatted with Shiv and the girls, but Bella was making Grace feel uncomfortable still in her grumpy mood she'd been in all weekend. Marlo was in and out flitting around laughing with a glass of champagne in hand. After a while Grace sat over out of the way with Ed, he reminded her so much of her father, the accents, the opinions, the love he had for his family, she loved it when they had talks about the old days and how much he missed her dad and her mother.

'You know Gracie, we were the best of friends, it's like half of me is missing. Shiv and I miss them every day,' Ed said as she sat on the sofa looking out at the harbour.

'I can only imagine,' she replied knowing the loss they felt, she missed her dad so much she felt like part of her was missing too. Life had gone on after her father passed, but it had never been the same, she lost the one man who really and truly loved her unconditionally, the one man who thought absolutely every inch of her was beautiful and perfect. Grace didn't have a mother to compare the love, all she knew was that her dad had been the person who she loved the most in the world. Tom King was a bull of a man, stern and blokey, but he adored Grace wholeheartedly and he'd melt to butter whenever she was around. He'd raised her single handedly with help of course from a young Marlo and loving Shiv.

'How's the new apartment Gracie - settled in yet?' Ed asked her.

'I love being back in the city,' she smiled.

Loving Grace

'Of course, you do,' he huffed like her ever moving away was ridiculous, 'You're born and raised a city girl.' He'd been nice to Michael, and he'd actually liked him, but now he wanted to skin him alive. 'Where are your boys anyway Gracie?'

'I don't know Ed, their supposed to be here.'

Gabe sat forward, 'They'll be here,' he smiled, 'They won't want to miss out,' he added.

Lewis and Jimmy came back into the living room, both with serious faces, Grace wanted to go to Lewis, but she couldn't, she really wanted to kiss his lips. Instead, she watched him chat with Shiv in the distance, they had this bond that was so admirable, she'd been his grandmother and his mother, she'd been there to bring him into the world, nobody had known him longer than Shiv, her hands had been the first hands to touch him. They looked to be in a serious talk, Grace had one ear on Ed and all of her attention on Shiv and Lewis as they sat face to face in deep conversation.

It got later and later and eventually they all sat at the long dining table, Grace and Lewis had two seats between them, Marlo, and Bella across from Grace with Scarlet and Angus too. Three empty seats at the table for Kristian, Luca, and Ross. Grace had sent two texts and then she called Luca and left a message.

'Leave it Grace, it's not a problem,' Marlo assured her as they took their seats. But it was a problem for her as everyone was asking after Ross and the boys and it was rude to not show up to dinner on a such special occasion as a birthday.

Bella was still mega shitty, her and Mac sat talking quietly like there was something juicy going on.

Jimmy and Louise sat between Lewis and Grace, Louise beside Grace, and even she'd been super quiet tonight... Maybe she was just paranoid, it happened. The table buzzed with small talk as the service for the first course started, when Marlo did a birthday dinner, it was an extravaganza.

As Grace's plate was placed in front of her, she smiled across the table to Bella who was looking sour as ever.

'What!' Bella glared at her. It was at that stage that Grace realised it was she who Bella had beef with, she frowned at her daughter, her rudeness was out of line, and her attitude was getting to Grace. Her feelings were hurt, Bella was one of few people who she could rely on to bring her down, she blinked her annoyance across the table, rather than say something she couldn't take back.

'Bella!' Louise said as the standoff between mother and daughter went on. If anyone were going to pull her up on her bad behaviour, it would be her aunties, Marlo, and Louise. As much as they loved her, they knew she gave Grace a hard time, and they both knew she was going through some things at the moment too.

Still with defiance in her eyes, Bella looked at Louise, 'What have I done wrong, why are you both looking at me!'

285

Loving Grace

'Not now Bella,' Louise said calmly like she knew something Grace didn't.

Grace pouted her lips wondering what was going on, her boys weren't there, neither was Ross, Bella was in a shitty mode, and everyone had been gossiping in groups since she'd arrived.

'Hmmm,' Bella huffed like she was about to boil over, 'I'm so over it!'

'Over what?' Grace was on the defense now and people were looking from both directions down the table. 'Am I missing something?'

A second of awkward silence and everyone looking at Grace and Bella.

'Kristian thought it would be a good idea to bash Dom last night,' Bella scoffed. 'That's were Luca and Uncle Ross are... bailing him out of the lock up again.' Everyone seemed to know about it accept Grace.

Bella glaring at Grace like it was her fault, 'And what do I come home to this morning... you two!' Bella hissing her words with anger, looking at her mother and then to Lewis with hate in her eyes. 'After Kristian went feral last night, I decided to come home. I saw the two of you.' She looked down the table to Lewis and then back to her mother knowing she'd gone too far, but she'd had the shock of her life seeing her mother and Lewis in bed naked asleep together when she'd come home at four in the morning. Obviously, they weren't expecting her home!

Grace rose from her seat slowly and calmly with all eyes on her as she gently placed her napkin on the table and glared at her daughter across the table for a chilling moment before turning and walking out the room, heading to the front door. Bella had purposely humiliated her and Lewis in front of everyone. Grace looked back at Lewis just before she was out of sight, he was excusing himself from the table of shocked family members. Not only had the whole Kristian drama been aired at the table, but so had their affair.

Standing in the foyer with her handbag, Grace was leaving, she was going to Uber it to wherever Kristian was. By the sounds of it, he'd finally gone too far.

'I'm coming with you,' Lewis rushed into the foyer to find Grace in tears.

'I'm so sorry,' she said knowing how this reflected on him. Even though Bella hadn't said she saw them in bed, it was obvious to most of the table. And if it weren't, it certainly would be soon enough. 'Stay here with your family, it's Shiv's birthday. I need to find Kristian.'

'I'm coming with you, and I don't give a fuck what they all think in there.'

'You will though,' she said softly between sniffs as she tried not to cry.

'Gracie,' he shook his head.

'I'll call you later. Promise.'

Loving Grace

'If I go back in there I'll have to explain us, and I don't want to. I'm more concerned about you right now, so, I'm coming with you, I'm driving you.' Lewis was certain, and as much as Grace needed to do this alone... she let Lewis go with her.

'Grace... Lew!' Marlo came into the foyer as they were leaving, 'You're both leaving?' she seemed shocked.

'I'm sorry, I need to go to Kristian.' Grace opened the front door.

Marlo looked at Lewis for his answer.

'I'm taking Gracie,' he stood looking at Marlo, 'We shouldn't have to explain ourselves at the dinner table,' he was slightly pissed that Bella had been a bitch about it, announcing it to the entire family rather than just confronting her mother in private. She had no idea what her outing them would do.

'But it's Shiv's birthday,' Marlo pleaded.

'My sons been arrested. Again. I don't give a shit about Shiv's birthday.' Grace was visibly upset, she'd been fine, recovering, getting better, but this thing with Kristian was just another upset to her, another disappointment, and another thing gone wrong. She didn't feel comfortable with leaving Ross to clean up her kid's mess over and over. 'I need to go.' And she walked out the front door.

Lewis held back a moment, 'Call me when everyone's gone tonight, I'd like to talk to you alone.' He thought Marlo had a right to know out of everyone. Bella's accusations had taken them all by surprise. Marlo was Grace's sister, and she would want answers from him.

Ross knew powerful people. This time it had taken more than his status to get Kristian off, there'd been money and bribery this time, something he wasn't proud of, but he had to do it, so Kristian didn't go to jail. Miraculously, again the charges disappeared. It never happened. Dom was paid off too, with Luca producing an air-tight agreements for all parties involved. Grace's gratitude to Ross was immeasurable yet again.

'I wouldn't do this for just anybody, you know that right!' Ross said to Kristian outside the station where he'd been held in a holding cell for fourteen hours. 'But mate, this is the last time I do it for you.' Ross gave Kristian a hug, he turned to Grace and hugging her too. 'I'll leave him with you,' Ross sighed before walking off, clearly drained, pissed off and Grace couldn't blame him.

'How about you come and stay at my place tonight, I think mum wants you close by,' Lewis said to Kristian who looked disheveled and tired.

'I think I've been evicted from my apartment anyway,' Kristian sighed with a mountain of regret, he'd had a rough night at his own doing. Grace rolling her eyes to Lewis who knew her pain. Her youngest son was volatile and unpredictable. He went through women like underwear lately and his violent outbursts were now an urgent issue. Lewis and Grace had discussed it on the way and decided Kristian needed professional help. At work he had an opportunity to take on the world. He made very poor decisions in his personal life though, like beating up his sister's ex-boyfriend on the curb outside a club in front of dozens of witnesses.

The fallout from Bella's dinner table outburst at Marlo's was huge, both Grace and Lewis had some answering to do, the Hunter King clan basically did an intervention style meeting to get to the bottom of it, and not everyone was completely sold by the end as it went down in Marlo and Ross' living room. In fact, there was a list of naysayers, starting with Shiv and Bella. Luca wasn't happy, which surprised Grace most of all. Marlo didn't love it, but she at least didn't show her distaste like the others did. Ross and Ed along with Gabe, Kristian, Jimmy, and Louise all said they didn't see the big deal. And thank God for Ruby and Scarlet, Grace's beautiful nieces who had her back and stuck up for her and Lewis unexpectedly when their grandmother said it was ludicrous and selfish. Shiv had told Grace she was being selfish because she couldn't provide children for Lewis at her age and suggested that Lewis had lost his mind. Scarlet and Ruby went in batting for their cousin, saying Lewis didn't want children of his own, he'd told them so on many occasions, they pointed out all the failed love affairs he'd had and said that maybe their aunt was the one who could actually make him happy. They even went to Grace and Lewis after the meeting to give them their support on their way home, and it was much appreciated. Jimmy and Louise did the same, it was like a follow-up meeting at Grace's apartment that was now all hers again after Bella moved out and in with Luca. Grace had been devastated. Kristian was as always in his mother's corner, he still had his tail between his legs, he wasn't in the clear yet but was seeking professional help, which was a start. Grace had told him she feared his temper and violent outbursts would land him in jail and help would be beyond anyone. He'd agreed.

It wasn't so much a divide in the family, just some noses out of joint. Marlo had slipped into neutral, she tried to understand, well she said she did, and she managed to make Bella and Luca see that they only had one mother who happened to be a great one, and that she didn't deserve or need their backlash. Shiv was still holding out, not speaking to Grace, and still very upset with Lewis. As for Grace and Lewis, their family's resistance only bought them closer. Bella had moved out, so they had no need to sneak around anymore, Grace literally spent every entire night in Lewis's bed. They were acting like a real couple and had even made some progress in their relationship. They were spending more and more time together and their sex had an extra certain element to it.

'Don't ya think it's weird that we're so into each other now, after knowing each other your entire life?' Grace gasped as she clung to Lewis enjoying a slow Sunday morning in bed together. He was way deep inside her and she was about to cum again.

291

Loving Grace

'It's not new for me, I had a thing for you when I was a teenager.' He laid over her and thought she hadn't really changed a bit.

'What!' she managed, flattered and yet cumming, which was a rush of emotions as she smiled, pulling him down to her so she could kiss him. Grace let him move in and out of her, she gazed up into his eyes, biting down on her lower lip as he thrust deep inside arching her back as she gulped for air right as she came again.

'I love you Gracie,' Lewis gasped as he filled her with his luscious cock and his cum. Tensing to her, it had been the perfect time to tell her exactly how he was feeling.

It came from nowhere and caught her off guard... she was vulnerable mid cum. 'I love you too!' And it was true, she couldn't see herself living without him now. Lewis been her rock from day dot, he'd had her back and helped her find her feet again in so many ways, how could she not love him.

Later that day it was time for Sunday night dinner at Marlo and Ross's, and it was one week prior to the girl's trip. All the kids were coming, Jimmy and Lou... Shiv and Ed had been invited but they'd declined tonight because of the rift between Grace and Shiv. Grace was still devastated that this had come between them. It seemed so many conversations had gone down in that one week and yet Shiv was still not coming around to the idea. Grace and Lewis felt since everyone knew they'd have to get used to them. No avoiding gatherings, no hiding. Just acceptance. They'd come too far to stop now.

None of Grace's children had arrived yet, she knew they were at lunch with Michael today, he'd told them it was super important they all went, much to Bella's horror. But it was time for them to talk things through with their father and maybe find a way of moving on with him in their life. Of course, there was a small part of Grace that hoped her relationship with Lewis would be mentioned.

The three kids arrived looking glum and just in time for dinner, they took their seats at the table, and nobody asked any questions of them, but Grace could see Bella was visibly upset and Kristian was out of sorts, it didn't look like it had gone too well. Luca seemed off too, he wasn't himself.

Marlo just couldn't help herself; she had to bring it up, 'How was lunch, was Tina there?'

'No, she wasn't there, lucky for her,' Bella snarled. 'Who's going to say it?' she looked at her big brother Luca.

He seemed hesitant, 'I will, I guess.' The awkwardness was obvious, and all three kids looked like the world had just ended. Luca looked at his mother with a regretful pain on his face. 'Lunch wasn't great. Kristian walked out, because he wanted to kill dad, again!'

Kristian couldn't look at Grace, he hadn't from the moment he'd walked in.

293

Loving Grace

Grace's eyes went from one son to another, 'Why, what happened?' she asked with the entire table listening in.

Luca took a huge breath in exhaled like he was about to die, 'Because dad told us something today.' He was dragging it out because the fall out was huge, but in this family most big things happened at the dinner table and better it happened now while his mother had everyone around her. 'We have a brother!' Luca announced looking away from his mother.

The table was in complete shock and silence.

'Since when?' Marlo spoke first whilst Grace wished the earth would swallow her up.

'Since five years ago,' Luca said knowing this was tearing his mother's heart out once again.

'What!' Scarlet scoffed loudly, they were all shocked, 'Is there no end to your fathers torture!' she was visibly upset at this latest claim.

Luca cleared his throat, 'Dad's the father of Bree's child. Did you know?' he looked at his mother, knowing this would set her back tremendously, it was another blow. Another secret. Another betrayal.

It took Grace a moment to register, 'No, I had no idea,' her tone matched the astounded look on her face. But she knew who might have known, her eyes went across the table to Lewis. She didn't need to ask the question because it was written all over his face. He'd most definitely known about this, he literally knew every other secret in Michael's closet, there's no way he'd missed this one.

Grace looked at all three of her kids, they all looked as worn out as she was from their father's indiscretions.

Her children were hurting, apparently Bella had told her father that Grace was seeing Lewis, because she knew this would pain her father. But it had backfired on her, Michael had seen red and again hit back in the worst way possible, with another secret, because that's what he did. When Michael was hit, he hit back.

The table was consuming it all, Bella spoke up, 'He's not with Tina anymore. They broke up when she found out about Bree's child with Dad.' The table was completely focused on what was going down, all eyes went to Bella, except for Grace, hers were firmly on Lewis.

'Hah!' Marlo was fuming, 'After all the hurt those two caused, and they can't even have the courtesy to stay together.' Marlo pushed her plate aside, 'See!,' she said looking at Bella and Luca. 'This is the sort of father we're dealing with here... A fucking idiot!' standing at the table Marlo slammed her hands down on it. 'And you have the cheek to banish your mother because she's moving on with her life.' Marlo's face was red, her heart racing. 'Your mother doesn't deserve to be treated like this by your father or from you,' she glared at Bella. 'I don't know how the hell she puts up with it, quite frankly.' Looking at her little sister who was still sitting at the table with her eyes at Lewis, Marlo was devastated by the latest instalment.

'Lewis was a shock, that's all,' Bella always had something to say.

'I don't want to hear it,' Marlo barked at her niece, 'I'm fed up and I'm sure your poor mother is too. That woman who happens to be my sister, has devoted her life to you children, and that poor excuse for a husband, and in return he cheats on her with her best friend. He lies to her for twenty years and then spends hundreds of thousands of her hard-earned dollars, racks up debt, and will probably end up taking half her fucking house too, and everything else she's worked hard for.' Marlo was mid rant and almost at meltdown stage, but nobody interrupted or spoke a word. 'Now he's got another child to someone your mother probably trusted, again... It's absurd... If you think it's hard on you, cut your mother some god damn slack!' With that she went to Grace and squatted down beside her at the table. 'I thought mentioning the car accident would be going too far,' she whispered taking her sister's hands in hers.

'You think,' Grace smiled at Marlo, she was teary, yet calm. 'I'm going to go home. Sorry I keep fucking your dinners up.'

This was too much and there were too many people for Grace to consume what had just happened, her life was once again on display in the most awful way, her family was falling apart for everyone to see. Michael had a child with Bree. *Who else was he fucking whilst they'd been married?*

Grace rose from her seat, and Marlo said, 'I understand you need to go; this is none of our business anyway my darling,' she turned and looked at Luca and Bella... not Kristian, in Marlo's mind he was the only one who didn't deserve her wrath, and she would apologise to him later privately.

'I'll take you home Gracie,' Ross stood from his seat, still shocked.

'I'll take her,' said Lewis standing.

'No!' she protested. 'Ross can take me.' A direct hit on Lewis. She was sure he had his reasons for keeping this humiliating secret from her, but it didn't matter now, he'd betrayed her by withholding such sensitive information, there was no other way to see it, his private investigator would have told him, no two ways.

'It's okay, I'll take my mum home.' Kristian rose from his seat and went straight to his mother's side, she was bewildered and devastated. Nevertheless, Lewis followed them out to the foyer.

'Grace!' Lewis never just called her Grace.

She faced him front on, 'You knew about this all along didn't you?'

'I found out after you had the accident and I didn't think you needed another setback,' he explained.

Loving Grace

'What I didn't need was another liar in my life Lewis.' She opened the front door, Kristian and Lewis following behind her as she went out to the street.

'Gracie. I didn't lie to you. I just chose not to tell you something that would hurt you even more than you already were.'

'And that's called lying!' she turned abruptly and looked for her son's car. 'Kristian, take me home please,' she headed for his car up the street.

'Will you stop!' Lewis understood her anger, she'd just found out about another lie, another woman and child. 'I'm not the arsehole here Gracie,' he was still trying to make her see reason.

'Mum!' Kristian wanted her to give Lewis a break, 'Listen to him.' Kristian actually liked the idea of his mother and Lewis, because of course he idolised him.

'No. I'm not interested in anything he has to say.' And then left two of the dearest men in her life standing there like fools as she marched off up the street past Kristian's car and all the way to her apartment.

An hour after she got home there was that familiar knock at her door, she didn't open it, however, she did speak through it, 'I can't see you Lewis. Please go away.'

'I'm not going away.' His muffled voice came back at her from the other side of the door.

'Let's just go back to a tenant landlord situation. I think it's best for us. This was never going to work out anyway.' Her voice was emotional.

He needed a minute to think, desperate to win her back, 'I'm sorry. I never meant to hurt you or make you distrust me. Honestly Gracie, I was trying to protect you.'

'I can't see you anymore,' she paused for a long moment with a gaping gash in her heart. 'If you want me to move out I will.' But he never replied and when she looked through the peep hole, he wasn't there.

'Fuck!' Abbey sighed with an element of sadness for her friend from the sofa, she'd arrived twenty minutes ago after Grace called her. 'Are you sure you have to do this,' Abbey wasn't sure Grace was thinking straight.

'I need to go to bed,' Grace was crying. This had set her back a mile. A double whammy so to speak. Another betrayal from Michael just when she thought he couldn't hurt her anymore, and now Lewis.

'You go to bed; I'll make you vegemite toast and a cuppa tea.' Abbey knew the drill.

Chapter Sixteen

Marlo had been wonderful as usual. A tower of strength and support, and to Grace's surprise she knew breaking up with Lewis had hit her sister terribly hard. Everyone was concerned for Grace's mental health; she'd been through enough. They were all on the plane to Rome, all of them, including Bella, who was sitting at Grace's side in the big plush beige leather seats. She'd made peace with her mother straight away; they needed each other more than ever. They sat quietly reading and watching movies. Abbey and Lou were drinking champagne with Marlo and Mac up the front, laughing loudly and kicking off the trip with a bang. Grace hadn't heard from Lewis, he was respecting her wishes, and she hadn't run into him in the lift although she thought she may have just missed him one day. He'd told Marlo he didn't want Grace moving out, and that he hoped they could one day be friends again.

It was the four grown up ladies and the two young ladies heading off on a Mediterranean girl's trip, Marlo had everything taken care of, her travel agent was on the payroll, which was how billionaires rolled. For mere mortals like Grace, Abbey, and Bella, this was the trip of a lifetime. Lavish beyond anything they had ever experienced in their lifetimes.

There was money... And then there was money!

Grace hadn't been to Rome for over ten years, she was looking forward to two days of just wandering around the beautiful city and taking it all in, she needed time away to clear her head, and time with the girls she loved the most to brighten her spirits. Ending things with Lewis had left her with many feelings, hurt, sadness and the obvious that she should have known better. Jumping into a romance so soon had been a huge mistake and she knew it, it had just felt so right at the time. Lewis felt so right, he had picked her up into his strong safe arms when she was at her lowest. Her heart was sore from the pain, only from Lewis... Michael couldn't hurt her any more than he had with Tina, and as for Bree that two faced little bitch, good luck to her and her poor child.

Arriving in three large black Mercedes at the hotel in Rome mid-morning and being greeted by two concierges specifically for Marlo and the ladies, it was obvious they had been awaiting their arrival and were completely dedicated to making the ladies stay the best it could possibly be. The thing was with a client like Marlo Hunter, she wasn't an A lister, she was the most

301

important guest of all... Mega wealthy and stayed with them regularly.

The ladies had rested on the private jet over, everyone was feeling excited and ready to take on the world. After an hour of showering and getting ready, they set off to lunch together, Marlo was in Rome several times a year, she was literally like a local. After lunch, the young girls set off on their own, whilst Marlo, Grace, Abbey, and Louise roamed the piazzas chatting and enjoying one of the most beautiful cities in the world.

Grace felt like she was in yet another recovery stage of her life, a week ago she'd been in bliss with Lewis, now she   felt empty and lost again, wondering if she'd bought on everything with Michael and Lewis herself. Had she been blind to her husband's ways, been so dumb that he'd thought he could get away with it... obviously. Then getting attached to Lewis, was she mad! Clearly she was. Grace didn't blame anyone but herself, she wasn't a victim, she was stupid and now she had to accept that and pick herself up again. One thing was for sure, she wasn't going to be a wet sock on this trip, even though she didn't feel much like talking or being with people, she knew she had to make an effort, the last thing she wanted was for the girls and her daughter to think she wasn't coping with the latest situation, even though they were all very aware she was completely and utterly heartbroken over Lewis.

Day two of Rome and Bella and Mac had their day planned out, they'd gone off together early to get a start, the weather was stifling, and they had so much to do. Louise had taken Abbey to the Colosseum for an early tour before it got unbearably hot, leaving Marlo and Grace drinking coffee on the balcony terrace of their palatial hotel suite overlooking the old city of Rome.

As much as Marlo thought Grace had rushed into things with Lewis, she knew the impact they'd had on each other in such a short time. Her sister again hadn't been herself since the breakup. Lewis was devastated and he told Marlo he was gutted. Once Marlo had got over her own initial shock, she actually saw the possible potential of their relationship. For the brief moment she'd known them as a couple, they'd seem connected and it was more than a sexual attraction, Marlo could see it, 'How are you feeling now you're here?' she asked as Grace stared off into the distance.

'I miss him. Is it weird I miss him more than Michael?'

Marlo sipped her coffee, 'Not at all.' She did think it was slightly weird.

'I felt better every morning knowing I'd see him at some point in my day and now I'm just hollow.' Grace had been trying her very best to be upbeat, happy, good company, but she knew she wasn't coming off that way. Michael and Tina weren't her problem. It was Lewis. And as much as she tried to not think about him or how it felt making love to him in those last few days of their time together, the loss was huge.

Loving Grace

'Well, this is your birthday holiday my darling, and I want to take you to some of my favourite stores and spoil you before we head off on the yacht. Would that be okay with you?' her adoration for Grace was ever present.

'You don't have to do that; you've given me enough with this trip and Abbey and Bella coming along. You don't need to buy me things Marlo.'

'Oh, yes I do. You're my baby sister and I love spending time with you, so, let's go shopping,' Marlo had an excited smile on her face.

They shopped for hours. Gucci, Valentino, and Chanel. Grace couldn't even calculate in her head what her sister had spent on her. Every time she touched something or tried something on, Marlo bought it for her, saying it gave her the best pleasure to buy her sister gifts. Grace was fine with it, so long as it wasn't out of pity. She didn't need her sister's pity.

'Grace, I have more money than my entire family will ever be able to spend, even if they lived lavish lives for the rest of time, please accept my gifts.' Marlo had said to Grace in Chanel, it was their last emporium, they had to get the shopping delivered to the hotel because they simply couldn't carry it all. Dropping half a million dollars in Rome on a shopping spree was a pebble in the ocean for Marlo.

Bella and Mac were having so much fun together, they'd arranged to meet up for dinner with some young Italians they'd met on their travels today, they were living their best lives. The four grown up ladies went out walking over the river to Trastevere for dinner, they sat among the forever ambient laneways at a candle lit table, the night was warm, the atmosphere so very Roman with gorgeous Italians waiting on them, drinking amazing wine and ordering fabulous food. This was going to be the holiday of a lifetime, beautiful Rome, a Mediterranean cruise finishing with a wedding in Tuscany, life didn't get any better!

Abbey had managed to changed her schedule and had accepted the invitation to the wedding even though she was exceeding the number of days which she could take leave from the firm. Abbey knew being at Grace's side she'd feeling better about attending the wedding in Tuscany. Lewis would be there, along with Shiv and the whole entire Hunter family, she'd be seeing them for the first time.

Abbey and Louise got along famously, Lou being the sister-in-law saw her sometimes tread a fine line with Marlo, never Grace. Louise was a straight up person, she had a bad poker face and said it how it was most of the time.

'I think you should reach out to Lewis before Tuscany, see if you can repair things.' Lou suggested to Grace as they sat sipping limoncello.

Instantly Marlo's eyes widened, 'Repair!' it was more a question.

Loving Grace

'Why not?' Lou said casually, she was interested in Marlo's take on it.

Abbey sat there keeping quiet although she and Lou had had this very conversation, they were both rooting for Grace and Lewis to get back together. They didn't understand the uproar from the family, and if Grace could get over Lewis withholding the information about Michael fathering Bree's child, then why shouldn't they be able to rekindle in Tuscany at the wedding. Lou had an insight into the family dynamics, and she thought their reactions were selfish and uncalled for, what difference did it matter if Grace hooked up with Gabe or Lewis! Shiv had double standards, and she liked things her way.

Abbey just wanted her friend to be happy and if that was a sexy younger man, then half her luck. What Lewis had done was not a betrayal.

'You're forgetting he lied to me.' Grace spoke up.

Abbey dropping her head to one side, 'I don't think he lied to you, he was protecting you.'

Marlo huffed, 'That's kind of lying.'

'It wasn't really a lie!' Lou said as if she didn't agree.

'It doesn't matter now what it was, it's over,' Grace said ending the conversation.

Chapter Seventeen

An abundance of super yachts lined the marina in the sweltering heat of the ancient Grand harbour of Valletta in Malta. The glorious one hundred-and fifteen-foot white luxury vessel awaited the ladies. Of course, Marlo knew people boarding the yacht beside theirs, a group of males young and old, Americans, apparently members of a famous band. With some brief introductions before boarding their respective yachts that were miraculously taking a similar route. Grace raising her brows at the younger guys who no doubt took note of Mac and Bella. The ladies boarded, the hot Maltese sun sparkled around the harbour as the crew introduced themselves, again, a few strapping young men who noted the younger ladies boarding. Grace would have to remember all their names, a woman in her forties who was the first officer and then two younger females who all seemed lovely. Excitement was in the air. Marlo had upgraded yachts at the last minute, now everyone had their very own suite.

'I just thought we might need our space. Ten days can be a long time on a yacht all together.' She explained before they all set off to settle in before a tour of the magnificent vessel. Grace,

Loving Grace

Bella and Abbey had never seen anything like it, they'd never been on a super yacht before.

'We disembark in half an hour ladies, so let's meet back here in five,' said the chirpy chief steward.

Looking around her suite, Grace marveled at the opulence, it was on a different level, this was how the rich and famous holidayed, she almost felt unworthy of such extravagance... Her private bathroom had a spa bath, and the closet was a gally walk through, the very first thing she noticed was a jewelry drawer built into the dresser, she gasped at the delight of it all. The entire suite was neutral with a light timber, designed with extraordinary luxury and style.

By mid-afternoon, they were eating lunch at the large round dining table out on level one's deck, delectable antipasto, cheese boards, fresh salads, roasted chicken, cold meats, fruit, bakery selections, and champagne, it was a feast fit for royalty. The afternoon was spent cruising up the breathtaking coastline of Malta, the scenery was spectacular, the Mediterranean Sea as blue as the sky as they lounged on a row of six sunbeds on the upper deck looking out over what was the island of Malta. They'd reached their first destination in no time and sat out off the coast of Gozo, a smaller Maltese island, the sun was setting over the ancient land, then the luxury yacht settled into the marina for the evening alongside the American's super yacht. Marlo had ventured over to visit her neighbouring friends with Mac and Bella leaving Abbey, Grace, and Louise sipping cocktails on the lower deck.

'They've just finished their world tour and are celebrating a divorce,' Louise informed the girls as they watched Marlo across the way in her bright yellow shirt and white flowing linen pants as she socialised. 'Marlo says Gus hasn't taken his divorce well.' Louise always knew all the latest gossip.

'Who's Gus and who's Pete?' Grace asked oblivious to their fame.

'If you're saying you don't know who the lead singer and guitarist are of one of the world's biggest bands, I don't believe you Grace King!' Abbey scoffed.

'I'm sure I'd know some of their songs if I heard them,' Grace sighed.

'Gus is like one of the biggest rock stars on the planet Gracie,' Louise laughed, 'He's got the long hair the beard... oh my god what a man... and he's freshly divorced, the other one with short blonde hair is Pete Webber. So cool. Happily married from what Marlo says, but not according to the tabloids.'

'Well, their sons took a good look at the girls, I saw that,' Abbey added with a snicker.

'Great, that's all I need. Bella hooking up with a random American,' Grace huffed with her straw in her mouth.

'She's young and in paradise, let her go,' Louise said with a cigarette hanging out her mouth. She smoked in Europe when holidaying, Grace fanned the smoke away.

Loving Grace

'I wonder what Marlo's talking to them about?' Abbey asked. Marlo knew the band because Ross knew them, they knew all sorts of famous people all over the world.

'She looks like she's flirting to me,' Grace sighed making the ladies laugh.

'It looks like she's telling them her sister is single, and look she's pointing at us,' Louise loved teasing, somehow they had to make Grace lighten up and enjoy herself.

'Very funny!' Grace sighed again.

'I wonder how many single men are over there?' said Abbey.

'Why? Do you plan on cheating on Dean?' Grace snapped at her friend's interest in the men.

'Relax,' Abbey chuckled, 'I'm just wondering. You don't have to take things so serious Grace, you're the only one single, besides the girls. Maybe there's one over there for you.'

'No thank you. I'm not here to pick up men,' Grace huffed, she was here to relax and although Lou and Ab's found it amusing, she wasn't here for men.

Ten minutes later Marlo and the girls returned, 'We're going onshore for dinner tonight, I asked our handsome neighbours to join us.'

The six men and six ladies looked like one big happy party at the long dinner table in the piazza restaurant, Grace made sure she sat at the very end off to the side, so she didn't have to engage in conversation, she ate her meal and as everyone socialised and got to know each other. The two band members Gus and Pete, who were in their early fifties, were with their sons Jude and Brad who were in their early twenties, and two crew members Jason and Zac both in their thirties. When everyone switched up seats, it threw Grace, she had been happily nestled up the end beside with Ab's and Lou and then along came Pete switching seats with Lou which meant now she'd have to speak to them. Pete was a rugged yet handsome man, some would say good-looking. A nice natured guy with a great personality that the women found adorable, he had Abbey eating out of his hand, Grace was standoffish, she wasn't giving much but interested all the same. Pete lived outside of Los Angeles, he was happily married according to him, and his son Brad toured with him whilst his other two kids stayed home in school with their mother. The Mediterranean trip was something they were doing to wind down after a five-month world tour before he and Brad were going to Greece to meet up with the family for a vacation.

'My son has had a bad year last year, a few rough patches!' Pete pointed out, 'I thought taking him along on tour would help and it has, he's found himself again... Not easy at twenty-two.' Pete was a genuine man; Grace could see him looking down the table checking in on Brad every now and then. When

311

he spoke about his son, he had a certain warmness, it was refreshing to see someone in his position being such a great dad. Funnily enough he and Abbey had something in common, she was a lawyer and Pete's father had been too, so they chatted endlessly about the legal systems in either country, boring Grace to smithereens, she was happy to zone out and take in her surroundings. It was hard not to wonder what Lewis was up to, how he was feeling, if he had got over her, she had no idea and it didn't matter, the less she knew, the better she figured. In her head it was the past she had to forget, it would never work, not with their family.

Day two of the yacht trip was spent on a much smaller yacht out in the Blue Lagoon at Camino Island, just off of Gozo. The lagoon was something to be seen, simply spectacular with its turquoise water and surrounding white cliffs.

The Maltese way was very relaxed and low key, the weather was phenomenal, and the food was fresh and plentiful. The Americans had somehow managed to put their smaller yacht nearby along with other private boats who basked in the dreamy waters as tourist filled the beach and rocks within the lagoon. Everyone, including Grace swam off the yacht in the heavenly water. The land was huge formations of sparce white limestone rock, it was stunning beyond any of their wildest imaginations. They swam, lunched, and laid out on the deck in the hot Mediterranean sun, all working on their tans and enjoying life. Bella and Mac snorkeled with the Americans, Grace could see Gus and Pete on the deck of their yacht, shorts and beers looking very relaxed taking in the beauty of the Maltese island. She wasn't a fan of the American accent and in general found them louder than Australians, friendly, nevertheless.

Abbey and Lou along with Marlo were in tanning mode, Grace was more skin conscious as she didn't tan easily, yet she had already caught some sun today. The ladies chatted about random topics from the wedding and how the guest houses on the property were just being finished as far as renovations went this week, just in the nick of time. To Abbey, wondering if maybe her Addison was having sexuality issues, to Louise wanting to move to New York, and of course Grace talked about Luca and her becoming a grandmother. There was no talk of Michael and Tina, which was a good change, and Lewis was never mentioned. Grace's issues were a long way away and that was good for the moment, she needed a break from it all. They were always present in her mind though, and she missed Lewis, she missed his touch and the feeling he gave her when she spent time with him, it was a feeling of contentedness, and of care. Something she'd only just realised she been missing for such a long time.

Another night in Gozo before they headed up to Italy, Marlo had been raving about Sardinia, which was exciting for Grace, she'd never been there. That night they'd dined on their luxury yacht and then walked up to the citadel, it was dark, and the tiny island had a mysterious air about it at night. The younger girls had gone off with the younger Americans to

313

experience a night spot apparently in a cave, Marlo warning them about staying together.

Grace was getting ready for bed alone in her suite when her phone rang. Shock horror. It was Michael. She stared at the phone for a moment, then answered it... what if something had happened to one of the boys.

'Hello!' she sounded startled.

'Grace, it's me,' his voice was painful for her to hear. Part of her would always love Michael, and part of her was still so angry at him for betraying her.

'Is everything alright, are the boys okay?' She was instantly panicking, why the hell was he calling her in Europe, something had to be wrong.

'The boys are fine.'

She recognized a slight slur to his words, 'Michael, why are you calling?'

'Please don't hang up. Grace, I- I need to speak to you about us,' he was most certainly drunk. 'I still love you Grace. I'm so sorry, I know I fucked up, but please forgive me. I can't just stop loving you Grace.'

Her instinct was to hang up on him, but she didn't. 'You're drunk Michael.'

'I still love you so much. Please, Grace, I want our life back. I want you.'

She hung up. Her body trembling uncontrollably at hearing Michael's voice. Her thoughts were mostly anger that he thought it was okay to call her without an emergency, and that he had unloaded his drunkenness on her. He and Tina were off, now he wanted his wife back! *Well, fuck you!*

Getting herself into bed, it felt like she'd taken twenty massive steps back in her initial progress with her marriage breakdown, she could feel her heart beating in her chest. She felt that sad and awful harrowing sadness that she thought would actually sink her at times, flooding over her as she laid in bed. She and Michael were so over it was way beyond silly, a sober Michael didn't want her back, and Grace didn't want him back, they were done. But hearing him say he still loved her and wanted her, had rattled her. She'd never fully ever be over Michael, he was the father of her children, the man she'd adored for nearly thirty years.

By late afternoon the next day they were cruising into Sicily, it had been a day of sun and relaxation, nothing but enjoying the Mediterranean Sea view, which was perfect for Grace as she got over Michael's phone call. She didn't tell anyone he'd called, how could she, it was ridiculous, and the humiliation would be excruciating. This one was best kept to herself.

Marlo spent a good portion of the day on the phone to Ruby sorting out the last of the wedding details, booking jets for the guest and stressing out as she so often did when she was under pressure. Grace had been in chats all day with Louise and Ab's, there was always something needing to be discussed, and todays load was heavy, Lou alluding to the fact that her and Jimmy weren't in a great place in their marriage, that she thought maybe he took her for granted and that she seemed to always have to fit in with his busy schedule, never the other way around. Grace got the sense Lou was on this trip to think about how she was going to move forward in her relationship with Jimmy. He was a good man, devoted to Lou, but she could see how being married to a billionaire could have its issues. Jimmy and Ross were absorbed in a life that was so rewarding and yet extremely addictive, they worked all hours of the day and night, they spent a lot of time consumed in their business. Marlo had always just made it work, she and Ross just had an understanding of each other, it was admirable Grace had always thought. Lou and Jimmy might have needed some time apart, this holiday hopefully was good for Lou, because if anything happened to their marriage, Grace dreaded the thought - Louise was like a sister to her.

The next morning Marlo and Lou headed off into Palermo to spend the day shopping, Grace, and Abbey along with the younger girls stayed on the yacht and headed out to a Sicilian beach destination for the day, the Americans close behind them. Their yachts sat just off the beach in the clear blue waters, the girls enjoyed jets ski rides and basked in the sun, even Grace was getting a tan. Life was good today, she'd woken upbeat.

Somehow Grace had found herself on a jet ski with Gus, whilst Ab's flittered around with one of the young American's.

Gus was a tall man, a gentleman, they sat out on the jet ski for some time, face to face, finding common ground chatting about their respective breakups, Gus declaring Grace's was the winner of the worst breakup! She couldn't help but see he was a handsome man, a little weathered from his lifestyle, but handsome all the same.

'I never once strayed out of my marriage vows, Grace,' Gus said as they enjoyed the water, the large jet ski allowing a good space between them. 'It just fizzled out.' He seemed at a loss, a little empty as he spoke of his divorce. 'Mind you, I had every opportunity to do the wrong thing, I just loved my wife so much and I was happy, so why fuck up a good thing!' He was one of those rock stars that all ages loved, but Grace wasn't seeing the rock star, she was seeing the man who was grieving his marriage breakdown. His wife had been the one to pull the initial pin, and Grace had the sneaking suspicion, that just maybe Gus didn't want to call it a day on their marriage.

'Well, that's a testament to you, it's a shame thing's couldn't work out for you and you're wife.' Grace offered supportive words. 'Why couldn't Michael have been like you?' she laughed at the notion. 'Oh well, if we were all the same, how boring would life be.'

317

Loving Grace

'Yeah,' Gus laughed too, 'I mean how utterly boring would it be if we were all stand up guys.' He had a grin that seemed to get how she felt.

They laughed together, it was light-hearted and yet sad at moments too, it left Grace wondering why she hadn't been enough for her husband. Was it him or was it her!

That night they again joined up with the Americans for dinner on shore for a Sicilian feast. Mac seemed rather friendly with Pete's son Brad; they weren't hiding the fact that something was in the air. Grace kept an eye on Bella, but she was more reserved about her affairs, perhaps sneakier. If she liked one of the guys, it wasn't obvious to her mother at this stage, they were young girls on a trip of a lifetime, Grace was happy to let her daughter be, if she had a holiday fling it wouldn't be the worst thing in the world for Bella, but she couldn't see a connection yet, unlike Mac who was marking her territory for all to see, not that Marlo seemed on board with the display of affection at the dinner table.

Later that night they all resumed back on the lady's yacht, they'd formed this little holiday pack, all getting along and enjoying each other's company, the crew making sure they had drinks and were entertained, which wasn't hard, the chatter was endless and the dynamics of the group enjoyable for all.

Marlo, Gus, and Pete had known each other for years, they told of how they had all spent time in LA and how she and Ross had been guests at a big show in London one time. Grace sat there listening to the way the rich and famous lived, private jets, minders, security, PA's, fancy restaurants, VIP all the way, she'd experienced some of it on this trip, with the jets and yachts, she'd noticed people recognised Gus and Pete out and about on shore, it was a whole other world for them, they were rich and famous.

Grace and Gus picked up on their conversation from earlier, he commented on what a well-balanced girl Bella seemed given her parents recently slitting up, so Grace filled him in on some of her daughter's finest bad girl moments.

'Look, no kid is perfect,' Gus agreed with Grace.

'My boys give her a good run for her money too. The middle one is the title holder' she told Gus as they sat out on a deck side by side.

Gus laughed, 'Boys are bad by nature, I think, I think about me at my sons age, and I was terrible,' he laughed. 'I take this one with me to keep an eye on him, his wilder than I ever was.' He pointed over to Jude who was keeping Bella and Abbey entertained with a magic card trick.

'Life is about experiences, isn't it?' Grace asked sipping her cocktail.

'Oh, for sure,' he sighed, 'My life's a little different now, things are changing, I'm getting used to living like a single guy.'

'I get it,' she agreed enjoying the warm night.

319

Loving Grace

They took a walk on the main deck to view the Palermo lights, the marina was bustling so they decided to venture off the yacht down to civilisation and take it in.

'You know my wife never liked travelling... my ex-wife I should say,' Gus said as they walked slowly. 'It was part of the problem I guess; she didn't like coming on tour with all the kids.'

'Did you holiday together, as a family?'

'You mean vacations... rarely... that was a problem too, because I'd finish touring and need time out – like I'm doing here now, and she'd never do it, the farthest I ever got her was to Mexico, now that's saying something,' he sighed.

They wandered up the marina and got a gelato, Gus was recognised again and gladly took a selfie with a fan briefly, 'Sorry Grace, I don't like to say no.'

'Oh, you're fine, go for it,' she said standing watching on.

They headed back to the yacht, Abbey giving Grace a funny look, Marlo raising a brow too, but for Grace, Gus was a man who shared common ground with her, nothing more.

Later on, when they headed off to bed, Abbey pulled Grace aside, 'What's going on with you and the rock star?'

'Nothing at all.'

'Yeah well I see his sneaky eye looking at you,' Abbey said knowing how good it was for her friend to be receiving attention from Gus, Grace needed as much flattering as she could get, she deserved it.

'I don't think so,' smiled Grace hanging onto her suite door in the hallway, wondering if it was true, she hadn't seen a sneaky eye!

'Well, you're mad if you don't jump his fucking bones... I tell you, I would.' Abbey was buzzing from her champagne.

'We talk about our ex's and kids, it's hardly romantic. We do enjoy talking though... a lot,' Grace had a low soft voice, and she thought about how well she and Gus got along.

'Well, I say go for it, but that's just me,' laughed Abbey.

'Good night my beautiful friend, you go and enjoy sleeping in your private suite on your luxury yacht.'

'I know!' Abbey beamed, 'How great is this trip... I will forever love your sister,' Abbey laughed swaggering down the hallway with her best sexy walk to make Grace laugh.

From Sicily to Tavolora in Sardinia, they didn't see the Americans for a whole day, but since the young girls had formed such good friendships with the guys, they were never too far away. Sardinia was stunning, they anchored off the coastline and enjoyed a day and night enjoying life. The young girls went assure with the young Americans which was no surprise, Marlo concerned by this stage, knowing Mac was most certainly involved with Pete's son Brad who she wasn't sure was such a great influence. Drugs were always prevalent in her mind.

Loving Grace

Louise and Abbey were back on the champagne, Marlo and Grace drinking dinner cocktails as the sun went down, in the distance they could see the Americans yacht and Grace couldn't help but wonder what Gus and Pete were doing tonight. Nevertheless, she enjoyed her night hanging with the girls, Louise was tight with the yachts crew by now and asked them to join them for drinks which gave a different dynamic again, it was good to get to know some new people, the people who had been serving to their every need for the past four days.

Grace woke up with a heavy head, she drank too many cocktails with her sister last night and had thoroughly enjoyed herself. Today, not so much as they pulled into the next destination, Spiaggia del Relitto at the top of Sardinia, crystal clear water and beaches to die for. They swam off the yacht and did lunch around the main deck dining table before basking once again in the Mediterranean sun. Boating it to shore for dinner at a beautiful beach village, this time on their own, no Americans.

The following day it was Spiaggia Test del Polpa, quiet and heavenly, paradise on earth as Marlo said at breakfast. She'd spent a lot of time up in the north of Sardinia, her excitement when they anchored was evident. 'This place is where Ross and I came once Hunter King hit the big time... we stayed her with the girls for a month and I think we even thought we might just move here and live here forever,' she explained, 'But then reality kicked in and we went home. And today we're fighting over the boys getting to Tuscany the day before the wedding instead of three days like everyone else.' The boys were Ross, Jimmy, Lewis, Luca, and Kristian. The rest of the family were on a separate Jet from Sydney.

'What! Jimmy promised me he'd be there by the time I got to Tuscany,' Louise looked surprised, she knew Ross and Jimmy were flying over together, what did this mean for her.

'Oh, don't worry, I'm putting my foot down with Ross, it's his daughter's wedding.' Marlo more often than not got her way. For Louise this was a prime example of Jimmy not being on board with her plans, he'd just spring it on her when the time came, and she'd be in Tuscany without him for three days.. Three days prior to the wedding had been the arrival time for everyone, now Jimmy was changing it, and Lou didn't know whether to cry or go with it, her marriage had holes, she knew it, but she loved her husband more than anything and couldn't bring herself to even entertain a life without him.

'So, who's arriving three days before the wedding, can you give me the run down?' Grace needed to confirm.

'Everyone!' Marlo said defiantly, 'There's no room for change.' And that was final from her. 'I know Ross, their business meeting will be in Monaco probably at the casino... Not happening! Nothing is ever enough for him; he always has to have more.'

The deck was quiet all morning whilst Marlo and Louise baked themselves and talked softly to each other about their husbands, Grace and Abbey enjoyed the peace. Then a jet ski

Loving Grace

arrived making its way from the Americans with Bella and Mac on the back, Brad driving it, the young ladies had spent the night over on the American's yacht. Their mothers had thought they were still asleep, in their own beds, here on their yacht.

'Those little shits!' Marlo said in a mood. All the ladies looked on. The girls were in their clothes from last night, all smiles and in good spirits as their aunts and mothers watched them do the jet ski ride of shame just before lunch.

'They're having the time of their life, let em be,' Louise sighed.

'I know, imagine being that age again, I'd kill to be in my twenties right now,' Abbey agreed.

'I hope their using protection,' said Grace as the girls came aboard.

'Oh, my god, do you think they're having sex!' Marlo huffed, the thought was unpleasant and shocking, quite frankly.

'Oh... relax you two, you'll kill their buzz,' Louise scoffed always and forever the cool aunt. Naturally, the girls went straight to their rooms, avoiding the main deck and their mothers.

Later in the day as they swam at a beach, the crystal-clear aqua water off the north of Sardinia, Grace was with Bella away from the others, this was her chance to get the gossip. They sat in the water at armpit depth.

'Good night last night?' she asked innocently... non-judgmental.

'The best.'

'So, do you like Jude?' Grace thought her question was valid.

'Yeah, he's okay.'

'Just make sure you're using condoms.'

'I'm not sleeping with Jude, Mum,' Bella chuckled.

'Oh, that's good,' the relief in her voice was evident.

'I'm sleeping with Paolo their leading deck hand.'

'Paolo!' Grace was instantly horrified. Paolo was in his thirties at least.

'Yes, Paolo... I'm sleeping with Paolo, you asked me the question, I told you.' Bella didn't seem fazed. 'It's sex mum, just sex. I'm having fun.'

'Well, I hope you're using condoms and I'm not sure you're supposed to be sleeping with the crew.'

'I'm not supposed to sleep with our crew. Their crew is fine.'

'Oh, I see.' Grace had to let it slide, she couldn't get into an age disparity with her daughter after Lewis, she'd never win. This was a dream trip for her daughter, she knew it and she wasn't about to be that mother, she'd leave that to Marlo who would be onto Bella as soon as she found out. Besides, as much

325

as Grace wanted to be that mother, she didn't have the mental capacity to be, her life was a disaster, she hated Michael and she missed Lewis, which made her question herself, was it easier to bring all her hurt from Michael over to her misery over Lewis. She thought so.

'Mum. Are you okay?' Bella asked casually. 'Are you dealing with your feelings?'

Grace lifted her sunglasses, 'My feelings! Which feelings are those?' she laughed.

'Dad. Lewis,' Bella felt awkward saying it.

A big sigh and a splash of cool water to her face, 'I'm trying.' It took all her might not to cry, her daughters questions had her emotional, and mostly because she just wanted to feel Lewis, to hug him or to kiss him, it was the weirdest thing ever. Her feelings for the man she'd been married to forever, were the least of her problems today.

'Okay.' Bella left it be at that. She could see her mum was upset. Maybe she shouldn't have mentioned it, her mother was struggling, and she didn't blame her, she'd been dealt some pretty crappy cards lately.

The ladies boat-hopped for dinner, all going over to the Americans yacht, their respective crews tag teaming and working overtime to make the dinner a grand affair. Marlo had been disgruntled all day, she was pissed with Ross and Mac, but now that she had a few champagnes under her belt, she was better. The ladies along with Gus and Pete enjoyed life as their exuberant yachts sat off the coast of Sardinia in a dream location. The company was good, the food was amazing, the champagne was endless and when Gus and Pete got out their guitars and started playing a private set after dinner, it went up a notch, even the younger girls and guys hung around and enjoyed the evening.

Grace and Gus chatted on and off, they now had a friendship, they talked about life and their failed relationships, basically all the bullshit everyone else around them was sick of hearing about.

'Hey, I thought we could go to Maddalena tomorrow, we'll be there for the next few days anyway. We can wander around, get some lunch, do a little shopping,' Gus suggested to Grace.

'I'm sure everyone would love it, run it past Marlo,' said Grace.

'I was thinking just you and me, it'll be less chaotic.' He smiled.

'Sure, that sounds great.'

When the next day came and Grace announced at breakfast she was heading ashore with Gus, she had everyone's attention, 'We're just friends going to do a little sightseeing.'

327

Loving Grace

The younger girls had already left the table, and her audience were thinking this was more than two friends sightseeing.

'I hope you and you're friend have a lovely day together,' Marlo had a hint of a grin on her face.

'Oh yeah, enjoy the day with your new friend,' Abbey teased.

'Gracie!' Louise couldn't hide it, 'This is so cute, this is unbelievable. Who would have thought!'

'Lou! We are only friends,' Grace confirmed again. It didn't matter, the ladies were acting like she was going ashore to lose her virginity or something, making such a big deal about how she looked, what she should wear and say, and do, as they all hovered in her suite as she got ready. By the time Gus picked her up in the smaller boat to take her to shore for the day she was happy to be leaving the yacht and escaping.

Gus was much taller than Grace, he was at least six foot two or three, his long trademark hair was tied back in a ponytail, she noticed his beard was freshly trimmed and he wore torn off blue shorts and a white linen shirt, he'd cleaned up for their day out together. Her soft blonde hair was fluffy and wavey, she wore a white sheer cotton dress shirt and carried a woven hand basket she'd bought on the beach a few days prior. Her white sandals where brand new thanks to the shopping spree in Rome with Marlo, she was looking radiant and feeling good. Grace had nothing to lose, she liked Gus, he was a good man, a gentleman and they had so much in common, he interested her with everything he spoke about, his band life, his kids, where he lived, Gus lived a different life, and she found him a joy to be around.

They wandered the boutiques so quaint and unique; they ate lunch at a seaside restaurant with the mild wind keeping them cool as they sipped on white wine and indulged on the local cuisine under the shade of an umbrella, immersing themselves in conversation and taking in the beautiful Isola Maddelena.

They both took bags of shopping home, they'd enjoyed a market were Gus had bought a handmade drum, and she'd bought some dresses made by the local women, their day had been perfect, and it had changed up yacht life for them, both agreeing the day had been amazing on the walk back to the yachts that were now at the marina just a short distance away.

Grace again had the gang in her room, Marlo standing with Abbey and Lou lazing on her bed as she showed them all her shopping from the day, question after question.

'Was it romantic?' Abbey asked.

'Do you like him?' Louise enquired. One after the other they quizzed her until she again pointed out they were just friends.

'Well, Pete thinks you're good for Gus,' Marlo pointed out.

'How do you know and why?' Grace asked frowned.

Loving Grace

'Pete thinks you're normal... I didn't tell him about how crazy you've been lately,' Marlo said joking. 'Pete thought it was lovely you'd gone ashore with Gus.'

Grace huffed, 'I'm not crazy!' Her sister was loving and everything else, yet she couldn't help reminding Grace that her life was actually fucked, that she was unstable as all hell.

Her day trip in all had helped in a way, just being away in paradise with someone who didn't really know her was good for her. After being with a really good man all day, Grace was angry with Michael and hated both him and Tina more than ever. Lewis felt like a whole different sadness, she felt like she should never had gone there with him, made friends with him, fallen for him, made love to him or wanted him at all. But she had and now she had to get over him... she couldn't erase him from her life even if she wanted to, he was part of her extended family. Grace would just have to get over them all and find a way to move on with her life, and after talking with Gus these past few days about how he was moving on after his marriage breakup, Grace knew she could do it too. The power was hers now.

Two more full days in beautiful Sardinia had past and they were on their last night celebrating the last dinner with the Americans ashore at a beautiful restaurant with lots of laughter and drinking, which seemed to be the pastime that they all looked forward to at the end of a hot day. Young Mac had totally fallen in love with Brad whilst Bella kept her sexual fling with Paolo under wraps for the most part. Grace didn't hound her with questions or ask how it was going, Bella appreciated her mother restraint.

Tonight, was the last night before two days of sailing back to Malta to disembark and then fly to Florence. The night was going out with a bang, they were docked in a marina for the night, and after coming home from the restaurant Marlo was even playing beer pong on the lower deck. Louise and Abbey were a cross between drunk and stoned, Grace had been drinking spritz' s all night and was past her limit too. So, when Gus asked her to go for a walk for a gelato, she obliged with a smile on her face, and they set off along the beach.

Chatting like they were the best of old friends, their friendship had gone from great; to close in such a short time, they'd confided in each other and built a trust that was comfortable. As they strolled back along the somewhat quiet beach, bare feet in the water, Grace had a short cloth dress on and no shoes, and Gus shorts and a T shirt, the night was sticky and balmy, so the stroll in the water cooled them down. Stopping halfway to chat and sat in the shallows of the water, Grace thought it was the most peaceful time in her life she'd had in such a very long time. She could see the stars shining brightly, the moon was big, Sardinia was breathtaking, and she'd loved her time there. The lights in the distant background flickered on the water, the marina ahead looked lovely with all the yacht lights. The soft waves rolled into their legs with a gentle calmness as they sat enjoying each other's company without pressure and expectations. Their shoulders nudged each other softly as they chatted and relaxed, there was most definitely chemistry, something a little more than friendship and they both felt it. Over the past few days, they'd become a little more expressional with their hands, a touch to the shoulder, a hug here and there, it was nice to have someone who understood where you were at in life.

'Grace, can I kiss you?' Gus had wanted to ask her for days, but he didn't want to ruin what they had, a friendship.

Her smile was easy, she knew it was coming, 'I'd like that,' she said looking up into his eyes, his hair pulled back behind his ears, his gentle face smiling back at hers as he leaned down into her.

Gus was an attractive man, a sexy rugged man who polished up well he when wanted to, his persona was huge, and now they were rolling around in the shallows of one of the most romantic beaches in the world. Grace's dress up around her waist, her underwear up in the sand along with Gus's sorts and underwear, his T shirt wet and hanging over her as they kissed amongst the soft rolling waves. It was romantic and sensual, but without depth or commitment. It was sex and Grace had nothing to lose.

She was sitting over him, her legs wrapped around his waist, she drew him in closer, pushing herself up towards his large manhood, ready and waiting for her as she let him sink inside her, the water rolling to them under the romantic moonlight. Grace didn't think, she just did what felt right, she rolled her hips into meet Gus again and again. Clinging to his shoulders she gave him her all. He was a large man, hence the large cock! She was being pushed to her limits as far as cock and vaginas were concerned, she let herself take all of him, Gus held her face to his, they kissed passionately, a bit of tongue which she usually didn't like, however Gus was very good at it. They let the beautiful sea take them away to a place that only they existed in, the water giving its own rhythm to their sexual escapade. For Grace this was different, it was sex without feelings, like when she'd been a teenage girl exploring her sexuality and learning how to pleasure herself as well as a man. Gus was like a special friend, and it felt right, she felt safe. At fifty she knew the road, and well. As she felt her insides swirl with heated fury, rubbing herself hard over Gus with a tightness that he could feel, his size and girth satisfying her efforts. His big hands roaming her back and body. He held her breast beneath her wet dress and griped her with a tense but erotic hand, she pulled her own dress up so he could suck at her nipple, she needed him to suck her strong and hard. Gus licking her nipple, nipping with pulling motions, driving her wild, she lifted from him and his big fingers explored her moist folds in the shallow sea, fingering her with swirls, stretching her wider as he sucked and pulled at her nipples. The wet dress was hanging around her neck, Grace falling back over Gus and engulfing his cock, rubbing herself vigorously over him, pushing him to the edge as she held Gus' shoulders and ground down hard over him as she reached her peak. He squeezed at her arse cheeks, and she lifted from him, he came to her folds, now rubbing

333

himself to her outer folds, their cum washing away in the sea, he never presumed he could cum inside her.

Walking back aboard the yacht to find Marlo asleep was a sigh of relief for Grace, her dress and hair wet, so were Gus's clothing and hair, they'd had amazing sex on this fine night under the moonlight in Sardinia.

'You're all wet!' Bella pointed out as Pete stopped playing his guitar and all eyes turned to Grace and Gus.

'Have you seen that beach,' Gus smiled, 'We went for a swim, you guys are all missing out.' He made out like they'd been swimming, and everyone seemed to believe it. It wasn't until a little while later when Grace and Abbey headed off to bed that Abbey questioned her.

'You had sea sex with him, didn't you?' scoffed Abbey.

'Yes!' Grace laughed quietly in the hallway.

'Oh, my god, you are on fire, I'm so jealous of your sex life right now, you are literally living out my sex dreams left right and center. First Lewis, now Gus.'

Grace lay in bed that night wondering what Lewis was doing. Had he had sex with someone else yet because she kind of had the guilts, her emotions were getting the best of her, warm tears rolled into her hair as she laid. Gus had been unexpected tonight, he'd been sweet and fun, and she'd enjoyed her time with him, she'd needed the sexual release, but she couldn't stop thinking about Lewis.

Chapter Eighteen

The yacht sailed slowly back down to Malta, the ladies spent the entire day and a half on the decks chilling out and enjoying the down time. The next time they would see the Americans would be perhaps at the marina in Valletta harbour as they disembarked, and only if the timing was right. As they basked in the sun relishing their final day, the conversations were inclusive of young and older.

'What about Paolo,' Louise sighed to Bella who hadn't been over chatty. 'Are you keeping in contact with him?' By this stage, everyone was in the know on Bella and Paolo.

Bella took a deep breath in and looked at her aunt, 'Absolutely not... I'm off men, their pointless.'

The comment took the ladies by surprise, particularly her mother.

'Oh, that's a shame,' Marlo said who had kept her opinion to herself to this point, she didn't like the idea of Bella seeing a crew member from the other yacht... you didn't mess around with the crew, it was a rule for the most part.

'It's no shame, I don't need a man to ruin my life. I just need sex every now and then,' Bella sounded serious and like someone twice her age.

'Good for you!' Louise said making a few eyebrows raise, but Bella and Lou had that kind of relationship, Lou had always been the fun aunt.

This thing with Bella was just another thing for Grace to take on board her very own guilt train, now Bella was a man hater! Until recently, she'd had the best example of a marriage and a stable home, and a good father figure. Grace had done her best to be the best mother she possibly could and that included a shining example of marriage, or so she thought. The guilt felt so heavy it was sometimes suffocating, even though she wasn't the perpetrator of the guilt, being the mother felt like guilt by association, especially when it came to Bella. Her daughter being a man hater was on Grace's mind until they reached Malta.

Standing at the marina after ten days of being pampered and seeing the most desirable destinations in the Med, Grace hugged Gus goodbye, he'd purposely hung around to see Grace. Their friendship was nothing more than a nice friendship that had gone to a sexual level... Just once. They promised to keep in touch and to talk soon, but Grace really doubted she would. He was a great man, and he let out hints of her coming to visit him in L.A. or them meeting up in some exotic place to see each other again, but Grace had her plate full, she'd agreed it was a great idea because she was a nice person, not because she necessarily thought there was anything between her and Gus. Maybe if the timing had been better, she'd pursue him, he was such a good man, and she'd certainly miss him.

The jet to Florence was a buzz with wedding talk, Bella coming out of her shell a little, over her man hating bad mood. Marlo had stopped stressing and was now on the phone to Paulette back in Australia, happy and content that all the wedding plans had been finalised. Mac and Louise were telling Abbey, Bella, and Grace all about the forty-bedroom Tuscan estate they'd never seen, it sounded surreal, and knowing Marlo and Ross it would be in full swing ready for the wedding guests to arrive. All the ladies were staying in the main house with the rest of the family, Grace was struggling to imagine the size of the property set out on 1000 hectares with three other complexes with their own pools and facilities. The scale of the estate was getting bigger and bigger with every conversation had. Grace's anxiety was escalating, seeing Lewis was on her mind, staying in the main house with him was even more stressful.

Arriving in Florence was beautiful, they got there in time to catch an early dinner at their hotel, which was one of the finest hotels filled with old antique furniture. Marlo had a private concierge at her beck and call everywhere she went all over the world; it was just how the rich rolled apparently.

337

Loving Grace

Marlo's version of a girl's trip left nothing to the imagination and at times it blew their minds.

All the ladies loved the Italian hospitality, particularly the two waiters who fussed over their every need at dinner and then promptly asked Abbey, Grace, Marlo, and Louise if they could accompany them out for drinks at a nearby café. Flattered as the men were considerably younger, heavenly to look at and charming to no end.

'They're players,' Mac huffed once the table was clear of the waiters, immediately taking the shine off what had been a flattering moment for all the older women.

'Let us have our moment,' laughed Louse.

'Yeah, it's not every day younger men want to take us out,' Abbey said.

'Maybe it's my mum, younger men seem to like her,' Bella winked at Grace, she had no idea that older men liked her mother too... Rock stars in fact. Grace had only told Abbey and Louise about Gus, she didn't see the need for it to go any further, some things were better kept private.

'It's her single scent,' Louise smiled.

'I'm heading up to bed, you guys go and enjoy the young Italian men, I'm done for,' Grace said smiling.

'Oh Mum, come with us,' Bella gave her mother an apologetic smile.

'Come on Grace, you only live once.' Even Marlo was wooing her out on the town. 'We are in one of my favourite cities. This is still your birthday trip.'

'We won't take no for an answer.' Abbey touched Grace's hand on the table.

'Grace, please!' Louise gave her a sad look begging her to come, so how cold she refuse.

The Firenze air was intoxicating, the ladies enjoyed drinks at the nearby piazza and yes the young Italian waiters did catch up to them after their shift had finished. Florence was fashionable, stylish and a hive of activity late into the night. Marlo was relaxed like Grace had never seen her before, Italy was definitely her place, she had no idea her sister spoke such good Italian until this trip, tonight she was chatting nonstop to the young waiters who'd join them. Grace looked around the table, all the women were glowing, Bella and Mac smiling and laughing more than they had all trip at the antics of Abbey and Louise playing up to the younger men. Even Marlo was flirting, conversing in Italian like she was a native which was very impressive. This had really been a great time in their lives, Bella and Grace fresh out of relationships big and small. Louise was her gorgeous bubbly self, however Grace felt Louise was on the verge of something big in her life. If her brother Jimmy was going to let Louise slip through his fingers after all these years of a wonderful marriage, all because he was so caught up in himself, Grace would be terribly disappointed... As soon as she saw her brother, she'd be telling him he needed to fight for

Loving Grace

Louise, Grace wasn't just letting this fall apart in front of her eyes, she loved both too much.

It was one of those nights that snuck up on you, the kind that wasn't planned and yet turned out to be outrageous and fun. A night that Grace didn't originally want to partake in, but then ended having the best time. It was just before midnight when they moved from the nearby piazza café with some random girls Mac and Bella had befriended, to somewhere very unexpected. Of all places in Italy, they end up in an Irish pub, Abbey winning a beer drinking competition and Louise dancing on the bar with Bella while Grace and Marlo chatted to two cute young English fashion students at the bar with Mac... Or more so, for Mac. Marlo sat crossed legged up on the bar in her Gucci dress and shoes with a Guinness in hand. They were all letting their hair down on this trip, Abbey and Louise rekindling their teenage relationship with weed, Marlo letting loose, the young girls having the time of their lives, and Grace making a special friend.

When the cars arrived mid-morning to take them to the estate, a one hour and twenty-minute drive away, all the ladies had sunglasses on, Marlo wore a big, brimmed hat, Mac commenting it was a disguise rather than a fashion statement after her mother's outstanding efforts last night. Marlo may have been the eldest by ten years, but she definitely received the most attention from the Italian men.

Louise, Grace, and Abbey went in the first Mercedes SUV, with Marlo, and the younger girls in the second, and a third Mercedes van for the luggage.

'Have you had a good time Grace' Louise asked once they were buckled in.

'Absolutely. The best time ever!' she sighed relaxing and pleased she had the next hour and a bit to gather herself before seeing everyone at the estate. 'It might take me all day and night to recover from last night, but it was worth it,' she managed to smile amidst her hangover.

'Are you worried about seeing Lewis today?' Abbey asked knowing too well Grace was more than worried, she was fretting. Louise looked at Grace, nobody had spoken about him all trip, not even Marlo, they all knew she'd taken the breakup hard. And it wasn't just Lewis she was trying to move past, it was the Michael scandal, all the lies, pain and hurt he'd inflicted on her and the kids. Not to mention the humiliation of it all that she was slowly getting over.

Grace looked at Louise, 'Did I hear that Immy is coming to the wedding?' Immy was one of Lewis' ex-wives. Bella had told her after Mac had mentioned it.

'I don't know about that,' Louise sighed, she hadn't heard anything. 'Ruby and Immy were good friends, so it's possible.'

'I hear she lives in Italy now, apparently he's bringing her to the wedding.' Grace looked at Abbey, 'Lewis' second wife... He

341

cheated on her.' She pointed out, it made her feel better that he was a floored man.

All of them found it odd, but wouldn't put it past him, he was rarely without a hot woman at his side.

'Don't let it get to you if he does bring her, or someone else,' Louise said softly knowing there was a good chance he'd bring a wedding date.

Grace couldn't help her mind racing, maybe Immy still loved Lewis, maybe she was still the most gorgeous looking woman on earth, and maybe Lewis still loved Immy! It didn't matter anyway, Grace couldn't accept he'd kept the Bree and the baby information from her, how could she forgive that! He was clearly over her now, if he was bringing Immy to the wedding.

'Have you heard from Jimmy?' Grace asked her sister-in-law.

'Yeah,' she paused uncomfortably, 'He's calling me later, he was busy this morning.' Louise didn't make a deal of it, although Grace could see she was hurting, and her brother was to blame. The entire trip Louise had been doing everything to keep her head above water. As always she'd been the life of the party, but her eyes didn't lie, and Grace was concerned.

'I'm sorry my brother is being such a shit right now.' Grace couldn't keep it in.

'It's okay, this isn't our first rodeo Grace,' Louise's eyes sparkled.

Grace nodded and smiled like she understood. But if she and Michael could disintegrate, anyone could. Her brother wasn't the perfect man she'd always imagined him to be... *Was anyone perfect?* The fact that Jimmy was a billionaire made Grace wonder if he'd been faithful to Louise all these years, having so much money sometimes made people think they could do and get away with anything, because basically they could. She'd seen it with her own eyes, Ross making Kristian's bad behaviour just vanish, without any consequences, and making her driving charges disappear after she hit Michael's car with hers. But then it went both way she knew, Marlo and Louise had access to a lot of money too, they could easily be hiding secrets of their own and nobody would ever know. It was then that Grace decided to stay in her own lane and keep out of her brother's marriage.

'Did I mention I got my period this morning!' Abbey said out of the blue. 'I'm over it, I'm too old for this shit every month. When is it going to stop, I'm having hot flashes!'

'Isn't it bizarre how we get a period all of our lives, and then we get fucking menopause, how wrong is that!' Louise sympathised with Abbey while Grace thought about her own period and how she hadn't had one for weeks... months... two months in fact. She'd never not had her period, not for one single month, she was perimenopausal, apparently.

343

Loving Grace

'You can't get pregnant in the change of life can you?' she asked flippantly.

'The change of life... What is this the fucking sixties!' Louise laughed.

'Can you get pregnant or not?' Grace took a breath and held it in.

'Yes the fuck you can,' Louise scoffed. 'My friend Wendy, fifty-two years old.'

'What happened!' Grace gushed.

'She got pregnant to her seventy-year-old husband.' Louise looked mortified, disgusted.

'Oh, please!,' Abbey huffed in horror. 'Women are born to be punished, I'm sure of it. You'd think that by fifty we could have sex and not worry about that bullshit, wouldn't you?'

'What did Wendy do with the baby?' asked Grace.

'She gave birth to it, and she now has a six-year-old and a twenty-six-year-old,' Louise scoffed with laughter.

'That's so crappy. That would be my worst nightmare.' Abbey shook her head.

'Imagine we could have sex like men!' Louise chuckled, 'The world is so lopped sided.'

'I missed my last period!' Grace announced matter of fact as they sat in the back of the SUV. Abbey and Louise just looked at her. 'I told you my boobs were hurting when we got on the yacht, and I thought it was because I was riding the jet ski.' Grace was in a panic. They went through all the dates and worked out Grace could well be pregnant, to Lewis, which sent them all into a quiet tailspin. Louise was in charge of getting a pregnancy test, Abbey calling her gynecologist friend from university to find out about falling pregnant when perimenopausal.

Anything anyone had said about the estate could not have prepared Grace, Abbey, and Bella for the sheer exuberance and size of what was going on here. As they drove along the driveway which literally went forever along the ridge of the hilltops, all you could see for miles was olive trees and vineyards. Then as they came down and around the hillside, the sprawling estate sat nestled eloquently into its surroundings. It was four stories high and bigger than any home Grace had ever seen, beautiful too! To the far left down the hill was a cluster of smaller villa type homes, more over to the right with rows of vines and manicured gardens distancing them from the main palatial home that was Marlo and Ross's estate. Gob smacked was nowhere near what any of them were experiencing. This was an outlandish extravagance at its finest. A row of luxurious cars lined the parking area as they pulled up at the front of the home.

A team of Italian staff met Marlo and the ladies in the grand foyer. Grace looking up at the painted ceilings and the art, there was so much to look at.

345

Loving Grace

'Grace, you're near me darling,' Marlo said smiling at her sister as the others all left with their respective house staff.

Still in awe of her surroundings, Grace was trying to come to grips with the car ride here. Her stress of seeing Lewis had diminished, it was now the least of her problems, then she thought about Luca having a baby and it was too much, the thought was more than her head could handle. As Marlo personally took Grace to her room, which turned out to be a palatial suite, Grace felt sick. Being pregnant would be the cherry on top of her fucked up year from hell.

'Are you alright Grace?' Marlo questioned as her sister stood in the middle of the magnificent room, looking out the large window over the most spectacular view.

'Yes,' she turned to Marlo, 'I need a shower and maybe a sleep, that's all.'

'Me too, I'm still hungover. Well, Manuella will look after all your needs,' Marlo looked curiously at her sister, 'Get some sleep because we've got a big dinner planned for tonight, everyone is going to be here.' A warning that if she was feeling weird about seeing Lewis, she only had the day to get over it.

Sitting on the edge of the huge dark timber framed bed with soft white linen, embroidery on the slips, Grace looked out the big window and doors to the terrace it led out to. Suddenly feeling so far from home and somewhat home sick even though she'd be with all her kids tonight at dinner, she couldn't keep her anxicty attack at bay a second longer. Her teeth tingled as she took deep breaths. Part of her thought it was ridiculous and part of her knew it was inevitable, one woman could only fight for so long, trying to constantly act normal had been an effort to say the least and now being here at the estate, which was so big and so unexpected, she felt like she was drowning. Knowing that Lewis was here or going to be here at some point today had her hyperventilating. He'd lied to her, and he hadn't tried to win her back, which in her mind was his way of getting out while he could. She'd spent the whole trip wondering if she'd overreacted to his with-holding of information, maybe she had, maybe she hadn't. Pride simply wouldn't allow her to want Lewis openly, and now with this latest instalment of self-inflicted drama, Grace was hoping she could stay clear away from him while there were here in Italy.

The afternoon had been busy with people arriving and being delegated to their rooms. The main house was for all Ruby's family, the Hunter's, the King's, and associates. Then the two complexes of guest houses were for the grooms family and their combined friends along with a select few of Ross and Marlo's friends. In total the estate had forty odd bedrooms, mind-blowing, the main house had twenty alone.

Late in the afternoon Grace and Abbey had gone for a long walk taking in the surrounding grounds as well as the breathtaking home in which they were guests for the next week.

Loving Grace

Dinner was off the charts, not only was it an over-the-top outdoor dinner party, but it was sweltering hot and in Grace's own head, she wasn't coping well with the heat, because maybe she was pregnant! Tuscany seemed to be super-hot compared to all the other hot places they had been in the past two weeks. Guests were still arriving and as Abbey and Grace made their way over to the pre-dinner drinks gathering at the big pergola by the swimming pool. Grace saw Shiv for the first time, they smiled to each other courteously, and then everyone watched as a helicopter made its landing far enough away to not disrupt the long and large dinner table set for a king's dinners. On board was Ross, Jimmy, Lewis, Luca, and Kristian, they'd made it by the skin of their teeth. Marlo and Louise were fretting all afternoon, unable to get hold of their husbands with no ETA. Well now they were all here, and it was time for Grace to face up to her fears with Lewis, she'd talked with Abbey and decided she needed to put on her bravest face and act like nothing had ever happened between them, like she was not possibly pregnant to her younger ex-lover. Grace was cool as a cucumber on the outside but a complete mess on the inside. Grace caught Shiv looking at her as the men all ran towards them, it was like a James Bond movie. Grace wasn't sure what Shiv's take on things was now, nor did she care anymore. No doubt Shiv was relieved by the demise of her and Lewis. It was no secret; Shiv had been the hardest campaigner against them.

Kristian was Grace's faithful, he went straight to his mother, hugging her like he hadn't seen her for months. Grace hugging him back, pulling on all her strength not to cry, she held her sons face and looked up into his handsome eyes, he looked well, as handsome as ever. 'I've missed you,' she said hugging him in.

'Me too. I love you mum,' he wrapped his arms tightly around her.

'Everything alright?' the words pained her, but she had to ask.

'Yeah!'

'I love you sweetheart; I've missed you so much.' And then before she could finish analysing Kristian, getting his vibe, she had Luca waiting for his turn. 'Oh, my gosh. My other sweetheart,' Grace smiled, there was no time for tears now hugging her eldest son who she could tell was in a good place. His posture, the way he smiled at her, Luca was great, which gave her some relief.

It seemed like there were so many people and such a big fan fair that Grace didn't even get to say hi to Lewis, not that she was looking for him. Whilst she was enjoying a good old catch-up with Jag who'd arrived earlier in the day, with his wife, Bella came and stood very close to her mother. Everyone was catching up and chatting, it was lovely, Bella stuck close to her mother,

'What's going on with you?' Grace rubbed her daughters hand in hers. But Bella just looked at her with big eyes, teary eyes. 'What?'

Loving Grace

'Why is there a pregnancy test in your bathroom?' Bella asked so nobody else could hear.

Grace was stunned, 'Why were you in my bathroom?' she said too fast.

'Mum!' The frown on her face was near tears. 'Is it for you?' The sheer bewilderment on Bella's face was too much to comprehend. Louise had earlier whispered in Grace's ear that the tests had arrived, and that she'd put them in her bathroom, and now somehow Bella had been into her bathroom and discovered them. It was the day that just kept on giving.

'It's not what you think,' Grace said shaking her head like there'd been a misunderstanding.

'Well, what is it then?'

'Not now Bella,' she tried to stall her, to appease her. 'We can talk later.'

'Are you pregnant?' but she wasn't appeased.

Grace took a deep breath in and held it, 'Bella!' she gushed, her daughter glared at her like she'd just sacrificed a sibling, then she walked off emotionally teetering. Grace couldn't say the tests were for anyone else, who would she blame - Abbey! It was ridiculous and Bella would see right through her. In a bid to not cause a scene and hold it together, Grace had to let her daughter go. Turning around she saw Louise and Abbey. 'Why did you leave the tests in my bathroom, and how many did you get?' she blurted out to Louise. 'Bella saw them!'

'I got three because you know, they say three is good luck,' Louise mumbled with a slur, she and Abbey had hit the champers hard.

'Good luck!' gasped Grace, 'How?'

'Three negatives would be good right?' Louise was floundering.

'Fuck. My daughter knows I could be pregnant. This is not good.' Grace was about to crumble when Lewis appeared at her side, she stopped breathing.

'Hello,' he smiled to all three of the ladies, his eyes stopping at Grace.

'Lewis, hi!' Abbey said surprised.

'Well, Hello,' Louise scoffed and then walked off into the crowd.

'I'll be at the bar,' Abbey followed Louise, leaving Grace and Lewis together.

Smiling with his own nerves, not sure of his reception, 'How'd the trip go?'

'Great. It was great,' smiling back for one second before tensing her shoulders and taking a deep breath, holding it in again as she let herself look up into his eyes. She'd missed him so much.

'You look tanned and healthy,' he paused, 'It's good to see you.' And just like that he was done with her, their conversation was over. Lewis had nothing else to say to her, nothing whatsoever. Grace stood there, gasping for air, wishing she could tell him how much she'd missed him, but he was walking away. He looked utterly handsome in his white linen shirt; his dark skin and eyes had mesmerised her for the few seconds she'd had his attention. Standing there unsure of whether she was going to cry or not, Grace knew she'd made a huge mistake breaking up with Lewis. Just another one to add to her list. Mistakes seemed to be piling up in her life. In that moment she didn't know where to look or go, she could see Bella with Mac in the distance talking with her brothers and cousins, Abbey at the bar in conversation with Lousie and Jimmy, Marlo hugging Lewis with one of her comforting hugs, whispering something in his ear. And where was Immy, was she here yet, Grace looked around getting herself together wondering how she was going to get through dinner let alone the next week. Walking over to the edge of the gathering and standing at one end of the large pool overlooking the valley below as the sun was disappearing for the day.

'It's all good and well to have all this, but all I ever wanted for any of them was good health and happiness,' Ed stood beside Grace, he'd seen her wander off from Lewis in a daze.

Her smile was warm and filled with emotion, 'I've never seen anything quite so over the top.' She smiled.

'My son and your sister make over the top seem normal... I'm even getting used to it,' Ed chuckled.

'At least they share their good fortune.'

'That they certainly do my dear,' Ed paused. 'If you want something in this world Gracie, you've got to have the balls and go get it, put yourself on the line, it's the only way.'

Turning to Ed she wondered if he had seen her and Lewis and the devastation on her face when he'd walked away from her, 'What if you don't have the balls to go for it.'

'Then you'll never know will you.' They were on the same page.

Chapter Nineteen

Bella had completely ignored Grace the entire night, keeping her distance, whether it was shock or disappointment she had to let her daughter be, and pick things up with her tomorrow. As for Lewis and Immy, she was nowhere to be seen, and he kept away from Grace too. Maybe the Immy rumour was just that, all Chinese whispers, or maybe she was arriving tomorrow. Thank God for Abbey being here, being single at these kind of gatherings wasn't easy, she couldn't have imagined being there without Abbey.

Grace made it back to her bedroom with Abbey in tow before midnight, they talked about the morning being the best time to take the pregnancy test, and Abbey agreed to be back first thing, so Grace wasn't alone when she took the damn test.

'If the first one is positive, we'll take the second, and then the third. If it's negative first up, we know you're not pregnant. How does that sound for a plan?' Abbey was tipsy.

'Should I just not do all three straight up?' Grace asked as they stood outside her door in the hall whispering.

'Oh god no, it's too confusing,' gushed Abbey.

'Really, how?'

'I don't know, let's just deal with one test at a time,' Abbey said kissing Grace goodnight and going off down the hall, 'I love you Grace. See you in the morning.'

Up unusually early, Grace had had a very interrupted sleep, and her body clock was out big time, so she dressed and went for a walk through the large home and then out by the pool and sat on a small table and chair taking in the morning glory, what a view. Every time her life had an upheaval, she felt like she was emotionally back at square one, this pregnancy thing had her unsure of everything. Even talking with Kristian last night, she was numb to the fact that her troubled middle son had been involved in yet another altercation with his father. Luca had told her that Michael and Tina were back together again, it had jabbed at Grace's heart just as viciously as it had the very first time. Michael had again tried to rally his sons just before they flew out to the wedding to mend bridges, but again he failed, and Luca ended up pulling Kristian away before things got too out of hand. Grace needed to talk to Kristian in depth about this last night but couldn't focus enough or didn't have the energy to get into anything deep. Luca had given her a blow-by-blow account of the incident and as much as she knew Kristian was wrong, a little part of her loved that he'd tried to thump his father... Again, and at least this time the police weren't involved.

'You're being too hard on yourself!' Ed appeared from a lower terrace, he'd been out for his morning stroll and spotted Grace, she looked like she had the weight of the world on her shoulders.

'Oh, Ed! You scared me.' Putting her hand to her chest.

'Can I join you?'

'Of course.' He reminded her of her father so much. 'I couldn't sleep.'

'Ross has offered Shiv and me to move here so we can get old far away from him,' Ed laughed, 'The odd thing is I would love to get old here in this serenity and beauty.'

'I'm thinking I might move here too, just so I can be far away from everybody... except you of course,' she smiled with a joked.

'It might just be you and I; Shiv would never move here. She'll be too far away to meddle in other people's lives.'

'Shiv isn't a meddler.' Grace thought that was a strange thing for Ed to say, he never spoke like that.

He looked at her, 'She meddled in your affairs.'

'You mean Lewis and I?' dare she say his name.

'I hope her opinion didn't persuade you to back away from my grandson,' Ed never really got into personal things, this was a rare exception for him.

'Actually, it was his behaviour, his lies that made me back away,' she huffed a little.

'You sure?' Ed looked her right in the eyes like he knew otherwise. 'Because for a minute there Gracie, I saw you the happiest I've ever seen you in your whole entire life.'

'Oh, well that was only for a week or two that I felt that happiness, I can assure you,' Grace was so matter of fact.

'Just be happy Gracie girl, life is too short not to be. I don't need to tell you that.' He reached out and put his hand gently over hers. She couldn't speak, Ed's words had touched her.

'Okay. Is your bladder full?' Abbey stood in the bathroom. 'Is it the first pee of the day?'

'I think so,' Grace pulled a face.

'Pee on this then,' she handed her friend the first stick.

'If I'm pregnant, I've made a plan,' Grace was beyond nervous. 'Well, I've got two plans. One is that I would stay here in Italy in one of these rooms here, nobody would care I'm sure. And I'd have the baby on my own.'

Abbey's eyes were wide open, she laughed knowing her friend was joking. 'But the plan that I think is more me, is that

Loving Grace

I'd not have the baby, I'd move out of my apartment, because I can't be around Lewis.' She still had the stick out in front of her. 'I can't even look at him without feeling sad, and I've got the whole week ahead of me, and it hurts so much,' Grace began to cry. 'And Michael and Tina are back together, and I don't have Lewis!' her voice heightened. 'He's ex-wife will probably show up today looking all gorgeous and young and super model hot and they'll be back together.' She was barely breathing. 'And I'll probably be pregnant at fifty and fucked.'

'Grace!' Abbey had to raise her voice; she was on a mad rant that was getting her nowhere but upset.

A nock at the door alarmed them both.

'It's me,' whispered Louise from the door as she came into Grace's room and then into the bathroom. 'What's the verdict?' She came in hoping for good news.

'Oh, my god. I can't do this,' Grace gasped stepping back to the wall, over dramatizing things.

'She's mid meltdown,' Abbey told Lou who could see things weren't going well. 'Michael is back with Tina and Lewis's ex is arriving today.'

'I don't know if she's coming or not,' Grace shouted turning in a circle on the spot, 'My life is a totally fucked!' she wasn't breathing, 'Am I supposed to tell him if I am pregnant?' then she dropped to the floor with a thud.

Waking up in bed to a handsome doctor sitting at her side with a huge headache, Bella at her other side, with Abbey, Marlo and Louise all standing at the end of her bed.

'Hello Grace,' said the nice doctor at her side in an alluring Italian accent, 'My name is Dr Mondello.' His smile immediately medicating her, seductive brown eyes mending sore head, he was bellissimo!

'Hello,' she sighed, a little confused.

'You hit your head when you fainted, we called a doctor when you wouldn't wake up,' Abbey stepped forward.

The doctor stood from the bed. 'I think you might have a concussion; you should rest for the day and try not to worry yourself too much. Your vital signs are all okay.' He had a permanent grin, gentle, friendly. 'The ladies will take care of you I'm sure, you need plenty of sleep to rest your brain.'

Marlo came to the bedside, 'Thank you Doctor Mondello for coming so fast. We'll keep an eye on her. I'll call you if we need you again.'

'Thank you,' Grace said, she wasn't completely sure what she was thankful for, but she said it anyway.

The doctor looked at Marlo and walked to the door with her, 'When your sister is ready, take the test, I'm a phone call away if you need me.' They both left the room and Marlo shut the door behind herself, leaving Grace with Abbey, Bella, and Louise.

Loving Grace

'What happened?' Grace asked.

'You scared the life out of us,' Louise said trying not to sound resentful, even though she'd literally thought Grace had died from a heart attack right there on the bathroom floor.

'Mum!' Bella was upset, she was right there on the bed with teary eyes, 'We were so worried.'

'I'm fine sweetheart,' Grace could feel the pounding in her head, she could feel the very spot she'd hit it, at the back, her vision wasn't clear, and she was so very tired.

Abbey and Louise had told Marlo and Bella about how worked up Grace had herself in the moments before she passed out, Bella asked if it was anything to do with the pregnancy test she'd seen in her mother's bathroom the night before, and they'd hesitated and then told her yes. Of course, this was all a big surprise for Marlo, and she had freaked out with Grace unconscious on the floor.

'Can we keep this quiet; I don't want your brothers thinking something is wrong with me.' Grace felt stupid, she was embarrassed, and she didn't want any of it getting back to her boys or Lewis. Marlo would be the one she needed to swear to secrecy.

'It's okay, we've already sworn each other to secrecy,' Louise said giving Grace some ease.

It was half an hour later and the ladies were still all in Grace's room. Bella was the most attentive, she hated seeing her mother unwell again. She understood just how hard the past few months had been for her mother, and she was hurting too, her father and Tina had turned all their worlds upside down. Bella didn't begrudge her mother's relationship with Lewis by any means, it just seem to happen so fast and accepting her mother was with another man was hard... whilst it lasted anyway. Now her concern was that her mother was having a baby, what did it mean for them all... No wonder her mother had passed out!

Marlo returned to the room, 'Grace, are you ready to take the pregnancy test?' she said without judgment. 'Doctor Mondello will come back if the test is positive to confirm with a blood test.'

The thought of it was enough for all the life to leave Grace's body, she was exhausted, 'Ab's will you stay with me while I do it?' as much as she loved these women, she wanted a little privacy, only Abbey could stay. The one person who never turned on her, or judged her, or passed comment on her decisions or actions.

'Of course,' smiled her trusted friend, 'I'll let you know how it goes,' she told the others, who all seemed to look a little insulted that Grace didn't want them around. And once they'd all left except for Abbey, Grace took a deep breath in, and then exhaled, looking at her lifelong friend. She didn't have to say a word, Abbey just knew how Grace was feeling and how the whole pregnancy thing was affecting her.

Loving Grace

'Go pee on that stick, you're killing me,' Abbey said humorously, but Grace didn't move an inch. 'The sooner you know, the sooner you can make a decision.' She went to the bedside. 'I know you're overwhelmed right now, but this is important. I know you're scared; I would be too.'

'This is the last thing I thought I'd be dealing with at fifty. A broken heart and a baby.' Grace felt like her mental health had taken ten steps backwards this past day. 'I'm really struggling with getting my head around it all,' she said crying. 'Michael was the love of my life and now he feels like a stranger to me... I can get over Lewis, I have to. I will,' a hint of positivity came through in her voice. 'But how do I go to a doctor at fifty and ask for an abortion?'

'Oh, Grace,' Abbey said softly. 'You will be okay no matter what the stick says.' Referring to the stick bought a smile to Grace's face. 'If the stick says you are pregnant, I will be with you all the way, I won't let you do this alone.' Now her eyes were misty. The moment of silence was Grace getting the courage to get out of bed, she needed to do this, and she needed to do it now. 'I'll do everything for you, except pee on the stick,' joked Abbey.

'Okay,' Grace agreed shuffling off to the bathroom, while Abbey sat on the bed waiting. Five minutes went by. 'Can you come look at the stick?' Grace poked her head out the door showing no emotion whatsoever.

Abbey jumped up and went straight in. She looked closely at the stick sitting on the benchtop. 'One line!' she looked at Grace, 'Maybe we should do another test to be sure.'

'I don't have any pee left,' Grace gasped holding her head, 'One line is negative. I'm not pregnant. Right?' It was the biggest relief of her life.

'You're not pregnant according to the stick and the stick is ninety nine percent correct,' Abbey wanted to jump up and down. 'You're not pregnant.'

'Oh, sweet god! this is the best news of my life,' Grace cried, she was tired and so very relieved.

'I hate to sound old, but you need to use protection when you screw hot guys Grace King,' a joke was Abbeys way of expressing her own relief. God only knows what she would have done if Grace had been pregnant at fifty. It wasn't unheard of, but it felt so foreign.

'Oh, don't worry. I'm never having sex again. I'm done,' Grace hugged her friend.

'I think you should sleep now. I'll tell the others the good news,' Abbey made sure she got into bed okay. 'Can I get you a tea.'

'No. I'm good, I'll try to sleep.' Grace was all smiles, the relief in not being pregnant was huge, not only could her life go on, but she could now enjoy her nieces wedding and the time with her family and friends.

Loving Grace

Whilst Grace slept, there was lunch time drama down under the pergola. The morning episode and news of a possible pregnancy had left her big sister Marlo emotional and unsettled, she'd gone straight to Ruby and asked about Immy and when she was arriving... She was coming, she was already on the estate. Bella wasn't in the best frame of mind, even after Abbey had informed them of the negative result. All the ladies were a little out of sorts, and when Lewis turned up to lunch with his ex-wife Immy, laughing and chatting, it triggered Bella and she was unable to hold back, she took Lewis aside and let him have it.

'Being here with your ex-wife is distasteful,' was her opening line to him as they stood under the vines of the pergola. 'You know my mum is up in her room recovering. She fainted and hit her head this morning. The doctor came because she may have been pregnant,' Bella hissed her words at a whisper to a stunned Lewis. 'With your baby!' She was angry and hurt and he was the perfect person for her to take her frustrations on. Lewis had caused part of her mother's misery and now him being here with Immy, was not okay with her. 'Stay away from my mum, do you hear me!' her voice got louder, and a few people heard her.

'What is going on?' Marlo was on the scene in seconds, just in the nick of time. 'Everyone can hear you,' she said looking at her niece with a disapproving frown.

'Is Grace okay?' Lewis looked at Marlo, 'Is she pregnant... Marlo!' Lewis was shocked and they now had Shiv and Luca's attention, as well as Ross and Scarlet.

'I just found out this morning,' Marlo explained quietly taking him by the arm and turning him away from prying eyes, 'She's okay. It's a concussion and she's resting. She's not pregnant.' The words were still thick in her throat. With that, Lewis walked off toward the estate house.

'You need to keep out of this one,' Marlo warned her niece as Bella went to say something, cutting her off. 'This is private, and we need to keep it that way.'

'He's here with his ex-wife while my mums up there, she's had enough, this won't help her Aunty Marlo,' an emotional pause, 'My mum can't keep getting hurt. She still loves Lewis, can't you see.'

Marlo grabbed Bella and hugged her in, they'd moved away out of sight and sound, 'Lewis is not here with Immy, her husband arrives tomorrow from Milan in time for the wedding.' She rubbed her niece's hair as she could feel her sobbing.

'He hurt mum! She was so upset this morning she fainted. I just want my mum to be okay.'

'Sweetie, she's fine now. And what Lewis did wasn't that bad in the scheme of things. Think about it Bella, he thought he was protecting her.' Marlo needed Bella to see reason.

There was no mistaking the knock at the door. Grace knew the three taps. When the door opened and Lewis stood in her

365

Loving Grace

doorway, as handsome and sweet as he'd ever been, she shuffled up in bed a little, she'd been in a light sleep.

'Can I come in?' he said with a gentle tone. Her smile was fragile as she nodded. Lewis went and sat on the side of the bed, looking at Grace with worried knowing eyes.

Instantly she knew he knew everything, 'I'm okay.' She assured him.

'Why didn't you tell me when you saw me last night?'

She rolled her lips, 'I wasn't about to tell you something I wasn't even sure about. That'd be a little dramatically tactical of me, don't you think?'

'You don't need tactics with me Gracie.' He was a little dumbfounded as to why she'd need tactics at all, and he had no idea she was aching inside for him. His dark eyes hadn't left hers. 'I get you don't like me again; I've accepted that. But I'd like us to be friends again.'

'I don't not like you,' she smiled.

He huffed a big sigh, 'Okay.' Not taking his eyes off her for a second. 'Were you going to tell me if you were pregnant?'

'I don't know. Probably not.' Her glassy eyes looked to his. 'I wasn't becoming a mother again at fifty, so I didn't see the point in telling you.'

A complexed grin came to his face, 'Well, I'm glad for you that you're not pregnant.' He raised his browns and got up from the bed. 'And I'm glad you only got a concussion this morning.

You gotta stop getting concussed Gracie, it's not good for you.' His smile widened.

'I'm fine, really. Thank you.'

'Um... My ex-wife Immy is here for the wedding,' Lewis stood and looked at her. 'Just so you know, Ruby invited her, she's not here with me. Her husband Marchello is arriving tomorrow, but she and I are still friends, and that's all.' Lewis felt the need to explain the situation to Grace. He was still in love with Grace and didn't want to cause her any more stress, even though she didn't want him anymore.

'Oh!' she made out like this was all new to her. 'Of course, Immy is friends with Ruby,' Grace shrugged like it made perfect sense.

'Will you be coming down to dinner? It's a fancy barbeque by the pool, Indian Italian style,' he chuckled, 'You know your sister.' Smiling knowing Grace would find it amusing.

'I'll see you later on,' she smiled back as he left. The door closed and she held her cry in for as long as she could without exploding. *Why couldn't she tell him she wanted him!* Her face was hot and red, her heart was sore, and she was still so in love with Lewis, but there was a huge roadblock keeping her from being honest with him. She'd trusted him once before and he'd disappointed her, how could she trust him again.

Loving Grace

When Grace came downstairs the house was preparing for the extravagant barbeque, there were people running around setting up for dinner. Marlo and Shiv stood out on the main terrace having a private conversation whilst Abbey and Louise sat at the lower terrace with a larger group all having drinks and enjoying the shaded afternoon before dinner. Grace held her head high, she knew everyone knew her business by now, it was just how this family was, and frankly, she didn't care anymore.

Phoebe had arrived from London and was in the pool with Mac, Bella, and Kristian. She waved down to the pool and blew a kiss to Phoebe then walked to the group, 'Hi,' she was all smiles as she stood beside Abbey. Phoebe's husband Nigel jumped up out of his seat and gave Grace a warm hug and kiss hello, he was a thirty something English gentleman who Grace had only met a handful of times but like him all the same, Nigel was sweet.

Ruby stood up and welcomed her, 'Everyone, this is my mum's sister, my Aunty Grace,' she said putting her arm around her. Ruby introduced her aunt, and then Grace saw her, as beautiful as she had remembered her to be. 'Aunty G, you remember Immy.'

'Hello Immy,' it was the performance of a lifetime, Grace was so cool, yet friendly as she smiled.

'It's so good to see you Grace. You look amazing!' Immy said sparking Grace's insecurities right off the bat.

'Thank you Immy,' Grace took the compliment with a wry smile, she didn't want to return the comment. It was her knew thing, no bullshit words to cloud the space. It was something Gus had talked to her about on the yacht one night, how people say random bullshit filling space with things they don't even mean. Ever since, Grace had noticed most people did it all the time, wasting words on things that they really didn't give a flying fuck about.

Louise moved over and for Grace and sat her between her and Abbey.

'You do look amazing by the way,' Abbey whispered to Grace, she'd seen the way her brow went up when Immy made the comment and knew exactly what her friend was thinking.

'Yeah!' her sarcasm couldn't be helped. 'Why the fuck does she care how I look?'

'She knows you did her ex-husband, that's why,' Louise smiled.

'Hmm.' Grace looked around, 'What do you think they're doing up there?' she looked up at Marlo and Shiv, who stood looking out over the estate and their family and friends who were enjoying it.

'I don't know, but Ross and Jimmy took Luca and Lewis off in the chopper somewhere a few hours ago. Said it was business.' Louise wasn't thrilled.

'What! did they fly to Rome for a meeting, that's crazy!' Grace laughed.

369

Loving Grace

'Golf disguised as a business meeting.' Lou was matter of fact about it. 'They'll be back for dinner.'

Abbey huffed, 'I think Jag looks alright for his age.'

'Definitely. Look at that body,' Lou agreed happy to change the subject.

'You know, some men improve with age, Jag is one of them,' said Abbey, 'If he wasn't married Grace, I'd say go for him.'

'You think?' Grace smiled as they watched everyone.

'Yeah I do, he's not bad at all. Hey, how'd it go when Lewis came up to see you earlier?' Abbey asked gently.

'Good.' Nobody knew how to take her.

'He must have been so worried about you.'

'Hmm.' Grace wasn't so sure.

Louise leaned in, 'Jimmy said he's not himself since you two broke up. That's what Lewis told him.' It had been a short love affair, but one that had everyone's attention.

'He told me he hopes we can be friends. I don't think I can, just be friends.'

'He what!' Abbey said louder than needed because she was alarmed.

Louise moved in even closer, 'Grace, you can't be his friend at all?'

She shook her head like she didn't want to talk about it.

'I don't know, it sounds like a whole bunch of bullshit to me!' Abbey scoffed. 'You said he was the best lover you've ever had and you're just letting him slip away without a fight.'

'Wow! Better than Ari Roth?' Gasped Louise like it was impossible.

'Better than Ari,' Grace kept her eyes on the pool. Lewis was better than anyone, he was better at everything, he looked better, he smelt better, he treated her right and yes, he was deliriously sexy, and he made her feel sexy too. Lewis was so good for her soul. But he lied to her while she was in the most vulnerable place she'd ever been in, and she couldn't seem to get past it.

'You are out of your mind?' Louise hissed, 'You're being stubborn, just tell him how you feel for crying out loud.'

'Yep, I think she's right Grace,' Abbey would never side against her friend unless it was necessary. 'If you miss this boat, you might never get another chance to sail it again.'

'Did you just make that up, because it was awful,' Grace frowned at Abbey's efforts.

Abbey came back at her as they huddled together, 'Lewis didn't sleep with Tina behind your back. He protected you when you needed protection. Just saying!' It was a no brainer for Abbey.

'So, you're on his side now!' Grace questioned.

371

Loving Grace

'Stop it,' Abbey protested. 'Don't cut your nose off to spite your face, is all I'm saying.'

'Oh, you're saying a lot today!' a smile came to Grace's face. 'You got all the one liner's going on.' She reached out to a passing waiter and took a champagne, she needed it.

Abbey and Grace walked down the large main staircase in their dinner outfits, Abbey in a blue silk pants and shirt and Grace in an embroidered white cotton dress she'd bought on her travels, they both looked radiant, and Grace was feeling better.

'Lucky I packed every piece of clothing I own. It's hard keeping up the appearance every day with three costume changes,' Abbey joked as she hung onto Grace's arm. They were the last to arrive at dinner, and heads turned.

'Are my nipples showing, why is everyone looking at us?' Grace said between her teeth with a smile and she and Abbey clung to each other.

'You're doing swell, they're looking because you look hot,' Abbey giggled.

'Jag's looking at you, I think he heard you say he was hot today.'

'He's a married man Grace King. Shame on you,' Abbeys laugh was naughty. 'Don't let me drink too much tonight, I can't be trusted anymore.'

'Ha, you better drink too much,' Grace teased her friend, 'And if I haven't told you lately. I love you Abbey. I couldn't have done the past few months without you.' Grace stopped and looked at her best friend, their connection and loyalty was beyond most friendships.

Abbey squeezed Grace into her side, 'I couldn't do life without you. So, we're even. Now stop being mushy and lets barbeque rich people style!'

The barbeque was fancy all right, and it was cheerful now that almost all the guests were in attendance it was party-like and very welcoming. There were three musicians playing instruments and a beautiful girl singing Italian folk songs. Everyone was now in holiday/wedding mode.

One by one Grace's children came to her and offered only warm hugs, none of them, not even Bella mentioned the pregnancy scare or Lewis for that matter, it was basically checking in on her after her day in bed, everyone knew she'd passed out, they just didn't know the circumstances.

It seemed that the chat Ross, Marlo, and Abbey had with them today had done the trick. From the minute Grace left their father, the boundaries sometimes got blurred, right now all Grace needed was their love.

'Mama you look beautiful tonight,' Bella gave her a big hug, 'I just want you to be happy,' she said to her mother's ear knowing she'd been out of line lately.

Loving Grace

'Sweetheart, I'm fine. Thank you for your concern, but I'm a big girl,' Grace kissed her daughter's cheek and touched her beautiful long hair. 'You need to concentrate on your own happiness.' Grace gave her a kiss on the cheek.

'This is nice to see,' Shiv was right there with a big smile on her face. 'How are you feeling Grace?' She'd heard all about the faint today and Ross had suggested to his mother that she stop being rude and start talking to Grace.

'I'm good. Much better thank you.' Grace hadn't been in the headspace to worry about what Shiv was thinking of her.

'I'm so glad,' Shiv stepped closer as Bella left them. 'You look lovely, white is stunning on you, your mother always wore white in the summer.' This was Shiv's way of apologizing.

Grace gasped, she loved hearing about her mother from Shiv, it was always loving and warm, they'd been the best of friends, much like she and Abbey. 'I wish she was here,' suddenly Grace was full of tears, sad and happy tears.

'I do to. She'd be so proud of the woman you are Grace. She'd want you to be happy... I want you to be happy, to be kinder to yourself, to follow your heart.' Shiv smiled, there was a message behind her words.

'It's time to sit down,' Marlo said to them both as the guest started to take their seats, 'Find your name and take your seat.' She looked at Grace with those big blue sisterly eyes.

Great! Concussed and now probably sitting next to some random person she'd never met, Grace sighed as she looked for her name, knowing her luck she'd be next to Immy or Gabe, Marlo would get a kick out of that, so it was unexpected when she was seated next to Lewis.

Was her sister playing cupid or was she out of her fucking mind!

For a second Grace thought she might fake a headache and do a runner, but that would be too obvious. She had to take her seat; it was too late. Sandwiched between the man she longed for and her favourite niece, the beautiful Scarlet. This wasn't by chance!

For Grace it felt nice being close to Lewis as awkward as it was, feeling his body warmth was comforting. Neither spoke many words, they exchanged a few looks and made comments on the barbeque chicken, had a laugh at Marlo's expense. He passed her some of the large salad bowls in the middle of their table and he smelt so good, Grace was at one stage lost in a flurry of heated memories that saddened her. She realised what she'd done, she'd lost him.

Between meals Lewis went to sit with Immy up on the far end of the long table, they sat close together smiling and talking privately. Grace couldn't look at them, even though Immy was married to someone else, she and Lewis just made such a great couple visually. Grace felt like an idiot, if they could be friends after being married and it ending badly, why couldn't she just be Lewis's friend?

375

Loving Grace

Exchanging seats with Luca was easy, he was happy to be going to sit next to his cousin Scarlet, and Grace needed to be with Abbey. Lewis had left his seat and gone to Immy, she'd taken that as a huge rejection, they'd been seated together by design, and he'd moved.

'What was Marlo thinking sitting me way over there!' Grace could be in Abbey's company all day and they didn't have to speak all the time, tonight they couldn't stop talking. Marlo had noticed when the main course came out that Grace wasn't in her seat. Lewis was now seated next to Luca, he'd returned to his seat and Grace was gone, so he took it as she didn't want to be seated near him.

'I miss Tina,' Abbey said out of the blue, catching Grace off guard after a few wines.

Grace sighed, 'It's like she should be here with us, but I never want to see her again in my life if I can help it - does that make sense.'

'It does,' Abbey agreed, 'I feel like I'm mourning her, but she's not dead, and I'm also certain I can't be her friend.'

'I still can't believe this has happened,' Grace shrugged, she still found it hard to believe. 'Sometimes I have to ask myself if it really all happened, did Michael and Tina really do this?'

'I know. When I think about it, she was never the person or the friend we thought she was.'

Grace took a big drink of her red wine, and then another gulp, 'The two of them completely fucked everyone over. What does that say Ab's?'

'It says they are awful people. Awful people.,' she repeated to stress the point. 'They lied to a lot of people, you, me, your kids and your family.'

Rubbing her face, Grace sighed, 'Sometimes I feel like I need to call Tina and tell her what I really think of her or go visit her and slap her face so hard it stings for a month,' she laughed at herself.

Abbey laughed too, 'Slap her for me too will you.' They laughed and talked the night away, drinking red wine and chatting with Lousie and Jimmy, Jag, and Gabe. At the end of the night Grace saw Lewis sitting over by the pool sipping wine with his grandparents, they seemed to be in deep conversation. When Grace was about to turn in, Marlo found her in the hallway of the estate house.

'I've got tea coming up, come and sit with me.' She took Grace through her large palatial bedroom suite and out onto the private terrace that she and Ross so loved. It had the best view over the whole estate, and at night the lights of the valley looked so peaceful and calming. When the tea arrived they sat, the only noise was coming from the pool where the younger crowd now congregated, it was too early for them to end the night.

'I didn't appreciate the seating plan tonight, by the way!' she told Marlo with sarcasm, and to Grace's surprise her sister didn't say a word. 'Did you think that was funny because it wasn't. It made me sad.'

'Why... Why would you feel sad?' Marlo wanted Grace to be honest.

'It's weird for Lewis and me, that's all.' They both looked out over the pool area. 'It hurts me to be near him. Is that so hard to understand. I still love him. I miss him. I want him,' Grace gushed.

Marlo looked at her in shock, she knew Grace still felt for Lewis, but she had never expected to hear her be so forward, and with such emotion, 'You need to tell him how you feel.'

'He lied to me,' she said loudly like it should have been obvious to her sister.

Considering her words carefully, Marlo wanted to be frank, 'You deserve to be happy and not all men are like Michael,' she paused. 'Just tell Lewis how you feel, maybe it could work out between you two still.'

Grace wondered why Marlo would think it could still work. Did she know something Grace didn't. 'I can't mentally afford to be rejected by him. And I think...' she stopped to get the courage to admit her next words, 'I think. I think maybe he's thinking he got out of it easily, that he's better off without me.'

'Why would you say that?' Marlo seemed dumbfounded.

'Because!' Grace could feel the tears welling. 'I'm older, I'm fifty and he's a younger man who could meet someone and have a family... you know he told me it was good for me that I wasn't pregnant!' Lewis' words had been playing on her mind. 'And he said it in a way that made me think, maybe he really does want kids of his own, even though he says he doesn't... I can't give him that.'

'Oh, you are way over processing this my darling,' Marlo huffed with a smile, 'Lewis has never wanted kids of his own. We've had this discussion so many times, I'd know if he wanted kids, and I'm telling you, you're trying to find any excuse to let him slip away because you are scared.'

The silence was uneasy,

'Do you blame me for being scared,' Grace looked at her big sister with worried eyes feeling the lump in her throat getting larger. 'After everything.'

'Grace! It took me a while to see you two as a couple, and when I did, I couldn't then not see it,' Marlo took a breath. 'You and Lewis made each other happy; you were like a hand and glove.'

Grace gave Marlo a look, she hated idiomatic expressions at the best of times. 'We're people, not gloves.' She whipped a stray tear from her cheek. 'And deep down in my heart, I know I'm not what Lewis imagined in his life as his lover or his partner... I'm just not.'

'Yeah, well, if that's the case, I don't know why he defended your relationship to his entire family when we all found out about you two.'

379

Loving Grace

'Maybe he felt sorry for me,' Grace said.

'Oh, stop being so ridiculous. Do you think a guy like Lewis would waste his time on someone he felt sorry for. Please!' Marlo was a little pissed.

That night Grace went to bed wondering why she'd fallen for Lewis after loathing him for years. And it was easy to fall for him, he'd been a beautiful caring man to her. It was simple.

The next day was more beautiful than the ones before it. Grace, Abbey, and Louise took a drive into the nearby village with Jimmy and Luca to get an early bite to eat before the afternoon saw them all preparing for the pre wedding dinner which was going to be more extravagant than last night, this was to get everyone ready for the highly anticipated wedding the following day.

Jimmy and Grace sat next to each other at the outdoor table in the quaint little café, 'I'm thinking of taking Kristian out to L.A. with me for a few months, Lou and I have decided to base ourselves there for a while after our trip. We need a change, so does Kristian.'

She looked at her brother for a moment, 'Oh. How long for?'

'We're not sure exactly. I'll be working with a new team for our new project, and I think it would do him good Grace, he needs a change of scenery. We all do.'

Luca overheard, 'I think it's a good idea mum.'

Jimmy needed his sisters approval, 'He can't go around punching his father out every time he sees him, and I think it's time to get him out of that circle of friends he's hanging out with. He needs a break from Sydney.'

'Lewis thinks it's a good idea too!' Luca added.

Instantly at the mention of Lewis her back was up, Grace looked at Louise, 'I don't know why you're all wording me up, if Kristian wants to go, he's a grown man, he can make his own decisions.'

Jimmy winced at his sister, 'I've asked him, and he originally said yes, and then yesterday he told me he won't be coming because he needs to be here for you.'

'Great!' Grace sighed with angst. 'So, it's my fault.'

'He's worried about you mum, that's all,' said Luca.

'So, I should try to be less of a worry.'

'Nobody is saying that honey,' Louise said.

'I'm just not sure what you want from me, why are you even telling me?'

'If he mentions it to you, maybe you could be positive and encourage him to go,' Jimmy suggested.

'Sure,' Grace said dismissing the conversation there and then. What did they expect, she'd let them throw up the accusation that her son was putting his life on hold because of her, she knew this had been a discussion prior to today and it was them softening her up to the idea, making sure she wasn't going to flip out.

When they got back to the estate, Grace and Abbey sat out on Grace's terrace in the shade and drank Pimm's and lemonade in tall glasses with ice and lemon slices in the heat of the day. They talked about a trip they wanted to take together next year to Spain, just the two of them on a discovery of good food and sunshine. Grace also mentioned to Ab's that she was thinking about moving back to her country house until it sold, she thought maybe it was time to go back.

'I don't think it's a good idea at all.' Abbey was not on board. 'Your apartment is gorgeous, and you'd only be moving so you don't have to see Lewis, and I just think that in time, the whole Lewis thing will be easier for you. So don't make any rash decisions.'

'Mmm. I'll see how I feel when I get back,' Grace took a big breath, 'I'm definitely ready to throw myself into my business I've missed working.'

'Well, that's good, you might be finally getting your groove back.'

'I don't know! Part of me still feels wounded,' she said looking at Ab's.

'You wanna hear what I think?' a pause, 'I think you need to cut yourself some slack. I'd like to see you smile a little more and yes, you'll have good days and bad days, but you'll never be alone.'

Grace frowned at Abbey, half a smile, half a frown, 'Okay!' She wasn't sure if she was offended or grateful, either way if it came from Abbey she was taking it on board.

'Look at where we are, this is like a fairy tale for you and me, let's have some real fun while we're here.' Abbey

Later in the afternoon, Abbey went to her room and showered and dressed for the pre wedding dinner that felt like it was the actual wedding, so much fuss was made of it. She came back to Grace's suite and found Grace with Marlo sitting on her bed, Marlo was in tears, beside herself.

'Come in Ab's,' Grace gave her the all clear, 'Marlo is just leaving,' she said as Marlo walked to the door, she gave Abbey a smile, amidst her tears.

'I'll see you two for predrinks,' she said leaving.

Grace shut the door, and it was just she and Abbey, 'She's okay, it's just Ross being Ross,' Grace sighed, 'He is flying in some surprise people tonight for the wedding,' Grace sighed. 'It's thrown Marlo's planning out, Ross wouldn't tell her who the people were, it's a huge surprise apparently, and this is their daughter's wedding, you know Ross, he's all about the good times. She's upset, I get it.' Grace loved her brother-in-law, but he could be too spontaneous sometimes. Her sister was a planner, she liked everything to run to schedule. Everything.

'Oh, Rosco! Women don't love those kinds of surprises, especially at weddings,' Abbey laughed it off.

'Men are so weird!' Grace chuckled as she went over to her hanging pink and green patterned dress and put it over her head. Her blonde hair was tied neatly back into a low ponytail, her makeup was natural with a nude lip and her tan looked stunning. 'I've got the terrace ready, lets drink, we're going to need to join AA when we get home,' she giggled. They sat sipping on their spritz' and making each other laugh... fits of belly wrenching laughter, telling stories of their youth and then they were hysterical about Abbey's first wedding and how her ex-mother-in-law was caught coming out of the disabled toilets with a much younger waiter by Abbey's gay cousin Freddie, that's all they could now remember of the actual wedding, which made it even funnier.

Again, they were the last ones to arrive to pre-dinner drinks holding hands and half cut, they'd been watching everyone arrive from Grace's terrace, commentating and giggling on the fashion and the people, luckily they were just out of earshot, not all of it was nice, but they'd had such fun doing it.

Instantly Grace saw Lewis talking with Immy, and a handsome Italian who had to be the infamous husband

Marchello. *Hmm*, Grace thought, *it had to be a tossup as to who was the better looking, Lewis or Marchello! Both tall, dark, and handsome, both utterly gorgeous!* With her spritz courage, Grace wandered on over to say hello, why the hell not, she was in such a great mood.

'Oh, Grace,' Immy took her by the hand and bought her into their circle. 'I want you to meet my husband Marchello,' she said beaming from ear to ear. 'This is Grace, Ruby's aunt.' Immy seemed to make a point of introducing her, the sudden smile on the stunning looking man's face was telling, he knew exactly who she was, probably because his wife told him she'd fucked her ex-husband, it was all rather amusing to Grace.

'It's a pleasure to meet you Grace,' his accent was divine. 'You have beautiful blue eyes like the sky,' his smile sparkled as he complimented her.

'Thank you Marchello, it's lovely to meet you too,' Grace spoke softly, then looked at Lewis. 'Hello, how are you!' she said giving him a huge smile and her friendly tone, Lewis could tell she'd been drinking.

Immy clapped her hands together getting their attention, 'Marchello and I have some news to share,' she was like a little girl, 'We are expecting our first child.'

Grace couldn't figure out why on earth Immy had waited for this exact moment to announce this news to her ex-husband, Lewis, who seemed overwhelmed with joy for Immy and Marchello, Grace couldn't tell if his happiness was real, or he was putting it on for their sake. She wasn't completely sold on the notion Lewis didn't ever want kids.

'How wonderful for you both,' Grace said giving them both a hug and kiss, she was happy for them genuinely, even though she barely knew them, they were clearly overjoyed.

'I wanted to tell you first,' Immy told Lewis, then she took her gorgeous Marchello by the arm and floating off on cloud nine to tell Ruby.

'That's nice for them,' Grace shrugged, a smile on her face as she spoke to Lewis.

'Yeah. Immy's always wanted to be a mum.'

'So, you never ever wanted kids with her at all. Ever?' Grace wasn't sure why she needed to know.

'No. I've never wanted kids. Ever.'

Grace stared at him, 'Mmm. I'm just curious,' she had a questioning smile on her face. 'The other day in my room you said it was good for *me* that I wasn't pregnant. You made a point of it only being good for me.'

He took a moment, looking at her, 'Gracie, I've never wanted kids. Regardless of what my grandmother might think, I know with all of my being, that I don't want to ever be a parent.' He was so sure as he shook his head.

Grace put her hands out to him, 'I don't have a problem with people not wanting kids. Parenting is way overrated if you ask me,' she was trying to be serious, but he could hear the humour in her tone. He smiled at her with a certain admiration in his eyes, a lusting adoration more to the point.

'Hey you two!' Louise came in between them with her bright than bright yellow dress, and super red lipstick. 'You're wanted for a family photo over there Lewis,' a giddy glint in Lou's eyes.

He looked straight back to Grace and put his hand to her arm, 'I'll see you later,' he told her with the most charming grin..

As he walked away, Louise looked at Grace who's eyes followed him, 'Am I missing something here? Did I interrupt something?' Louise was her bubbly self.

'No,' the smile on Grace's face resonated through her voice. She was happy.

'You two seem friendly, that's all.'

'We are trying to be friends Lou.'

'You're in love with him!' Lou whispered softly to Grace's ear.

'Oh, you have no idea,' sighed Grace feeling her heart twinge.

By this stage all the wedding guests had all arrived and there was some commotion over by where the family were taking photos, Ruby had a photographer taking shots since they'd arrived, he'd been flown in from New York City and was apparently the ultimate - as everything to do with her wedding was.

387

Loving Grace

'What the hell is this!' Abbey gasped coming to Grace and Louise as a chopper landed out on the distant lawn. Grace could see Marlo and Ross having words right before he left the group photo and rushed out to the chopper with Jimmy at his side, Marlo left behind looking less than impressed. The three ladies looked on with intrigue, wondering who the surprise guests were.

'Marlo is freaking out about these surprise guests!' Grace said to Lou.

'Oh, it's a surprise all right,' Louise said smiling.

Grace glanced at her, 'Who are they?'

'Take a look,' Louise said like she already knew. It was Gus and Pete along with their mini entourage getting out the chopper and greeted Ross and Jimmy. Grace and Abbey stood there; mouths open in disbelief.

They'd been flown in to do a special acoustic set at the wedding tomorrow night. Ross thought it'd be nice for Ruby and Sam, since they are their favourite band.

Grace and Abbey looked at each other dumbfounded. Was it going to be a little weird for Grace to see Gus after their little holiday sex romp in the ocean? Maybe.

The buzz under the big white pergola poolside got louder when everyone recognised the lead singer and the guitarist from one of the world's most famous bands. It had made perfect sense to Ross to invite his good friends Gus and Pete to his estate for his daughter's wedding when he heard Marlo, and the girls had been yachting in Europe with them. They'd accepted his offer and now they were here.

Grace's eyes darted to Ruby to see her reaction, and well her father was right, she was crying with excitement at the mere sight of Gus and Pete, she didn't even know they were here to perform at her wedding.

Two hours later Grace was sitting next to Gus chatting about the past few days and how they'd ended up here at the wedding together, was it fate or just sheer luck.

'It's fate, can you believe it!' Gus had a sparkle in his eyes sitting relaxed and very at ease with Grace now in his company again.

'I actually can believe it, my brother-in-law is always pulling stunts like this,' Grace smiled.

'You know why I couldn't say no to him?' Gus had a playful grin, his long hair messy, his hand resting on Grace's at the table.

'Why?' she smiled.

'I wanted to see you again.' He had a look in his eyes that was casual and possibly hopeful, which made her immediately anxious. They'd parted their yachting holiday as friends. 'I felt like we had this amazing chemistry, and we didn't give it the attention it perhaps deserved.'

Loving Grace

'Oh, I thought we kind of did,' she laughed it off, assuming Gus was joking, at least hoping. 'Well, one particular night in the shallows of Sardinia anyway,' she continued down the not so serious road for want of not knowing what else to do or say.

Abbey had been watching from a far, the main course was over and now as people gathered in groups and seat swapped, she was in a small group on the other side of the table to her friend, with Lewis at her side. Abbey wondered if he was watching Grace too. She wondered if Lewis knew that Gus was making a play for Grace, she could see it a mile away.

Gus reached out and touched Grace's hair, pushing it back behind her ear, she almost pulled away from him. 'We had such a good time with you gals, we just had to come here.'

'Well, it's good to have you here,' Grace shrugged, looking over at Lewis in the depths of conversation with one of Ruby's single friends from Sydney. They looked comfortable, they made more sense than she and Lewis did.

When Grace went back to her own seat were she wound up now next to her niece Scarlet. Her belly had grown in the last few days and Grace felt she had this closeness with her niece now that she was becoming a mother, a closeness more so than they had before. Scarlet was a woman now; she was mature and sensible and lovely like always.

'Aunty G!' she had this look on her face, sceptical and somewhat hesitant. 'What's going on with you and Gus, it looks like you two are best buddies?' She pulled her dress away from her chest in the warmth of the evening.

'We hung out a lot on the trip, he's a great guy.' Grace had a luminous smile, a combination of drinking, the atmosphere, and the fact that Gus and Pete were here, the place was buzzing.

Scarlet kept staring at her aunt, until Grace stared back at her, 'You know I love you,' she sighed like she was thinking deeply. 'I don't want you to make a wrong decision, or choice.'

'What are you talking about?' It made her laugh, Scarlet being so serious.

'Lew and the rock star.' Scarlet didn't laugh. 'Don't do anything you might regret... My mum told me you and Gus got on like a house on fire on the yacht, and she also told me you still love Lew.'

'Oh, your mother has the biggest mouth ever!' scoffed Grace knowing she should never have opened up to her sister. 'She's such a gossiper.'

'Do you love Lew?'

'Scarlet!' Grace gasped looking at her niece, the smile began to fade from her face. 'What would it matter if I did? He lied to me, and not to mention his history. It was stupid and desperate of me to even go there with him in the first place.'

'Funny, you're not the desperate type. And his history isn't that bad,' Scarlet would go in batting for any of her family, she was loyal, and her heart was among the purest.

Loving Grace

Grace moved her body to face her niece, 'He cheated on poor Immy with the housekeeper, he told me so himself.' This was her rationalising the situation to appease her poor heart.

'Oh, come on, there's more to that than him just cheating on her,' Scarlet laughed defensively. 'Did he tell you she instigated them having sex with other couples on numerous occasions, or that she had asked him for an open relationship more than once! No, I didn't think so. And did he mention she also had sex with the housekeeper before he did. Ha!' Scarlet felt triumphant. Grace on the other hand was a little surprised.

'It doesn't matter what you say Scar, there's nothing between us anymore,' Grace was adamant.

'I'm just going to say it, because you need to hear it,' Scarlet held her aunt's hand, 'You two made such a good couple once everyone got over the initial shock, and he hasn't moved on. But you're putting up this wall and he doesn't know what to do.'

Grace knew Scarlet would know exactly how her cousin was feeling about her, Lewis confided in Scarlet, they were great friends. Frankly, she was shocked to hear he was still in the game. 'He's also a liar, and I have to remember that.' It was awful... Grace couldn't stop her barrage of why Lewis wasn't the one for her.

'Aunty G!' Scarlet wiggled in her seat. 'You're being impossible. You're self-sabotaging your own happiness, it's ridiculous.'

'I know. I know.' Grace admitted then paused. 'I don't know why I'm so hung up on the whole liar thing. He thought he was protecting me, and I get it, I really do.' Grace suddenly found herself tearing up as Scarlet reached out and rubbed her hand. 'I'm scared Scarlet.' There, she said it.

'Of what? Lewis didn't do anything wrong - I mean I know he probably should have told you in the beginning about Bree's child. But he fell hard for you, he didn't want to see you hurt any more than you already were,' Scarlet let her emotions take over, she was crying in the softest voice, her eyes watering and her face flushed. This beautiful pregnant young woman was absolutely gorgeous.

'Oh, sweetheart!' Grace wiped her tears away with her hand.

'I was your supporter from the start,' Scarlet was fully crying now. 'If you do still love Lew, you're mad not to give him a chance. He really loves you.'

Grace looked at her niece who she adored, 'Please stop crying, you're too beautiful to cry,' she smiled gently.

'What have you got to lose?'

'I'm too old for him,' Grace gave it a last ditched effort.

'Age is just a number,' Scarlet sniffed.

'Did Lewis tell you that?'

'Yes, actually he did,' she laughed wiping her tears.

Loving Grace

'I don't know how to be with him.' Grace was still making excuses up.

'Yes, you do. He makes you happy. You know he does.' Scarlet wasn't letting her aunty off the hook. 'Try. I wouldn't be telling you all this if I didn't think he was right for you. I love you so much, please Aunty G,' she got emotional again. 'Please!' Her words were penetrating to Grace.

'You are a beautiful heart,' Grace hugged her. 'You're also my favourite, but you already know that.' She held onto her niece lovingly. 'I'll see how I go with getting over myself,' a little laugh eased them.

Chapter Twenty

The wedding morning saw the estate house in chaos, dresses being rushed in and out, hairdressers and florists coming and going. Caterers and people carrying loads of chairs in their arms... chairs, so many chairs! Out by the pergola a stage was being constructed, it was all very elaborate.

Abbey, Grace and Lousie decided on a morning walk through the estate grounds, only to run into Lewis and Luca who were doing the very same thing.

The joined forces and headed off to escape the madness. They took the outer trail that rimmed the property and went through the main vineyard and into a much larger neighbouring vineyard, nobody was in a hurry to get back and while the heat hadn't yet set in it was perfect walking weather. Abbey and Louise were in front talking to Luca about Jasmine and the baby and how things were going. The situation was getting better and now at least Luca had a chance to be in his child's life.

Walking at a slower pace, Grace and Lewis admired the surroundings and talked about the land and the grandeur of Marlo and Ross's estate, it was extravagant and so very beautiful, they both agreed on that.

'I think I could actually live here, I love Italy,' Grace said as she waved a fly from her face.

'The food and wine alone does it for me,' Lewis said looking relaxed and handsome wearing a black T shirt and white linen shorts with black joggers, his sunglasses on his head. Grace loved his style; he didn't have to try.

'I've been thinking about it. I mean, I could design my jewellery here, there's no need to be in Sydney. And I could attend the European expo's and break into the market here.' She smiled having it all figured out in her head.

'Seriously, you'd leave your kids behind!' he questioned her, he liked that she always had these ideas spinning around in her head, Grace was a dreamer.

'Maybe, they're all growing up and living their own lives now.'

'Bella's still a baby,' Lewis looked at her.

'I know, she can come with me if she likes,' she smiled. 'I don't know, anything seems possible to me at the moment. I'm floating in the universe.'

'You're not sold on the harbour view are you?' he joked.

Grace laughed, 'It's had its ups and downs,' she played along. Had Scarlet already told him about their conversation last night, she couldn't be sure. 'Can you believe Ruby will be waking up a married woman this time tomorrow?'

Lewis let out an amused huff, 'It's always felt weird, those girls are like sisters to me. Scarlet and I got married the same year you know.'

'Wow, you two are almost like twins,' Grace found it funny, it was the age thing.

'We are close,' he was matter of fact and looking at Grace. 'In fact, her and Angus have asked me to be the godfather of their baby.'

Grace stopped in her tracks, 'Oh, that's amazing. I think they'll be great parents; you know she's my favourite, right!'

'I know, you've told me several times,' he chuckled comfortably, thinking it was so Grace to pick a favourite niece, that's what he loved about her. They looked at each other right in the eyes for the first time today. 'I think you're her favourite person too, besides her husband, just between you and I,' Lewis said.

'What makes you say that?' Grace's eyes sparkled as she delved.

'I just know so.' He shrugged cutely trying to get out of it.

Loving Grace

Grace gave him a long meaningful look, one of her looks were her eyes narrow as if she was thinking hard, 'What has Scarlet told you?' she knew there was something going on, Scarlet had said something to him already this morning. He pondered for a moment, and she could tell he didn't know if he should go any further or shut it down now. Her eyes devoured every incredible inch of him in those few seconds.

'Nothing really,' he lied.

'Tell me!' she asked with a hint of excitement.

'Never you mind.' His smile oozed sexiness, her body had this incredible want that was killing her.

They went on to talked about Kristian and how he was doing, then they tried to guess what flavour the wedding cake would be, this went on for the entire hour of the walk until Louise declared it was way too hot, and she needed to head back. One walk had seen them both come a long way, this morning had been a chance for them, to just to be them.

Bella was part of the wedding, Ruby had wanted her and Mac to be at her side, along with Pheobe and Scarlet, which made Grace and Marlo very proud of the tight relationship their girls had. The day had begun early for the bridal party, eight a.m. was kick off with a special yoga class, then breakfast by the pool just for them, massages, and facials, then hair and makeup followed by photos and bridal party drinks in Marlo's suite where they were all getting ready.

Abbey and Grace reconvened on Grace's terrace before they headed down to the late afternoon wedding. In a beautiful teal blue slip dress, Abbey looked stunning, Grace curled her long hair with a wand and did her eyebrows with a pencil. The baby pink Italian silk dress Grace wore was soft and flowing yet bought in at her waist to show off her curves, she'd straightened her hair and wore it behind her ears, she wore large gold earrings, her dark lashed blue eyes were smoky and seductive as Abbey put it.

'Have a look down there, it's unrecognizable. These people are outrageous!' Grace said as they watched over the large pool and pergola below, they'd eaten there every night as it was truly a large, beautiful area, now it had been transformed into wedding bliss. White flowering plants and trees had appeared overnight all the way from France and the Netherlands, the tables were long and white with long elaborate centerpieces of white flowers and candelabras, gold accessories and gold chairs sparkled.

'What would you do if you had all this money Grace?' Abbey asked as they sat comfortably on their plush chairs sipping French champagne in their pretty frocks.

'I'd buy a nice villa in the Med somewhere, and I'd do nothing,' she sounded dreamy.

'I've been thinking about this the whole holiday, and I'd do exactly the same. I'd have a full-time housekeeper and a chef, both male, both exceptionally sexy.'

Loving Grace

Grace laughed, 'I wouldn't expect anything less.'

'Imagine having this much money!' Abbey beamed with the thought.

At four p.m. all guests were to be down by the side of the estate house to be seated for the ceremony, it was the greenest grass with the best views of the estates rolling hills of Tuscany. The sun was starting to subside, and the setting was something from a fairy tale book, an Italian garden fairy tale book. Rows of vineyards and green trees as the backdrop, stone farmhouses scattered, the view was peaceful. As for the wedding, it was beautiful and romantic with white seats and large stone urns overflowing with white flowers that cradled the altar, it looked like a floating white cloud of floristry.

Ruby walked down the center with her parents on either side of her, she was gushingly gorgeous as all brides are on their very special day. Musicians played the violin and harp as an opera singer sang in Italian, everything was so beautiful, Grace wanted to cry. As they reached the altar, and Ruby stood beside her husband to be, Grace glanced over at Lewis a few seats along, and he was looking at her. They settled their eyes at each other for a moment, there was something there, she simply couldn't deny it - besides him being breathtakingly handsome, something she'd always known yet couldn't admit. His eyes comforted her as she sat there on her own next to Abbey. This was the first time Grace had been to a wedding without Michael at her side and for some reason it felt strange. Seeing Lewis though, made all her angst and strange feelings fade away. He smiled and she instantly knew all was okay.

Throughout the ceremony, she was distracted, if one smile from Lewis made her turn into a marshmallow inside, he had to be worth it. Michael had given her those feelings for almost all of their marriage, she had adored the ground he walked on, to the point she'd missed his flaws and all the warning signs. There were no guarantees in life, Grace understood that, but she wasn't sure if she was brave enough to take a chance on finding love again. Or was she!

After the happy couple kissed and became husband and wife, Grace looked around the gathering, her daughter standing beside one of Sam's cousins from England, Bella looked so much like her father, still so young with the world at her feet, Grace could only hope she'd find her place in the world and flourish and be proud of herself. Then Luca was standing with Lewis and Kristian. Her boys were now men, Kristian had a long way to go, but maybe the move to L.A. would be just what he needed. Grace had already had the talk with him and given him her assurance that she would be fine with him gone. And Luca, well he was embarking on a stage of life that she was sure he would relish in. He was a good man, a caring and smart man who knew right from wrong even in the most difficult of times.

Her sister stood discreetly wiping the stray tears as they fell from her eyes, Marlo stood proudly with Ross who was not only her husband, but her best friend, they had their moments, and they were solid as a rock.

Jimmy was Jimmy, Grace thought as she watched her big brother and with his arm at Louise's back lovingly, they were leaning into each other with the ease of a happily married couple, Grace could only hope they were. Maybe she'd judged her brother too harshly because of her own experience with men.

And then just as her thoughts went all the way back to Michael and the fact he wasn't here, Abbey tucked her arm into hers.

'We're going to have a great time tonight Grace, I can feel it in my bones,' Abbey had the biggest grin on her face, 'I'm so excited.' She was like a little girl about to go to a party, and yes, it was a party and yes, it would be spectacular.

As they walked around to the upper terrace enjoying drinks, the allure of music was phenomenal. The terrace looked out over the below wedding festivities where on the far side of the pool on the stage, a small orchestra were playing, the sound was everywhere as everyone was gasping with delight as the opera singer from the ceremony was now fronting the orchestra with Adele's One and Only.

'Oh. My. God!' Even Abbey was lost for words. Not only did it sound out of this world, but now as the sun went down a million candles lit all the tables, and scattered fairy lights filled the trees. The scene was beautiful and rustic, very Italian with an air of excitement, everyone was dressed up and in their finest, it was truly spectacular.

Grace was called away for family photos of which she felt again, strange because it was now just her, and in the moment, luckily Ross knew exactly what she was feeling, she joined him and Marlo for a picture with Louise and Jimmy, Ross wrapped his arm around her, she was solo in this photo, and he understood it couldn't have been easy for her.

'You're doing great kiddo,' he pulled her into his side as they stood casually for the photo.

'You know what,' she said to him, 'I feel great.' She would rather be standing here alone than with Michael, a man who took her goodness for granted for so long, he humiliated and hurt her more than she thought anyone ever could.

Ross leaned down to her, 'Can I tell you, Gracie, you look the best I've ever seen you look right now. You're looking full of life and radiant.' He kissed her head and gave her another squeeze into his side. 'I'm so proud of you.'

'Thank you - I think,' she smiled, it was nice to hear. 'The past few weeks have given me a chance to breathe, to think and to find myself, and believe me it wasn't always easy.'

'Gracie, it never is easy.' Ross and Grace stood arm in arm until all the family got in the next shot, the Hunter's, and the King's, all together. 'I'm just going to give you one piece of advice my sweetheart,' he had a glint in his eye, he'd given her so much advice in her lifetime, but Ross felt this advice was above all valid. 'Don't sweat the little things, they're not worth it.'

At first Grace just took it at face value, the little things, there were so many little things in life. But then she thought about it, she looked at Lewis as he maneuvered his way into the photo next to Kristian and Mac. Was keeping the Bree and baby information from her a little thing or a big thing? It was absolutely a big thing, but it wasn't Lewis' doing! He didnt have a baby with another woman behind her back, he's done what he thought was right, protected her from another awful Michael scandal. Now in contrast to everything Michael had done, Lewis' part in it was a little thing. Lewis had made a mistake, only because he cared for her.

The style and sophistication of the wedding left nothing to the imagination, the food was served in large share bowls all down the long candle-lit tables. Lewis was seated two seats up from Grace, she was next to Abbey and Gabe, which made for interesting dinner conversations. In the back of her mind, she knew Shiv was probably behind the seating arrangements, she'd probably switched the name cards around, although it was a lovely mix of family and friends on the table. Regardless, they all shared plenty of laughs, the red wine was flowing, and the night was warm and still, it was the perfect night to celebrate a wedding in Tuscany. A traditional wedding, as they ate dinner the orchestra played James Bond songs, softly in the background, and then Gus and Pete got up after mains and did a set too.

Once the cake had been cut it was time for the bridal waltz and some speeches of which Grace found herself in tears as Ross made mention of how there were two very special people missing from tonight's celebrations, the brides grandparents... Claudine and Tom. This very public recognition of Grace's parents was beautiful and yet confronting. No matter how much time passed, there was guilt on her behalf, although she had nothing to be guilty for. Her entire life Grace carried the guild of her mother's death. Marlo and Jimmy and everyone who had loved her mother were without her because she was born, and nothing would ever change that. She was away and lost in her thoughts as the bride and groom danced to the orchestra's operatic version of Fly me to the moon by Frank Sinatra. The next dance was the bride and father of the bride, Ross, who encouraged everyone to join the dance floor as the orchestra turned up the vibe with Happy by Pharrell Williams.

Grace sat in her seat sipping her iced mineral water with lemon as Gabe went to dance with his mother, and Abbey accepted a dance with Luca who insisted. If the night were more perfect, Grace would have to pinch herself, her sister was floating around the dance floor smiling and happy now that it was done, and she could do nothing but enjoy her daughter's wedding now.

Grace felt the warm hand on her shoulder first, instantly her heart began to pound, 'Would you dance with me?' But it wasn't Lewis. It was Gus. She smiled hoping she'd hidden the second of disappointment that swept over her.

'Sure!' She knew it wasn't the most definite answer, but it was the only one that would come out. And as she put her arm up around Gus's shoulder, she saw Lewis dancing with Mac, he was trying not to notice her dancing with a rock star.

Taking a deep breath in, Grace wondered why she wasn't blown away by the attention from Gus. He was charming, he had a fantastic personality and even though he was American, she enjoyed listening to him talk, because he always had something interesting to say. Gus was without doubt a great man, a good man, sexy too. Her eyes glanced over to Lewis as Gus spun her around, then she looked up at Gus, he was a strong man who knew his place in the world, and how he got there, his story as a human was solid, and his eyes were genuine.

'I love an orchestra, and these singers are so special, do you realise how lucky we are to be in their presence?' Gus said as his eyes twinkled with joy.

Grace smiled up at him as they danced perfectly together in the wedding buzz on the dance floor.

'Let me tell you ma lady - you're blessed tonight, we all are,' his happiness came through his tone, Gus was a music lover it was in his soul, he loved all music.

Her smile was looking for something, he didn't know her well, but he knew that look. 'I know!' he said cheery, 'We are both blessed to be in each other's arms tonight.' He was half joking, but mostly serious.

Grace wondered if Gus turning up at the wedding was a sign. Had she been backing the wrong horse? *Was Gus the one?* Again, she questioned her attraction to him. Maybe he made all women feel like this, like they were special.

'Don't look at me like that Grace. Or I'll have to kiss you.' His ever-pleasant way made her get goosebumps.

Did she want him to kiss her? She thought about it. She'd actually thought about it more than she wanted to admit. 'Why did you really say yes to Ross?' The question snuck up on her.

Gus took a moment, 'You know why,' he said innocently as they smiled and danced slowly to the beautiful Italian opera, they'd gone into the second song and still hung onto each other.

She knew there was a split second to know whether she wanted him to kiss her or not, 'I can't kiss you Gus. I'm not ready. As much as I'd like to be, I have too many things happening in my life right now.'

'I figured so,' he paused still with that gentlemanly smile, covering up the disappointment. 'When you are ready, you know where to find me.' They danced to the end of the song, until Ross asked if he could kindly dance with his sister-in-law.

'Rosco,' Grace gasped turning into his arms, 'This is one hell of a wedding.'

Loving Grace

He swept her up into a big spin as they floated around the dance floor. 'I hope so,' he was content and enjoying himself. 'Are you having a good time Gracie? Cause you know that's important to me.'

'Of course, I know,' she beamed brightly noticing her brother-in-law had been enjoying his red wine.

'How great is Gus?'

'Oh! He's amazing,' she said as they danced amongst the now crowded dance floor. Grace realised that Ross was analysing her reaction, looking for something. 'What!' she laughed.

'Nothing. I just wanted to check in on you - make sure you're all right.'

'I'm perfectly fine,' she smiled. 'I'm a big girl.'

'I just like to know you're doing okay, not falling for famous musicians who think you're a bit of alright.'

'A bit of alright!' She laughed, her voice getting louder. 'Did he tell you that?'

'Not in so many words, but I know when a man's trying to pick up my sister-in-law,' Ross was talking with a slight mumble, something he did when he'd been drinking. 'I mean you could do worse. You have done worse,' he joked.

'I'm lousy with men,' she sighed with a big smile as they danced.

'No, you're not, but sometimes Gracie ya gotta take a punt in life, make a move, you know what I mean?'

She kind of did, 'I think so.'

'One day you'll thank me,' he huffed hoping he'd said enough.

Grace danced with both her sons, Ed and then Abbey before ending up in Jimmy's arms. He'd been by Louise's side most of the day, they'd been dancing making and having fun together, which was good to see.

'How are you?' he asked his sister. 'You look good. Are you having a good time?'

'Why, thank you. It's not even my wedding and yet everyone seems very interested in how I am.'

'Like whom?' Jimmy asked out of curiosity.

'You. Ross. Are you two up to something?'

'Not at all,' he smiled at her like she was silly, which pissed her off.

'Because if you are. Stop now. I'm fifty years old, I don't need you two doing whatever you're doing, so stop it please.' She was as frank as needed. 'Seriously you two are ridiculous.'

Jimmy laughed out loud, 'What! The only thing I would ever tell you is to be true to yourself. Do what is going to make you happy Grace. You deserve it. Make good choices.'

Loving Grace

She looked at her brother, 'What are my choices Jimmy?' Both Ross and now her brother had told the same thing.

'Don't fly off with some rock star because you're flattered when you've got something really fantastic right over there,' Jimmy huffed.

'Over where? Who, Lewis?' Grace squinted and stopped dancing. 'If he wanted me, he'd try a little harder.' She pouted looking away, only to see Lewis with a group of guests, he was standing close to a tall, gorgeous redhead who seemed to be at the wedding alone.

'I don't want to say it, but I will,' a pause from Jimmy. 'Why are you being so stubborn? Give him a little hope and maybe he'll surprise you.'

Her mood had changed, 'I don't want to be surprised Jimmy! I've had enough surprises to last me a lifetime.' Grace stopped dancing and stepped back from her big brother, she'd had too much to drink, everything was suddenly spinning, and she needed air, urgently.

'Are you okay, do you need a water?' asked Jimmy.

'I'm fine,' she huffed and turned away and wandered off to the edge of the party. Leaning up against a post she could taste the red wine on her lips as she watched out over the darkness of the valley. Everyone seemed to be having their say on her love life. The thing was, if Lewis wanted her, he'd had the past three days to tell her so. Seeing him here wasn't easy, but she'd realised tonight that they were over in every way, despite the efforts of their family. He'd had every chance to speak with her, to spend time with her, to reconnect with her.

Reaching out to the table behind her, Grace picked up a random glass of wine and turned back around and drank it as she looked out at the stars, her eyes welling with pitiful tears of love lost. She couldn't even have a good bitch to anyone, they were all team Lewis, even Abbey. Sniffing the tears back she took a huge gulp of somebody else's red wine and went out into the night to sit on one of the fancy bench seats. Grace knew she was drunk, and she knew she needed a moment on her own to gather herself. Just her and her glass of random wine. What did it matter? The cake had been cut, the formalities were over, Abbey was dancing, and Lewis was happily chatting up the redhead.

'Hey you! What are you doing out here on your own?'

She looked up and it was Gus, instantly a smile swept across her teary face mid cry.

'Let's walk!' he suggested and put his hand out to her, took her glass of wine and placed it under the bench seat. They walked slowly along one of the candle lit paths within sight of the wedding. 'I'm not going to ask why you've been crying,' Gus said softly knowing Grace wasn't in a great way.

'Good, because I don't want to tell you,' huffing a slight laugh. She felt better just hanging onto his hand, he was safe and had nothing in his power to hurt her or make her feel sad. They were friends, good friends and she trusted him with the vulnerable mood she was now finding herself in.

'Did you like the two sets we did, be honest, did you like the music?' Gus asked swinging her hand as they continued walking.

'Yeah, it was pretty good, you were great,' she slurred her words.

Gus couldn't help but laugh, he'd had a few drinks himself, and two joints with Pete, Ross, and Gabe over the other side of the pool. 'Now that the orchestra has finished, it's time for partying and dancing, I thought you'd be enjoying yourself with your family.'

'I think I'm ready to go home,' she paused, 'Back to Sydney I mean. I miss Sydney... It's been a long few weeks away and I want to go home.'

'You're home sick!' he said with a smile.

'I don't know.'

'I get home sick all the time when I'm on the road, not that I've got an actual home to go home to anymore. My new place is just a house were my things are.'

'What's wrong with us!' Grace couldn't help the wide smile across her face as they stopped in the moonlight, she sniffled on the edge of crying.

Gus looked at her, they faced each other, 'We're navigating not being married to the people we loved anymore,' Gus expressed with all seriousness. 'I don't think it's supposed to be a walk in the park,' he said smiling down at her.

'Absolutely not!' she sniffed in hard to keep her composure, and as she did, Gus leaned in and kissed her on the mouth, his hands at her arms. It was a gentle kiss, not forceful or assuming, very caring.

Grace's arms went up around his neck and as he wrapped her in his arms, this kiss had more feeling to it, more meaning. They understood each other, however, that didn't mean they knew exactly what the other wanted. As her breaths became fast and heated, Gus lifted her feet off the ground and she hung there in his arms, her lips to his for a few seconds before they both began laughing.

'I'm sorry if you didn't want me to kiss you,' Gus said, always the gentleman which played at her heartstrings, he was a good man.

Shaking her head, her smile was disguising her emotions that swirled around like a tornado inside her body. Her heart wasn't there, and yet she was so grateful for Gus and all his kindness.

'Our timing just isn't that great is it?' he let her down, so her feet touched the ground.

'The timing is shit!' she laughed with tear filled eyes. 'It's not you Gus,' she felt so cliche saying it, but it was true, 'It's me. I've got a lot going on in my head.' Grace put her hands through

413

her hair and pushed it all back off her face. 'You are a lovely man, but…' She began to cry; she was in love with another man.

'What about we go back to the wedding and get you a soda water and we sit out on the quiet side of the pool, you can put your feet in the water, I can smoke. How does that sound?' As much as Gus wanted Grace, he knew she didn't feel the same way.

'I think I want to go up to my room, I need to sleep this off. Will you walk me up to the house, I don't want to see anyone.' She'd stopped crying, but the tears still twinkled under her eyes.

'I will,' he said smiling and taking her hand in his. They walked the entire way around the wedding festivities, so Grace wouldn't have to see anyone, they said goodbye to each other at the front door of the estate, Grace went up to her bedroom and cried herself to sleep while Gus went back to the wedding and continued to party.

A knock at the door woke her in the early hours of the morning. Jumping up, throwing her beige silk night wrap around her body she rushed to the door and opened it, still in a daze.

'Mum, I've been looking for you,' said Bella holding her shoes in her hand, her smile was loving, and Abbey standing beside her.

'I wasn't sure where you'd gone, are you okay?' Abbey could tell her friend had been crying.

'I had a little too much to drink, so I put myself to bed,' Grace smiled.

Abbey kissed Grace on the cheek, 'I've danced so much I don't think I can stand a second longer.'

'Goodnight.'

'Mum, can I sleep in with you tonight,' Bella's voice was demure and sweet as her mother opened the door smiling.

Mid-morning and the wedding festivities started over again. This afternoon, the newlyweds would head off on a honeymoon of Greek island hopping whilst everyone else packed to head off home tomorrow.

Grace and Bella had slept in until noon, only woken by a chopper flying over the house, which was Gus and Pete leaving. After lunch they joined everyone by the pool for a lazy afternoon, Grace a little weary, but then so was everyone.

The wedding night had been joyous and gone right through to daylight for some. Now Abbey sat with Louise and Scarlet on sunbeds on the far side of the pool. Most of the guests who weren't family had left or were in the midst of leaving. Grace went and sat down on a sunbed next to Scarlet, they went over last night's events and the standout highlights of all the ceremony and Ruby forgetting her lines, the dancing and the orchestra and Gus and Pete. Then they settled in and the four of them lay peacefully in the sun.

Loving Grace

'Lew left for home early this morning,' Scarlet whispered to her aunty. 'Did something happen to you two last night, he just got up and left, which was really odd.'

'We didn't even talk at the wedding,' she turned her head to Scarlet.

'Oh, I just wondered. He wasn't supposed to go home until tomorrow.'

Grace left it at that, although Lewis was all she could think about all afternoon and for the rest of the evening as she packed her cases and got ready for an early morning departure, and why had he left early!

As she lay in her bed alone for her final night of what had been truly an amazing trip, she was grateful to Marlo and Ross for their generosity as always. She had a good sister, no two ways about it. She'd got to spend time with her family, her best friend, her children, and her gorgeous nieces. She'd met some knew friends, seen and experienced fabulous places. Being with her family was always a blessing, Grace never took it for granted.

Chapter Twenty-One

Unlocking her apartment door and walking in really felt like being home. Grace shut the front door behind her and took a big breath in, then released it. She'd been contemplating moving; she was still undecided although she did love being in the city and had vowed and declared never to go back to the country house. Here she was close to her sister and children, the fact that Lewis was upstairs wasn't a plus... they were in a very strange space between friends and ex's. Grace doubted they would even see each other in the building often at all, she barely saw the other neighbours. Trying to figure him out was beyond Grace, she just needed to accept that they were over, and when she saw him at Marlo's for dinners, she'd have to tough it out. The worst thing was that this coming weekend was Mac's birthday. Yes, another Hunter birthday that would be over the top. Marlo had said it was a low-key Saturday night gathering... which would be a party, it always was.

Being home meant some changes, Kristian would be going to Los Angeles to live in a few weeks. Luca would be a father in about six months. And Bella, well she was Bella. She'd talked about maybe moving out of Luca's and into Grace's again but wasn't actually committing.

Waking up on her second day home, she was feeling brighter, more positive, Grace decided she'd up her days at Marlo's shelter from Saturday mornings to Tuesday and Thursday's too, the shelter seemed to center her. It bought things into perspective a little and having a purpose other than herself was good for her. She'd think about setting certain work hours aside for her business, Scarlet had suggested that one while in Italy, they'd done a little lite brainstorming. Wanting to be positive was one thing, having the drive to follow through was another for Grace. One minute she was feeling great, the next she wanted to go back to bed and sleep for a week. She'd thought that by now she should be over herself... Shouldn't she be! By the afternoon, doom had set in, and she spent the night on the sofa binge watching series two of Sex Education.

The next morning, she had no drive to get out of bed. Friday's had for a long part of her life been her favourite day of the week, however, this one was not. This particular Friday was Michael's birthday and as much as she hated him, she still loved him. Normally she'd make a big deal for birthday breakfasts, she got pleasure out of making his birthday's special. Today was very different. She wouldn't even be wishing her husband of nearly thirty years happy birthday, in fact, she hoped he had an awful day.

Saturday morning, Grace woke up feeling good, the days were like roller coaster rides since being home. Today she was spritely. Bella decided to stay the night, she had got in around two a.m. and then woken up hungry, so they went on foot to the local farmers market together, Grace buying French bread and pastries, coffee for their breakfast, they sat on a park bench together enjoying the mid-morning sun.

'I met such a nice guy last night Mum,' Bella said with a mouth full of croissant. 'His name is Harris.'

'And?' questioned Grace.

'Normal height, blonde hair and very sweet. I think he's the one,' Bella was glowing, and Grace couldn't help but smile at her daughters happiness. 'Yep. I'm having dinner with him tomorrow night,' said Bella, she'd been a different girl since their trip away, loving towards Grace, happier with life in general.

'Did he pick the restaurant or did you?' asked Grace.

'Of course, I did,' Bella smiled going on to tell her mother about him for the next fifteen minutes while they ate.

Loving Grace

They walked past the makeup store and bought Mac a nice present for her birthday and then pottered home stopping in a few more stores to do some more shopping on the sunny Saturday that it was. Time spent as mother and daughter alone was wonderful. For Grace it felt like her daughter, although only nineteen, had done some growing up on their trip to Europe. Not once since they'd come home had Bella been nasty to her or blamed her for something.

'If it's okay with you mum, I'd like to move back in permanently with you,' she'd said as they walked back to the apartment, arms full of shopping bags.

'You never have to ask. My home will always be your home.' Grace said pressing the lift button as they waited in the lobby of her building.

'Great, because I love being here.' Bella smiled at her.

The lobby door opened and in came a hot and sweaty Lewis in his running gear, Grace was a little stunned. 'Morning,' he gasped for breath coming to a halt beside the girls.

'Afternoon, don't you mean?' Bella gave him a look. 'How far did you run today Lewis?' she asked to be amusing.

'Fifteen K's.' He answered panting for breath.

Grace wondering why he didn't take the stairs; he usually did after a run. Mostly she wondered why he hadn't looked her in the eye. *Was it all in her head?*

'I'm moving back in with my mum,' Bella announced to him as he stood looking slightly uncomfortable.

'That's great,' he puffed as all three of them got in the lift.

'Yep.' Bella said smiling proudly. 'You going tonight?'

'Yeah! I'll see you ladies there,' he said as the lift stopped at their floor and they got out.

'Bye Lewis.' Bella waved.

'See you tonight,' Grace said softly turning to him and giving him right as the lift door closed. Not wanting to seem unfriendly even though it felt like he'd done his best to completely ignore her. For some reason she felt he was offish with her, he certainly looked okay - very okay.

Inside the apartment Bella and Grace put the shopping away. 'Do you want to move in straight away?'

'I do if that's okay with you. I was even thinking of getting my things now from Luca's.'

'Would you like me to help you?'

'That would be great.' Things seemed to be on the up. With Bella moving in, it would force Grace to organize her workspace a little better out in the living room, it was time to get a desk. She wanted to be more organized, the demand for her jewelry in the past few weeks since the trade fair was high, it was time to throw herself back into her business.

Loving Grace

For the afternoon at least life felt normal, hanging out with Bella, and moving her out of Luca's and back into her apartment was just like old times. Luca announcing, he was bringing Jasmine his pregnant friend to Mac's birthday party tonight at Marlo and Ross's home, which was exciting for all of them.

Sometimes Grace looked in the mirror at herself and liked what she saw, tonight was one of those nights. Being fifty was settling with her, she was a good fifty, her skin was clear with a glow, bouncing blonde hair, her eyes blue and clear, she felt confidently well.

The weather was pleasant, so she'd put on a knew white dress that was flattering in all the places that counted at fifty. Wearing all her own jewelry designs was something Grace didn't do often, but tonight she just felt like it... Why not! Her makeup was spot on, natural with nudes as her skin still looked sun kissed from her holiday. Finally putting on a pair of clear pumps and a final spray of perfume, she was ready to go. Kristian was dropping past in his uber in approximately five minutes time, so she and Bella would wait out the front at the end of the small street for him.

'I want to tell you something mum, but I don't want to upset you, or for you to be angry at me.' Bella looked stunning in her red dress.

Grace now felt her good spirit dwindling fast. She didn't speak, she listened to her daughter. 'Tina called me a few days ago to see if I'd have dinner with her and dad for his birthday last night,' Bella looked at Grace, like she was expecting a reaction, but she didn't get one. 'I said I didn't want to go.' Bella was a little flustered, like she was telling her mother out of guilt, which Grace didn't like. 'But then Tina asked me how I was doing and how the trip went, and how you were.' She was looking to her mother for some kind of approval or for her to say it was okay she'd given Tina the time of day. 'I told her you were good.'

It took Grace a few moments to respond, 'You shouldn't feel bad about talking to Tina.'

'I didn't want to talk to her, she called me!' Bella gasped awkwardly.

'Sweetheart you don't need to explain yourself to me.' It hurt, it really hurt! 'Don't feel bad about talking to Tina, or your father for that matter.' Grace had already thought about this very moment, when Tina reached out to Bella, because she knew at some point she would. Tina loved Bella like she was her own and it would be killing her to not have contact with her. Grace knew that for certain.

'Well, I don't want to talk to her. Or dad. I didn't even wish him happy birthday yesterday,' the hurt in Bella's voice was evident.

Loving Grace

'I want you to know,' Grace said taking the higher ground even though it killed her. 'That you need to do what feels right for you in this situation. Not for me.' Just then, Kristian's uber pulled up and they got in, driving up the end of the street and around the bend to Marlo and Ross's house. She sat next to Bella in the back of the uber, proud she was able to say what she thought was right, and not get upset or say something she couldn't take back, or worse, make her daughter feel bad about something she had no control over.

Marlo's apparent get-together was indeed a flashy party, lots of people enjoying the sun going down over the harbour, a DJ, not to mention a lot of young people who looked like they were all out to impress each other with their uniqueness, that was Mac's friends.

Grace looked around as Bella and Kristian literally went in two different directions leaving her alone by the terrace doors. Huge glass bifold doors opened up one entire wall of Marlo's living room and the house became part of the outdoor party. She stood there scoping out were the cool older people were, or if there were any at all. It depended on who she thought was cool. Ross and Gabe were about as cool as it got from first glances, then she saw them with Marlo's friend Kitty and decided to settle for Louise and Shiv talking to some random people she'd never seen before.

'Oh, Grace, I want you to meet someone,' Marlo said rushing past her, not stopping just giving her sister a peck on the cheek.

'Sure,' She felt the overwhelming sensation of being at the party on her own, she took a drink from a passing waiter and headed to Lou and Shiv. Welcomed with hugs and introduced to the random people, Grace was a quiet observer for three drinks and what felt like way too long. Until Lewis arrived with what could only be a date. A young, attractive woman who was without doubt beautiful to look at but so very young, it was an insult to Grace. It was inevitable that this was going to happen at some point. Six months ago, she'd never even notice Lewis walking in, she'd never have talked to him, and she'd never have imagined he'd make love so fucking sensationally well.

Grace's lungs collapsed as she looked away, a strange tremble came over her as she took a deep breath to settle her emotions that threatened tears. She was devastated, and yet not surprised that he'd moved on. Watching him out of the corner of her eye, he walked a little further into the crowd with his new young and very sexy friend by his side. Louise couldn't see, she had her back to Lewis. Shiv saw and gave Grace a quick look but never said anything. Now that Lewis had his back to her, she watched on wishing it were she at his side, not some young girl barely out of high school! She took another breath, maybe he was better off with a younger woman, rather than her. *Yep!* Grace told herself as she reached for a reddish coloured cocktail from the passing waiter. As she took a gulp, it was strong, the rum was overpowering but just what she needed. Grace didn't drink rum. Suddenly she did, taking big gulps and downing her cocktail. Eyes flickering from the conversation between Louise and Shiv and the nice randoms over to Lewis and his sexy young date. Then when Marlo went up and gave the sexy young date a kiss on the cheek and a hug as Lewis introduced them. Grace was mortified! 'What the fuck!' she actually said out loud making both Shiv and Louise look at her. 'Sorry!' she apologised shaking her hand apologetically out in front of herself, her eyes going back to the action. How could her sister do that, be so warm and kind! Unable to take her eyes away from the scene as Lewis introduced his date to everyone, even Bella! Then Luca arrived, he gave his mother a wave from the far side of the terrace and made his way straight into the eye of the storm, he went straight up to Lewis' sexy young date and kissed her cheek. This was absolutely absurd and unacceptable.

After drink number four, Grace was ready to have her own introduction, so with her best confident and sophisticated walk, Grace fluffed her blonde bob out and went over. How could this young woman be that interesting, even Kristain was in on it now, they were all chatting and laughing, smiling and kissing and hugging. *How could they!* She stopped and stood behind Kristian, looking at the group, unable to hear what was going on. Luca, the sexy girl, and a few others were in the depths of conversation, when Lewis saw Grace. Without thinking she frowned at him, squinting her eyes, pursing her lips. She tried not to look agitated, giving her head a slight flick.

Lewis frowned back at her and raised his brows at her questioningly.

'Mum!' Luca interrupted her thoughts. 'Meet Jasmine,' he said putting his arm around the sexy young girl – who wasn't Lewis's date at all. 'Jasmine, this is my mum, Grace.'

Her mouth dropped open, with nothing coming out, Grace sucked in air for a moment, 'Uh... oh... hello.' The last thing she wanted to do was look stunned meeting the person who was carrying her grandchild for the very first time, so Grace snapped into action. 'It is so lovely to meet you Jasmine.' She took the young girls hands in hers and held them, smiling.

'It's nice to meet you too – can I call you Grace?' Jasmine said as if she was unsure of Grace, suddenly this young girl looked so pretty and kind.

It was love at first sight for Grace, in her head she prayed this beautiful young woman wasn't a devil in disguise, that she would always be as lovely as she in this moment. 'Of course, please, call me Grace.' Not taking her eyes off Jasmine, she was captivating, and it was obvious what her son had been so attracted to. From there the conversation flowed. And when she asked Luca on the side why Jasmine had arrived with Lewis, he simply explained they'd picked Lewis up on the way and then he got stuck out the front on a business call, so Jasmine had walked into the party with Lewis instead of waiting on the street with him. Delighted was an understatement, this girl was young, yes, but she was polite, smart and Grace watched closely as she looked up into Luca's eyes with adoration. Cautious adoration naturally, but there was something true in her young eyes and Grace felt ease in her heart. And just like that, her world was coming back into focus, her stomach had been unknotted, and her chest wasn't tight anymore.

'She's fabulous!' Marlo whispered into her ear as they both watched on as the younger generation enjoyed the party.

'So far,' Grace said softly. 'I really hope she is.' Then Grace felt a familiar hand on her shoulder.

'I need to talk to you, if you've got a minute?' Lewis questioned her, rather than asked her. He looked concerned.

'Of course,' she replied looking surprised. She followed him into the living room and then down the hall and into what Marlo called her private sitting room, which was really her office. A room filled with books, expensive art, a plush red velvet sofa, and an impressive desk, the room had seriously been styled of the charts.

'How are you?' Grace smiled with confidence and control.

He looked at her and paused, 'Not that great. I don't think.'

Her smile turned to a frown, 'What's wrong?' she examined his troubled face, something was up, she'd never seen him quite like this.

'Are you okay?' he counter questioned her with a tone she hadn't been expecting.

'I'm fine!' Grace gushed, confused, she narrowed her eyes at him. 'Are you upset with me?'

'Kind of.'

'What have I done?' she was oblivious.

Again, Lewis paused and looked uncomfortable, he shrugged a little frustrated, like he wanted to speak but didn't know what to say.

'Lewis. What's going on?' She huffed. 'You said you needed to talk to me.'

'I need to ask you something,' he paused hesitantly. 'In Italy I wanted to talk to you in private, but I never got the chance.'

They stood looking at one another for some time before either of them spoke.

'This really isn't the best place to talk, but I...' he huffed a laugh, looking at her with sexy as eyes. Calming her a little.

Grace shrugged her shoulders and laughed too, 'If you've got something...'

Just then, he leaned down and kissed her mouth before she could finish. His gentle lips over hers, controlling the narrative immediately, taking the lead, giving her no way to back out. Both breathing into each other.

If Grace objected to his actions, she wasn't letting on, wrapping her arms up around his neck and pulling his body to hers, gasping at his mouth in the privacy of Marlo's sitting room. The heat between them was like they'd never been apart for one single second. Lewis felt like home to Grace, and she was all he'd thought about the whole time they'd been broken up.

He kissed her, walking her backwards into the nook were Marlo's desk sat, lifting Grace to the wall out of sight should the door open. Pressing his body to her, Grace could feel his masculine and disciplined body beginning to arouse hers. Who in their right mind would stop now. She went with him move for move. Her beautiful white dress was bunched up around her thighs as Lewis kissed her urgently, his hands ruffling through her dress fabric to touch her legs. Grace now lifting herself to his neck as he ripped her underwear from her body and then reached down to his own pants to unbutton them frantically. The music from outside buffering their sounds. The heat was on and there was no stopping this steam train..

It was sudden and abrupt, Lewis was inside Grace with one determined thrust, she gasped at the intrusion. Immediately thrusting deeper and deeper, as she jolted up the wall, her body so sweet and warm. Lewis grunting with desire every time he pounded himself into her body. They spoke no words. Eager hands swirling through his short dark hair as she was overcome with the sensation of him deep inside her stomach, buzzing from head to toe with his goodness as their mad sex romp went from frenzied crazy, to slow measured and intimate lusting love making. Tender kisses to her neck as she groaned with what could only be described as relieved pleasure to have him inside her again. Nobody had ever made love to Grace the way Lewis did. As his cock pushed gently into her body, she felt him stretching her open, evoking every sexual sense of her being. Such strength and care all at once was as sexy as it was comforting. If she only made love to one person for the rest of her life, he was the one.

'Lewis!' Overpowered by emotion, Grace felt her body responding, cumming to his girth, her eyes watering as he stilled long and hard inside Grace, her warm flesh contracting to him, burning around him as he came inside her.

'Gracie!' he panted for breath, his head resting on her shoulder.

Only for a second did they stay in each other's arms, 'How do we get out of this without making a mess?' Grace smiled as Lewis looked at her.

'What about that scarf thing on the sofa,' he suggested looking around the room.

'No! Not my sisters scarf.'

'I'll get her a new one,' Lewis said shuffling over a few steps, still holding onto Grace, and still inside her, so he could grab the scarf.

Grace stood looking up at Lewis for a moment before they re-entered the party, 'I feel terrible about my sisters scarf.' She bit down on her bottom lip.

Loving Grace

'She'll never know it's gone. I promise you,' the glint in his eyes as he laid a kiss on her lips made Grace want him again. It was hard to ignore the impulse she had to take Lewis into another room and fuck him again. Once he'd been the epitome of her dislike, now the complete opposite. 'I'll replace the underwear too.' He gave her another kiss to the lips.

Standing in the middle of the living room on the edge of the party, minus her underwear that Lewis had ripped off her body, and with a now very creased beautiful white dress, Lewis at her side, both assessing the party before re-entering the hive of activity.

'Can I take you for a drink and dinner tomorrow night?' Lewis asked as they both looked forward.

'Absolutely.'

'I'll be at your door at five.'

'See you then.' And with that, they both walked off in different directions.

'Where have you been?' Louise gave her a grin as Grace joined her group.

'In the kitchen talking,' Grace told a white lie.

'Everything okay, you look flushed?'

To Grace it felt like everyone was constantly checking up on her. She loved that she was loved, the past few months had been her hardest, and everyone had shown up for her. But it also made her feel like they all thought she was incapable of being happy, which wasn't true, it was just how she felt sometimes. Finally, she could smile and honestly say, 'I'm really well, thanks Lou. What about you, are you good, is everything good with you?'

'I'm good,' Louise said checking her out. 'Clearly not as good as you though, by the look on our face,' Lou paused and couldn't help but grin. 'What have you been drinking?'

'Hahaha, wouldn't you like to know!' Grace teased. From then on the night looked up, it was like old times, the two of them getting up to mischief, drinking too much and talking a bunch of bullshit as they danced and entertained each other. Mac's birthday party turned out to be one of the most successful and fun-filled parties Marlo had ever hosted. Grace didn't mention her sexual encounter with Lewis to a sole, she wanted to keep it for herself for now. The rest of the night they didn't speak, there were however, a few long sexy looks through the crowd to one another.

At ten a.m. Marlo pressed at Grace's door buzzer like the building was on fire, she'd set out on a walk and stopped by her sisters to see if she wanted to come along. Marlo loved going out for a walk the morning after a party at her house, it was like a reset for her.

'Really!' Grace buzzed her sister into the building with one eye open.

Loving Grace

As Marlo got to the door, Grace put her finger to her mouth for her sister to keep the noise down, 'Bella is sleeping... I was sleeping too, we didn't get home until daylight,' she grumped as Marlo gushed by her and spun around in the middle of the living room. She looked perfect, fresh, and ready for the day, whereas Grace had hair in a birds nest, her night gown was hanging off her shoulder and only one eye was fully open.

'I thought you'd like to walk with me. It's a beautiful Sunday morning,' Marlo had this slight edge to her voice.

'I don't think I'm up for walking today. I drank a lot last night, I'm kind of hung over,' Grace's voice was husky, she'd partied hard with Lou and was paying the price this morning.

'Yes, well, I'm feeling great.'

'Good for you,' Grace cleared her throat. Her sister took that many vitamins and potions to prolong aging and life that she rarely had hangovers.

'Well then, I'll go on my own.' She walked to the door. 'Glad you had a good last night, Mac enjoyed herself.' Marlo lingered at the door. 'Oh, and you won't believe it!' she gasped shockingly, 'Fiorella found my Hermes silk scarf from my sitting room in the rubbish bin this morning, messed up with body fluids of a sexual nature... With a pair of torn women's underpants wrapped up inside it.' Marlo glared at her. 'Fiorella was mortified!' She held her eyes at Grace's waiting for her reactions. 'I mean who would do such a thing, and in my sitting room!'

'Wow!' What else could Grace possibly say.

'Fiorella said she'd seen the underwear before.' She was looking at Grace so intensely, so accusingly.

'That's awful. How disgusting!' Grace paused, 'Must have been good sex!'

'No. Not good sex,' Marlo was seriously pissed, speaking at a whisper but so bent out of shape. 'Not with my Hermes scarf. Not in my sitting room.' She went to the door. 'Are you coming to dinner tonight?'

'No. I'm out tonight.' Grace held her breath.

'Right. Well, have a nice time... I'm heading up to see Lewis now. Will he be there?' Marlo was pissed but playing with Grace all the same.

'How should I know!'

Marlo did the long stare at her sister like she was onto her and her antics of last night. 'Enjoy your date tonight,' Marlo said looking at Grace with curious eyes.

'It's not a date!' she shook her head.

Marlo shut the door.

Grace huffing and puffing with relief that her sister had gone, she went to make a cup of tea, she had the afternoon to get ready for her not a date with Lewis, she wanted to do a face mask, a hair treatment and pick out the perfect outfit. This dinner with Lewis felt important, although not a date, not even Marlo could derail her today.

Chapter Twenty-Two

Bella sat on the edge of the bath in Grace's bathroom watching her mother get ready, 'Anyone special?' she asked noticing her mother was taking extra special care with her makeup and hair tonight.

'Yes, actually. It's someone very special,' Grace continued with her mascara.

'Oh. Wow. Very special!' Bella smiled, pleased to see her mum so happy. 'Someone I know?' Her eyes widened with hope.

'Maybe.'

'Oh my god! It's Lewis, isn't it?'

Grace didn't answer straight away, that would show too much excitement, and if it turned out that Lewis was only wanting dinner to make sure he and Grace could just be friends moving forward, then she didn't want to get too ahead of herself or hurt. 'I'd rather not say.' She started to put on several gold bracelets on the one wrist, clustering them.

437

Loving Grace

'So, it is Lewis... Mum why won't you just say it's Lewis?' Bella sounded confused, she was happy it was maybe Lewis, could her mother not tell!

'Because!' Grace was being very guarded.

'Well, I hope it is Lewis,' Bella said to her mum, 'I know you care about him a lot and that he feels the same way about you.' Her words soft and caring making her mother look at her. 'He told me when we were in Italy.'

'It's just dinner Bella.' Grace shrugged hoping she wasn't setting herself up for heartache again.

'Mum, why don't you see what everyone else sees.' They were still in the bathroom having this conversation.

'I'm not sure what you see exactly,' she smiled fidgeting through her tray of jewels. 'Let me guess, a lady who's been a tad crazy lately!'

'My mum is smart and self-made, she's sassy and sexy – not to mention her beautiful heart.'

These words made Grace bite at her bottom lip, overwhelmed that her daughter could be so kind and loving. Bella had been a hard one to crack, more so than the boys and at times Grace felt like she'd missed out on the connection she so desired with her daughter. Until of late.

'Self-made!' Grace laughed, doubting the pedestal her daughter had her on.

'Yeah, you are. You've taught the boys and me we have to work hard for what we want in life, and how to get back up when we fall.' Bella spoke softly and with such meaning, she was very understanding of how far her mother had come. 'You're a great woman mum.'

'Thank you.' Grace was in a state of shock, lovely shock.

'Tonight, be yourself. You deserve someone like Lewis, he sees your goodness and worth.' *Was this a pep talk from her daughter!*

Without saying so, Bella was comparing Lewis to her father who had betrayed her mother at the highest level. Bella didn't know if she could ever forgive her dad, he'd caused them all so much pain, most of all her mother, and it hadn't been easy for her or her brothers to watch.

Grace took the hands of her daughter, 'Thank you so much for everything you just said, it means more to me than you'll ever know.' Her eyes filled with tears, 'Everything I've ever done in life is for you and your brothers, and lately it's been hard I know, I've had to do things just for me, just so I can get out of bed every morning, and I couldn't have done it without you,' she paused, 'So I need to thank you my beautiful girl. Having you around has made all the difference.'

Bella battered her kind eyes tearfully, 'Oh, Mama!' They embraced and hugged, the connection between them was stronger than ever.

Loving Grace

That familiar knock at the door was right on five o'clock, just a few minutes after Bella had headed off around to Marlo's for Sunday night dinner,

'Hi.' Grace's eyes were sparkling as she stood there in her tailored jeans, black blazer, white silk shirt, and heels. Her delight in seeing Lewis couldn't be hidden, not even if she tried. It was like every sensory in her body was stimulated with pleasure just by seeing him.

'Hi,' he said softly, calmly and with the same sparkle in his eye. 'You look great. Really great!'

'Thank you,' a smile as she looked away from Lewis and then back to him. 'So do you.' She stepped out the door and closed it behind her. They both knew if they didn't leave this very minute, this strange yet very family feeling would lead to something more. Lewis had booked a car to drive them into town, the evening weather was mild, and he wanted to take Grace somewhere he'd never taken her before. They went to a new bar that wasn't far at all from the restaurant he'd chosen.

Sitting at the bar Grace drank a martini and Lewis went for beer. Her hair was blow dried with a hint of her natural wave taking over, she had her usual nude makeup on, blazer off, white shirt open low at the front. Never did Grace try to be something she wasn't, she was elegant and current, she didn't feel the need to dress younger than her years to impress anyone, and that was true style in Lewis' opinion.

As they sat, Grace appreciated Lewis for the exceptionally good-looking man he was. Younger, yes. Sexy, yes. Would other women be looking at him tonight, yes. It was hard not to notice Lewis Hunter, she could now admit that freely to herself. The time had passed when she felt people would look at them and think she was so much older than he, this wasn't prevalent anymore. Things had evolved between them, those kind of thoughts were behind her now. For a split-second Grace imagined unbuttoning his linen shirt, then as he spoke her eyes went to his.

'About last night,' he said. Grace didn't say a word, she let him go, if this was his let down, she was prepared, she was going to be cool about it. 'I hope you didn't think I just wanted sex.'

She sighed, 'I'm not sure what I thought. I was a happy and willing participant. Did you notice?' her humour shone through.

'I know you were,' he smiled at her. 'I'd never use you for sex,' Lewis was coy, yet serious.

'Oh!' She fumbled. 'Good. I guess. I'm glad - unless you didn't like my sex.' She was distracted by his smoldering eyes.

He couldn't help but laugh at her response, 'Gracie. I loved your sex.'

He was making her nervous. As much as she thought she'd prepared herself for whatever he said tonight, she was overwhelmed. In her heart she'd wanted him to want her, but she'd also talked herself into accepting that maybe he didn't. At this point she was none the wiser.

Loving Grace

'Gracie!' Lewis prompted her as she sat in her own thoughts.

'Mmm.' She wasn't sure if this was his way of saying he liked her or just the beginning of a huge let down. 'Oh, um. I love your sex too.'

Lewis gave her a funny look, he sensed her anxiety, 'I really didn't want us to be over. I know you had to do things your way, I get it, I really do,' He was saying everything right, everything she wanted to hear.

Grace was so aware he had the capability to woo women at the blink of an eye, she didn't want to just give into his charm, and yet she didn't want to push him away again. This sabotaging her own happiness had to stop tonight.

'Lewis,' she smiled at him, sparkling eyes, a dreamy look, 'I didn't want it to be over either,' a pause as she thought her words out carefully. 'It wasn't you. It was me getting scared. Me not trusting that you weren't that kind of man. A man I couldn't trust.' The conversation had gone back to being serious.

'I wanted to give you space. Normally I wouldn't have let you discard of me like that.' His cheeky little smirk was playful and delightful.

She had to smile, 'Normally, I wouldn't have discarded you.' If sexy was her intention, she was kicking goals. 'You realise I'm not sure if I'm worthy of you Lewis, right!' Her eyes never left his. 'I'm a fifty-year-old woman, not overly confident within myself. I'm slightly crazy for good reason,' she laughed.

'And I've got kids with adult problems I'm trying to navigate... I've got baggage.'

Lewis looked at her with his caring eyes, 'I don't have the best relationship track record. I'm set in my way. I'm weirdly overly dedicated to my job, and I've recently discovered I have a thing for older women,' he smiled at her. 'Especially cute little crazy blonde ones.' He had to give her humour back, she was expecting it, and it worked so well for them. 'You make me happy in ways I never knew I could be Gracie.' He took a breath. 'And I think you're amazing, and you are more than worthy of me, in every way,' he chuckled.

As deep as it was, Grace wished she could record this for Abbey to hear, she'd freak out. A mere sentence from him had Grace feeling like she was on top of the world... *She wished she were on top of him!*

They stayed at the bar, ate a hot bowl of chips and aioli, and talked about everything from Kristian moving to L.A. to Lewis and his newfound love of making dumplings. The chatter didn't stop, they laughed about how lavish the Italy Tuscan estate was and how very Marlo and Ross it was. Grace opened up to him about her business and how she had this newfound energy to expand and take it to the next level. He was a go-getter, Lewis loved that Grace was striving for more success, she was vibrant, and she wanted more.

'Can I take you home?' It was ten thirty and they had talked for hours, and the natural flow of the evening seemed

Loving Grace

like it needed to head back to one of their apartments and do what they'd each been thinking about all night. When Lewis looked at Grace he saw a smart sexy independent woman he'd admired from a distance for years and years. She was realistic and never put expectations on him. The sex he had with Grace was real and meaningful, it wasn't just sex, it was so much more. Their relationship was so much more than sex though.

Grace insisted on paying for the bar tab, they had enjoyed themselves so much they never left the bar and went onto the restaurant.

Lewis was a good man at heart, he was more than she'd ever given him credit for over the years, and if there was a barometer for sex appeal, he'd blow it up.

They stepped out into the calm Sydney night; they held hands as they walked to the end of the street to meet the car that was taking them home. It seemed like everything was right in the world tonight, until!

It was a blink of an eye and Grace came to a stop in the street, she had walked head on into Tina. She was right there in front of her, they both came to a standstill. They'd been walking in the opposite direction to each other, what were the odds! To make the moment worse, Michael was at Tina's side. The world had stopped, and the seconds felt like forever. Here they were the four of them, Grace and Lewis hand in hand, and Michael and Tina together, all facing each other in the middle of a busy night CBD street.

'Grace!' Tina gasped; she was shocked yet the happiness in her eye to see her long-time ex-friend was evident. Her eyes going from Grace to Lewis, who'd she'd always had a thing for, then back to Grace who needed a moment to gather herself. 'You look well.' Tina broke a small smile; she'd forgotten she'd betrayed her best friend in the most unforgivable of ways - literally now flaunting it in front of her. Tina missed Grace in a way that was so profoundly deep.

'Hello, Grace!' now Michael had plucked up the courage to say something even though his archrival was standing there glaring at him and holding what was still his wife's hand. The outrage of it! Michael had heard about Grace and Lewis; he'd thought it was over and done with, but clearly not.

Grace was speechless, she couldn't breathe, unable to take her eyes off Tina, she wasn't ready to look at Michael, to give him the satisfaction of her eyes.

'Grace... I'm...' Tina floundered in her own pathetic space just as Grace found her words.

Looking straight at Tina, she said, 'You did always say you never attract anyone special,' a pause from Grace with a smile, 'How insightful, you were so right!' And with that said, Grace looked up to Lewis who stood looking too damn hot and sexy for his own good, smirking at her killer words. Finally, she glanced at Michael, her eyes penetrating his for only a mere painful second before she turned away and walking off down the street with Lewis holding her hand in his.

Loving Grace

Her inner core had wanted to punch, kick, scratch, bite, kill... Whatever it took to hurt both Michael and Tina, but instead, she walked away an empowered woman who'd shown restraint. Again, she looked up to Lewis with a triumphant smile, he couldn't hide his pride. Proud of her class and integrity. Grace hadn't lowered herself to their level and been a spiteful bitch.

'Let me take you home,' Lewis said oozing tenderness and compassion. Grace was so in control, so feminine and strong in the way she'd taken back the power.

They'd contained it in the lift even though the air was thick with sexual tension. He'd opened his front door and held it open for her, watching her as she walked into his apartment in her tight sexy jeans, black blazer over her shoulder, clutch bag under her arm. Twirling on her heels she looked back at him, her smile had a sweetness, a calmness that made him want her.

'Thank you for tonight,' she said softly.

'Which part, the beers and hot chips or keeping my mouth shut when I really wanted to smack that dickhead in the head.'.

'All of it,' she sighed putting her blazer on the sofa and taking a big breath. 'For making me laugh, and for holding my hand in what I thought was supposed to be my worst moment ever, facing them!' she sniffed her composure. 'It was a good night.' She was cute and cool, her hair fluffy and wavey.

'You did well Gracie. I gotta tell you, very smooth baby.' Lewis smiled.

Trying to stop the emotional tears welling in her eyes, they were from pride, from happiness, from relief. 'Thank you.'

Lewis walked to her, the white silk shirt was showing her hardening nipples beneath, the bronze glow of her European tan turning him on. A gold chain with a pearl drop hung just above her cleavage, his hand reached out to her shirt top button. With a gentle hand he unbuttoned his way down the shirt, it fell open, his eyes admiring her softness, her beauty. 'The whole time we were in Italy, I wanted to you desperately,' Lewis's words were quiet and measured, his fingers pushed her shirt gently off her shoulders and then her bra straps. Leaning forward he kissed her shoulder as she stood in the middle of his living room, dim lamps lit the room. The lights of the harbour the backdrop.

'I've never stopped wanting you,' Grace began to unbutton his shirt, eager to feel his body at hers.

Lewis looked deeply into her eyes, letting her take his shirt off, he undid his own pants and kicked them off, then he went to his knees and peeled Grace's jeans down her legs as she stood silently in front of him, she stepped out of her heels. Resting his hands at her hips out in front of him, fingers slipping inside her knickers sliding them down her thighs to her knees, she stepped out of one leg and put her hand to his shoulder, carefully pushing him back onto the sofa, she sat over his lap, his hardness between them, his body warm at her front, Grace stared into his eyes, their breathing the only sound.

Loving Grace

Lewis leaned back and pulled her up into his arms and let her settle down on his hard stiff cock. His end pressing into her soft moist pussy as she sank over him, warmth flushed through her, an inner happiness as she felt him inside her body that she hadn't felt for a while came back to her sole. His hands roamed her back as she rolled herself into his hips, feeling him deep in her stomach too soon, but the pain of his cock imbedded in her body was the most beautiful and erotic sensation ever.

'Gracie!' Lewis gasped to her ear as he pushed himself inside her. 'I want you in my life... more than just friends.'

Wrapping her arms around his neck she ran her fingers through his hair, her lips curling with happiness, 'Oh, I think we're more than friends.' His penetration was consuming her.

'I need more than friends,' he panted, 'I need to make love to you,' he kissed his words to her mouth.

'Is that what we're doing, making love?' Her entire body was about to orgasm as she felt Lewis' hands move to her front, cupping her boobs in his hands and tantalizing her nipples between his thumb and finger. 'No, no, no, no,' she begged for reprieve from his infliction.

Her wetness was all over his thighs, 'I'm in love with you Gracie. I need you in my life,' he gasped as his desires were coming to a head.

'Tell me more,' her lips curled to his mouth as she kissed him, their eyes open. For Grace, the moment was almost tantric in a sexually overwhelming way, all her senses were coming together in one huge emotional orgasm as Lewis declared his love for her, his arms now crossing her back, his hands entwining in her hair, pulling gently at it.

His lips never left hers, 'I love you Gracie. I need you,' he was about to cum with explosive fury. 'I want to love you like you should be loved.'

'I love you too,' she let herself go to him. 'I love you so much and I don't want to be without you, not for a single day,' she gushed in a desperate bid to let him know she was there, that his words were everything she'd hoped for.

Their bodies meshed to one another, cumming together with such ferocity. Grace's legs wide apart, her body falling over him as he dug deep inside of her. She ground down over him, clenching her insides to his cock to pleasure him until the very end.

Then it was just them wrapped in each other's arms on the floor of Lewis' apartment, their skin glistening with a sexual sheen, he kissed her forehead and stroked her hair away from her face.

They'd come to this place, the long way around, but that was how they knew this was right for both of them. In the still of the night, they didn't need any more words, a peace had come over them. There were no obstacles in the way anymore, they didn't need to hide from anyone or sneak around. Age wasn't a factor, they knew were they stood with each other, and what they could expect from one another, any reservations had diminished. They'd expressed their feelings, and they were more than clear. As unlikely as their relationship was, it worked. Love had been declared and now the only important thing to either of them was that they were together.

P.F. SCOTT

Loving Grace

Acknowledgements

Thank you to my husband Anthony for your unwavering love and care. You are always there for me in every moment, good, bad, happy and sad. I love you so much.

Thank you to my precious children Charlie and Isobel for teaching me some of life's most important lessons.

Thank you to my beautiful girlfriends De, Jo, and Lisa, for your encouragement and interest, it means the world to me.

A special thank you to Vicki and Sheridan... I think you both know why!

To my family and friends... thank you for all your support.

www.ingramcontent.com/pod-product-compliance
Lightning Source LLC
Chambersburg PA
CBHW070858260626
47162CB00007B/2492